TYCOON

TYCOON

TERRY PRINGLE

TYCOON

A NOVEL

ALGONQUIN BOOKS OF CHAPEL HILL

1990

Published by

Algonquin Books of Chapel Hill

Post Office Box 2225

Chapel Hill, North Carolina 27515-2225

a division of

Workman Publishing Company, Inc.

708 Broadway

New York, New York 10003

Printed in the United States of America.

Design by Molly Renda.

Library of Congress Cataloging-in-Publication Data

Pringle, Terry, 1947–

  Tycoon: a novel / by Terry Pringle.

  p.   cm.

  ISBN 0-945575-30-0

  I. Title.

PS3566.R576T9   1990   89-28125

813'.54—dc20   CIP

10 9 8 7 6 5 4 3 2 1

First Edition

To

Louis D. Rubin, Jr., and his unfailing sense for fiction,

Bob Compton and his unfailing sense,

and

Sheila Taylor and her—no, I better not say it

ACKNOWLEDGMENTS

Many people introduced me to that part of the industry they fondly referred to as the "oil patch" during the years I spent moving around Taylor, Shackelford, and Stephens counties. Neither they nor I knew at the time that I'd write this book, but they were educating me anyway. Some of them I'll remember because they respected the land on which they drilled and produced, and looked after it in a manner that probably pleased the good Lord. Some of their names will always stick with me because of their character or diligence or their repertoire of stories. Others I'll remember just as long because they didn't care; they didn't care where salt water ran or even their oil—until the price hit forty dollars a barrel.

When I started this book, I realized I didn't know nearly as much as I thought about the oil field and almost nothing about real estate. So I picked the brains of a number of people, and I feel compelled to thank them by name although none of them is responsible for the details of this story.

David "Repo" Rhodes, my good friend, former neighbor, founder of the Abilene chapter of FFGFYG Society, and absolutely tireless talker, spent more hours than either of us could now count discussing booms, busts, banking, and just plain "bidness." Also I infringed on the time of Eugene Hasten in Arlington, J. W. "Red" Butler and Brent Schkade in Abilene, and Bob Miller in Dallas, not to mention an endless number of friends.

I thank them all.

1964

1

"Remember me?"

The question was asked by a young man of indeterminate age standing in front of my desk. I'd never liked being asked that question, and being put on the spot, but in this case, I did remember him. I just couldn't immediately think of his name. We were approximately the same age, and I could remember exactly his picture in my high school yearbook. At the age of eighteen, about five years ago, he'd looked forty with a face elongated and mature enough to have a great deal more life behind it. Some wit had scribbled beside his picture in my yearbook, "Whose father is this?" The answer, provided in blue ink that had smeared: "Abraham Lincoln's."

The young man with the same long face was wearing a green suit, an olive drab almost, and his haircut—very short—made me think he'd just walked off an army post in the last day or two.

He was waiting for me to identify him, and I wondered, what was he doing, just wandering Abilene asking people if they remembered him?

The god of names didn't smile on me, but he certainly leered. I said, "Sure I remember you. Frank Dick."

Two guys who had barely known each other shouldn't have had an inside joke, but we did. The first time I'd ever seen him, we'd both been about ten years old and he'd been in the custody of the local police in the parking lot of a football stadium. The policeman had relieved him of his purloined hubcap and was reading him a rather solemn riot act: if he didn't reveal the name of all his accomplices, who had managed to scatter and hide or escape, he'd have to take the rap for every hubcap that had ever been stolen within the city limits since the turn of the century. No telling when he'd get out of jail. But the young criminal not only refused to name his partners, he wouldn't give the policeman his own name.

I'd stopped to watch this parking lot interrogation because I'd been unable to imagine a kid my age with balls that big. I would have given my name, my parents' names, my address, phone number, my favorite teacher at school—anything. But he was standing with a look of real obstinacy, which he didn't lose upon giving his name.

"Frank Dick's my name," he finally said. Then he added this rather confusing statement: "And I ain't saying nothing else till I been incriminated." In later years, I'd never been able to decide whether he'd known what he was talking about or not.

I'd seen him off and on through the years, but I had never spoken to him until we'd both arrived in high school. In the hall one day, I'd said, "Aren't you Frank Dick?" And he'd given me the same response then as he gave me now: first a blank look, then a small laugh, and, "Oh, yeah, I almost forgot about that."

I still couldn't remember his real name, so I stood and shook his hand and asked how he was doing; it'd been a long time. I made the assumption he'd graduated along with me and said, "I haven't seen you since graduation."

"I'm doing great, just great," he said, but he was dissatisfied. "You don't remember my name, do you?"

Now the god of names smiled. "Stanley Gaines."

He nodded, pleased I remembered all his names. "Stan. I go by Stan now."

"No kidding? Well, sit down, Stan, and tell me what you've been doing. You look like you just got out of the army."

He sat beside my desk, which was along the edge of an open office on the second floor of the Brewster Building in downtown Abilene, Texas. My father, the owner of Brewster Drilling, didn't believe in private offices any more than he believed in excessive leisure time for his son. Secretaries and bookkeepers didn't need their own offices, and anybody getting paid more than the clerical help was supposed to be spending too much time in the field to warrant an office. One of the old man's favorite lines was, "I've worn out many a steel-toed boot, but I've *never* worn out the seat of my pants." The furniture was appropriate to the times—gray metal desks and beige floor tile—because the drilling business was slow. But it had looked exactly the same during the boom of the fifties. The old man didn't like expenses.

"I'm out of the army yesterday, looking for a job today," Stan said. "You're my first stop."

Why, I wondered, would a man just out of the army choose an off-the-rack suit that was olive drab? And why would he make his first stop Brewster Drilling? We hired floorhands and swampers occasionally, those guys who worked on the rigs and the trucks, but we didn't need anybody at the moment. Then, I didn't think Don't-call-me-Stanley-anymore was here to apply as a worm anyway. He wanted something more. His manner, the intense way he stood and even sat, made me think the old man would like him. Stan wasn't the type to ever wear out the seat of his pants.

I invited him to go to lunch, and if he seemed like one of those tightly coiled, purposeful types my father liked, I'd introduce them.

We walked to a downtown restaurant; there were only a couple even though the boom of the fifties had changed Abilene, almost doubling the population from near 50,000 in 1950 to almost 100,000 ten years later. But now, postboom, it had returned to that sleepy town that wasn't far removed from its beginnings just over eighty years ago, when saloons and whorehouses had lined the railroad tracks, when the bones of thousands of buffalo had been piled along those same tracks, awaiting shipment to fertilizer plants. The prairies had been littered with the carcasses, dropped by the hunters who had taken the skin, robbed the hump of meat, and then left the animals to rot.

People who visited here for the first time expected to see it sitting on a landscape as flat as a table top, but it really occupied what seemed a natural lake bed in the hills of the Callahan Divide. The view from some places in town was that from the center of a plate, looking toward the upturned lip, the hills to the south and west providing the rim. I'd always expected water to flow down from the north and fill up our lake bed, but here all the creeks ran backwards, when they ran at all, south to north.

Abilene was a working town, with 500 hundred businesses related to oil, but we also had a lot of ranching and farming. It was a place as contradictory as my father and grandfather, a town with three church-related colleges and an untold number of churches, all trying to contain, or at least hide, that residual spirit of the frontier that still poked its

3

head up. We'd just learned that in the first nine months of the year, almost as many people had filed for divorce as had applied for marriage licenses.

Now Stan and I made our way through the slow noonday crowd to the restaurant, and Stan had to restrain his steps. He was in more of a hurry than anybody else. We entered the restaurant and wound our way to a table, stopping to greet those I knew. Abilene is a talking town. People stop to talk everywhere, in the banks, on the sidewalks, everywhere. A trip to the bank or post office is usually four short and one lengthy conversations long.

The waitress, who was probably kin to Stan, walked by our table quickly and dropped two battered menus between us. I handed one to Stan, but he waved it off.

"I'll just have a hamburger and french fries," he said, sitting sideways in his chair, one arm resting on the table, the other on the back of his chair, ready to bolt at any time.

"Have a meal. You probably need one after all that army food. This one's on Brewster Drilling."

He shook his head. "Nah, thanks anyway." He looked around the restaurant as if to determine who in attendance he knew.

Apparently he didn't see this meal as a part of a job interview but as a delay. He twisted a couple of times in his chair as though trying to screw himself to the seat, and then ended up facing me, both elbows on the table.

"You're not going to college?" I asked.

"No, I don't have time," he said, then smiled, adding, "Of course, I didn't have time for the army either, but the draft board didn't care."

I started to ask where Uncle Sam had sent him, but the waitress arrived, pencil and pad in hand, prepared to take an order. A redhead in her early forties, she was padded in all the right spots and tested the elasticity of her white dress in two specific areas. She was the kind of woman who engendered fantasies among boys under the influence of their hormones, and at the age of twenty-three, I wasn't immune. I'd asked her out once and she'd said, "Let me see here. What would a rich kid want with an older woman who works as a waitress? Oh, I know. You want me to help you with your homework."

She looked Stan over, measuring his cheap suit and short hair, and then said to me, "Well, Billy Boy, I guess the FBI finally got you. This your last meal as a free man?"

4

Before I could introduce Stan, he'd jumped up and offered his hand. "Hi. Stan Gaines, just back in town."

The waitress looked partly amused, partly pleased, to see one of her customers standing and offering to shake her hand. Not even politicians did that. She dropped her pencil into the pocket of her small apron and shook his hand, giving him a long look. They engaged in some abbreviated chitchat while she took our orders for hamburgers and french fries.

Stan watched her swish off and said, "She seems like a real nice lady. I'd ask her out but she probably thinks she's too old for me."

"No, you've got it backwards. She's not too old for you; you're too young for her."

I expected him to pursue the matter of the dress-stretching waitress, but he launched into a monologue on the oil business, touching on governmental regulation, foreign imports, and falling prices. He sounded for all the world as though he'd just read a magazine article ("The History of Oil in Six Paragraphs"), and I was impressed not by his knowledge but by his earnest manner. I'd seen such people at my front door trying to sell me magazines, often reading their sales pitch from a sheet of paper.

The waitress returned with two glasses of iced tea and Stan quickly reverted to the previous subject. "I've been out of circulation so long I can't remember what people do around here. So why don't you show me? Besides, Billy doesn't think you'll go out with me."

She shook her head. "People around here don't do anything. They never have. And if you're just out of the army, you probably ought to take a cold shower and get a pint of his granddaddy's hootch," she said, jerking her thumb at me. "And if that doesn't work, move to Fort Worth or Dallas."

Stan had leaned back in his chair, looking up at her. "Oh, there's got to be something new around here. No new houses? How about taking me around and letting me look?"

Hands on hips, she looked closely at him, then switched her gaze to me. "He's asking me out."

"Sure sounds like it."

Her eyes narrowed, and she fixed me with a suspicious stare. What was a stranger doing asking her out two sentences after an introduction? "What're you telling him about me? You had to tell him something."

I shook my head. "All I told him was that you're a greyhound in a world of basset hounds."

She looked Stan over, obviously evaluating him. She waved off a customer complaining about his dry coffee cup; she handled all complaints the same. She was, she said, like Lyndon Johnson: she didn't get ulcers, she gave them. Stan responded to her long look with a smile, the one he hadn't used for his senior class picture in the yearbook. The waitress again looked at me.

"Think I oughta go? Will you vouch for him?"

Did I? Would I? I didn't know anything about him other than he'd once been Frank Dick, ringleader of the notorious Hubcap Kids gang. All I could tell her was that this was Stanley Gaines, who'd pounded the pavement every weekday morning of the school year, his head down, in a hurry as though the school might relocate before he got there. And regardless of the temperature, he'd never worn a coat. I'd stopped on some rather cold mornings to offer him a ride, and he'd invariably refused with a shake of his head. But now I said, "Sure, I'll vouch for him."

"Well, Mr. GI, why don't you come back here about three and we'll talk about it."

"Great!" Stan said.

We watched her walk off—she was always accompanied by tom-toms in my ears—and he said, "What was that remark she made about your grandfather?"

My grandfather, the first of three William C. Brewsters, had been born only a few years after the last Indian raids, the son of an open-range cattle herder, who'd taken his longhorns to wherever the grass looked good, and he'd grown up with a strong desire to join the trail drives to California. Unfortunately, barbed wire and trains killed any possibility of that wish being fulfilled, and he'd found himself in his early twenties, married with a child (my father), when he'd heard the news of the first gusher at Spindletop. He'd found his calling. If he couldn't make trail drives, he'd go to Beaumont. And for the next thirty years, he'd made every boomtown in the state. Which was why I called him Boomer. And it was also the key to understanding his politics. He believed the government had only one legitimate function—to protect the frontier from the Indians—and if it engaged in any other activity, it overstepped its authority. The Second Cavalry patrolling the area had been fine; the existence of a regulatory agency concerned with the production of oil couldn't possibly be justified.

He lived with my parents and could tell stories longer than anyone could listen, everything from Uncle Hat—who'd been the victim of a partial scalping in his youth and had worn a hat to cover the hideous scar—to the buffalo hunters and bone gatherers and

6

the lawlessness of the town of Ranger in the 1917 boom.

His son, who had grown up wondering why his father was never home, had developed a rebellious attitude. Everything Boomer hated—stability, regulation, predictability—became my father's code of honor. He waited to marry until he was forty, hoping to put enough money away so he could insulate his family from the wild economic cycles his father thrived on. Boomer made and lost fortunes as though they were pocket knives.

The stories the two men told were as different as they were. Boomer would tell me about the time he'd rented a pool table to sleep on in Beaumont, with every room, cot, and barber chair already taken. He'd spent the night with his hands on his money and a small pistol he carried, only to awaken the next morning to learn his boots had been stolen right off his feet. My old man would counter with a story about the time he'd plugged a well with drilling mud all by himself, carrying it in five-gallon buckets by hand from the mud pit, a process which had taken a week. And somehow he thought these little fables were competition for Boomer's stories. Right.

Boomer was now eighty-five, and he didn't get out much anymore, and he kept a pint bottle of whiskey in his boot beside his bed, covered with a sock as though it were hidden, as though only he, and not the entire town, knew of its existence.

Stan listened to me in his Dale Carnegie manner, asking questions and nodding and smiling, and I found myself hoping the old man hired him. I'd always admired people who tried, probably because I'd never had to.

After lunch, I escorted him into the presence of the second William C. Brewster, who occupied the only private office on the second floor of the building. He looked nothing like Boomer, just as I looked nothing like him. Each generation rebelled. The old man, steadfast as a mule, had given himself over to that stabilizing force called gravity. He'd been pulled to the ground, a solid rock and just as bald. Boomer, dedicated to everything fast and loose, was thin as spaghetti and had enough hair, even though it was yellowish-white, for five younger men. I fell somewhere in between.

Stan didn't realize my father had the world's most sensitive bullshit detector, and he hadn't said two sentences before I began expecting the old man to toss him right out the door.

"Mr. Brewster, I just want a chance. I'm the hardest-working guy you've ever seen, and I can't prove it to you without a chance. All I can tell you is, you won't ever be sorry you hired me, not now, not ever. I came by here because I want to learn everything there is to know about

7

the oil business. I want to be taught by the best, the very best. I know you and I know your reputation. My mother asked me when I was ten years old what I wanted to do when I grew up, and I told her—I wanted to work for Brewster Drilling.

"I hit town yesterday; I'm here today. I would've been here earlier but I bought this suit at Penney's yesterday afternoon and the pants were too long. They wanted me to pick it up next week. I had to talk to four people to get it ready this morning. I'm only telling you this because I want you to know, this is where I want to work, right here, with you."

The old man, to my utter amazement, sat up straight behind his metal desk and smiled. But what had I expected? In his early years, the old man's nickname had been Rooster because he'd always been waking people up in the morning, demanding to know if they intended to sleep their lives away. They were wasting time, the best part of the day. Then too, he was partial to people who weren't so educated they couldn't make decisions.

"Stan, I like a man who believes in hard work." He then preached a short sermon on the virtues of labor and energy and dedication that was meant for my ears and then told Stan he was my replacement. It was time I learned more of the business than just lease acquisition.

Actually, I wasn't sure I wanted to learn more of the business. I'd started the University of Texas as a geology major, but I'd decided that going out to desolate places in search of oil would doom me to a lonely life, so I'd changed to accounting. But when I graduated and actually began working for the CPA of the company, I'd discovered that poring over paper could be as lonely as looking at rocks.

So I'd become a landman for the production end of the company, one of those guys who went out and acquired leases from little old ladies so we could drill on and, hopefully, produce the oil and gas under their land. And I liked the job, although I was still fighting the paper, digging through courthouse records, keeping track of all the leases.

To me the old man said, "Take Stan with you and go see old lady Miller." To Stan he advised, "Billy's a good landman but he visits too much. He tends to forget why he's there and instead of nailing down prospects, he's drinking lemonade and looking at picture albums. And he's real bad with the old ladies. So you don't have to follow his lead to the letter."

I'd already visited with Mrs. Miller three times, had started out offering her three dollars an acre, then five, then seven, which was high for a thousand acres that looked promising to only one person, the old man.

8

Still, we hadn't come to any agreement. A local drilling contractor, no longer in business, had drilled a dry hole several years ago. The old man had bought their seismic study and our geologist thought he'd found a promising-looking structural trap, but I thought the real reason my father wanted the lease was because he believed he was being thwarted by a little old lady and his own lethargic son.

"You want me to offer her *more* than seven bucks?"

"I want you to lease the goddamn land is what I want you to do. Don't come back until you've got her signature."

With that admonition, the old man dismissed us, and the newest employee of Brewster Drilling and I set off to Albany, which was thirty-five miles northeast of Abilene.

I liked going to Albany because it required crossing the old frontier. Once away from town, there were miles of landscape that must have looked exactly as it had when the first settlers had arrived. The irregular rising prairie was empty except for an occasional lone and very lonely looking tree. There were no power lines out here, no pumping units, no houses, not even many mesquite trees. It was rocky ground with sparse grass and brush, occasionally disrupted by the breaks of some long-forgotten river that had flowed across here. The prairie and overwhelming sky were the two great facts of nature out here, and they would have overwhelmed a normal person, which was probably why most of them had stopped at Fort Griffin and Albany.

The prairie rose for over twenty miles and then peaked in the hills above Albany, overlooking a range of buttes and mesas that ran all the way to the blue horizon. This part of the state had a strong hold on me. Every time I went too long without seeing it, I felt adrift. My four years in college in Austin had been entertaining and interesting, but basically I hadn't liked living there. It had been too busy, too populous, too hectic.

We were halfway to Albany before I remembered Stan's second interview of the day, the one with the red-haired waitress. "What about your date?"

"I'll talk to her some other time."

He seemed nonchalant not only about the date but about his salary as well. He hadn't been out of my hearing since he'd walked in the front door, and he hadn't even asked about salary.

"This is great," he said, sitting back in the car and looking out the window. "A chance to learn from the best company around. What more could you ask for?"

"Well, how about a salary and a company car?"

He shrugged, a jerky motion, almost a tic. "Your father'll pay me what I'm worth, whatever that is. I don't know anything about this business, but I sure plan to learn."

"Just as long as he doesn't start paying everybody what they're worth."

I was in fact getting $750 monthly, and I assumed Stan would start at something less, but then, I wasn't sure. He seemed to possess that elusive quality the old man looked for—fire in the gut. That was worth more than education or family connections, probably. But Stan would have to prove he had staying power before the old man would consider any real rewards, I thought.

I started Stan on the basics as we drove. The only thing I did well was talk, and I'd delivered this spiel to investors before. My father had to admit he liked listening to me, but on the other hand, my glibness irritated him. His son, the dilettante. Still, I was eloquent singing the praises of that most wonderful element carbon. Without it women would never smile and school kids couldn't erase their test answers to make them agree with their neighbors'. We were, of course, talking about pure carbon, diamonds and graphite.

Combine four hydrogen atoms with one of carbon and you hit west Texas right in the gut, not to mention wallet. Hydrocarbons, the basis of all petroleum products. I lost Stan somewhere along the line, probably when I began talking about saturated compounds. He wasn't interested in history or science; he wanted to talk about getting the stuff out of the ground.

"How do you find it?"

"Only one way. You drill."

As we drove down Nine Mile Hill, a long but rather steep descent into Albany, I explained our mission at Mrs. Miller's, which was to be the same with any other landowner who'd retained his mineral rights. Normally we paid a certain amount to lease the land, called a bonus, and left the landowner with a royalty of an eighth. We executed a lease and retained the right to drill for a period of years, preferably five, and when we found oil we held the rights thereafter as long as it was produced.

"I talked to one old man and told him we'd leave him an eighth royalty, and he bowed up and said, 'Yeah, the hell you will. I know how you oil companies work. You offer an eighth but settle for something more. I want more than an eighth. I want at least a fifteenth, hell, maybe even a twentieth.'"

Stan laughed, and I told him it was an old landman's story.

We passed through Albany, a small oil-field town in rugged country. I'd heard a lawyer say once that when a jury of twelve men raised their hands to be sworn in, he couldn't count more than thirty-five fingers. The others had been left lying on the floors of drilling rigs and pulling units, given up in one kind of accident or another.

Mrs. Miller lived between Albany and the site of old Fort Griffin, a wide-open frontier town and important stop on the Western Trail to Dodge City. Her place looked, from the road, like a small settlement of white buildings in a valley between the road and the peaks of the Antelope Hills. She was a spry little lady who wore formless dresses and white athletic socks, and she was full of good humor. At the age of seventy, she lived alone and had no trouble taking care of herself.

And she remembered the previous drilling contractor too well. He'd run over a fence, uprooted some of her scrawny mesquite trees, and left trash on the location. And he'd refused to pay the land damages he'd agreed to in advance.

I stopped in front of her white frame house, which was patrolled by the largest and friendliest, and therefore most useless, watchdogs I'd ever seen, dogs that lay around in the dark hoping for a trespasser upon whom they could shower their slobbering affections. It was difficult to arrive on Mrs. Miller's porch in a dry condition.

We left the car in pre-Halloween weather, a day that contained no hint of frost or cold weather. It was one of those long blue and thoroughly pleasant afternoons that made me happy I wasn't engaged in regular or arduous labor. We fought through the huge, cheerful dogs toward the long porch.

Mrs. Miller pushed open her screen door, wearing a blue dress that had no waist. "Well, we're getting serious now, I see. You're bringing reinforcements."

"He's from *Reader's Digest*, Mrs. Miller. He told me if I showed him the nicest person in the world, he'd give me a lot of money. So here we are."

She had several wooden rocking chairs on the porch and we sat. I wanted to stay some afternoon and watch the sun sink behind the hills to the west. My father said I had two speeds—slow and stop—but I really had three. The third I called whiff, and I moved only if the air pushed me. It was a good speed for looking at sunsets and girls.

Mrs. Miller kicked off, pushing her rocking chair back, her white athletic socks flashing, and said, "I thought of that other drilling company, that one that made all the mess. Southwind. That was it, Southwind. I should've remembered because every time the wind gets out of the south, I start sneezing." She laughed, rocking as though she intended to receive the full benefit of her chair, pushing off just as a child would in a swing.

I told her Southwind was out of business, as were many other oil-field companies, because things were slow. "My grandfather says there's not much point in drilling when you can't make any more than you could in 1920. The price of oil's about the same."

"It may very well be what it was in 1920, but it's fluctuated a right smart amount in the past forty years too," she said, showing me I wasn't dealing with just another bumpkin.

By now I felt as though I knew her family. She had a daughter in Dallas and a son in Denver. I asked about her grandson in Denver, the one who'd had chicken pox, and her granddaughter who'd been preparing for a dance recital. She gave me an update and then went to the kitchen for iced tea, which she served in glasses so old the blue and white ornamentation had faded. We visited for a while, pushing the dogs away, and they lay in the dirt between the porch and car and attacked each other without enthusiasm.

When there was a pause, I said, "Well, you know why I'm here. My father sent me to get your John Hancock. I can't go back to Abilene until I do. So if you're feeling contrary, I hope you've got extra beds."

"Why, I'll be more than happy to put you boys up. It's so seldom I have company. And maybe you can chop me some wood 'cause it's going to get cold here pretty soon." She pushed off again, rocking so far backward that the top of her chair hit the house. "I've been trying to figure out why your daddy's so anxious to drill out here. I'd guess he knows something. So what does he know? Whatever it is, it's worth more than seven dollars an acre."

"He doesn't *know* anything, Mrs. Miller. My father's one of those guys who gets gut feelings. Sometimes they're right and sometimes they're wrong. But there's really nothing to know, and if it was me, I wouldn't pay even seven dollars."

She rocked and shook her head, her eyes fixed on something only she could see. Empty pipe dope buckets, maybe, or big ruts from truck tires. "I don't know, I just don't know. That other drilling company, they just tore up everything. I had to get a lawyer after them just to get the land damages they'd already agreed to. And that took over a year."

Before I could say anything, Stan, looking half soldier and half civilian

12

in his green suit, stood up and said, "Mrs. Miller, the reason I'm here is to keep you happy. Mr. Brewster's personally assigned me to you. We'll get an aerial photograph of your property, and we'll find out where every rock is, and when we're through, we'll put every one of them back in place. We'll plant weeds to replace those we pull up. Mr. Brewster told me when I left, 'Stan, you get up there and see what makes that little lady happy, and when you do, you agree to it.' And that's why I'm here, to make you happy."

"Well, I'll tell you what'll make me happy," Mrs. Miller said, her rocking chair again banging against the house. "Ten bucks'll make me pretty doggone happy."

"Then ten bucks it is," Stan said, waving his hand as though he were a magician making the money appear.

I was trying to get my mouth closed, utterly surprised not only by this coup of Brewster Drilling's two-hour employee, but by the fact that this old lady had been doing nothing more than negotiating, holding out for more money. And all that time I'd thought she was concerned over her property. But the biggest prick in my pride was a vision of my father's face. His amused expression matched Mrs. Miller's.

"Wait a minute," I said. "How long are we talking about?"

Mrs. Miller, now rocking like crazy to inch her chair away from the side of the house, said, "Oh, I couldn't go more than a year."

"Then we'll have to withdraw the offer," I said, standing up so Stan would realize he wasn't on a plane higher than mine. He was a worm, a boll weevil, a new guy.

"Oh, I already accepted," Mrs. Miller said. "He offered me ten dollars and I accepted right off. I guess you weren't listening. Keep talking, Mr. Gaines. I like what you're saying."

Stan said, "Mrs. Miller, do me a favor and go five years. You know, when you said ten, I didn't say, no, I can only go eight. Or eight fifty. Or nine. Or nine fifty. I agreed to ten right off. So do me a real big favor and say you'll go five years."

"Well, there's something to what you say, all right. And you didn't come out here trying to butter me up by asking about my grandkids and trying to make a deal that'd make your father proud—"

"Wait a minute!" I yelled to the lady who was rocking so vigorously she was spilling iced tea on her dress.

"Oh, just hush up. Me and Mr. Gaines are settling this."

I left the porch, angry about damn near everything that had ever happened to me. I wanted to tell the old bat that I hoped her granddaughter broke both her arms in her dance recital and I was sorry as all get out that her grandson had recovered from the chicken pox. I hoped he had horrible scars. I couldn't remember being so pissed off. And when Stan didn't immediately follow me to the car, I started it, gunning the engine and raising dust.

Stan. The same guy who'd worn the Frankenstein mask to school one Halloween and refused to remove it. It had been one of those rubber masks that fit over the entire head. He'd apparently been proving a point to his mother, who had come to the school wanting to speak to the assembled student body about the evil inherent in the celebration of Halloween. Of course the school had refused her, and Stan had managed to make his point, I guessed, by embarrassing his mother in the same way she'd humiliated him, all of which had seemed a rather strange method of communicating back then, just as it did now. Obviously, I was going to have a difficult time understanding this guy.

I didn't speak to him when we left, and when we got back to Albany, I turned left toward Breckenridge, and a six-pack of beer, rather than back toward home. I not only wanted a beer but I wanted to delay Stan's triumphant return to the office. I wasn't prepared to hear him tell the old man that a two-hour employee—a person who wouldn't have recognized a lease agreement if it had jumped up and bit him on the butt —had taught the owner's kid how to do his job.

Stan didn't say anything, either. He knew I was mad. But after about five or six miles I couldn't stand it any longer.

"What's with you and all your bullshit?" I yelled. "Aerial photographs, weed transplants, not to mention this burning desire you've had for fifteen years to work for Brewster Drilling. I couldn't *believe* that line of crap. I figured the old man was going to throw you out on your ear when he heard that. Man, I just can't believe you."

Stan, having hoped for congratulations, wasn't happy to hear me accuse him of severe deficiencies in the sincerity department. "Hey! None of that was bullshit."

"You're telling me that one day when you were ten years old, your mother asked what you wanted to do when you grew up, and *you actually told her you wanted to go to work for Brewster Drilling?* Do I look like a complete and utter idiot? You really think I buy that?"

Stan waved his finger sideways; it said no. "You're wrong there. Listen, I *always* figured Brewster for a good place to work. Always. And I couldn't tell your father why I really came by. I came by because—well, you probably won't even remember this. Back when we were in high

14

school, you had a black '55 Chevy, and you were the only guy in school that ever offered me a ride. Ever. And I would've taken you up on it but you always had a bunch of guys that were real snobs, I mean guys with their noses stuck up on the roof of the car. I could tell they didn't want you stopping and offering me a ride, so I never went. And I used to see your father on TV, and I always thought he'd be a good guy to work for. And I was probably about ten when I first saw him, and I may have told my mother I'd like to go to work for Brewster Drilling. I sure couldn't say it never happened."

His words eased my irritation somewhat. I did remember offering him a ride on a few occasions, and I remembered too that none of the guys who rode with me were enthusiastic about my stopping, partly because of his mother's periodic religious crusades. She'd been to the school on another occasion, which I'd just remembered, once when the English teacher had assigned a TV program she'd wanted us to watch. Mrs. Gaines hadn't believed in TV and had visited the school to say so.

"Hey," he said. "I was just doing what I thought your father wanted me to do back there. She was just an old lady holding out for more money, and I wouldn't have known that if you hadn't told me everything you did on the way up there. So I appreciate your help on my first day. And I thought it we did all right, don't you?"

I shook my head. We. Oh, the generosity of a two-hour employee. I couldn't believe it. Worse, I couldn't believe I was going to have to tell my father that Stan had accomplished in a few minutes what I'd been working on for a month.

I was so happy.

2

My mother told me often that the only exciting dinners at home nowadays were those I religiously attended every Thursday night. My father and grandfather had been feuding for over thirty years, and Boomer saw that the ill will was resurrected every Thursday night at 7:00 P.M. The issue that had always divided them was proration, and it encompassed their clashing philosophies. Every time a major field had been discovered, the massive supplies suddenly flooding the market drove the price down to almost nothing, in some cases as little as two cents a barrel, and my father had always been a hardcore proponent of proration to support prices. Boomer, however, believed that those who demanded regulation were crybabies and sissies. He wanted the world running wide open. He'd like the oil field where he could step from the floor of one wooden derrick to another. A man should be allowed to produce as much and as quickly as he could.

In the thirties, the two of them, along with a third from Abilene, the grandfather of my girlfriend, had been involved in the Yates Field, one of the most productive in the country, and they'd formed one of the few independents that had benefited from the enormous reserves there. My father and the third man had supported one of the first proration plans that had ever worked, and Boomer had left them, disgusted that they'd call themselves independents and then support a plan proposed by major oil companies.

"Shit," Boomer had reportedly said as he'd walked off. "Change the name of this operation to Turncoat Oil Company."

I always wore a suit and tie to the Thursday night dinners, and my mother insisted that we eat in the dining room with china and silver to prove that we still possessed manners and could act civilized, an admirable notion that succeeded only in theory.

On this night, my father was happy with his latest business decision, that of hiring Stan. After feeling somewhat guilty and childish for having deprived Stan of an immediate and glorious return to the office from Mrs. Miller's, I'd returned him to the office. And there the old man had let drop a bit of information that he'd neglected to tell me at all until that moment.

"Well, of course she wanted more money," he'd said, looking at me as though I were both blind and deaf. "She told me the first time I talked to her she wasn't ever letting anybody on her property for a lousy three bucks an acre. I told you that."

Of course, he hadn't told me any such thing, and I'd gotten irritated all over again, this time transferring my ire from Brewster's newest employee to its oldest. And I went to dinner looking forward to repaying the old man for his oversight.

Boomer was already seated at the dining room table when I arrived, napkin on his lap, fork in hand. He was invariably the first to arrive at the table, smelling of whiskey from his boot, and he had nothing to say until he saw food appear. He thought conversation would delay the commencement of the meal. I said hello to him, and he nodded without looking at me. With his yellowish-white hair and leathery face, he looked

16

every bit of eighty-five years old, and although he still had a clear voice, he often mumbled for the sole purpose of making my old man mad.

The dining room could easily handle large dinner parties, and I always felt a little strange when we gathered on one end of the long table to eat. My father sat at the end, my mother to his left and across from Boomer, and I sat beside my mother, facing the mirror over a buffet so I could watch myself eat. I could also see in the mirror the large crystal chandelier overhead, and I could tell when events began really heating up because the little glass tassels on the light would vibrate.

My father came in through a swinging door from the kitchen and dropped a magazine on a vacant chair. "Well, I think we found a winner in Stan."

"How much are you paying him?" I asked, already seated, my mother's empty chair to my right.

The old man caught the challenge in my voice and responded with a raised-eyebrow look that said he was equal to any challenge I attempted to mount. "You know my attitude about discussing salaries."

"Oh, I don't want any specific figure. Just tell me you're not paying him more than you're paying me."

He didn't answer, taking his seat at the head of the table just as my mother walked in with the first of the food, a plate of baked ham. She was, I thought, an incredibly classy and beautiful woman with just enough gray in her hair, at the age of fifty-five, to add dignity, just dark-skinned enough to looked tanned and healthy all year long.

The appearance of food liberated Boomer, who now felt free to speak. He reached for the plate of ham and swiped a piece with his fork before the plate hit the table. "I'll tell you what, Billy. The best thing you could do is go find a real job and leave the oil field to the girls who changed it. You work for the turncoats, you get shot in the back."

"How is it," my father said, "that an old man who never does any more than get soused while he watches TV can know so much about the present state of the oil field?"

My old man had either never figured out, or refused to believe, that Boomer never responded to anything directly. He couldn't argue with Boomer using logic; Boomer disregarded logic because it belonged in the same realm with good posture, virginity, and other examples of moderation.

I'd left the office earlier while my father and Stan had still been talking, and they'd undoubtedly discussed Stan's salary. Let's see, I thought. How would he figure it? What was the equation? Fire in the gut plus the acquisition of Mrs. Miller's lease two hours after reporting for duty equals more than someone as useless as Billy gets, let's say $775. Could he be paying Stan more than me? Sure, he could. We were talking about Turncoat Oil.

"Stan's been in Vietnam," my father said. "He tells me we'll end up bombing those people back into the Stone Age, just like Goldwater wants to do, because we aren't used to fighting in the jungles. They are. Been doing it for years and years."

"So how much you paying this war department employee?" Boomer asked.

My old man pretended he hadn't heard and instead briefed my mother on Stan. Since he knew very little of a personal nature about Stan, and that was all my mother was interested in, he deferred to me when my mother started asking questions, none of which I could answer. And to raise questions about the old man's judgment, I told them about the Frank Dick incident, which made my mother's mouth open in amazement. And I pointed out that none of us knew where Stan lived, who his parents were (an absolute for my mother), what he'd done between high school and the army, or even his age.

"Did he graduate with you?" she asked.

"Not that I remember."

"Oh, oh, oh," she said, looking immediately thoughtful, her eyes fixed on the chandelier. "I remember a Melissa Gaines who worked for the Hendrix and—who else—Ford families. But I don't think that could be the same person. I hope it wasn't anyway. But she'd probably be about the right age."

"Who was she?" I asked, as intrigued about Stan's past as my mother was but for different reasons.

"Just a maid," my mother said in a manner that meant, obviously, the lady had been more than a maid. Or had more impact than a maid normally had. She wouldn't say anything else though so I dropped the matter.

I was thinking about something else, anyway. Stan had managed to save about a thousand dollars in the army, and now he wanted to find his own lease and put together a group of investors and drill. At that point in the discussion this afternoon at the office, when the old man had agreed to drill a well for Stan for half the cost and an eighth interest, I'd left. I couldn't believe it. Instead of giving Stan advice on the necessity of learning the business, he was encouraging him to put together an oil and gas package, even though before today Stan had thought oil was something squeezed out of a Three-In-One can. How crazy could all this get?

Boomer mumbled something. It was almost but not quite a sentence

18

that contained distinguishable words. It sounded like, "The birds buzz
the rutabagas before the young dogs get their wallets."

"What?" my old man said.

"I said, how much you paying this goddamn doughboy?"

My old man failed to answer and Boomer worked on a slice of ham,
mumbling as he did. My father tried his best to ignore him but just
couldn't do it. Almost coming out of his chair, leaning over the table, he
shouted, "*What* are you saying?"

"I said, he sounds like a fellow I met in Ranger during the boom.
Came into a saloon one day saying he'd developed the rock bit and
Hughes Senior had stole it from him. That was his claim. He elbowed
his way up to the bar and was about to down a shot of whiskey when his
mama came in. She grabbed him by the ear and said, 'You simple son of
a bitch. I send you after your sister and you end up in a bar.'"

I laughed, but my father refused to acknowledge any parallel between
Stan and this simple son of a bitch in Ranger. Boomer gave me a big
smile while he chomped on ham; he liked to know his stories were
heard and received with amusement.

"Well," I said, "he can't be paying Stan as much as he's paying me. I've
got a degree and I'm a longtime employee. I was painting rigs when I
was twelve. I was a floorhand at sixteen. I worked derricks every summer during college, and that's how the system works. You reward your
longtime and loyal employees. You give a new guy a chance but you
dang sure don't pay him more than your longtime and loyal hand."

When the old man refused to even voice basic agreement with this
philosophy, I thought: I'll be damned. He's paying Stan more than he's
paying me. I had to refigure the equation. Fire in the gut plus Mrs.
Miller's lease equals a shower of shit on the owner's kid. I was getting
mad all over again.

Mumbling from Boomer, who was eating salad. This time it sounded
like, "The range fires will sap the strength of the committee on bird
dookey."

"*What in the Sam hell are you saying?*" my old man shouted.

"I said, you oughta be ashamed, paying some Oriental more'n your
own flesh and blood. This boy here was painting rigs before he could
walk. Took both hands to hold the paint brush. Had to get somebody
else to move the bucket. Show him some appreciation. Give him a damn
raise. Pay him at least sixty dollars a week."

My old man's jaw tightly wrenched. He was not only angry over having what passed for a discussion with a man thirty years behind on the
wage scale, but because he thought the attack was unfair. He believed

he should constitute a majority, sufficient to establish a tyrannical rule. One man, one rich and successful and hardworking man, shouldn't have to tolerate assaults from two yoyos who thought work was an optional activity, something like going to a movie or taking a walk.

Boomer pointed his fork at me and said, "D. Jack Owen wouldn't do something like that, no way in hell. *That's* why he's still respected."

Owen had been dead for twenty years, a fact Boomer had forgotten or chose to overlook, and I said, "You've seen his tombstone, haven't you? You know what it says? His epitaph is, 'He served God, loved his family, and never, but never, overpaid a new guy.'"

I was taking a growing satisfaction in the trend of the fight. To shut us up, my old man was going to have to tell us that he wasn't paying Stan more than me. We were proceeding on the assumption that Stan's salary was higher, and the old man hated erroneous assumptions.

My mother, whose dedication to good manners and civilized behavior was always overshadowed by these weekly resumptions of the feud, seemed distracted, and I knew she was still trying to place Stan and his mother.

"I'll tell you who would do it," Boomer said. "Mister Benedict Arnold. Shows you what loyalty and faithful service mean to Turncoat Oil. They take some little North Korean soldier and start throwing money at him, just like that, and they don't even know his name. I'll tell you what. You ask that kid tomorrow—if he speakee any English—you ask him how much he's getting paid. And if he's getting more'n thirty a week, you come see me. By God, I ain't too old to get back in the business. We'll get us a rig, call it Willie's and Billy's, and we'll put *somebody* outta business."

My old man didn't respond, staring at his plate as he finished eating. I knew Boomer would start mumbling again because he believed my old man contained stores of untapped ire. And sure enough, Boomer mumbled something that sounded like, "You can suck the honey out of a vine but you can't shit a house dog."

My father slapped the table with his fork, sending a small bit of ham flying up at the chandelier, and yelled, *"What is it you're saying, you old fart?"*

Boomer, innocent as a newborn, looked around as though trying to identify the person to whom my old man had addressed himself. He asked, "Me? You talking to me? Why, I didn't say anything."

"If you'd said something, I would've heard you," I said. "And I didn't hear you say anything."

My father shook his head. He wouldn't admit it, but he knew Turncoat Oil had been drilled by Willie's and Billy's.

My mother, as though emerging from the fog, looked at me and said, "Ask this new boy if his mother's name is Melissa."

"Okay. Who was Melissa Gaines?"

She shook her head. "Just a maid, that's all."

I fully intended to ask Stan about his mother the next day, among other matters, but I got disoriented as soon as I walked into the office. There he was sitting at my gray metal desk, going through all the drawers like a scavenger. What was he looking for? Or had the old man given him my desk? I quietly walked up behind him and noticed he had a tablet on the desk, the top sheet covered with what appeared to be notations in code. Or some secret script. Or he just couldn't write legibly.

When he sat back, unable to find whatever he'd been looking for, he noticed me standing behind him. "Hey. Don't you have some preprinted lease forms?"

He'd dressed "normally" today. His pants were plaid and his shirt was striped and he wore white athletic socks just like those Mrs. Miller wore.

"What're you doing?" I asked.

"I need some of those preprinted lease forms you were telling me about."

He told me why. After his conversation with my father about acquiring a lease of his own, he'd returned to Mrs. Miller's, in his new company car, a white Oldsmobile two years old that had belonged to the drilling superintendent; and with the help of his elderly friend, he'd located 180 acres in Coleman County, to the south of us. The premise of drilling for an interest had seemed a divine revelation, too good to be true. Mrs. Miller had a relative who'd previously leased her land, but the operator had neither drilled nor renewed the lease. It was waiting to be picked up by Stan Gaines on his very first day in the oil business for three dollars an acre.

"Wait a minute," I said. "Mrs. Miller held out for ten bucks but she put you onto one of her relatives for three?"

Stan smiled. "Not bad, huh?"

"How'd you manage that?"

"I cut Mrs. Miller in for a thirty-second as a finder's fee and then just let her negotiate it over the phone last night. Anyway, I've already got three guys lined up, some guys I knew in the army with plenty of cash.

The last thing they told me when I left them was, 'Hey! Make us rich in the oil business.' I talked to them last night and two took a quarter and one an eighth. I've got three thirty-seconds left. You want in?"

He caught me with my mouth open again. Stanley Gaines, who knew less about the oil business than Howdy Doody, was off and running. I'd been uncomfortable talking to investors until I'd learned every angle, every risk, every bit of information a sensible person needed to know about drilling and completing and producing and operating a well. And here Stan was soliciting money for a venture he didn't even understand. My God, the guy was a menace and I was responsible for turning him loose on the public. Now I knew what Jack the Ripper's mother felt like.

"Stan. How'd you explain the risks to these people?"

"Oh, they understand we've only got about a one-in-ten chance of hitting a biggie." He tapped his paper. "I intended to give you an eighth, but I've only got three thirty-seconds left. Do you have any trouble with the idea of less than an eighth? I should've taken care of you right off, but these guys who wanted quarters threw everything off. But, hey, three thirty-seconds is nothing to sneeze at, not down there. This is a great-looking piece of land, probably traps all over the place. It's got easy access for a rig and two shut-in wells from the twenties. I don't see how we can go wrong. And I'm sorry I didn't take care of your eighth first, but the thing started moving so fast." He shrugged. "You know."

This was a replay of yesterday. Would every day be the same? I wasn't sure I was up to it. Every time he opened his mouth, I thought of so many questions they all seemed to merge and come out as: What the hell is going on? Had he explained the costs of completing the well, costs Brewster wouldn't reduce by drilling for an interest? Had he told these foolish investors that even a completed well didn't always produce enough oil to justify the expense in operating it? When had he examined this "great-looking piece of land"? Mrs. Miller's house was probably eighty miles from the lease. When had he eaten, slept, changed clothes, showered, and shaved? When had he *thought* about what he was doing?

The guy was destined for one of two fates—extreme riches or impoverishment. No, make that three—prison had to be one of the alternatives. He was selling something he didn't understand, and although that wasn't an illegal practice, it seemed an easy step from selling something you didn't understand to something that didn't exist.

"Stan, what'd you sell these guys? A quarter of the well? A quarter of the working interest? A quarter for a third? What'd you sell these guys?"

His hesitation was brief but long enough to tell me he didn't remember everything he and my father had discussed. "Well, the guy who took a quarter gets a quarter."

"That's what I'm asking you, Stan. A quarter of what?"

"Well," he said, pointing at his paper. "This deal."

"Okay," I said, sitting on the desk behind mine. "Let's try it this way. Will the guy who took a quarter pay a quarter of the drilling costs?"

"Yeah, sure. He'll pay a quarter of the drilling costs."

I sighed. "Stan, you've got three parties here with royalty interests, and they're not paying any expenses. Brewster Drilling has an eighth, Mrs. Miller's got an override for a thirty-second, and the landowner's royalty is an eighth. That leaves twenty-three thirty-seconds working interest, and since your man with a quarter is only paying a quarter of the drilling, you're going to end up paying nine thirty-seconds yourself, and you won't have any interest yourself. You'll get zilch, nothing, for paying over a quarter of the drilling costs yourself."

He laughed and punched me on the arm, thinking I'd pulled some mathematical sleight of hand merely to confuse him. I thought, the old man hired this guy; why isn't he explaining this? He probably had last night, but obviously the lesson hadn't taken.

"Congratulations," I said. "You've come up with a brand new way of putting these deals together. I figure by midafternoon, everybody in town will want in on one of these."

To show him I wasn't playing tricks with his calculator, we went over the fractions until he understood what I was talking about, but it really didn't matter because he simply shrugged.

"Okay, okay, look here. Here's what I did and you confused me. I told these guys we'd just split up the costs based on the percentages." He circled all his addition as though that wrapped the matter up. "See, all these guys know they're going to have to pay the drilling costs. They understand. I'll just break it down based on the percentages."

"I've seen some strange deals, but nothing this strange."

"Hey!" he said, smiling. "These guys are strange."

If I hadn't been responsible for setting Stan loose on ignorant investors, I'd have enjoyed watching him. He liked going to the same downtown restaurant for lunch when we were in town, and he introduced himself to people while they were eating, often while their forks were midway between their plates and mouths, or while they were trying to chew tough roast beef. "Hi, how are you? Stan Gaines," he'd say to a person balancing peas on his fork. Abilene was an informal place and few took offense; in fact, like me, they started watching him just to see what he'd do next. He was crude and didn't know it. His clothes clashed like cymbals and he could easily have fallen into the clown category, but people didn't see him that way; instead they viewed him as energetic and friendly. They did, however, comment frequently on his clothes.

"Who dressed you this morning, Stan? A drunk Indian?"

I think he was thrilled to find the society of commerce much more democratic than that of high school, and more than once he said, "You know, deep down, everybody's pretty much alike, aren't they?"

He'd talked the red-haired waitress out of resentment over being stood up and took her to play tennis several times. One day he asked how her arm was, and she said, "Better, but I'm not ever playing with you again." To me she said, "Have you ever played with him? Well, don't. He's not any good, but I've never seen anybody play like he does. He'll wear you down to a nubbin."

I played with him once and discovered what she meant. He was all determination and lacked any semblance of finesse. It was whack, whack, whack, hit the ball over the fence, straight up in the air, off cars driving down the street. His constantly chopping motion with the racket reminded me of an executioner trying to remove the head of an unwilling victim, someone rolling all over the chopping block.

He couldn't tolerate silence and he asked questions all the time, not so much out of a desire to know as a desire to hear sound, voices. Maybe he'd learned the fine art of questioning in his Dale Carnegie course, and I didn't mind answering questions, but I did mind answering questions when nobody was listening. One day when I knew he was just rattling, desirous of noise, I told him blowouts were caused by stuffing a well full of matches and then setting them afire with reflections from a mirror. He said, "Umm hmm, umm hmm."

I couldn't find out anything about his mother other than her name was in fact Melissa, and she'd worked for two families on our side of town many years ago. My mother said, "I was afraid—I mean, I thought so." And that's all she'd say. I told Stan I thought my mother might know his, and he said, "Yeah, she might. Mine worked as a maid a long time ago."

I couldn't even find out where the guy was living. I thought about following him home once, but he never seemed to go home. And I asked him outright where he was living and he replied, "Oh, just some apartment until I can work out something permanent."

We occasionally seemed to drive each other crazy, for different rea-

24

sons. He'd look at me and say, "Now here's a man who's got the world by the . . ." and clench his fist as though he'd firmly grasped the planet Earth's gonads. "You've got it all, Billy Boy. Some day this company will be all yours. All yours. You'll be riding high and all you've got to do is wait. Now is that something or what? That's something."

I told him I never thought about inheriting a drilling company, and now that he'd mentioned it, wasn't sure I wanted to. I'd have preferred it to be Brewster's Bawdy House.

"Billy Boy, you're one of a kind. If I was you, all I'd think about was having this business some day. You're about the luckiest guy I've ever known and you don't even care."

Besides his superficial attitude toward his function in the world of investments and exploration, he managed to irritate me physically. His favorite trick, if he thought I was ignoring him, was to reach over and twist the hair on my arm. More than once I warned him against engaging in such childish antagonism.

"Hey! I just want you to remember I'm still here."

"I'm not likely to forget that, Stan, and if you do it again, you're not likely to forget I hate that kind of crap."

I'd almost expected him to take advantage of either me or Brewster Drilling, a poor kid who'd finally located the vault and now could collect compensation for his years of deprivation, but he was strict about paying for lunch on alternating days and taking his car if we'd used mine the previous time out. I wasn't sure what difference it made whose car we rode in since both belonged to the company, but he insisted anyway.

He asked a number of questions (and listened to the answers) about the country club, about memberships, dues, the decor, the cost of food and drink, so I invited him out there one afternoon for a drink. I didn't know what he expected, something magical and mysterious like a house of mirrors, but it was nothing more than a pleasant place to socialize and play some gin and a little golf. It was a big two-story building that was down a drive lined by pecan trees.

We entered through the front into a large room furnished with overstuffed chairs, all in groups of four around small tables. Stan looked around, checking out the light fixtures, the mirrors, the ceiling. There was nothing in the place that couldn't be found in any of a hundred, maybe a thousand, houses around town. I tried seeing the place through his eyes, but Stan was so completely different from me, in every way, that I couldn't imagine what he saw. I may as well have been trying to read the mind of a zebra.

I greeted a passing waiter, a young black man in a starched white jacket, and asked for two beers. He pointed at me, smiling, and said, "You got it, Mr. Brewster."

Stan giggled quietly. "*Mister* Brewster. I wish somebody'd call me Mister Gaines."

We sat and Stan got comfortable, having dressed up for the occasion by wearing a striped jacket over a plaid shirt, making himself look like an optical illusion.

"Well, what do you think, Mister Gaines?" I asked.

He shook his head, still looking around. "This is the life, right here, Billy Boy. This is it."

The waiter brought two bottles of beer, placed them on the table atop napkins, and poured part of Stan's into a glass. He knew, uncultured bumpkin that I was, I preferred drinking out of the bottle. One of these days, I thought, I'd become cultured, a patron of the arts, an expert on music of the nineteenth century, and all-around Renaissance man. But until that future date, I'd still drink beer from the bottle.

When the waiter left, Stan took a drink of beer and said, "We start drilling in two weeks."

I thought he'd spoken a little loudly; possibly he had even waited to make this pronouncement until he'd seen others passing through the area. But maybe I was only imagining things. And even if I wasn't, so what? Mr. Gaines was only giving himself a Christmas present a few days early.

"So you're about to become Stan Gaines, operator."

"I sure hope so, as much money and people as I've got involved in this. I told them all there wasn't much more than a 10 percent chance we'd end up with a producing well, but they keep calling and asking if they're rich yet. Are they making money? Not yet, I tell them. Be patient." He took another drink and then said, "I sure hope this sucker's not dry."

I didn't see any sign of real worry on his face. He was having too much fun to worry, getting calls all the time. He hung around after work each day getting full use of the telephone. If it rang after the receptionist left, he yelled, "It's for me." And it usually was. Next year in the phone book, under the listing for Brewster Drilling, it would read, "See Stanley Gaines."

He believed he was going to drill a flowing well. Flowing, hell, he was expecting a gusher like those captured in photos at Beaumont and Ranger. He was expecting a shower of crude in which he could wallow and then go visiting like Jett Rink had in *Giant*. He was eager, a hustler, but he never talked about his dreams and aspirations, never mentioned plans. All of a sudden, he'd simply be involved in some venture he'd never even talked about.

He was patient in fielding calls from those who'd invested in his well, but he was also inaccurate most of the time. I'd heard him explain to one man that once the well was drilled, the Railroad Commission came out to make a survey and determine the reserves. The Railroad Commission was involved in the oil field in a number of different ways, but they didn't visit the location and they didn't estimate reserves. He told another man that if his baby was born before drilling operations commenced, he'd name the well after the baby. This was a practice which hadn't yet hit the oil field. Wells were named after the lease, and Stan's already had a name—the #1 Lowell B. Brooks Estate. I tried keeping him on track by later introducing these same subjects for general discussion, but these remedial lessons were of necessity late.

Sally Ann Wells came bouncing through the room in a tennis outfit, headed toward the front door. She had dusty blond hair and although she wasn't actually beautiful, she had a look that the mind always translated as exquisite beauty. The same mind was always surprised when it was next in her presence and realized she wasn't quite as beautiful as it had thought.

I'd known her all my life (her grandfather had been the third member of Turncoat Oil) but hadn't seen her in several weeks. I rarely thought of my past apart from her. Each of us was an only child, and we had functioned as cousins when we were children, although at the age of eleven I'd discovered there was more to the relationship than I'd thought. I'd bought a girl an ice cream cone, and Sally Ann had socked me in the eye. Then, after hitting me as effectively as any guy would have, she'd taken me to her house and lovingly applied an ice pack as smoothly and as easily as if I'd been battered by someone else.

We'd gotten together after dates in high school and critiqued our separate evenings when we weren't dating each other (always her choice, never mine), and we'd passed every important day of our lives in each other's company. When we'd played together as children, back when she'd merely been known for being "bossy," she'd insisted in the summer that if I could go without a shirt, she could too. And she'd continued the practice even after the difference in our chests had become apparent.

27

Over the years, she'd given me more confusing and pleasurable emotions than any one person was normally capable of. We could be discussing marriage one night and the next morning she'd have left the country. After our sophomore year in high school she'd broken my heart by attending a private school in Dallas, and then she'd returned to Abilene in time to accompany me to the University of Texas, only to transfer to S.M.U. at midterm.

She approached our cluster of chairs from behind Stan and said, "Billy Bastard, you old brewster."

I stood up and she gave me a hug. So I could fully absorb the sensations of contact with her long and lovely body, I closed my eyes and held my breath and tried to feel every curved and cushioned part of her. Then I inhaled the scent of midnight flowers and soft powders. A girl in a tennis outfit could have smelled sweaty, but she was much more interested in the attire than the sport.

"How was France?" I asked.

"Oh, Billy. The wine, the food, the sun. I didn't want to come back."

She gave me a smile, one that was half mysterious, half friendly, a facial gesture symbolic of our relationship. Half the time we were good friends, half the time lovers, and she could behave so unpredictably she normally was driving me crazy. Her reasoning always was, "I'm trying to keep things interesting."

"You should've gone with me," she said. "You would've loved it. Topless bathers. Miniskirts. On the beach in Cannes they have these little partitions, and women just take off their bikini tops and sunbathe to their heart's content. You'd have had a perpetual hard-on."

"I probably would've gone but I wasn't invited. I don't remember you asking me to go."

"That's why I didn't ask you—you'd have had a perpetual hard-on."

She took a chair and poured part of my beer into the empty glass beside the bottle, then sat back and crossed her legs.

I finally thought to introduce her to Stan, and he obviously remembered her from high school. When he heard his name, he popped up as though he were the clown in the jack-in-the-box, and he fell back into his chair, kicking the table between us and rattling the bottles. The poor guy simply lacked coordination. I'd watched him flip a coin once and he'd shot it off into space at a thirty-degree angle.

"You're working for Brewster?" she asked.

"I sure am," he replied happily, sitting down normally this time.

"And so what're you doing right now?"

Stan for once was speechless, looking at me as though we'd been caught by someone hired by my father to monitor our work habits, to make sure we stayed out of the country club until six in the evening. And he didn't know whether she was joking or not. He seemed to alternate between thinking everyone was alike and thinking "The Blest" were different. He'd used that term, the blest, several times before I ever figured out what he was talking about, and then I didn't know whether he intended it satirically or not.

Now he was apparently of the opinion the blest were *much* different, and he ran, the first time I'd ever seen him avoid any situation. He told Sally Ann, the blessed of the blest, that he was glad to see her again, and he loped off toward the front door, getting outside before he remembered that he'd accompanied me to this sacred place and he had no car. I gave him my keys so Sally Ann would have to take me home.

Once Stan was gone, she pushed my foot with hers and said, "Tell me what you've been doing. And don't leave anything out."

There wasn't much to tell. Other than work, I'd had a few dates the past few weeks, although I made it clear that all the girls were terribly inadequate stand-ins for her. She smiled and asked about a tall redhead named Carrie, an athletic girl who loved dancing and whose physical prowess and gymnastic abilities had always stirred my imagination.

"Can she kiss?" she asked. For a reason. She knew I loved her mouth. Sally Ann had the most kissable-looking lips I'd ever seen.

"She kisses like this," I said, making something up on the spot and avoiding the truth. I gave her a demonstration of the way in which Carrie supposedly kissed, pulling my lips back in over my teeth and imitating a toothless person. "Weirdest thing I ever saw."

"Maybe she was afraid of biting you."

"She kept grabbing my tongue with her lips."

"Well, the important thing is—did you find out she was capable of multiple positions?"

I shook my head. No way was I going to tell her the truth. She may have acted nonchalant, but she wasn't. Not ever. I'd made the mistake of giving her truthful answers before, and she invariably gave me the emotional equivalent of a black eye. Once, sounding both miserable and disgusted, she'd said, "My God, Billy, *why'd* you tell me?" She hadn't spoken to me for weeks, and may never have resumed the relationship, had I not undergone an emergency appendectomy.

She'd stayed in the hospital with me for three solid days and nights, even though I hadn't found her a great deal of comfort after the first night. And true to form, what I remembered most about that experience was her behavior and not my appendectomy. The details of the surgery were gone, faded from memory.

She'd awakened me in the middle of the night and asked, "Did I wake you up?" When I hadn't answered, confused by the question, she'd said, "I was afraid I woke you up. I was having a dream about falling and I screamed. Or thought I screamed. And I just knew I woke you up. I didn't?"

She sat on the edge of the bed and said, "Billy, I've got to tell you this because it's the grossest thing I ever heard. A nurse told me this afternoon. She said they had this man up here who was really burned bad, and when he healed up, he had all this scar tissue under his arm. You know how it looks. She called it a web. Isn't that the most terrible thing you've ever heard, to call that a web?" She shivered. "Anyway, he had this scar tissue, this web, on his arm and side and under his arm, and he couldn't lift his arm very high at all. Maybe this high. And it was just driving him crazy, so he'd put his hand on the wall and then try to stretch the web. But it wouldn't stretch; it would only crack. And he'd stretch it until it would crack and bleed." She shivered again, this time clasping her hands, squeezing them together in the darkness of the hospital room. "That's just the grossest thing I ever heard and I can't stop thinking about it. I just can't. Unless I go to sleep and then I dream I'm falling."

She lifted my hand and pressed it to her lips. "Billy, promise me you won't die before I do. Promise. What would I do if you died?"

This was care provided by Sally Ann. She was supposed to comfort me, I thought, not speculate on her future after my death. "I thought for once I'd be the center of attention."

"You are," she said, kissing each finger. "You're all I've been thinking about. Except for that man with the burn. That is *so gross*. I hate that nurse for telling me." The sudden tremors of repulsion ran down her arms and into my hands. "Billy, do you ever think about dying?"

"I can't say that I do."

"What're you thinking about, right now?"

"I'm thinking these pain pills make me sleepy."

She gave a little gasp. "Great. If you're so sleepy, just go back to sleep. Don't let me bother you."

"Good night. Again."

"That's just fine. You go back to sleep and I'll go sit in the corner and fall to death."

Now, both in good health, we left the country club, headed for her house. She drove her car, a red Triumph convertible, without a lot of care, the same approach she took to most activities. Her window open on this warm December day, her hair blew freely in the wind. She knew exactly what I liked; she knew because she made me tell her even though I had to guess at her preferences. She was very selective about what she let me know. And we both knew I loved her neck and the wispy hair that I could see as she drove.

She lived in the house her grandparents had owned; it had been left to her by her grandmother, the last to die. Physically, Sally Ann and her grandmother had been nothing alike. The old lady had been short and fierce looking, as intense as an Indian woman who'd been abused by too many white men. She'd always worn black hats that looked like derbies. But emotionally, the two women had been similar, strong willed and demanding and absolutely certain of what they wanted. Her grandmother, however, had apparently possessed some reservations about the grand-daughter's maturity because although Sally Ann was incredibly well pro-vided for by a trust, which consisted primarily of oil-producing proper-ties in west Texas, she'd never be allowed to touch the body of the trust.

We went sliding into the driveway of the big house and squealed to a stop. The house was two-story, the front walls covered with ivy, and it wasn't particularly well kept because Sally Ann never seemed able to spare the time to look after it.

She cut the engine and looked at me. "Are you hungry?"

"Sure. What have you got?"

"A sandwich. Sally Ann on satin. With I scream."

I laughed. One night we'd been making love, sitting up, Sally Ann on my lap facing me, and she'd got us into a position in which the sensa-tions were almost too good, too acute, and the nearer I got to ejacula-tion, the longer I was holding my breath. And when the release finally came, I not only exhaled all that pent-up air, but I'd screamed. Ever since, we'd never finished making love in any other position. We may have started in a different one, but we finished sitting up with a shout. Mine.

The big house retained the flavor of the grandmother in several of the rooms. Sally Ann refused to change the furniture or decor, but the bed-room was definitely the granddaughter's. It was dark and sensual and contained a huge four-poster bed, one big enough to sleep a family of six. But the best part of the room was the existence of my picture, an eight-by-ten, sitting on her dresser. It was a sign of hope.

I followed her into the bedroom, and she hit the switch on a reel-to-reel recorder, part of a large collection of stereo equipment against the wall. It had been a casual-looking move, but one that I knew had been purposeful when I heard the song. She'd been expecting me because the tape started on "Be My Baby," which was, as she said, our song.

I listened, waiting for my favorite lines.

> We'll make 'em turn their heads
> Every place we go.

All I wanted was to go places with this girl. My desire was a well-defined vision, seen through a haze—she and I went swinging through a crowd of people that opened as we went, all heads turning, moving to the sound of "Be My Baby." That was all I wanted. But the song had a bittersweet effect on me because I didn't think I'd ever achieve my goal. She'd never marry me. I didn't know why; I just knew she wouldn't.

She walked across the bed on her knees, throwing the bedspread down as she went. Then, still on her knees, she pulled off her shoes and pitched them toward a closet door, then removed the tennis dress, showing me what I called her athletic underwear. Wanting to slow things down, wanting to exist forever in this present state, I sat on the end of the bed.

"I just figured something out," I said. "It's the violins."

"The what?"

"The violins in that song that make it about half sad. I always thought it was because I knew you'd never marry me, but maybe that's not it at all. Maybe it's just the violins."

She refused to give the encouragement I wanted to hear; instead she made a temporary offering of the flesh by stripping.

She was nothing short of perfect. Or maybe she wasn't really perfect but was just exactly what I wanted to see, a model of balance and the picture of good health. Her breasts were as crisp as apples, the lines definite and clean, and their weight seemed to give the right definition to her collarbones. She was tall, five feet seven inches, in high school, and she'd swept an election for the best body parts, even for arms, disappointing a large number of boys who'd been immensely proud of their biceps.

Still on her knees in the middle of the bed, hands on hips, she watched me watch her.

"France was good to you. You're as sleek as a greyhound."

"Why're you always comparing things to dogs?"

"Well, I guess because I wouldn't want to compare you to a cow or, say, a tree."

"You could just tell me I'm beautiful."

I shook my head and crossed the mattress, my knees punching the white satin sheets. "That doesn't cover it."

I lay down, pulling her with me, and for a moment she hovered above me, on her hands, her arms straight, looking into my eyes. Her hair was almost long enough to brush my cheeks.

I'd been born to privilege, one of The Blest, and couldn't remember ever really wanting anything I hadn't gotten. But what I wanted more than anything—to marry Sally Ann Wells—was somehow going to be forever just beyond my grasp.

"Did I tell you how glad I am to see you again?" she asked.

"Don't tell me. Show me."

Her head dropped slowly and she kissed me.

3

Spud date, the date drilling was to begin on Stan's well, brought rain, a fairly normal occurrence in January. Stan considered this good luck, however, because the temperature was moderate. "Hey! It could be snow or ice," he said of these forty-degree nights and fifty-degree days. The climate in our part of the state was somewhat confusing. We had two seasons, summer and winter, and spring and fall came at odd times throughout the year for brief periods.

He and I drove to the lease in the afternoon to check on the condition of the location, as though it might have washed away in the drizzle or been stolen. Stan wanted to make sure it was ready to receive Rig #3. His spirits didn't reflect the gray and gloomy weather; he was getting anxious.

"This is gonna be great," he said. "We've got a producing well in our future, I just know it. I don't know how I know it, but I do."

I'd quit trying to make him realistic. He assumed because there were two plugged wells on the property he'd find oil at 3,700 feet, which was the anticipated total depth of the #1 Lowell B. Brooks Estate. And maybe since Stan had a beginner's naïveté and enthusiasm, he'd also have beginner's luck, even though I didn't think there was any such thing.

The lease was about sixty miles from Abilene, close to nothing, on land that had once been partially farmed but was now overgrown with yucca and goatheads. Part of the property was a big hill, and much of the rest wasn't suitable for anything, full of gullies and rocks. In fact, Lowell had dug a tank for his cattle before he'd died, and the process had required more blasting than digging. The giant shards of rock were still piled beside the tank.

We drove onto the lease on a gravel road and followed it to the location. Off from this gravel road was a brand-new one, for the rig, made of caliche, and it was almost glowing white in the gray afternoon. The pits had been dug and everything was ready for Rig #3. It would come in assorted sections to be assembled here, a moving task that required eighteen truck loads. Moving a rig was a routine operation, but it was a massive undertaking.

Stan knew all the possibilities of this producing well in his future because he'd used a mile of calculator tape figuring, checking, and double-checking. I'd pulled this immensely long tape from his trash can one night after he'd gone home (wherever that was) to verify what I'd suspected. He'd calculated the possibility of everything from ten barrels a day to a hundred. And I'd been surprised to see that he'd stopped at a hundred.

His figures broke down this way: Brewster had contracted a turnkey job to drill a 3,700-foot well for $29,600 and an eighth interest; the landowner, Mr. Brooks's estate, retained an eighth royalty; and Stan had granted Mrs. Miller a thirty-second out of the goodness of his heart for her altruistic efforts in securing this lease. Those two would pay no expenses regardless. Stan, after checking his bank account and an unknown source of credit, had decided to take only a sixteenth. The rest had gone to his various well-informed investors.

The expenses would be borne by those investors, and once Stan had started calculating, he'd begun to regret giving Mrs. Miller her thirty-second as a finder's fee. "Live and learn," he'd said. "The old bat oughta be paying her way." One of the investors in for an eighth was going to get a bill for $5,148 for drilling. Stan's sixteenth would cost him half that much.

The unknown, which often ran from 25 percent to 100 percent of the drilling costs, was the expense required to complete the well should it look promising. They'd have to set casing in the hole, cement it in place, perforate it to allow oil entrance, and set the equipment necessary to pump the oil to the surface, then erect the necessary tanks to store the oil until it could be picked up by a truck.

There was, of course, no guarantee that the well would produce anything, or that it would produce anything but salt water, or that it would produce oil in conjunction with gas or salt water. Additional equipment would be necessary to separate oil from salt water or gas. And although gas could be marketed, just as oil could, there were no gathering lines in the area.

If completion costs ran half the expense of drilling, the investor with an eighth would get an additional bill for $5,148. He'd also get a bill each month for the cost of operating the well and for any repairs or workovers.

In return for his investment, he received tax advantages as well as revenue. He could deduct the costs of drilling from his income, could depreciate the costs of the equipment, and he received 27.5 percent of his return tax-free under the depletion allowance. Should the well produce thirty barrels a day, his monthly return would amount to $393.75, as long as oil was selling for $3.50 a barrel. If the production was greater, at a hundred barrels a day, his return jumped to $1,312.50 a month.

But first Rig #3 had to find oil.

Sitting in the car on this dismal afternoon looking at this freshly dozed and packed location, Stan said, "That's it. That's the spot, right there."

"Randy'll be glad to know you approve his work." Randy was the geologist.

Then, an amazing event occurred. We were facing west, and a crack in the clouds appeared; blue sky shone through the otherwise solid gray wall. I couldn't believe it. Even God was on Stan's side. The drizzle had quit, and I figured with the way things were going, the temperature by midnight would be eighty, the relative humidity zero, and by morning cracks would have appeared in the ground because it was so dry.

Stan, his eyes fixed on the magic location, said, "That girl, Sally Ann. You serious about her?"

"I try not to be. It doesn't pay."

He didn't say anything for a moment, but I knew he was going to, because this wasn't the first time he'd brought her up as a topic of conversation. I thought he was laboring under a misconception. The world of business was much more democratic, much more fair to Stanley Gaines, than high school had been, but Sally Ann wasn't a democrat. It was difficult to say what she was, but not quite as hard to say what she wasn't. He wanted to ask her out, and I didn't know how to discourage him, but I didn't think there was any more chance she'd date him than there was that she'd marry me. The only comment she'd ever made

35

about Stan had pertained to his clothes. "He's the only person I know who buys his clothes at a joke shop. Look at him more than a few seconds and you get vertigo."

"You mind if I ask her out?" he said. "If you don't want me to, I won't."

"Be my guest," I said, thinking he wouldn't heed a warning anyway. "One thing though. Before you do, you need to know she said something about your clothes. You need to work on coordination."

He looked at me, smiling, and I swear that the slice of blue sky in the west was suddenly shaped into another big smile.

"She was talking about me, huh?"

"She was talking about your clothes. Fashions by Dizzy Green. Your geometry clashes, Stan."

"How about that. She was talking about me." He turned toward me as the great smile in the sky enlarged. It even seemed to be showing teeth, like a laughing mule. "Hey. Why don't we go to the country club again sometime and kinda run into her like we did the first time. Give me a chance to talk to her. I'll even show her some coordinated clothes. Maybe a navy blue suit and a nice red tie. What do you think?"

I suddenly lost my complacency. Undoubtedly, Stan had left the army and a number of people who'd suspected his intention of getting into the oil business, only to be called a few days later with a proposal on an oil and gas package. Here was a guy making $600 a month—I'd asked him—with no experience in anything, much less in the oil field, and yet we were in a car sitting on his lease. This was the same guy who dated the red-haired waitress, who'd flatly refused my invitations, and who had almost displaced me as son in the Brewster family. He'd walked in and exposed his fire in the gut and given my father a tangible standard against which to measure me. And to find me wanting.

Now he was after Sally Ann.

I had to listen carefully but I heard it, I definitely heard it. The mule face in the sky said, "Heh heh heh."

For the first time in the history of our weekly family dinners, an outsider had been invited. Good old Stan. I'd suggested more than once bringing company—usually Sally Ann, who was almost a relative—and my mother had always said, "Oh, let's just keep it family." But now the old man had invited his new son. I walked around muttering to myself. One of these days I'd walk up to the door of my apartment and find a sign on the door. "Under New Occupancy. Signed, Stan Gaines."

Worse, Stan picked the Thursday our enlarged family would eat together to also visit the country club so we could "kinda run into" Sally Ann.

As he drove us, he said, "Hey, what're we having for dinner?"

"My name's not Hey."

He smiled, knowing deep down that I wanted him to twist the hair on my arm and call me Hey. Probably I secretly wished I owned geometric clothes.

"So what're we eating?"

"I don't know."

"You said your mother's a good cook, and I'm really looking forward to this. Besides, I've never met her."

This was the way in which the old man had decided to commemorate spud day for the #1 Lowell B. Brooks Estate. He and Stan were going to drive out to the location after dinner, and Stan was taking several cases of beer for each tour, hoping to lubricate some good luck out of the guys. If I'd tried such a tactic, one of them would get drunk while working and get his arm ripped off at the shoulder.

We "kinda ran into" Sally Ann in the parking lot of the country club, as she was arriving for a hot game of gin rummy. She wore black pants and an orange sweater, which added color to a winter day that seemed to lack light. The sky was clear but the sun wasn't very bright.

Stan had bought a navy blue suit with a red tie, just as he'd said, but the problem was—at least I hoped it was a problem—that the nicer he dressed, the more homely he looked. He needed geometry to keep people from looking too closely at his face. I hoped that Sally Ann noticed that he looked not so much like Abraham Lincoln, as I'd once thought, but a formally attired basset hound. If she didn't notice, I'd point it out.

"The working men," she said, meeting us between two cars in the parking lot. "That'd make a good movie title, wouldn't it? Except they'd never find a man who knew how to play the part."

"As though you'd recognize work," I said.

She stopped to talk, as though she knew what Stan wanted, and propped herself up by an elbow on a white Cadillac. I wanted her to say something about Stan's clothes, maybe ask if the joke shop had closed down, but she didn't. Instead she gave him an opportunity to talk, and he launched into the story of his drilling venture, telling her this was the biggest day of his life. He explained drilling operations as though they were foreign to her, and maybe they were. I watched her, hoping to see some concrete signs of disdain, but I didn't. She very politely listened, which wasn't like her at all.

He ended his monologue by telling her he was headed for the rig later, hoping the beer that made Milwaukee famous would get him started on the road to riches. "So wish me luck."

"I'll not only wish you luck, but I'll make a prediction," she said. "You're going to get a show at twenty-seven hundred feet."

A show was evidence of oil. My God, I thought. I'd just heard Sally Ann Wells wish him luck. She wasn't always a kindhearted person, and with the majority of the population, she'd probably have sneered at the request for good wishes and prayed they'd drown in a veritable sea of salt water at 2,700 feet. This was another example of a process I just didn't understand. Everybody seemed to fall right in line hoping the basset hound would succeed. Maybe it was his careless enthusiasm, or his childish sort of naïveté, that made it easy for others to offer their support.

And then it hit me—I'd been one of those pulling for him until I'd begun to resent him for his efforts at inhabiting my body. At least I felt as though he were try to take my place. He'd displaced me in the family and now he was trying to take my girlfriend.

He stuck his hands into his pockets, pulling his suit coat open, and leaned against the dusty car behind him. "Well, that'd sure make me happy. Maybe for *real* luck, we should go out and be there when they get to twenty-seven hundred feet."

I'd been silent so long I was about to become anonymous, so I cleared my throat and moved around, scraping my feet on the pavement of the parking lot. "What's magic about twenty-seven hundred feet?"

She looked at me as though she wasn't certain of my identity. "It's my favorite number."

"Well, no kidding? Mine's three hundred ninety-six thousand four hundred and eight. What's yours, Stan?"

She gave me a look of disgust. "My favorite number's *twenty-seven*." She dismissed me with a shake of her head and turned her attention back to the big dog. "I think that'd be a good idea. You tell me when they get close to twenty-seven hundred and we'll go pay homage to the patron saint of the oil business. Who is that?"

"Saint Dino," I said. "The dinosaur."

I was witnessing what I hadn't been able to believe would happen, the worst, the very worst. Sally Ann could be interested in Stanley Gaines. He wasn't going to possess me; he was going to make me invisible, nonexistent, a nonperson nobody would even remember. At family reunions, my relatives would come up to my mother and pat her on the shoulder and say, "I'm so sorry you were never able to have kids. But young Stanley's probably a real comfort to you, isn't he?" My mother would nod and blot her tears of joy with a tissue.

The Blest, my ass. It was the mean and hungry who counted.

Now Stan was holding forth on a theory he'd just developed, or just heard, and that was that the five-year-old alliance of petroleum-exporting countries would eventually learn how to control the price of oil, and west Texas would boom again. I listened to him, thinking, unbelievable, absolutely unbelievable. An expert with less than three months in the business.

Then, as though he'd suddenly remembered he was in a hurry, he pushed himself off the dusty car, his navy blue suit spotless instead of coated with the red dust of west Texas, and said, "Okay, Sally Ann Wells, when we get near twenty-seven hundred feet, I'm going to come get you and we'll go to Coleman County."

"Maybe the man with the great big lucky number will agree to go with us," she said, looking at me.

"He ought to," Stan said. "He's responsible for this whole thing."

"Don't be telling your investors that, Stan," I said, thinking things would have to turn around soon. We had to be at the nadir. He'd taken my job, my waitress, was working on my girlfriend, had renamed me Hey, and was now on his way to assume his role in my family. What else could happen? Now he'd have to start working on someone else, and I'd be able to identify his next victim. It'd be some poor guy named Yo.

The newly restructured family met at seven to eat, and I was slightly surprised to see Stan across from me at the dining room table and not sitting in my father's spot. I could hardly see myself eating in the mirror over the buffet anymore. What bothered me more than anything, though, was to see Stan sitting by Boomer. My grandfather, in black pants and white shirt, all he ever wore, hadn't yet acknowledged Stan's existence. No food was in sight, and he wasn't about to start talking until it was.

Stan and my father were in a hurry, as excited as kids going to the county fair with pockets full of money and heads full of ideas. Was this fire in the gut? I wondered. Getting stirred up over the drilling of a well?

My mother set salads before us in white bowls and Boomer popped a cherry tomato in his mouth before asking, "So this is the doughboy, huh?"

If the term confused Stan, he didn't show it. "Yes, sir, that's me, Mr. Brewster. And let me tell you, it's an honor to be eating with you. An honor. You're one of the heroes of the industry."

"Well, I've been called that," Boomer said. He'd never been strong on modesty.

For the next few minutes, he gave Stan a brief history of the cycles of his life, the booms and busts. He'd been up and down more than anyone I knew, or, as he put it, more than any dance-hall girl in Ranger. He'd formed companies and sold the stock on street corners, everything from God Help Us Oil Company to Lady Luck Petroleum.

Stan hadn't yet touched his salad. "God Help Us Oil Company?"

"Yep, easiest stock I ever sold. People thought success was as sure as the Almighty. I tried Ask and Ye Shall Receive Petroleum, but those damned heathen in Wichita Falls didn't recognize scripture when it bit 'em on the butt."

He jumped from stock to shooting, having never felt compelled to make smooth or logical transitions in his stories. Once wells had been drilled in the old days, the crew often called in a shooter. He lowered a long bucket of nitro into the hole, often containing as much as thirty quarts. The object was to get the unstable explosive to the bottom of the hole and then set it off, thereby stimulating production.

A major problem arose if the pressure in the hole pushed the bucket back up toward the shooter, a frightening occurrence signaled by the line to the bucket going slack. If the downhole pressure was strong enough, it blew the bucket out of the hole, right up to the crown of the derrick, and the entire structure, along with anyone on it, was blown to bits. When the line went slack, thinking men ran like hell. Others, like Boomer, stuck around to catch the bucket as it exited the hole. Or so he said. I'd never met anyone who had actually witnessed him doing so.

"You really caught those things?" Stan asked.

"Oh, hell, yes. Wasn't nothing to it. Lots of guys were scared of the stuff, but not me. I was one hell of a shooter, in demand all over the country."

My old man usually added a disclaimer to Boomer's stories, but tonight he was too busy eating. He wanted to get to the lease.

"How's your mother, Stan?" my mother asked.

"She's fine, just fine," he said and began eating.

There was something to this Melissa Gaines business, something scandalous, and my mother wouldn't tell me what it was. The only way I could encourage her to tell me was to make her believe I'd somehow manage to pull the curtain on the past through ignorance and bumping around in the dark. After all, how could I refrain from talking about something if I didn't know I wasn't supposed to? So I said, "How is it you know Stan's mother?"

"You went to school together," she said, as if somewhat irritated by having to state the obvious. But of course I knew the reason for her snippy answer. I wasn't supposed to be asking such questions.

"Were you room mothers together or something? I don't remember you ever talking about her."

I heard my mother exhale through her nose, a sign of anger. She was sitting right next to me, staring at her salad, and I knew she was trying to figure out some way to shut me up, and she apparently decided the best way was to ignore me. So I turned my attention to Stan, who was also guilty of withholding information. Either his mother's name wasn't Gaines anymore or she didn't have a phone. One night, in the course of looking for him, I'd called every Gaines in the phone book and not a one of them knew Stan.

"Does your mother still live here?" I asked.

Stan dug a crouton out of his salad with his fork and looked it over as though he'd just found something unexpected, like part of a shoelace, right there in the lettuce. "Are these things made out of bread?"

"Where's your mother live?" I asked.

Still examining the crouton from different angles, turning it this way and that as if to catch the light, he said, "She's been here all her life and I doubt that she'll ever leave."

He couldn't answer one of my questions like a politician and get away with it. If the guy expected to move in and take over every relationship I'd ever had, he'd have to answer a few simple questions. "And she lives where?"

"Hellfire," Boomer said, "why don't we interrogate the son of a bitch? Any Hebrews in your family, doughboy? How many generations back are clean? Ever traveled to the Holy Land? Ever been denied permission to enter Egypt? *Is your middle name Moses?*"

Stan laughed, making Boomer show his dentures in appreciation, and Stan, smarter than I thought he was, asked if Boomer had made the boom in Desdemona, a question that started Boomer back on the old days and effectively shut me up and my investigation off.

I couldn't remember Boomer ever aligning himself with someone other than me, and I was feeling even worse now, knowing he had a new grandson, knowing I'd been almost completely displaced. Still, I wasn't prepared to hear him say, "I believe I'll ride along with you boys out to see the number-one doughboy. I ain't been out on a location since Christ was a corporal."

My father stood. "Salad's all I want. You ready?"

Boomer and Stan stood as well, leaving me and my mother with a meal prepared for five people, and I briefly entertained a thought I'd never even considered. Maybe I'd join the army. Better yet, the marines. I'd go to Vietnam and maybe take one in the gut and return to join this inner circle of hot dogs, guys who caught nitro, drilled wells when they couldn't spell, much less define, geology, and who had once been nicknamed Rooster after a desire to deprive others of sleep.

Once they were gone and my mother and I were sitting silently at the long table, she gave me a long look.

"You're not going?" she asked.

I shook my head.

"Why?"

"Because you're fixing to tell me about Melissa Gaines."

Shaking her head but knowing she was caught, she said, "You make me mad sometimes, you know that?" She sighed and sat back in her chair, looking at us in the mirror over the buffet. "You keep in mind, I don't *know* any of this. But years ago, probably before you even started school, she was working for the Hendrixes, and she and Mister Hendrix were—" She waved her hand back and forth as though directing me in a song. "You know."

"And what about the Fords?"

"Don't you ever forget anything? It was kinda the same situation but she didn't leave the Fords as fast. Mister Ford was supposed to be, I don't know, intrigued with her."

"What'd she look like?"

"I never saw her so I don't know."

"She liked rich guys," I said, because Hendrix and Ford were both wealthy, one in ranching, one in oil.

And I remembered another Stanley Gaines story. In high school, probably early, a guy had called Stan's mother something scurrilous, a whore maybe, and Stan had paid him back. In the boy's rest room, there had been a long urinal and two stalls against one wall. Stan had stood at the end of the urinal, facing the stalls and the rear of the rest room, and watched the slandering malefactor enter the first stall. Then, standing tiptoed, arched backward, Stan had shot a rainbow arc of urine into the first stall, showering the kid who'd maligned Melissa Gaines.

42

No one had ever called Stan's mother a whore again.

"What're you smiling about?" my mother asked.

"You don't want to know."

"You're probably right," she said, standing and picking up her salad bowl. "I don't want to know."

At 1,100 feet, Rig #3 lost circulation.

Stan and I had been at the courthouse in Albany clearing the title to Mrs. Miller's land, and we walked back into the office to hear the tool pusher shout over the radio, which sat beside the receptionist near the front door, "Call Strawn Mud and tell them to get this numbnuts off my location before I peel his ears off."

The receptionist, an agile young lady who handled both the radio and telephone, often simultaneously, told the tool pusher, "Okay, Don. Okay. I'm calling right now. Base, out." She replaced the microphone on the table beside her and started dialing the phone in the same motion without consulting a phone book. She had a hundred phone numbers memorized. And while she was doing this, she said to us, "Lost circulation."

Stan immediately looked at me for an interpretation. I explained that the drilling mud, which was circulated down the drill pipe and back up the hole outside the pipe, lubricating the bit and removing cuttings from the well bore, was disappearing into some channel or fissure in the formation. I knew they'd been using a lightweight mud because they'd been drilling through shale, and, more than likely, the mud engineer, a Mr. Numbnuts who had an earless future before him, had been negligent in watching the cuttings returning to the surface. They'd probably passed into limestone without adjusting the mud.

"Let's get down there," Stan said.

Why not? I wondered. Stan not only could use the education, but he could watch Don Rains, the tool pusher who supervised Rig #3, in action. Rains had given me a harsh introduction into the real world of manual labor when I was in high school, and he'd cured me forever from any desire to work with my hands. He'd been a driller then, and when he came by to pick me up on my first day, my father had said, "He's just a worm, Rains. Keep an eye on him." And Rains had cast a hard glance my way and said, "*He* better keep an eye on me."

The rig was sixty miles away, and, since Stan was driving, I figured the trip would take about forty-five minutes. As we drove, I pointed at the road, reminding him that he was driving and that other cars often used the same highway, and also explained that the crew would have to reestablish circulation by sealing the thief formation with some solid material in the mud, something like pecan hulls. If they couldn't reestablish circulation, then the hole would have to be cased and cemented, an extra expense which also cost diameter.

Rig #3 was sitting idle over the hole, rising 120 feet in the air over the late Mr. Brooks's land, a blue and white digging machine with its snout 1,100 feet into the earth. Rains was sitting in the white company pickup with the blue Brewster logo on the door. He sat sideways on the seat, the door open, feet on the floorboard, bending forward and taking extremely quick drags from a cigarette, looking like a freight train with a real head of steam up.

"Don't park too close to him," I said. "He's pissed now."

"You mean he wasn't a while ago?" Stan asked, pulling into the goatheads near the pickup.

"No, he yells all the time. He hates silence." And he did. He didn't want to hear the wind moving through the weeds or the birds singing. He wanted to hear diesel engines roaring and iron clanking. And he didn't like delays of any kind. If the old man wanted 3,700 feet of hole made, Rains intended to give him 3,700 feet of hole before any other human could possibly get it done.

I rolled down my window and said, "Pipe's stuck, isn't it?"

He gave me an affirming glare, telling me the shale had started swelling and had a death grip on the string of pipe in the hole.

"So where's Numbnuts?" I asked.

He pointed as though identifying a target. The mud engineer sat on the ground beside one of the tanks, his knees up and resting his head on his arms, no doubt humiliated by Rains and made to wonder why he'd chosen this particular occupation. This was a nice January day and he could have been having a picnic with the family. Instead he'd been threatened with the loss of his ears, and probably other parts of his body. Rains's size was deceptive. He was small and wiry, and one never suspected that he could deliver curses as he did.

He lit one cigarette off another, his eyes still fixed on the mud engineer as though contemplating sadistic pleasures. "Strawn must be hiring retarded sons of bitches. If we ever use them again, I'll know your old man's lost his mind."

The crew—four of them—milled around on the floor of the rig, casting nervous glances our way. When drilling operations were interrupted, Rains would hover around, showering them with bits of his frustration, and he wouldn't leave until normal operations were restored.

44

The mud engineer lifted his head to look around. A mistake. Rains shouldn't have been reminded that the man was capable of or interested in movement, because he was out of the pickup like a shot, jumping from the cab and landing fifteen feet away. "Where're the pecan hulls, boy? If they aren't out here in two minutes, I'm gonna rip your arms off and grind up the bones. I'll use your fucking *bones.* I'll use your wife's bones, your kids' bones. I'll use your *fucking dog.* Where in the hell are those pecan hulls?"

The victim hurried to his car to use the radio, locking the doors once he was inside. Then he leaned over, resting his elbow on the seat, and tried to hide as he talked.

Stan watched all this silently until he said, "Is that guy mad, or what?"

"He's pretty close."

Stan left the car, smart enough to stay away from Rains, and took a circuitous route to the rig, probably so he could see if the crew had enjoyed the beer he had delivered. I leaned over and turned the key so I could listen to music on the radio.

I had a more distressing development than lost circulation to consider. I hadn't really thought of Stan's arrangement to bring Sally Ann to the rig when it neared 2,700 feet as a date, especially since I was going to be along, but now he had arranged an official date. They were going to a party together, a traditional post–New Year's, pre-Easter party we'd been having for years, one that had started as a crutch to help us get over the blahs caused by the distance to the next holiday.

In his usual blind optimism, Stan had dropped this bomb on me and suggested I find a date so we could double. I had just about as much interest in spending all night seeing Stan and Sally Ann together as I had in disturbing fire ant beds with my foot. First I'd considered boycotting the party, then changed my mind and asked a girl named Jill Denton to go.

She was pretty in an unexciting way, and she rarely experimented with clothes or looks; about the only time her appearance changed was when freckles broke out across her nose in the summer. I'd dated her off and on for years, just about every time Sally Ann dumped me or disappeared. And she wasn't a scintillating date. A friend had put it succinctly several years ago: "She'll probably make somebody a great wife, but she's a lousy date."

She was the daughter my mother wanted, and the two had always been on very friendly terms, regardless of whether she and I were dating or not. I'd gotten the idea more than once that they were conspiring against me, ushering me toward the altar. My mother didn't dislike Sally Ann; she just thought my old friend was probably perfect for some other guy. Jill, on the other hand, wanted to be a Brewster, and my mother had extended her arms, welcoming her to the family.

A flatbed truck from the mud company finally arrived, its bed stacked with bags of pecan hulls. The truck came bouncing quickly over the gravel road across the lease, the driver either acquainted with Rains or having been warned. But still he wasn't going fast enough; Rains ran toward the road making big circles with his right arm, waving it on.

The truck stopped near the rig and Rains immediately climbed onto the bed, throwing off the sacks, showing everybody in attendance that they weren't working hard enough to suit him. The mud engineer, believing he was safer on the truck than on the ground below the human cannon shooting sacks of hulls, assisted.

Stan walked back toward the car and said to me, "Can you believe this? Here we are in 1965 and we're using pecan hulls. Unbelievable."

After two hours of inactivity, the rig was busy again, the diesel engines running, drowning out the sounds of nature. The derrickman ascended to his perch ninety feet above the ground. They would attempt to restore circulation and then probably spot the pipe, mixing oil with the mud to free the drill pipe from the swollen shale. Actually, the quickest way to free the pipe was to let Rains stick his head down the hole and curse it. Not even a formation millions of years old could withstand that kind of torment.

"I can't believe you don't think this is exciting," Stan said.

"It's kinda like breathing. It keeps me alive, it's necessary for me to continue living, but I don't get very excited about it. Do you?"

"Oh, yeah, sure I do."

"You get excited about breathing?"

"Sure. If I think about it."

Poor Sally Ann. She'd never have a conversation with the guy that would mean anything. She and I had spent hours talking, discussing and dissecting life on her bed while we listened to music, on a mesa at her grandmother's ranch, anywhere we'd ever been alone. No subject had ever been too sacred; we'd talked about everything.

Why, oh why, had she agreed to date Stanley Gaines?

The pecan hulls worked. Stan and I left just after dark, headed for Abilene and, for me, a long boring night.

· · ·

46

I began to think Sally Ann and my father were collaborating. The old man decided they needed a core sample at 2,700 feet. I started to ask him if that was his favorite number, but he'd located the man who had operated the two wells, both plugged long ago, and after a search through his garage they'd found the man's records on both wells. And so, after a little research and having consulted with St. Dino, he'd decided to get a core sample at 2,700 feet.

As promised, the three of us—Stan, Sally Ann, and I—drove to the lease the night the rig neared 2,700 feet. I thought Stan had a very strange attitude toward romance, if that's what he had in mind. He seemed happier with my presence in the front seat of his car than with Sally Ann's, and he kept talking to me about things going on at work. The thought that his overwhelming interest in wheeling and dealing precluded any real interest in romance made me feel much more tolerant toward him.

Sally Ann, in true and confusing form, rode between us, her right hand between my leg and hers, applying periodic pressure against me by making a fist. At times she seemed to be sending me a coded message. We were all dressed casually, and she wore Levis and a plaid flannel shirt. And her manner of dress confused me as much as Stan's attitude. Both seemed bent on proving this was a nonsexual event.

So why'd they have a date lined up?

The rig, its derrick lighted, was visible from a distance, and Stan grew almost reverent as we approached through the night over the old gravel road that ran the length of the 180 acres. We arrived as the crew was tripping back into the hole, having already changed bits. To get a core sample, they had to stop drilling at 2,700 feet, lift all the drill pipe out of the hole, breaking it out in three-joint sections of about ninety feet each and standing it in the derrick. They then had to switch over to the coring bit and reenter the hole. Tool pushers like Rains believed coring operations were a gift from God; the crew was required to work its collective ass to a frazzle.

Stan parked near a thicket of small oak trees not far from the rig and killed the engine.

"This is it," Sally Ann said. "This is where you get a show."

Stan made no comment, surprising me. Where was his cheery optimism, his back-slapping assurances, his glib words? Was he sick?

"You don't think so?" I asked.

"Actually, and I'm sorry for this, but I hope we don't. One of those old wells produced nothing but salt water, and the other went great guns at first. A hundred ninety barrels a day. It did that for about two weeks and then started tapering off. Bad. The entire year it produced less than five thousand barrels and then it was done. That's not what we want. Its pay zone was right at twenty-seven hundred feet."

My God, I thought. Was Stanley Gaines getting realistic? Was it possible? The prospect of a dry hole or a well that wasn't economically feasible to produce had a way of making a person realistic, especially when he had investors calling him, wanting to know if they were rich yet.

"But," Stan said, shaking his finger, "we're definitely going to do it at thirty-seven hundred. No question."

So much for caution, I thought.

The lights from the derrick provided some illumination for us, but the lower parts of our bodies were in the shadows. Sally Ann moved her hand onto my leg. What was she doing? Encouraging competition? Making a statement in braille about her relationship with Stan? I turned to get three beers from a cooler in the back seat, curious about where her right hand would end up as I twisted to my left, toward her. But she moved her hand. I pulled three cans from the ice, got a church key from the glove compartment, and opened the cans of Bud. The scent of beer *swooshed* into the car.

I distributed the cans. "Well, here's to good luck at whatever depth." Then I poured some out the window onto the ground. "Libations for you, Saint Dino. Don't roar, don't kick, just give us about a hundred barrels a day for the next seventy-five years."

"I'm going to see how they're doing," Stan said and left the car.

When he departed, I was afraid Sally Ann would move away toward the steering wheel, but she didn't. I shifted, turning slightly toward her, and laid my arm across the seat behind her.

She said, "Stan says you're not going to the party with us."

I shook my head, watching Stan approach the rig, and wondered how she could so easily talk about dating someone else. I didn't want to discuss the party, Jill, or Stan; I didn't want to do anything but take this girl home and listen to music with her.

"Are you going?" she asked.

I nodded.

"Who're you taking?"

"I haven't decided."

"Jill?" she asked and almost laughed, masking the urge by looking at the beer can and biting on her lips. "Mrs. Jill Brewster. It has a certain ring to it. And she's such a *sweet* girl." She smiled to reinforce the slur, then released the laughter she'd been suppressing, in the same instant collapsing against me.

Why, I wondered, if she wouldn't marry me, was she going to do everything in her power to make my departure from her life as difficult as possible? And I understood how terribly hard this was all going to be when she dropped her head back on my arm and then slowly let her head roll to the right, putting her face only inches from mine. Very lightly she blew on my lips.

I shivered and said, "Some day you'll be sorry for all this."

"I already am," she said, rising, moving the few inches necessary to kiss me, a short but meaningful kiss. "But then, some day you'll forgive me."

"Marry me. Make me happy."

"I can't marry you, Billy. That'd be like incest." To prove she was joking, she kissed me again, this time in a very nonsisterly way. Her hand fell into my lap. "I'll love you all my days and nights, but I can't marry you."

Her manner had changed, slightly but definitely, as she rested against me, the top of her head against my cheek. She'd shifted into the honesty mode, the one in which she talked to me when we were doing nothing but talking, and it suddenly occurred to me that she wasn't trying to make my departure difficult; she was trying to kick me out of her life with a satin shoe rather than a steel-toed boot. This was it, the end.

How could it happen? Our lives were irrevocably twisted together, as tightly as strands in a rope, and she was going to unravel us. "Do you know, when I see you, I see a ten-year-old girl in shorts with no shirt out there on the mesa, and I see you, too? I see the best friend, the best girlfriend, the best lover I could imagine. I see the sky out at your grandmother's ranch. Do you know that the only times my life ever seemed to make sense was out there with you? I can't explain what it was like for me out there. It was religious. It was more than religious."

Her response was another kiss. I pulled her against me, feeling her shirt move so smoothly over her arm and back that it should have just slipped right off. I undid the top two buttons over her chest and then inserted my hand into the warmth, letting my fingers slip into her bra where it fell away from her breast. For a moment I wished Stan would return to the car and catch us, but that wouldn't have done any good; he would have simply asked if we were having a good time. Stanley Gaines wasn't the problem. Sally Ann Wells was.

"Do you trust me?" she asked, rubbing her nose on my cheek.

"Sometimes. It depends on who I'm talking to. I don't always trust Sally Ann the lover. Who am I talking to?"

"It's Sally Ann the lover you want to marry, isn't it?"

"Not necessarily. I want to marry all of you. I want to sit with you on your bed and drink wine and talk and listen to music for the rest of my life. Except for a trip out to the mesa every once in a while."

"If you trust me, you'll know I'm doing what's best for both of us. And you won't ask me about it anymore because you'll only make us both sad, and I know you don't want to make us sad. We have too much fun together to be sad."

She kissed me again, this time lightly, teasing. "You know what you should do, don't you? Marry Jill and move to Dallas. Quit piddling. You're the biggest piddler I know, and you're capable of so much more. And all you want to do is sit around on the mountain and think about the Indians."

I supposed she had identified the problem. I did like sitting on the mountain contemplating the Indians. Her grandfather had shown us a spot on the ranch one day where two raiding Indians had been caught and killed after stealing horses, and I'd dug around in the dirt all day trying to find traces of their blood. It had seemed important for reasons I hadn't completely understood, and I'd been unable to explain to Sally Ann why I couldn't leave until I'd found the blood.

"Why do you want me to marry Jill? I'm asking Sally Ann my best friend."

"Sally Ann your best friend doesn't want you to marry Jill. She wants you to come live with her forever." As if to prove she spoke the truth, she burrowed into a spot between me and the seat as though she needed protection. And maybe she did. From herself. I pushed the strap of her bra down over her shoulder and pulled the cup away from her breast, holding the softest part of her, a perfect handful. I'd never made out with a girl sitting a hundred feet from a drilling rig while her new boy-friend watched the rotary table turn, but it seemed absolutely natural.

She pressed my hand to her breast and said, "Your best friend knows she'll never meet anybody else she loves as much as she loves you. And the lover wants you to know you've brought her lots and lots of pleasure she'll never know with anyone else."

"Who does that leave?"

"The part that can't marry you."

"Hell, take a vote. It'll be two against one. We can get married. Tonight."

"Billy," she said in the same tone she'd used when requesting that I not make her sad.

"Are you going to marry Stan?"

"I don't know enough about him to say."

"You think he's good looking?"

"Not really."

"Sexually attractive?"

"He doesn't think about sex so he can't be sexually attractive."

I thought if I kept hitting negatives, she'd finally understand that she couldn't possibly be the least bit interested in Stanley Gaines. Then we could take his car and go find a justice of the peace in Coleman and get married. I did possess fire in the gut—for her. There was very little I'd ever wanted badly, but marrying her was something I dearly desired.

"I don't suppose you'll ever explain this to me, will you?"

"The only thing I can explain right now is this immensely warm feeling my heart is getting from your hand."

"And this is the last time it'll ever be there. Right?"

"I didn't say that."

What on earth was she saying? That she was going to marry Stan, or someone else, someone I didn't know, and keep me in reserve? Was she going to keep me in her closet? "Why don't you just *tell* me what you want me to know."

"Okay, here's what I want you to know. I love you," she said, making it sound as though it were the first in a series, interrupting the revelation for a long and wet passionate kiss. Then she finished with, "And I want to look at the moon."

And with that she was sliding across the seat toward the driver's side, leaving her can of beer on the floor and getting out of the car. I followed. The night was barely cold; it was mildly winter, a night without clouds. I stood with her leaning against the front of the car as the crew made a connection. They'd collect the core sample in a few minutes, and it would be taken to a lab and run through a number of tests. I wished I could get a core sample on Sally Ann, find some part of her that would give me the unvarnished truth and tell me exactly what she wanted, what she thought.

Stan wandered over to us rubbing his hands together as if anxious to start collecting the financial benefits of his deal. "Well, you kids having a good time?"

I challenged the night: figure him out. It was a double-dog dare.

· · ·

51

The core sample showed Stanley Gaines's desires were stronger than Sally Ann's intuition—the rig was digging through limestone and wasn't in a paying zone. Now that was a real change—Sally Ann had met her superior, and her magic number hadn't been magic at all.

All we got for our night of watching the rig was fatigue and, in my case, depression over Sally Ann's decision to move on. When I went to pick up Jill at her townhouse, she opened the door to find me yawning on her steps.

She looked as Sally Ann had said—sweet—in a navy blue dress with a matching ribbon in her light brown hair. My feelings toward her were confused; she seemed to embody all the contradictions of the world in which we lived. On the one hand, being around her gave me a special kind of pleasure, making me wonder why I was so resistant to establishing a serious relationship with her. I always forgot how much I liked sweet until I was in her presence. Once there, I didn't want to leave. On the other hand, our relationship seemed almost as cut-and-dried and businesslike as a family-arranged marriage. Then too, I was never positive she was as sweet as she looked. Sally Ann had always considered her a faker, someone always posing.

And at times she seemed not only overly practical but almost cynical. She'd told me once in high school that a guy had offered her a large amount of money if she'd write all his themes in English. I'd asked her if she was going to do it, and she'd said, "No, probably not. I'd get in trouble if I got caught." Obviously, people shouldn't be judged on the basis of one statement, but I'd found her response curious. She wasn't going to refuse because of the moral or ethical questions; she'd worried about exposure.

Now she backed away from the door, inviting me in. "I'm not quite ready."

"You look completely ready."

"Just come in and relax. I don't want to get there before everyone else."

I entered the townhouse and stood in the living room as she disappeared down the short hall toward the two bedrooms and bath. The furniture was as conservative and carefully selected as her clothes or hairstyle, as tasteful, as appropriate.

"You look tired," she said from somewhere within the townhouse. "Like maybe you've been out all night drinking on some lease."

"Where'd you hear that?"

"It floated in on the telephone. On Sally Ann's voice."

Suddenly I was alert. Why would she and Sally Ann be talking? They'd never been more than acquaintances, representing opposite ends of the female spectrum. Sally Ann intimidated Jill, both with her height and attitude. Jill was several inches shorter, but the disparity, measured by her attitude, was greater than inches. She suffered from varying degrees of resentment and admiration.

I walked down the hallway and located her in the bathroom. She stood before the mirror looking at herself. Passing time. She didn't want to arrive at the party too early. And she was shocked that I'd venture this far beyond the living room; silently, she shooed me back down the hall.

"What'd Sally Ann have to say?"

"Oh, I don't know. She thought you've been a little down lately. She hoped we'd have a good time tonight."

I sat at the bar that separated the kitchen from the living room, taking one of two stools there. "Yeah? Did she give you any tips on how to insure we have a good time?"

She gave me a smirky sort of smile and walked into the kitchen, stopping at the refrigerator. "Do you want something to drink?"

I nodded, knowing that a drink in this house meant iced tea or Coke. Occasionally she might have wine with dinner, but she didn't consider the act of sitting around drinking appropriate behavior. And she'd never drink a beer unless it was disguised as something much less working class and male oriented.

Generally, she avoided any behavior that would embarrass her if on Sunday morning her minister stood before the congregation and said, "On Thursday night at ten o'clock, Jill Denton was seen . . ." I doubted that she was a virgin, but then, I couldn't say for sure. She'd almost married during her senior year of college, but with me, she'd never engaged in anything more than some light petting. I didn't object to her dedication to chastity as much as I worried about her lack of response to me. I was like Sally Ann; I wanted my partner screaming, panting, her chest heaving, ripping off her clothes in a frenzy. But Jill was always firmly in control, her mind on the Sunday morning announcements.

She delivered the iced tea and sat beside me at the nonalcoholic bar. We stared into a spotless kitchen, looking at gleaming enamel and floor tile.

"Why don't we just stay here?" I asked. "Forget about the party."

"I don't want to forget about the party, not after I'm dressed."

"Can't waste those clothes, can we?"

On top of all her other faults, she lacked the good humor of Sally Ann, who had laughed at stupid jokes with me until we'd cried and made our stomachs hurt, our faces freeze. I'd stopped telling Jill jokes at all because she'd never cracked a smile. Once she'd said, "That's pretty funny," with a straight face. I'd seen her laugh in the company of girlfriends but not with me.

"Why'd Sally Ann call you?" I asked.

"Why don't you ask her? You spend a lot more time with her than I do."

"Come on, what'd she say?"

She shrugged as if to say she didn't owe Sally Ann any allegiance and therefore wouldn't break any confidence. "She was telling me about Stan Gaines. Did we go to high school with him?" When I nodded, she added, "You were all out on this lease of his drinking beer last night."

She wasn't going to tell me what I wanted to know, but I could almost guess the reason for Sally Ann's call. She was trying to usher me out of her life and I wasn't cooperating. So she was enlisting Jill's help. She hadn't said anything as obvious as, "Jill, you take old Billy to bed and you've got it made," but she'd uttered similar words, I'd bet on it. And there was an easy way to find out.

I ran my hand up the back of Jill's neck, sliding beneath her hair, and stroked, simply to see how she responded. In the days before she'd been hired as a Brewster remover, she'd have moved away. But today, the conscientious hired hand, she tilted her head back and closed her eyes.

Thank you, I thought. Those were very loud unspoken words.

It was all set, engineered by Sally Ann, certified Life Planner. Jill and I were going to a party and then returning to this townhouse to make love. In the next year we'd meet Sally Ann's objective and get married. I'd have been swept out of her life as smoothly as ashes from a fireplace.

My stroking hand on her smooth neck was having an effect on me I'd not expected. Suddenly I remembered guys in high school sitting around in a cluster watching Jill walk by, speculating on what she looked like naked. I wasn't any different; I was curious. And the contact with her neck was having a real impact on my desire and curiosity.

I stood and pulled her from the stool; she came, her kiss enthusiastic, openmouthed, wet. And I realized that I was going to be the one ripping my clothes off in a frenzy. I was already panting.

"We can go to the party for a while and then come back here," she said, whispering into my ear, right before she kissed it.

When I saw the certified Life Planner, I wouldn't know whether to kill or kiss her. Had she sent me sliding down the rainbow toward a pot of gold? I thought so at the moment. Or felt it in that part of me that was coated with desire.

A guy in high school had professed to having seen Jill in the nude when she'd come to spend the night with his sister. He'd observed her in the shower and reported back, "You know how some girls are kind of mushy-looking and some kind of hard-looking? You know, kinda like the difference in a biscuit before you bake it and after. She looks like after. She hasn't got an ounce of baby fat on her."

I was in the middle of confirming that his observation applied to all parts of her body when she again whispered in my ear.

"Are you going to keep seeing Sally Ann?"

Even though I was riding the crest in a sea of hormones, I wasn't so far away from land that I didn't resent the timing of her question. The girl had much more control than even I'd thought. I whispered back, "I'm trying to forget her but . . ."

"Some things you need help with," she said and resumed the kiss.

She clamped my thigh with hers, giving me some idea of the type of assistance she'd provide in eradicating the memory and influence of her competition. And I not only confirmed my high school friend's observation on the texture of Jill's body, but I also confirmed that parts of her body that had been closed were now open and ready for business. In fact, they were advertising with neon lights. I touched her everywhere. More than once. And the kiss seemed scheduled to last until one of our obituaries was written.

She suddenly backed off as though she was having difficulty in overcoming the suction that had applied her to me. Sighing, blinking her eyes, she said, "Well, are you ready?" Before I could respond, she added, "to go to the party?"

The party was still held in the same house as it had been in junior high, when we'd discovered a way of dealing with the emotional malaise that followed the holidays. It had the looks but not quite the size of a colonial mansion. Usually we partied indoors because of the weather, but with the unseasonable warmth of the night, someone had opened two sets of French doors and the crowd had overflowed onto the patio. There were probably sixty or seventy people in attendance, and a high-school band was playing music from the fifties, music they'd never heard before practicing for this party.

Jill, the eternal helper, disappeared as we walked in, a characteristic (or pose) that had endeared her to my mother. I walked outside and fished a beer out of a tub of ice. The night was pleasant, and I wasn't at all sorry to see winter temporarily halted. Beyond a swimming pool, now covered, was a line of gaslights and then the darkness of big pecan trees.

Stan and Sally Ann looked like matching end pieces, both dressed in black even though the party wasn't a formal one. But Stan, unfamiliar with parties, had already bought a black suit, and so Sally Ann had dressed to match. I'd barely managed to open my beer before they descended on me, the assault led by Stan.

"We should TD tomorrow," he said.

TD was total depth; the rig was approaching 3,700 feet. The next step was to log the hole with a wireline, a sensing device that would log information regarding the formations and their characteristics. Stan's smile told me he was still enthusiastic, a true believer.

"You're getting close to the truth," I said, looking at Sally Ann but getting an unreadable expression in return. "I myself hope to TD tonight."

Stan smiled. He thought I spoke in code most of the time, and he never inquired into my meaning. Besides, all he wanted to hear was sound, and even code satisfied that requirement.

We stood for a few minutes watching the crowd, most of them laughing, boisterous, already recovered from their malaise.

"You remember any of these people?" I asked.

"Some of them," he said.

These were the same people who had ignored him in high school, or ridiculed him for his mother's religious and alleged sexual activities. And now that he was in their midst, even though I liked most of them, I hoped he'd better them all, make more money and go farther. I didn't hope, however, that he'd marry better. My goodwill was confined to economics.

He picked off a couple wandering by, introducing himself as though he were new in town, a tactic that was probably wise, and left me standing with Sally Ann. She looked better in black than any other color, maybe because of the contrast with her dusty blond hair, maybe because the color reflected the state of her heart. And I knew that as we stood there in this unfamiliar way, giving each other a tentative look, that nothing Jill could ever do would make me forget Sally Ann Wells, or make me want her any less.

"Let's TD," I said.

Her response was one of questioning, raised eyebrow.

"We have to dig out the truth," I said, taking her arm and leading her

56

toward the back of the yard, into the darkness. She came holding her drink, a napkin wrapped around the glass. We passed around the swimming pool, through the picket line of gaslights, and into the pecan trees beyond.

I pulled her to a stop in the shadows of the second big tree we came to and asked, "What'd you tell Jill this afternoon?"

The back of the house was lighted almost like a football field with floodlights on the eaves in addition to the gas lamps, and she'd found a shadow to hide in, one provided by the tree. She looked down and pulled her dress away from her legs. "I told her I was wearing this dress." When I didn't respond, she moved into the light so I could see that she was smiling. "I'm giving the obvious a push, Billy."

"I already knew that. What'd you tell her?"

She slid back into the shadow, all but disappearing. I couldn't see her face, couldn't even tell what color her hair was. "I told her you couldn't sleep with a girl without falling in love with her. I didn't make you sound promiscuous or anything, but if you have a good time tonight, you can thank me later."

"Damn," I said, not knowing whether it was her nonchalance about our relationship or her willingness to betray me that bothered me the most. She was right, of course, about my falling in love with horizontal women, and there were two people who knew that—she and I. And she'd used intimate knowledge against me. A traitor, that's what she was, a true descendant of Turncoat Oil.

I breathed evenly for a minute. If I got visibly upset, she'd shut up and I'd never get the whole story. "You didn't just call her up and drop that little tidbit on her, did you?"

"Oh, no, we had a long conversation, probably thirty minutes or so. That's long for me and Jill."

"And what'd she say when you told her I fell in love as soon as a woman's feet came off the ground?"

"Oh, you know Jill. She doesn't think I'm the kind of girl she should be talking to about that. Or anything else, really. I mean, her lily-white reputation could get dusty if one of her friends even found out she'd been on the phone with me."

I couldn't figure out which Sally Ann stood with me under this big tree. She was being truthful, something the friend in her was capable of, but the friend wasn't the one who'd booted me out of her life and then hired Jill Denton to take care of the carcass. Or was she? Damn, but this girl was confusing.

"Billy, she's been waiting on you for years. She's not the kind who'll chase you, but she'll wait forever. She'll wait like nuns wait on Jesus —forever. You know why she didn't get married before? Because she was down picking out wedding invitations when she heard you and I fell apart. That's why. She came home to give you another shot. You went skiing on spring break. Remember? Your last year of college?"

This was getting spooky, not only because Sally Ann knew so much but because her knowledge was accurate. I never wanted to know my life was programmed, but it was certainly beginning to look predestined. A group of college students from one of the churches had gone to Colorado on a skiing trip, just as Sally Ann had said, and Jill's best friend had invited me. Jill had gone too, and neither of us had been members of the church sponsoring the trip, but we'd spent a considerable amount of time together, getting warm and playing touchy-feely. And Jill hadn't gotten married.

Sally Ann entered the light from the shadow as she took a sip from her drink, watching me. "You do remember that skiing trip, don't you?"

I wanted badly to prove her wrong. If she wasn't playing the role of God, she certainly seemed to be sitting on his right hand, possessor of too many facts. And now she had taken her big pen and drawn two lines, the lifelines of Jill and Billy, and they were headed for an intersection. "Giving the obvious a push," she called it.

That was what I needed to know, and now I could let her know how mad I was. "Goddammit, you're acting like a traitor, telling her things about me, things only you know. And I can't believe you're doing it just to benefit yourself."

"Oooh," she said. "That hurts." She gave me an opportunity to exit, to stomp off and make it easy on her, but I didn't. "You know I'd never do it under ordinary circumstances, don't you? Last night I asked if you trusted me and you never said. Do you? Trust me?"

"Sometimes, but not when you're giving Jill inside information just to get rid of me."

She took my hand and squeezed it with a warmth and friendliness that was very difficult to resist. "I know way down deep in my heart that this is the best thing, the very best thing, for both of us. I *know* it and one day you'll agree, Billy, you will, even though you don't think so now."

"Damned if you don't sound like my mother."

"Well, your mother wouldn't lie to you about something like that, would she? And neither would I."

I pulled my hand from hers and walked away, back into the trees, because I was beginning to believe her. She sounded *just like my mother*. Why did I never win when this girl was involved? I'd been skunked long ago and the game should have been called, but I was still on the field, still losing. I walked back to her and she stood beside the tree as patiently as my mother would have, waiting for me to see the light.

"This is just all screwed up," I said, throwing my hands around in the air. "You're the one who decided this was best, not me, so why should I believe you? Damn you, Sally Ann, you've always made me do exactly what you wanted, from the day I met you. I feel so—" I made fists and shook them at her. "Frustrated is the only word I can think of."

She took both my fists and held them against her cheeks, coming close to me and saying very slowly, "I'll always love you, and I hope and pray we're always best friends. And I hate to say this, Billy, but the one who knows the most has to decide, and I know the most."

"Bullshit," I said, even though I believed her. "That's just bullshit."

I walked back toward the house by myself as though victorious in argument, wishing I knew how to even begin salvaging the relationship. She'd evicted me from her life, as surely as I was headed back to the house, and I couldn't even think of a good line of reasoning to use against her.

Damn, damn, damn.

I spent the next hour inside drinking and sitting beside Jill on a love seat near the unused fireplace. Sipping a Coke, she wrapped her arm up in mine and made comments on those walking by. I didn't hear much of what she said because I was watching Stan and Sally Ann. A person unacquainted with this crowd could walk in and immediately suspect that the older-looking guy in the black suit must have been the class favorite all the way through school. Stan was making real strides. He was backslapping and laughing and kneeslapping and drawing a crowd, and the look on every face was basically the same—this can't be the same Stanley Gaines who used to pee-pee on people in the boy's rest room.

But for me the strangest sight wasn't Stan; it was Sally Ann taking a back seat to another person. She was generally observant in an unobtrusive way, and her eyes never strayed far from Stan. And regardless of what she'd told me the previous night, I no longer had any doubt as to whether she'd marry him or not. She probably already had the date set.

"Has she actually fallen for Stanley Gaines?" I asked.

It was a rhetorical question but Jill provided an answer anyway. Leaning on me, her chin almost on my shoulder, she said, "She thinks he's the best show in town."

I almost said, "I do too, but I don't want to marry him." In fact, I couldn't think of a worse fate, having to live with Stanley Gaines and on a daily basis put up with his superficial attitude toward his work and life. I didn't feel compelled to change him, but neither did I feel compelled to approve of him. And I'd never figure out Sally Ann's willingness to do exactly that.

"Aren't you trying to forget about her?" Jill asked.

"I'm talking about Stan, not Sally Ann."

"Oh. Right."

Stan was obviously having a fine time, now telling a story and then standing back, one hand in his pocket, to listen to the appreciative laughter of his audience. Dale Carnegie would have granted him a Ph. D. on the spot.

"I'm ready if you are," Jill said quietly.

I turned to see her face because she'd made a major statement of intent. But her face revealed nothing of that intent; she simply stared at me with pretty brown eyes, a half-shy, half-alluring smile on her face. At times I thought possibly the smile was the basis of my attraction to her; it drove me crazy, as a veil would, as a semitransparent promise would, one that hinted at the depths of passion and spirit.

Taking her arm, I escorted her through the crowd, watching the kiddie band return on the opposite end of the room, now tanked on beer, ready to once again attempt the music of the past. I steered her away from the Stanley Gaines road show, avoided his most devoted female fan, and led her into the night outside.

My car was parked down the street but I wanted to walk. There was something about this carefully planned sexual event that made me feel as though I were en route to a football game. Maybe she'd lined up an announcer and pep squad. As far as I was concerned, the worst thing possible a person could do about sex was plan it.

As I opened the door of my car and let Jill get in, I felt as though I was already married. Me and the old lady. We'd go home, she'd shave her legs, put on panties that were stretched out of shape, and I'd fall asleep within a matter of seconds once I was in bed.

She moved over to my side when I got in. The car was cold; it seemed colder inside than it had outside, and suddenly I needed warmth from her. I stuck my hand between her legs, nestling there between nylon knees. She covered my hand with hers, squeezed her legs together, and gave a satisfied sigh.

60

I kissed her. She was apparently interested but she was also more restrained than she'd been earlier at her place. Without the obstacle of the party to keep us out of her bedroom, she wasn't going to kiss my ear. This simply wasn't going to work.

She rested her forehead on my shoulder for a moment and then said, "I'm not as experienced as some people, but that doesn't mean I'm not passionate."

"What're you talking about?"

"You told Sally Ann I wasn't passionate."

Without thinking, I yelled, "That fucking bitch!" She'd told Jill everything about me she could think of. Everything, probably including, but not limited to, the positions I liked and how to make me shout with utter delight. I couldn't believe it. For a minute I sat contemplating a return to the party. I'd choke Sally Ann with both hands, shaking her head like a rag doll's, and murder her in front of fifty witnesses. What a mistake our entire relationship had been.

I had to make a concentrated effort to control my breathing before I spoke. "Listen, I didn't tell her anything of the sort. Let's make a deal. We'll just pretend neither of us ever knew her, never talked to her, never knew she existed. All right? Just forget her altogether."

She kissed me several times, attempting to soothe my anger with light, sweet kisses, and she succeeded. "Think about *me*, not her. If you're mad, I know you're still thinking about her." She managed to tame the beast by stroking my neck. There was something about necks that I loved, and touching hers was as stimulating as feeling her breast. I thought. Actually, I'd never been allowed to let my hand remain in contact with her breast for more than a moment. She had a practiced move —slipping her thumb into my palm and twisting my hand into a hand-holding position. She was smooth. She could have taught classes, could have patented the move. The Jill Denton Palmar Deflection.

Her attitude changed with mine; now that I was calm, she was nervous. "This all makes me nervous. I'm afraid you'll give me a failing grade."

"Listen, let's just go back to your place and see what happens. If it does, okay, if not, so what? I don't plan on raping you. Or giving you a grade."

She nodded and turned toward the dash. "Okay."

I drove, thinking the night had been irreversibly fouled, first by Sally Ann, now by Jill. Why was she afraid I'd grade her? Why was she nervous? Because this night had economic as well as romantic implications?

61

All my life I'd managed to attract "friends" based solely on the fact that my last name was Brewster. My family had money; they lived in that big house on Tanglewood. I'd never gone so far as to wish I was poor, but more than once I'd strongly desired a world in which no one knew my background. And now Jill was acting as though she was being screened. It was time for one of the Brewsters to act on her application for admittance to the family. And the vaults.

I decided I was overreacting; what I needed was to calm down again. This was Sally Ann's fault, not Jill's.

Once we were at her place, she engaged in what I'd heard a lawyer call "capricious dilatory tactics." Anything to delay what she believed was inevitable. She made popcorn, she checked more than once to see what was on Abilene's two TV stations, she told me about her students at school, she got up and then sat back down a hundred times, she smoothed her dress, fiddled with the ribbon in her hair, took her shoes off and put them back on.

Finally I carried my empty popcorn bowl to the spotless kitchen and set it on the counter. "It's late and I need to go."

Still on the brownish gold couch, she looked at her hands. "I don't want you to go."

"I know, but you don't want me to stay, either. And I'm not going to make you into a basket case over something that's really not very important anyway."

"I do want you to stay," she said, patting the spot I'd just vacated. "Please."

I returned to the couch, and for a few minutes we engaged in a very domesticated game, kissing and touching nonerotic spots. And it was fun. I didn't want to do it every night for the rest of my life, but for this particular night, nothing could have been better. It made me feel young and frustrated and excited over future possibilities. I'd forgotten how pleasurable innocence could be.

"Tomorrow night we advance to deep kissing and fondling above the waist."

She looked at her hands. "Don't make fun."

"I wouldn't make fun of you for anything. Besides, I'm enjoying this too much to want anything more right now."

I sat up straight and pulled her over, placing her head in my lap. Looking down at her hair spread over my pants, seeing that half-smile, I put my hand just below her ribs and with my thumb brushed her breast. A slow windshield wiper, rising and falling, it didn't draw the Palmar Deflection.

"Do you know guys used to sit around lusting after you in school? You never wore clothes that showed much of your body, and we all knew you were hiding centerfold material. We just knew it."

"I wish I had been."

My thumb, the windshield wiper, remained at its outstretched position, presumably atop a nipple, which I hadn't yet found. Maybe she didn't own any; maybe she simply didn't respond. My hand closed on its thumb, in the process covering her breast. I was just about to engage in exploratory fondling when I felt her thumb in my palm. The deflection. She sat up, breaking all contact.

"Did you want more popcorn?"

4

The evidence on #1 Lowell B. Brooks Estate was promising. It showed the well had not one but two potential pay zones, one around 3,150 feet and another near 3,600. Both zones were in limestone, and the permeability and porosity looked good. In fact, there could be enough pressure in the lower zone to make a flowing well, one in which the oil didn't have to be pumped to the surface. Stan wouldn't have a picture of himself standing Jett Rink—like in a shower of crude for posterity, but his first venture into the oil field appeared it would be everything he'd hoped for.

Word got around quickly, most likely because Stan talked about it everywhere he went. His optimism drew listeners, and everyone assumed he knew what he was talking about. And maybe he did in a general sort of way.

He and I were sitting at my desk and I was explaining the specifics on the logs we'd obtained, when the old man walked in. He was carrying a Styrofoam cup of coffee that was almost empty, a sign, along with his tardiness, that meant he'd been eating breakfast with someone. He never left a restaurant in the morning without coffee for the trip to the office, even though he was never more than ten minutes from the office regardless of where he was in Abilene.

Wearing khakis and obviously intending to spend the day out of the office, he stopped beside my desk. "This is the day of decision," he said to Stan. "You think you're up to it?"

Much of Stan's behavior around my father was automatic. He said, "Sure," without thinking about it, and also stood. But neither of us knew what the old man was talking about. The decision to case the hole and perforate the lower zone had already been made. If the lower zone produced, the upper would be left for later. And he had our attention, especially Stan's. The newest Brewster had obviously been to the store with Sally Ann. He was wearing light green pants and a darker green pullover shirt, dressed and ready for action.

The old man took his last sip of coffee and dropped the cup into a trash can, then sat on the desk across the aisle from mine in this big room of desks. The three of us were the only ones who'd arrived so far. My father rubbed his head with the palm of his hand as though polishing the dome.

"I've already heard from two hungry operators this morning. Jay Lerner and Sam Anderson. Both of them invited me to breakfast, but Anderson called first so I met with him. They do their exploration in coffee shops these days."

The old man was a lot like Stan; a deal always interested him. The amount of money didn't have to be large, just as long as there was a deal, one person wanting something another had and willing to negotiate a trade. The old man loved dealing without, I thought, knowing why. Or even caring. And now he wasn't going to reveal his story until Stan expressed an interest.

Stan did. "What'd they want?"

"They wanted to know more about your well," he said, acting the part of a fisherman, reeling in the bait, watching Stan swim after it.

"You tell them?"

"Sure, I told them. Anderson liked it so much he made you an offer."

Stan could have been slapped to attention; he heard the magic word —offer—and all the implications made him stand up as straight as if a rod had been inserted into his heel and run up to his skull. "An offer? What kind of offer?"

"The best kind—money," the old man said, smiling at the rapt face of his student.

"Money?" Stan asked. "Money?"

"Money. He'll pay you fifty an acre for the lease, all the drilling costs, and thirty thousand."

"Jesus!" Stan shouted. His legs engaged in spasms, his knees locking and unlocking as though he were about to catapult himself toward the ceiling. Before saying anything else, he ran around me and to the desk,

64

jerking the calculator toward him. His finger flew over the keys, hitting the wrong ones and causing him to start over several times. I watched, and finally he got it right. If he took the offer, he'd make a profit of $8,460 on the lease and get $1,875 for his sixteenth interest in the well. He ripped the tape from the calculator and stared at it, at the time unable to stand still. He looked like a four year old who needed to go potty but couldn't bring himself to leave his company.

"Jesus. What do you think we should do?"

"Wait," the old man said, "just wait. Let the boys bid the price up. Like I say, these two do their exploration over breakfast. You're the one who took the risk, so pass it on to them."

The lease and potential well wouldn't attract the kind of attention and interest it would have in the fifties, not in the present declining market. But Lerner and Anderson had adapted to the conditions. Lerner engaged in various creative tax schemes, to the benefit of himself and his wealthy investors in Dallas, and Anderson operated his leases to the detriment of his investors, making money while they didn't. His wells got more rod and tubing jobs, more new pumps, more attention than any wells in west Texas.

Stan was transfixed, still staring at the tape; if he removed his eyes from that paper, the numbers would rearrange themselves. He'd lose money by looking away; the decimals would dart to the left like children playing hide-and-seek. "Don't you think they oughta break a hundred on the lease? A hundred bucks an acre oughta be a good price for a hundred eighty acres where you can drill three more wells." Then, in an instant, he'd gone from analyst to child. He looked up at me, finally convinced the numbers were real, stationary. "Ain't this great? Just great?"

The phone on Stan's desk rang, right behind him, and he whirled, facing it as though it were a rattlesnake with a sack of gold tied around its neck.

"It's probably Lerner," the old man said.

Stan reached for the phone, hoping he could grab the gold before getting bitten. He answered and then gave us a big smile with the fingertip-to-thumbtip okay sign. "Yes, sir, Mr. Lerner, how're you?"

The old man pulled me toward his office, down the main aisle through the sea of metal desks, and we stopped about fifteen feet away from Stan. "Well, let's see what the boy's made of."

My father was the best trader I'd ever watched, and he was naturally interested in Stan's potential. The old man automatically adapted his manner and speech and personality to the person with whom he was dealing; he was intuitive in his approach and always knew what would work. I'd seen him drink tea with little old ladies whose leases he'd wanted, and I'd watched him and Rains, the hard-nosed tool pusher, stand toe to toe and scream in each other's face, arguing over the price of a bird dog Rains wanted to sell.

"To tell you the truth, Mr. Lerner," Stan said, "I hadn't given any thought at all to selling until right now. It's my first lease and first well, and, shoot, my heart's out there. I know sentiment shouldn't play any part in this, but I can't help it. This is a first. Really, it's a double first."

My old man elbowed me on the arm, proud of his newest employee, because we both knew where Stan's sentiment lay, and it wasn't in Coleman County on the Lowell B. Brooks Estate lease. I watched him twist as he talked, waving the tape around like a ribbon. He was so obviously excited I expected him to break out in hysterical laughter, but his voice remained calm and businesslike.

"He's doing all right," my old man said.

"I don't know where you got your information," Stan said. "But it's accurate. You got a spy on one of our crews?"

He listened, nodding, then his eyes bulged. He tried opening the center drawer of the desk to get a pen and jammed his fingers. Grimacing, shaking his hand, he then got a pen from the desk. When he began writing, I moved toward the desk to see what his second offer was. But I couldn't read his writing. It looked as though he'd been stricken with right-handed nerve palsy.

By the time he hung up he was panting, his tongue out. "A hundred seventeen thousand, two hundred on a three-year payout." Almost with the words, he was spinning toward my desk and the calculator, saying, or praying, "Jesus, Jesus, Jesus." Momentarily confused on how to compare the two offers, he stood, finger on the machine, biting his lip.

The old man had already calculated mentally. "He topped Anderson by nineteen thousand, but you've got to discount some of that because of the three years."

I could see visions dancing in Stan's head. By lunch H. L. Hunt would be on the phone with a multimillion-dollar offer, and by midafternoon, Iran and Mexico would have raised the offer into the billions. Tomorrow morning, Stan would make the front page of the *Wall Street Journal*.

"I hate to be a party pooper," I said, "but we've got a pissed-off lady near Westbrook who's expecting us at nine-thirty. Why don't you stay here and take your calls and I'll go pay her for some dead oak trees."

Stan nodded agreeably, ready to shove me out the door, but he looked at the old man. And like a test proctor who'd spotted him just as the thought of cheating had crossed his mind, the old man was waiting to see what Stan would do. Would he exert the discipline necessary to remain on the job, or would he go twisting off with the first sign of good fortune?

He took a deep breath and said, "Mr. Brewster, what if I asked you to handle any of these calls and I'll go with Billy to get these trees taken care of."

The old man nodded. "That'd be fine."

Stan beat me to the office door by fifty feet, and as we rode the elevator to the first floor, he said several times, "I love this business, just love it. I knew it'd be just like this." He carried the evidence of good fortune, the calculator tape, and danced a jig down to the ground floor.

As usual when we were in a hurry, I let him drive. I rode and prayed he'd keep his eyes on the road because he drove too fast under normal circumstances, and when he got in a hurry, he tended to bury the speedometer needle. And the company cars had a lot of hard miles on them; who knew when a wheel would go flying into the ditch? Still, I didn't want to slow him down.

"Billy Boy, I'm glad your father was there. Damn glad. I'd have taken the first offer if he hadn't been. If he hadn't been watching me. I'm no horse trader, not by a long shot, never have been and probably never will be. My problem is, I get too nervous thinking, what if these guys change their minds? What if somebody walks in their office with a better deal? What if he's drilling a well and it comes in at a thousand barrels a day? He won't need my little well. So I want to take the money and run. You know what I mean?"

He talked nonstop except for those short interruptions to ask why I was directing his attention to the road or why I was reminding him that this interstate had only two lanes westbound, not three. He was driving on the shoulder. We blew down the highway toward the horizon, the earth flat here, running all the way to the point where it met blue sky. The center stripes came at us so fast they seemed to be one continuous white line.

"You heard those phone calls, didn't you?" he asked. "They really did happen, didn't they?"

"Yeah, they really happened, but they won't matter if you run under that truck."

We were approaching the rear of a trailer, a big silver barricade, and I entertained a vision of our car stuck under it, the top of the car and our heads sheared off.

Patting his leg as though trying to coax more speed out of a horse, he switched lanes to pass the truck and said, "You ever want to buy your parents something, but think if you wait, you can do better? No, that's pretty dumb thinking your parents need anything." He smiled sheepishly as though apologizing for having forgotten. "But I figured, hey, I can buy my mother a car. She needs one. I take her to get groceries on Thursday nights, and the rest of the time she rides the bus if she needs to go anywhere. But then I think, you know, if I hold off, if I put *all* this money back to work, then pretty soon I might be able to buy her a house. She lives in a pretty ratty neighborhood. A bunch of wetbacks just moved in across the street. And she really needs a new house more than a car. So what do you do? Billy Boy, this money really creates problems." He smiled to let me know he was joking.

We rode for a moment in silence, and I didn't want to appear as though I were interrogating him, as Boomer had one night suggested I was doing, but after a respectful period of time—ten seconds, more or less—I asked, "You live with your mother?"

"Yeah, but don't let it get around. I never give out anything but the office phone number, and when people ask for my home phone, I tell them I'm in the middle of moving to a new apartment. One guy told me the other day I move more than anybody he knows, but, hey, I figure if you're twenty-three years old, you shouldn't be living with your mother. But it's paid off. I used my savings on this lease instead of on an apartment or furniture, and it's paid off, it's paid off." He pulled the calculator tape from his shirt pocket to prove his words.

I tried picturing his mother but couldn't form a good image. All I could remember was a woman with somewhat pointed features and very fine hair, nothing at all like Stan's coarse black hair. I'd only seen her by accident, arriving at the office of the high school simultaneous with her visit when she wanted to deprive us of Halloween.

"Your mother's pretty religious, isn't she?"

He gave a two-syllable laugh, and for the first time since I'd met him, refused an opportunity to talk. I wasn't, however, going to let him off the hook that easily.

"You don't get along?"

"Oh, we get along all right, if you can get along all right with somebody who gives you a sermon on spiritual strength every time you say you're tired. Oh, she's all right, she's just . . . religious."

"How about your father?"

"Dead. He got killed in a wreck on North First, got run over by a

68

drunk at five in the morning. He drove a milk truck, home deliveries, you know. I was only four."

He changed the subject, unable to stop talking about his deal. "How much more do you think we can get out of this? I don't figure a lot, do you? I think we ought to go ahead and shake hands, kiss each other, whatever we need to do to finish it off."

"I wouldn't think a lot more. Some, but not enough to make you rich, not with all this cheap foreign oil around. But you're probably not through yet."

"What do I tell my investors? To sell?"

"Definitely. You don't want to leave any of them with Lerner or Anderson. With Lerner they'll get such complicated tax problems they'll have to hire a CPA full time, and with Anderson, they'll get operated to death. Tell them to sell."

Smiling, he said, "Jesus, I can't believe all this."

We settled the matter of two oak trees that had been knocked down by a dozer building a road to a location. The landowner's wife handled the claim, and she kept shaking her cigarette at us. She had ashes all over herself and the living room floor. Mostly she wanted to throw a few darts at the oil industry and complain to a captive audience. So we listened for a few minutes, paid her $175, and then shot back toward Abilene as though rocket-propelled.

In the course of the visit, Stan's good cheer and happiness over wheeling and dealing had been replaced by acute worry over both Anderson and Lerner either losing interest or backing out for some other reason, leaving Stanley Gaines with nothing but a meaningless calculator tape in his pocket, a near miss. I tried convincing him on the way back that it was unlikely either of them had lost interest in the space of a few hours, but he was dissatisfied with my attempts to reassure him, mostly because I was using the word "unlikely" and not "impossible."

During the visit with the disgruntled landowner's wife, he had graciously allowed me to handle the negotiations while he considered reasons his deal would collapse: Lerner and Anderson discovered they were bidding against each other, something they hated doing; Lerner's wife died an hour ago and Anderson had gone to Honduras; Mexico had increased its exports by forty million barrels a day and the price had gone to a tenth of a cent; the bidding had grown so heated that Lerner and Anderson had murdered each other.

When we got back to the office, Stan parked the car in front of the building and jumped out before putting the car in park. It finished its course, bumping into the curb and dying. I waved him on into the building, cut the engine, and got his keys.

By the time I got upstairs, Stan was calling the calculator Jesus, trying to coax information out of it without having entered the correct figures, and the old man was sitting on a desk looking very amused and satisfied.

"Lerner dropped out," Stan said. "Anderson's offer is a hundred and ten an acre, all the drilling costs, and forty-five thousand. You know what that comes to? That's a profit of twenty-two thousand seventy-two dollars and fifty cents." Wide-eyed, he repeated the figure. "That's the goddamn salary of—of a goddamn bank president. On one deal. One deal. I can't believe this." He turned to the old man. "Let's call him right now."

The old man stood and shook his head, a twinkle in his eye. "Squeeze him. Squeeze him like he does his investors. Make him pay. Hit him for another ten thousand."

Stan was bordering on a stroke; he didn't know what to say. In his hand was evidence of the most wondrous offer he could conceive, but the old man wanted him to squeeze Anderson. Basically, it came down to this—Stan wanted the money, but he also wanted the stamp of approval from William C. Brewster, Jr. So he took a few deep breaths and pulled the chair away from my desk to sit and contemplate his strategy. Scratching his head, he muttered the name of God's son several times, then reached for the phone.

For a moment, he did something that I would have considered him incapable of—making small talk with Anderson. For a few minutes, they discussed the difficulties involved in keeping landowners happy.

"Mr. Anderson, I really do appreciate your interest in this lease, but I've got to tell you, I've been working on my investors for a long time. I started long before I got back to Abilene and started working for Mr. Brewster. These guys wanted in for the long haul; they want the write-offs and the depletion allowance. None of them are really after a quick profit. And you've got to remember, all these guys are in southern California, and we're not talking about the kind of money that's going to impress them when the figures are broken down. If I go back and tell them they're getting a little over five grand for an eighth, they'll probably just shrug. When you're in southern California tooling around in a Cadillac convertible looking up at the palm trees, you know, five grand isn't all that glamorous. Being in the oil business is. They can walk around and tell people, 'Hey, I'm in the *all bidness.*' I try to think like they do."

The old man nudged me and smiled, but he wasn't as impressed as I was; he hadn't listened to Stan enumerate the ways in which this deal could fall apart all the way home.

Stan, nodding, acted as though he was listening but he was simply waiting for an opening so he could speak again. With his free hand, he had made a fist and his fingers had turned white. "How much is kinda hard to say, but I decided before I called you that I didn't feel like I could go to them with less than an offer of seventy-five hundred for an eighth. I mean, it's still only four lousy figures, but I can sell them on that. You know, these guys live out there where movies are made and they don't know reality from mesquite trees."

Nodding, nodding vigorously, he walked away from the desk as far as the telephone cord would allow him to go, then returned. "Okay. Sure, that's fine. Let's just assume we have a deal on those terms. I won't have any trouble with my investors, and let's just consider it a deal. Fine, see you later." He started to hang up and then seemed to be hit with the thought that maybe he hadn't made himself clear. He squatted and hollered at the phone, right before he hung it up, "Yeah, it's a deal!"

He sat, then stood, then turned in a circle. "Oh, hot dang, hot dang, I can't believe what I just did. I mean, I had the best offer I'd ever heard, right in my hand, and I *squeezed* the guy. *Squeezed* him. I just cannot believe this." He was getting louder, his voice shriller, and finally he leaned back and uttered the first rebel yell ever heard within the walls of Brewster Drilling.

The old man was proud of his student. He'd gone the old man one better, wrenching not an extra ten thousand out of Anderson but fifteen. He shook Stan's hand and said, "Not bad, not bad at all. I think you're catching on."

I pumped the wheeler dealer's hand and said, "Mister Oil and Gas." He shook his head. "I just can't believe it."

As it turned out, Anderson got a flowing well, one in which there was sufficient pressure to push the oil right to the surface without any man-made assistance. And for his trouble and money, he was getting seventy-seven barrels a day. That made his investment look very good, especially when he considered there was another potential zone of production behind the casing.

Apparently the profit of $23,010 had a romantic effect on Mr. Oil and Gas because he told me one afternoon over a drink at the country club that he was thinking about asking Sally Ann to marry him. He delivered this bit of news on a day when the weather suited my mood. We sat near the front windows, watching an early spring rain fill the parking lot with puddles.

"What do you think she'll say?" he asked.

I decided I was uncommonly adept at hiding my feelings if Stan felt free to ask me such questions. Why didn't I tell him the prospect of a wedding that involved Sally Ann and excluded me as groom made me miserable beyond words? Because he would have said, "Hey, Billy Boy, it's no big deal, just a wedding." Besides, there was no reason for him to be asking me to predict Sally Ann's behavior. Obviously I didn't know a thing about her. The part of my youth that had involved her obviously came under the heading of misinterpreted history.

Then too, I wasn't feeling quite as paternal about this guy. His hair had grown out, his clothes were coordinated, and he'd accomplished more in six months than I'd even thought about in twenty-three years.

"Are you losing your good old optimism, Stan? Afraid she won't say yes?"

He shrugged. "You know her better than I do. I just wondered what you thought."

"If I had to guess, I'd say she'll probably say yes."

He sat forward, resting his elbows on his knees, his eyes bright. "No kidding? You really think so?"

I nodded, wishing he'd found someone other than Sally Ann because the guy did intrigue me, no question. He'd been periodically humiliated in public by his mother as a child, grown up across town, pissed on people in the restroom, had grown up with nothing, not even a phone, but here he was on his way to some fantastic end, and he'd be in the company of the most wondrous woman I knew. Why, I kept asking, had he chosen Sally Ann? The answer, I supposed, was as simple as it was unacceptable—because this was life, the great contradictory affair we were all in the middle of, like it or not.

"Where do you think I ought to ask her? Out here? This is where we met."

"That's right, Stan, you did meet right over there, and I remember because I introduced you. Do *you* remember?"

"Well, sure I remember. How could I forget that? Jesus, everything I've done was because of you."

"Well, I'd say it probably doesn't matter where you ask her. She's not the sentimental type."

"Thanks for the advice, Billy Boy." He lifted his glass. "To the guy who taught me everything I know."

Without a great deal of enthusiasm over this toast (which had been misstated anyway; it should have been, "To the guy whose life I have now acquired"), I clinked my glass against his and looked out the window at the rain hitting the puddles on the asphalt parking lot. I tried to make myself feel better by thinking how unlikely it was that Sally Ann had even kissed Stan. And I knew he hadn't screamed with delight and near exhaustion with a naked Sally Ann on his lap. Of course, neither had I lately, not with her or anyone else.

In fact, I thought Jill's anxiety over sex was something of a dodge, a method of keeping me out of her pants but slowly reaching for the zipper on her skirt until I managed to grab it in the bedroom of our honeymoon suite. And I hadn't pushed her because the thought of sex with her seemed a sacrilege, even though I couldn't figure out why. We'd danced all around the issue, and in the process had settled one matter. I knew what she looked like naked, and my friend's biscuit metaphor had been right on target. Which, like everything else, was another problem. Her baked biscuit texture only provided the contrast I didn't need with Sally Ann's sleek softness, another reminder of what I'd lost.

Stan suddenly jumped out of his chair and looked at me as though he'd experienced a revelation. "I just had one hell of an idea. One *hell* of an idea. Let's have a double wedding, really set this town on its ear. Can you imagine—Billy Brewster and Sally Ann Wells getting married on the same night? The most eligible bachelor and, you know, whatever they call girls, most eligible girl, even though they aren't marrying each other? Now that'd be something, wouldn't it? The paper'd give it an entire section. Biggest deal of the year."

The guy was a maniac, a man obsessed, and it seemed at that moment, as I watched him get glassy-eyed with a vision of *the* social event of the year, I'd have to kill him for the greater good. And short of that, I had to immediately discourage him from even thinking about any such double wedding.

"Stan, don't *ever* mention that to anyone. Don't even think about it."

"Why not? You're going to get married sooner or later, and you might as well do it sooner. Let's do it. It'd be one hell of a deal."

"Stan, listen to me. Listen to these words. Don't bring it up ever again. Forget it. Don't mention it. *Ever.*"

I didn't tell him, but I'd already decided on a definite course of action once Sally Ann uttered the word yes to Stanley Gaines, once she made the decision to marry him, because she'd never change her mind. The war in South Vietnam was heating up. Communist attacks against Americans, even against the embassy, had resulted in stepped-up bombings against the north and the infusion of additional U.S. troops into the south. The navy was instituting coastal patrols to disrupt the Communist traffic and supply lines. And I was going to enlist in the navy. Part of my desire to go was a simple patriotic urge, to do my part, something I wouldn't have expressed to anyone, but mostly I wanted a complete change in my life. If my first and only choice was beyond my reach, if life with Sally Ann wasn't possible, then I wanted a total relocation. Total.

"You did hear me, didn't you, Stan? Don't ever say anything to anybody about a double wedding."

"You really don't like the idea?"

"Don't even think about it."

"No problem."

5

Upon hearing the news of Sally Ann's engagement to Stanley Gaines, my mother proposed a dinner in honor of them, and of course Jill and I were invited. Had I stuck to my schedule, I wouldn't have been there because I'd have been in San Diego or Great Lakes in boot camp. But I was discovering what a procrastinator I was. I'd visited with the navy recruiter once, told him I was interested in the small boat units patrolling the coastal waters of South Vietnam, and was almost ready to go. He'd thought I was kidding. A college graduate who not only didn't want to be an officer but who wanted to go to South Vietnam?

I was learning how easy it was to be rich and indolent, how difficult it was to walk away. I kept intending to return to the skeptical recruiter and sign my name, but I hadn't. Nor had I told anyone about my intentions, not my parents, not Jill, even though by the time of the dinner I'd spent a considerable amount of time rehearsing conversations with Jill about my departure. I hadn't actually initiated such a discussion though because I knew that if I ever said, "I've got something to talk to you about," she'd automatically assume I was going to propose. It was in her eyes, which she batted more and more often. And Sally Ann had been right; this girl would wait until the last spark in the universe went pfft and burnt out.

The dinner was quite an affair, with hired help, a French menu, even a spiffy-looking young Mexican-American waitress, a cute dark-eyed girl I wanted to ask out. I wanted some passion, some zest, not a woman whose standard answer to every question was, "Whatever you want to do," even though she didn't always mean exactly that. We sat in the dining room under the big chandelier, my father in his usual seat at the head of the table; my mother, me, and Jill to his left; Boomer, Stan, and Sally Ann on his right. Boomer had dressed up for the occasion, the first time I'd seen him wear a suit since a funeral fifteen years ago. It was black, an old wide-lapeled double-breasted number that almost swallowed him. I hadn't realized he'd lost so much weight.

He stood with his glass of champagne and said, "If I was sixty or seventy years younger, I'd take both you girls away from these two boys." He took a sip of champagne to lubricate the speaking machinery. "I remember these two sweet young things—"

My father interrupted him. "You're standing up so just go ahead and make a toast. Don't start in on one of your stories."

"Don't interrupt me. This *is* a toast." He dismissed my old man and put his smile back on for Jill and Sally Ann. "I remember these two sweet young things in Galveston just before the turn of the century. I was just a kid, like these two boys here, and these two young ladies had ridden the train down to the beach, and they decided to take me home with them to Houston. Of course, I put up a real fight." He grinned, then emptied his glass of champagne and handed it to Stan for a refill. "Anyway, these two girls gave me the summer of my life, and God bless 'em if they're still alive. And if they're not, I hope they're looking down on us. Every time I see you two girls, I think about that summer. I was a kid, just a kid, looking at a brand-new century coming up. And you two make me feel young, and that's the best thing you can do for an old fart like me. So here's to you two girls," he said, lifting, then downing his refilled glass.

The waitress, looking as delighted as Jill and Sally Ann in her crisp white dress, mimicked the two who'd been toasted and gave a clap of joy.

As I sat watching this celebration, feeling as old as Boomer sixty-two years too soon, I had to agree that the two ladies toasted looked like feminine wonders. Sitting across from Sally Ann, I could see her easier. She wore a light green dress that made her hair look blonder than it really was.

My old man, without a glass in his hand, stood and looked for a moment as though he might deliver a sermon. But then he smiled and

75

said, "Here's some news for you to digest along with this French food Sally Ann likes so much. As of June first, we're spinning off the production department of the company and making it a brand-new corporation. We're going to call it Brewster-Gaines Production Company, and Mister Stan Gaines is going to run it for us."

I gave what had become my normal look—openmouthed—and watched Stan to see if he was as surprised as I was. But all he did was smile modestly at Sally Ann, who returned the gesture. Both of them knew. Bitch and Son of a Bitch acted as though they'd been keeping this secret for some time and were relieved to be out from under the burden.

I couldn't believe it. I didn't care if Stan ran the production department or a new corporation; in fact, it was probably a good idea, the best way of avoiding conflicts of interest since no one knew if he was acquiring the best leases for himself or for Brewster Drilling. And the old man had always liked rewarding energetic and ambitious people, a philosophy hard to disagree with. But since when had they started keeping secrets from me? And when did they plot these moves? At four in the morning when they were stoking the fires in their guts?

I stood up, looking directly at the old man, who was to my right and still standing, wanting my mother to think these were joint announcements we'd all conspired in. "As long as we're talking about changes, I've got something to tell you. Tomorrow morning I'm joining the navy." I gave my father my best confidential smile, the same kind Stan and Sally Ann had just exchanged. "The navy's setting up small boat units in South Vietnam, which is where I want to go." I raised my glass. "So here's to changes."

Well, I thought, I'd sure as hell gotten their attention. A hush had fallen over the room as a knife onto a cutting board, just that quick and cleanly.

The first person to speak was my mother. She grabbed my arm and pulled me into my chair. "You're joking, aren't you? Aren't you?"

I shook my head, looking again at my father as though he were responsible, as though he might have brainwashed me by playing tapes each night. "Go to war, go to war, go to war." At the moment, I hated that short bald-headed son of a bitch, and I wanted my mother to hate him as well, and I didn't want her to ever believe he was innocent, no matter how loudly he protested. He was squinting, confused, trying to unscramble the signal I was sending.

Boomer looked at Stan and said, "The navy. Can the boy swim?"

I had more to say, just to prove I hadn't decided to enlist because of

76

hurt feelings over Stan's ascension, but Jill left the table, headed for the nearest doorway, which led to the hall. She was an innocent victim, one I hadn't intended to hurt, and I hurriedly left the table to follow her.

As I headed down the hall, Boomer said, "Well, hell, the boy didn't even say good-bye."

Jill had disappeared into the living room, but I hesitated at the door before joining her, to eavesdrop on my mother.

"Bill Brewster!"

"What?"

"*There's a war* going on over there."

"He got a wild hair somewhere, and *I* don't know where he got it. I've *never* talked to the boy about the service."

My mother was as pissed off as I wanted her to be. She always avoided public arguments and debate, but now she shouted, "That's my *son* we're talking about."

I had to wipe the smile from my face that this exchange had brought before I entered the living room because I didn't want Jill thinking I was laughing at her or enjoying her discomfort. She was across the room in a wingback chair, hands in her lap, sitting like a zombie in front of a dark fireplace. She'd bought a new dress for the occasion, a yellow and white frock that reminded me of Easter, and I wished there had been some way to avoid hurting her, but there she sat across the big room as forlorn as anyone I'd ever seen.

"Why didn't you tell me?" she asked.

"I didn't know how without you taking it personally. You'd think I was running out on you when that's not it at all. I've just got to get away, that's all, from this town and my family and the rut I'm in."

Very quietly, without expression and looking at her hands, she said, "Because Sally Ann's getting married."

I turned and looked away, unable to deny what she'd said, looking around at the living room and realizing for the first time I was actually going to leave. Making such an announcement made the decision more or less irrevocable. And what I remembered about this room was Christmas, with all my aunts and uncles and cousins, a day of nonstop activity and food and gifts. And now I was leaving, for the first time, really, because this wasn't like going to college.

And suddenly I was very nervous.

Jill stood and said, "Will you take me home, please? And get my purse from the dining room?"

I walked quickly down the hall, making a turn into the dining room and fixing my eyes on her purse, which sat on the buffet in front of the mirror. Silence prevailed here, broken only by the occasional clink of fork against plate. Five people attempting to eat without making any noise.

Jill was already at the car, standing in the spring twilight, her face frozen in that so-close-yet-so-far-away expression. She wanted into the family and I wanted out, and I wished I could have simply arranged a trade, one son for a daughter.

I looked at her as she got in and thought I'd watched too many movies, watched too many Hollywood soldiers going off to war, leaving on a train as their wives and sweethearts ran beside the departing train, pledging their eternal love, promising to write every day. That was what I wanted, not a similar scene at a train station but one last night when we both knew everything had changed, when all those bittersweet and tormented pressures would bring us together in a heightened frenzy of love and lust and loss. That wasn't, however, what I was going to get.

I told her something of a half truth as I took her home. I wasn't joining the navy now because Sally Ann was marrying Stan. The key word in the sentence was now, which I hoped she wouldn't catch. I let the statement hang and then gave her a number of other reasons why I was leaving, hoping she'd think these were the exclusive reasons. "I've been living off my family, my family's money, my family's reputation, all my life. I've got to do something that's not related to family. I've got to. For my self-respect, which I don't seem to have."

I stole a glance at her to see if she was buying, but I couldn't tell. She could have been playing poker with corpses.

Even when we arrived at her townhouse, she said nothing. Before I could get out to open her door, she was gone, and the only way I knew she wanted me to follow was the open iron gate to the small courtyard around her front door.

I walked in her living room to see her wipe her forehead with the palm of her hand as though she'd been sweating.

"I don't know what to say," she said, her voice cracking.

"I don't either." I didn't know what to do, where to stand, whether even to stay.

She stood by the coffee table, still looking stunned, her eyes fixed on some point between her feet and the baseboard of the far wall.

"I love you," she said, making it sound as though the sentiment may or may not mean anything; she didn't know. "I don't want you to go."

Then she started crying. I'd thought her shock was bad, but the tears ripped my heart. I walked the few steps necessary and put my arms around her. The girl in her yellow and white Easter dress started to say something, then changed her mind. Instead she took my face in her hands and kissed me at least a hundred times, all over the face, the mouth, the eyes, cheeks, everywhere, and when she pressed her slick and salty lips to mine, I remembered something she'd once told me. She had passion. And on this night she did. Her hand on the back of my neck, I thought she was trying to pass through my face. With her other hand, she was undressing me, and I realized something else.

She was going to give me the send-off I'd wanted. And the leaving was going to be more difficult than I'd thought because suddenly I didn't want to leave her at all. My attraction to her was greater than I'd known.

"Spend the night," she said, breathing harshly in my ear. "Stay with me."

She had unbuttoned my shirt and her dress and apparently pulled her bra up or down because I could feel her breasts against my chest. She was hugging me as tightly as she could and was biting my neck.

Dang, I thought. Maybe I should make an announcement every day.

Grasping her just below the ass, I lifted her, and she wrapped her legs around me. In that fashion, I carried her into the bedroom, having to turn sideways to pass through the doors. She was about to suck the vein right out of my neck, and I decided she wasn't giving me a hickey; she was branding me. But I didn't care.

In the bedroom I fell with her onto the bed, landing on top of her.

She grabbed my hair just above my neck and pulled my head back. "You're not going to forget me," she said fiercely, jerking my hair and popping my head back. She was crying again, her face shiny in the light from the hallway, her tears smeared, coating her face. "You're not going to forget me."

We didn't finish undressing and I didn't realize until it was too late how a zipper could damage you, but I didn't care. I'd arrive at the war scraped and bleeding, already wounded, my neck scarred, but I just didn't care.

And she was right: I wouldn't forget her.

★

1969–1971

6

I dreamed about the rain. This wasn't a west Texas cloudburst; it was the rain that had sent Noah to the ark, and it was causing twenty-five-foot seas on the river, great swells of water that washed away everything in its way, trees, people, wooden piers, boats. I kept going under . . . under . . . under. I could never quite make sense of the dream because what I remembered of Vietnam wasn't the rain but the bone-aching tiredness and the soul-sapping heat.

I'd made a mistake going twice. The first time, as unseasoned grist for a brand new kind of navy, one that was propelled over the rivers in fiberglass boats with Jacuzzi engines, I'd learned and seen and felt all I'd needed to know. But the corporate navy of Mayport, Florida, where the only challenge was to prevent bored drunks from burning down the barracks, proved to be worse than the heat and fatigue of Vietnam. With sixteen months to go, I volunteered to return, partly because I felt as though I'd lost something over there and if I went back, I might find it.

But the war had changed, just as the country had. LBJ had more or less resigned in search of peace, and the war was a holding action, fought with dope-smoking hippies and serious lifers side by side. The debate over the war had moved from the floor of government into the streets, and I who had done my duty returned to find I was a baby killer.

I arrived in Abilene a month late with a very bad attitude.

Jill had waited, but at times I wished she hadn't. We needed to get reacquainted and I didn't want to make the effort. I was suffering from an aloof sort of aloneness that I didn't let her penetrate, and I wasn't good company for anyone. I stopped watching the news in the company of other people because I went insane watching hippie motherfuckers with long hair and flowered shirts and beads who were asserting that I was the moral inferior of the Viet Cong, who were burning the U.S. flag, who were chanting, "Hell, no, we won't go."

I had a constant problem with winding down. For the second month —I'd spent the first with a friend in San Francisco trying to catch up and wear out body parts—my mind and body were out of tune with peace. The back of my neck was still in the war; it gave off sensations acquired there.

I'd never fully realized my life and the lives of my friends were no different from anyone else's—subject to sudden cessation—until one night we'd been setting up on the river for an ambush. And that night, we'd become the ambushed, the target, and our chief had lost his arm to a B-40 rocket. He'd become a one-armed madman in green fatigues soaked with his own blood, a crazed amputee demanding that we kill all the slopehead slime we ever again saw in our lives.

After that experience, we were all much more realistic about the risks, the stakes for which we were playing; and that strange sensation, that peculiar combination of anticipation and dread and excitement, would settle on the back of my neck and cause my hair to rise. And now it wouldn't go away, even though I could be sitting in an air-conditioned theater with Jill in Abilene. I was playing tricks on myself. I'd freeze, and for a moment wouldn't know where I was or why or how I was to protect myself. And there was no way to adequately explain to Jill what was going on, particularly since she didn't want to hear about the war or my part in it.

A secondary problem was my inability to figure out how Stan had marched into the offices of Brewster Drilling a day after his release from active duty, emerging from the same environment, although from an earlier and less inflamed war, and presented his optimistic and naively cheery self to us. Not only couldn't I understand it, but I held it against him. Somehow, even while recognizing the irrationality of the feeling, I planted on Stanley Gaines the guilt of a rigged war, one that had killed and wounded my friends at the rate of 30 percent on the dirty rivers of a primitive little country.

Like one who failed to fit into any world, I spent most of my time drinking and reading paperback mysteries and westerns. During the school year, at four o'clock each afternoon, I'd walk to my car like a robot and go pick up Jill at the junior high where she taught. I'd saved a year's tax-free salary and was in no hurry to return to any function in a society that I simultaneously loved and hated. Jill seemed afraid of me, Stan was very polite but cautious, and Sally Ann was acting as she had when I'd been in the hospital with appendicitis.

The pattern was the same. The first time she'd seen me, she'd been solicitous of my mental health; on the second, she'd been civil but impatient over my reluctance to woo her; and by the third, she'd been downright irritated that I was acting differently.

I met her at a shopping center one day on my way to replenish my supply of reading material, and I'd said the first thing that had popped into my mind. "Why don't we go to my place and fuck ourselves silly?"

She'd looked like a dream wearing a black miniskirt and sleeveless white blouse. Dropping her sunglasses down on the end of her nose, she'd looked at me over the frames. "Is that something you heard in a movie?" When I didn't answer, unable to relate to dreams anymore, she'd said, "You watched *The Pride of the Marines* one time too many. If you'd quit acting like John Garfield, I'd do my part in welcoming you home."

Was I playing John Garfield, the World War II vet who'd been wounded by the Japanese and who could hardly adjust? I didn't think so, but Sally Ann wouldn't have believed me. If I hadn't been, according to her, I'd have already come sniffing around, remembering her scent. What I wanted had nothing to do with Sally Ann, something she couldn't have comprehended. I wanted to know exactly what had happened to me, what I had lost, why I seemed to hate everyone regardless of who they were. I wanted to watch the chase scene in *Bullitt* without having to worry about B-40 rockets coming from the darkness.

I went on in this manner for several months, until one night Stan invited Jill and me over to eat steaks he was going to grill outside. I didn't really want to go—I didn't want to *do* anything—but I realized that I couldn't very well withdraw altogether and expect to remain sane. So we went.

The Gaineses lived in Sally Ann's house, the one left her by her grandmother. Many of the antiques had been displaced by more modern, Stanleyish furniture, much of it black glass or chrome, and it no longer seemed the place where I'd spent so much time talking and listening to music and screaming. In fact, I wasn't sure I knew Sally Ann at all anymore. The past was hazy.

We arrived to find her puttering in the kitchen, checking baked potatoes and looking over a big glass bowl of green salad as if to determine whether she'd made enough. I could see Stan at the grill he'd had built in the backyard, his eyes obviously irritated by smoke blowing right into his face in the warm fall evening.

"Do you eat your steak raw nowadays?" Sally Ann asked.

I set a grocery bag full of beer on the counter, next to a bottle of red wine Jill had brought. "I'm not interested in raw meat."

"It's hard to know what you like anymore. And I can't remember *what* John Garfield ate."

Jill was puzzled by the exchange and I didn't elaborate. Instead, I got a beer from the bag and walked into the backyard, wondering about the sex life, if any, of Stan and Sally Ann. The prospect of their engaging in sex didn't bother me as it once had. And knowing Stan, I figured Sally Ann was hornier than a thirteen-year-old boy, which was probably why she'd do her part in welcoming me home if I'd quit playing the wounded war vet.

Stan, in command of the red brick grill, was determined he wasn't going to move just to avoid the smoke, and he was waving his tongs as though he might change its course. Dressed in slacks and a knit sportshirt, he looked prosperous, and the longer hair in fashion improved his appearance. He was like a commodity that mellowed with age; he'd always looked forty, even when he was ten, and the closer he got to that age, the less harsh his features seemed.

I gave him a wave and dropped into a redwood lounge chair with plastic cushions.

"Hey," he said, waving his tongs still. "Glad you could make it."

I nodded but couldn't think of anything to say. Somehow I'd lost my ability to make small talk; I was incapable. So I looked up at the sky, typically endlessly blue. The yard, except for a pool they'd added, was a grove of huge pecan trees.

"Don't run off after you eat," Stan said, still engaged in his futile battle against the smoke. "I want to show you something."

"Show me."

"Hey," he said with a smile. "Don't act like me. Besides, I need a few drinks first."

I was intrigued. Stan had something he could reveal only after some lubrication? The suggestion made me more comfortable for some reason, and I sat back, trying to relax, telling myself to be nice all night long. None of these people had done anything to bother, much less harm, me, and I didn't need to release the free-floating hostility that constantly hovered around me.

"Ready to come back to work?" he asked.

"Nope."

Stan still didn't like silence; he was frustrated by people who weren't conversational, a fact which had accounted for the shortness of our visits to this point.

"So how's it going?" he asked.

"All right."

"What do you do all day?" He smiled to make the question seem less aggressive.

"Oh, not much. Read, drink, jack off. You know."

Stan acted as though he hadn't heard. "Well, these steaks oughta be just about ready."

We ate at the kitchen table, informally and silently. I cut into my steak and watched a thin red lake form on my plate. Stan, completely in character, had wanted the steaks cooked faster than they naturally would, and they were well done outside, raw within. I wasn't particular.

As I ate, I looked out the bay window of the kitchen into the huge backyard, thinking back fifteen years and more. Sally Ann and I had bought hammocks one summer and had hung them with one end of each tied to the same tree so we could lie head to head but wouldn't see each other. I'd lain there and couldn't remember feeling a pressure of any kind. My mind had been as empty and as restful as the sky.

Stan, his mouth full, said, "Somebody say something."

"Why?" Sally Ann asked. "Nobody wants to say anything because Billy will just disagree."

"The hell I will," I said.

Jill, first disturbed by the bleeding cut of steak, now gave me a nervous look. I smiled to let her know I'd been joking.

"This used to be a happy foursome," Sally Ann said.

"You've got a lousy memory," I said. "This foursome rarely ever got together. We were happy twosomes and threesomes occasionally, but never a happy foursome."

"You see what I mean," she said, sitting back as though I, and not her steak, had made it impossible for her to eat. She crossed her arms over her chest and stared at me.

"He's right," Stan said. "We were twosomes and threesomes and hardly ever a foursome."

Jill giggled and placed her napkin over her mouth. When we all looked at her, she said, "Well, it sounded funny. Twosomes and threesomes and foursomes. It sounds like something off 'The Beverly Hillbillies.'"

Sally Ann shook her head and said, "Now he has her disagreeing."

"You're the only one being disagreeable," I said, looking at her through the upper part of my wine glass. Her features were distorted, grotesque, the way they should have been on this stranger across the table. She wasn't the one with whom I'd lain head to head in hammocks.

I seemed to be the only one eating. The others, including Stan, had pushed their plates away, as if thinking the meat might find the energy required to mount a counterattack.

"This steak sucks," he said. He stood, glass in hand, and looked at me. "Come on. Bring your glass."

I stood and followed him. He carried not only his glass but a jug of wine from the refrigerator into his study. It was a heavily masculine room with pine paneling, bookshelves, and a very large desk almost in the center of the room. Stan closed the door behind us and opened a closet door. I sat at his desk, which was a disaster, a massive pile of geolographs, plats, and drilling logs that hid the surface. It was storage for a man who just couldn't get organized. On top of this paper mountain Stan balanced the bottle of wine and his glass, standing back to make sure they didn't fall before he turned his attention to the opened closet.

Without saying anything, he began removing everything in it, working toward a corner. Out came unused golf clubs and tennis rackets, parts of a stereo, an empty picture frame. He was apparently after a chicken box, one of those heavy pasteboard boxes with waxed surfaces. I sat at the desk but pushed my chair into a position so I could see what he was doing.

Finally he backed out of the closet with the box, setting it on the floor beside the desk and removing the top. My God, I thought, remembering my intrigue with this guy, the real Stanley Gaines is in that box. I wanted to throw him out of the room and rummage through the box at leisure. He pitched a big black Bible into the upturned top of the box. Beneath it was a small manila envelope he picked up, the object he'd been after. He sat back on the floor, leaving another photo revealed, one that was too big for the envelope.

It was an eight-by-ten glossy black and white, and it revealed that at least once, Stanley Gaines may have succumbed to lust. He was sitting at a table, obviously in a bar, with an Oriental girl wearing a slinky dress. Neither of them was smiling. I'd not only seen such pictures, but

I had one of my own, and the quality was always borderline, overly grainy. Stan stared blankly into the lens. And I'd been looking at it for some time when I realized he wasn't wearing an army uniform but an Australian bush outfit.

"This is what I was going to show you," he said, now holding a snapshot he'd taken from the envelope. "I don't know why I started dreaming about this kid when you came home, but I did. I mean, just about the time you got back."

Looking somewhat grim, he handed me the picture. It showed Stan in khaki shorts and jungle boots, spindly legs and all, standing beside an Oriental child possibly ten years old. Both of them looked happy, but the child was more than pleased. He was proud. Barefooted and wearing nothing but shorts, he tilted his head back, sticking his chin at the camera. He was ready to conquer the world.

"This is a little hard to explain," he said.

"Where was this picture taken?"

"Chu Porn Mountains. Laos."

"What the hell were you doing in Laos?"

"That's the part that's hard to explain." He stood and got his glass from the desk and poured wine, then sat again. "You ever hear of ICA? Or USAID? Well, in 1962, the Geneva Convention supposedly banned all foreign troops in Laos, which meant that most of them just changed clothes. Except the NVA. They didn't even do that. We went to work for USAID. And the CIA. We were training Meo tribesmen. Mostly they were opium farmers, but some of them were damn good soldiers. They'd been taught by the French. I was helping resupply them, but for a while, I was making raids with them up in the Sam Neua Province, which was under PL control. Pathet Lao."

He sipped wine for a minute and looked at the picture. "The boy's name was Pham, and he was a Meo. There were two things he wanted —to be an American and a soldier. He was a hell of a good kid, just a real good kid. A Special Forces sergeant had given him a knife and he never went anywhere without it. And this kid who wanted to be a soldier so bad learned how to whittle. Can you imagine that, taking one of those knives with an eight-inch blade, both sides ground down with a blood groove, and using it to whittle? But he was great. He could carve trees and all kinds of stuff. I got really attached to him, just like you would a little brother. He'd do anything you asked him. Anything. He'd tell people we were brothers and his name was Jimmy."

He stopped for a moment and looked as though he was experiencing an attack of indigestion, which he treated with a long drink of wine, his eyes still fixed on the picture, on the kid with his chin stuck out.

"One day we were setting up for a parachute drop and he didn't show up. He never missed one because it was like an air show. He loved watching the planes. And not only didn't he show up for the drop, he didn't show up all day. Or the next day. I went to the village and couldn't even find his family. They were out scouring the countryside, and all they ever found was a tree he'd been carving and that knife down by the river. He had this spot of his own where he'd go to carve.

"Man, we looked everywhere, but we never found anything but the knife and tree. We looked, we asked, we called in favors, we tried everything. And got nothing. It was the worst thing that ever happened to me. I looked for him off and on until I left, and we never found even a small clue. He'd just disappeared."

This was a brand-new side of Stan, one I'd never seen before. A serious side, one that understood life wasn't just one deal or another that he wanted to chase after. He scratched his head and looked off to the side as though deliberating on whether he wanted to continue.

"I've been having this dream, and I've been having it since you got back. I'm standing by a river in the evening, just about half light, and I see these two guys coming. At first I think they're carrying a stretcher, but then I see it's just two sticks. But the sticks are close together and there's something on them. It's too dark for me to see just what it is, but it looks like a coconut. And the two guys stop just a few feet away and this thing on the sticks rolls off and stops at my feet. I bend down to look at it and then all of a sudden it comes into focus. It's Jimmy's head, and his mouth is open like he's screaming. A silent scream. The kid looks terrified, just like he would've looked if he'd been on his back and seen somebody about to hack his head off.

"I don't know what to do and all I can do is just stare at this terrified face. And then the two guys pick his head up, put it back on the sticks, and they walk off down the river."

Stan took a deep breath and then exhaled, blowing. "Man, I wake up soaking wet with sweat and scared shitless. My hands are shaking, I'm panting like I've been running for miles, and for a few minutes I can't even get myself under control. I get up and get a drink, and I swear in the morning I'm going to Laos to find the poor kid. I've got to know what happened to him. I want somebody to tell me he showed up one day and he was all right. But I know that won't happen, and I know if I go I won't find him. Hell, I couldn't find him then; how could I find him now?"

He rubbed his forehead, looking tired, older than his normal forty years. I wasn't glad to see him suffering or hear of his problem, but I was glad to see he wasn't the one-dimensional curiosity I'd always believed him to be.

By the time we finished talking about his dream and about the sensation that kept lighting on my neck, we'd finished the jug of wine. I didn't know what the girls were doing but I assumed if Jill wanted to go home, she'd find a means of getting there. At the moment, I didn't want to leave Stan's study, didn't want to see either girl. I didn't want to hear any comments on John Garfield or on the grossness of war or questions on why we'd done what we'd done.

The longer we talked, the better I felt, and I thought about the part of the navy I'd liked—the camaraderie. I'd learned a lot, most of it related to the primary activities of drinking and playing poker and the secondary pursuits of fighting and fucking, but the friends I'd made were those who'd helped me put it all in perspective, usually at night, looking at the stars. In that unreal world halfway around the globe, I'd found strangers I'd grown to love, guys in whom I put the ultimate trust, that of my life. We'd talked about anything and everything, from love and hate to God and girls. In fact, at the end of my catch-up month in San Francisco after my release from active duty, I'd found it more difficult to leave one of those friends than it had been to leave home. It seemed a loss of too many important friendships.

Stan and I talked until five in the morning, until we were through, and still I hesitated leaving his study, partly because I was too tired to move, partly because I didn't want to leave.

Still on the floor, back against the wall, Stan asked what I was going to do.

"I don't know. I really don't."

"Your father wants you back. You know that, don't you? He thinks one hell of a lot of you. While you were gone, he'd bring your letters to work and read me parts of them. I remember once he said your boat was playing chicken with another boat every time you met."

Stan's voice was still strong even though his eyes were closed and he could have been asleep, his head against the wall. I remembered how surprised I'd been when I came home on leave to discover the old man knew as much about the patrol boats as I did. He'd known their armament and armor, their methods of propulsion and the makeup of their crews. Since I'd been home, he'd asked several times about my intentions, but he'd never once directly invited me to return to Brewster

Drilling. I didn't know whether he wanted me to choose my own course or whether he didn't want me back. Whatever, I hadn't yet decided what I was going to do.

"Before you leave," Stan said, pushing himself off the floor with an effort, grunting, "I want to show you something." He stood beside the desk, wavering for a moment, blinking his eyes open, and then dug into the papers on the desk. He found a magazine and then flipped through the pages until he located the picture he wanted to show me. It was a military leader, a foreign soldier carrying a riding crop and looking pleased with himself. The caption identified him as Muammar Qaddafi of Libya.

"Things are changing, Billy Boy. We've got revolutions and radicals everywhere, and this guy's the latest. You know what's going to happen? Things are going to get worse over there, not better. And we knew twenty years ago world oil production was shifting to the Middle East."

He fell against the desk and had to prop himself up. "You know what the worst combination in the world is? Religion and greed. One way or the other, these supplies are going to get disrupted. Hey, nobody believed Mexico and Iran would nationalize the oil industry. Nobody believed Venezuela would demand 50 percent participation. And even after they did, nobody believed the Arabs could pull off the same thing. Hell, the Seven Sisters figured they were stronger than the camel jockeys. They forgot there were all these smaller guys who figured 50 percent of the pie's better than no pie. The Italians thought 25 was all right. Religion and greed, don't get in their way."

He nodded, almost asleep. "Listen, Billy Boy, there's only one thing that'll make people cooperate—greed. And there's one thing that'll make them fight every time—religion. One or the other's going to disrupt the supplies and cause the price to skyrocket, and whatever it is, whether they figure out how to limit production and raise the price, or if they start blowing up each other's refineries, it's not going to be fixed very easy. And the price'll go up, up, up."

The speech exhausted him, and he slid to the floor. Lying down, he used the bag of golf clubs for a pillow on which to lay his head. He sniffed and rubbed his face and I was sure this time he was actually asleep, but again he spoke. "Come back to work. It's going to get exciting one of these days. I'm so sure of it I told your father I didn't want a salary and bonus, I wanted a draw against the profits. And I told him why. I don't know if he believed me, but one of these days, the sand niggers are going to make me rich." He seemed to possess enough strength for one more statement. "Come on back and we can work some deals while we're waiting."

He fell asleep. I knew because he started snoring, his mouth open. He wasn't a pretty sight. Still, I expected him to wake up and continue his spiel, or to continue it in his sleep, but he didn't say anything else.

I mustered enough energy to push myself out of the chair and left the room, opening the door very quietly to find the rest of the house quiet. A light burned in the kitchen, providing dim illumination for the maze of hall and rooms, and the house had gotten cold.

I found Jill on the couch in the living room, covered with an afghan. For a moment, I watched her sleep in the semidarkness, her breathing slow and steady. One strand of brown hair was about to slide onto her lips, and I started to move it but didn't want to wake her.

Taking my empty wine glass to the kitchen, I turned just inside the doorway, headed for the sink, and ran right into Sally Ann. A wave of fear ran up and down my spine as water in a shaken jar.

Holding her arms, I said, "*Dang.* I thought you were a ghost."

She laughed, her hand over her mouth to muffle the sound. Barefooted, she wore a short green robe, and, judging from the fact that her dark blond hair wasn't messed up, her makeup was still on, I didn't think she'd been sleeping. Or even to bed.

I started to ask what she'd been doing, but before I could, she kissed me, a long probing kiss. She hadn't been to bed but she had undressed because beneath the robe, she wasn't wearing anything at all. She broke the long kiss, added two short ones for good measure, and whispered into my mouth as she held my head, "Welcome home."

I think we expected the same thing—that I'd be swept away with that old familiar desire, the mind-numbing want, but I wasn't. I didn't feel as if I even knew her, this girl with whom I'd discussed every passage of my life. And she hadn't even asked about the most important. All she cared about was that I wanted her as much sexually as I had five years ago.

It didn't take me long to figure out what she'd been doing and why she was welcoming me home. "You've been listening to everything we said."

I'd released her arms and she backed away, puzzled by my lack of response to the best she'd had in the category of wet kisses.

"Not everything. I waited until Jill went to sleep. And then my butt got tired from sitting on the floor outside the door and I had to walk around some. So I didn't hear *everything*."

She backed up, leaning against an island in the middle of the kitchen. The light behind her shone through her robe, making a triangle of light between the shadows of her legs. And looking at that play of light and darkness, I worried for a moment about my lack of response to her. I didn't even want to kiss her.

She decided to try again. "Do you know how much I've missed you? If you ever leave me for that long again, I don't know what I'll do."

I laughed, quietly, without amusement. "If you'd wanted me to stay, there was an obvious way."

She said nothing and I began to think I'd been emotionally emasculated, had been drained of my hormones. She had great legs and I should have wanted to touch the shadows, should have wanted to run my hand beneath the robe, all the way to the top of the triangle, but I didn't.

"I'm glad you came home such a crab," she said. "You made it easy for me to ignore what my body was telling me."

"What'd it tell you?"

"It was like a magnet that hadn't been around any metal for a long time. Suddenly it started feeling something metallic and hard in the air."

She was trying to help me remember that I knew her but not very strenuously, telling me she understood partly why I seemed to be John Garfield but unwilling to put it in words. She'd welcome me home with her body.

"I remember when we didn't play games," I said, walking to the counter where she'd left a drink. I was extremely thirsty and downed her drink, crunching on the ice that was left.

"I remember when life was simpler. Before there was a man on the moon and before race riots and drugs and cult murders."

"What're you telling me?"

"That life isn't simple."

"Thanks," I said, putting the glass back down. "I hadn't realized."

Now I'd irritated her. She gave me a smirky look and got her glass, the one out of which I was eating ice, and took it to the sink, emptying it. "I don't think I even know you anymore. I kept asking Stan when you were supposed to be home and you were a month late. You not only had a beard, but you were drunk as a skunk. And the only thing you've said to me in six months was that we ought to go to your place and fuck ourselves silly."

"And what were you telling me just now with that welcome-home kiss? That you may be married to Stan but you *will* fuck yourself silly? What were you telling me?"

She obviously didn't like the course of the conversation, didn't want this quest for truth inserted. She walked from the sink to where I stood, looking up at me. Without her shoes, she seemed much shorter than her five foot, seven inches, and smaller. Minutes ago, pressed against me, she'd felt larger, twice as large, big enough to consume me. Now, close enough for me to smell the residue of perfume she'd put on hours ago, she didn't touch me. She wanted me to touch her.

"You tell me," I said. "You just sat outside the door and listened to hours of uncensored and unrehearsed conversation. Do you know me?"

"Do you want to know the truth?" she asked, now walking off since I hadn't accepted the offer to touch her. She stopped at the island in the center of the room again. "You didn't say anything that surprised me. But my own husband? I always thought he'd been in Vietnam and now I find out he was in Laos." She shook her head. "I wondered why he was getting up in the middle of the night to get a drink. I figured it had to do with work."

I wanted to talk about Stan and Laos, but she didn't, not right now. She returned to me, thinking surely that I'd get her message, that even my thick skull couldn't forever block the offer she was making. Obviously that was my problem—I hadn't yet understood what she was prepared to serve. She stuck her forefinger inside my shirt and stroked my stomach.

"Why won't you tell me you're glad to see me? You haven't said it since you got home. You are glad to see me, aren't you?"

This was the most frustrating conversation I'd ever had. I took her hand in mine and placed it on the counter, wanting her finger out of my shirt, and remembered thinking years ago, when she'd taken up with Stan, that I had misinterpreted our entire relationship. And I began to believe the same thing now. In all those years, had she only cared about my sexual interest? I wanted to talk to her, wanted to discover if I knew her still, and all she wanted was for me to exhibit an old sexual obsession.

I decided the only way to get to the truth was to make her mad, so I said, "You know what? You can't have it all. You can't have two husbands, one official, one unofficial. I'm not going to come over here and fuck you while Stan's at work. I'm not even going to lust after you."

I turned as though I was leaving and walked to the doorway into the living room, seeing Jill on the couch in the same position. She didn't seem to have moved even a finger. And I knew Sally Ann would never allow me to leave and have the last word too.

She didn't. "Bil-ly," she sang quietly, just as she had twenty years ago in the backyard of this house.

I couldn't even make her mad. Suddenly the weight of the wine and

93

fatigue and frustration settled in my shoulders, and I grew so quickly tired I wanted to lie down immediately, just as Stan had in the study, just go to sleep on the spot. I shook my head and kept walking, followed by Nemesis.

I stopped at the couch, looking at Jill under the orange and green squares of the afghan. I bent to awaken her with a kiss, not only to irritate Sally Ann but to recognize the fact that this sleeping beauty had caused me so little grief. She'd waited, she'd suffered uncomplaining through my long and unexplained silences, she'd made no demand that I tell her, show her, I was glad to see her.

With the kiss on her cheek, she came suddenly awake, blinking and glancing around in alarm.

"You're okay," I said. "I'm taking you home."

"What time is it?"

"Almost time for breakfast."

I lifted her up. Once oriented and in my arms, she seemed to consider a thought: how does one properly exit a house in this manner? She decided a sleepy wave would suffice and gave in to the apparent safety of my arms. Her arms around my neck, she emitted a whimper of satisfaction.

Sally Ann opened the front door, letting cold air in, then stood without expression, a significant look to a seasoned observer such as I was. She watched me turn, maneuvering through the door with my load, and said, "You know, some things bother you more than you think they will."

"Like what?" I asked, knowing what she meant—seeing Jill in my arms—but I wanted to hear her say it, just as she wanted to hear me say I was glad to see her again.

"Oh, I don't know. Just things."

I was suddenly enjoying this standoff because I realized she had lost that old grip on me, and she couldn't kick me into the mire of unfulfilled desire. So as I carried Jill out the door, I stepped on Sally Ann's toes, then looked apologetic.

"Oh, I'm sorry."

"You don't know how sorry you really are."

94

7

The offices of Brewster Drilling hadn't changed a bit in four and a half years, but there did seem to be slightly fewer occupied desks. The drilling business continued its long decline, and had it not been for the old man's reputation and relationships, there would have been even fewer employees to count. Inflation was running higher than in any year since 1951, and the cost of drilling a well continued to rise; the price of oil, however, didn't.

The change was on the third floor, where the offices of Brewster-Gaines Production Company had moved. The second floor hadn't been able to hold Stan, and I realized why when I stopped at the front door to the offices. There were five new companies listed in gold letters on the dark wooden door. BG Oilfield Supply. BG Well Service. BG Pump. BG Testing. And one that surprised me—Brewster-Gaines Properties. Properties? The other companies made sense. Not only could the old man make money selling to and servicing other oil-field businesses, but they could save money by providing equipment and services to their own leases and rigs. But Brewster-Gaines Properties? Stan had been a very busy young man.

I introduced myself to the receptionist and she buzzed Stan to announce my presence. "Mr. Gaines has a visitor but he said for you to come on back."

Stan had diverged from the old man in at least one area—office decor. There was a world of difference between the second and third floors of the building. The furniture here was rather plush and it matched his gold-leaf wallpaper. The floor was covered with carpet, not that hideous beige tile, and the desks were wood, not metal.

When I arrived at Stan's corner office, I saw why he wanted me to come on back even though he had a visitor. I recognized his visitor from high school, a guy who'd been a year ahead of Stan and me. He was one of those guys who'd always been campaigning for some school office, and his constant need for attention and reassurance had been construed as "leadership qualities," at least by the editor of the yearbook. I'd seen examples of such leadership qualities in the war from guys who adhered to the philosophy, "When in danger or in doubt, run in circles, scream and shout." And now, his leadership qualities shining like a black bra through a white blouse, he was running for the state House of Representatives. Although the primary wasn't until next spring, he was apparently getting prepared, soliciting assistance from a person who'd represented the antithesis of leadership in high school.

Stan's office was nicely furnished with a brown leather couch and two matching chairs, a coffee table with glass inserts, and several examples of western art on the wall, paintings of Indians and horses and buffalo.

The visitor stood, rising from the leather couch, when I entered. "I heard you were back from Vietnam and I want to tell you how much I appreciate what you guys have been doing over there."

"Hell, you should've skipped law school and come on over. You missed one hell of a big bash."

Stan, standing at his Cypress Street window, mimicked the president who occupied the office just below his by lacing his fingers together and extending his arms to stretch, palms out. He looked at me and said, "That reminds me of something I've been wanting to ask you. When you were there, were they still choppering hookers in to the hot zones?"

"Oh, yeah," I said, taking one of the leather chairs and making myself comfortable. "They'd load those helos up with naked women and just bring them in. Unless the LZ was hot. Then they'd jump. Hell of a sight. You look up and see naked women floating down in parachutes. That's where that old saying, 'Twat's up,' comes from."

Stan looked at the would-be representative very seriously and said, "I'll tell you something but you've got to keep it to yourself. The newspapers keep talking about the troops being out in the bush. I bet you didn't know what that meant, did you?"

The guy wasn't sure how to react, wasn't sure we were merely kidding, but then, he'd never been either quick or smart. So, ignoring what we said, he jumped for the pose that had got him this far, that of campaigning. "It'll be a tight race, Stan, but I really think your endorsement would give me the edge I need. I think just you alone could put me over the top."

"The top?" Stan asked. "The top of what?"

"Oh, you know," the guy said with a nervous smile and a glance at me, explaining with a flip of his hand. "If you give me an endorsement, I think I can win. I can give us the kind of representation in Austin we need. You're the kind of businessman—"

Stan interrupted him, leaning forward on his desk. "I'll tell you what. You scratch my back and I'll scratch yours. Your father's on the city council, right? Well, you get him to pass a treason ordinance and I'll vote for you. I want to see Senator Fulbright hauled into municipal court. You know how much support he's giving our guys? Listen to this; here's what he said: 'We ought to welcome North Vietnam's preeminence in Indochina.' That's a quote, a direct quote, from the front page of the paper published right here in town. So you help me get him in the Taylor County jail and I'll endorse you."

The visitor flicked his tongue across his upper lip, looking from Stan to me, wishing one of us would help rather than confuse him. "Well, Stan, that's a federal matter—"

"Not when it's printed here, it's not. Besides that, the post office is federal too, but we have mail delivery *here*, don't we?"

I wasn't sure what this guy had done to Stan but it had been fairly severe in Stan's sight, because I'd never seen him quite this wound up. I tried thinking back to high school but couldn't remember specifically if this politician had been the one who'd called Melissa Gaines a whore or not. Probably not. I doubt that even a politician would solicit funds from a man who'd pissed on him in high school.

Stan was still giving him examples of federal matters that existed within the city of Abilene. "And I know we've got people *right here* who are getting Social Security."

Abruptly finished, Stan shot his hand out, offering to shake with the blinking, frowning man, extending over the desk so the visitor would have to stand to shake. "Hey, it was good of you to come by. I'll invite you to speak at the FFGFYG meeting next month."

The politician stood, shaking reluctantly as though Stan might have one of those practical joker's buzzers in the palm of his hand. He shook without a great deal of enthusiasm. "The FF—what'd you say?"

"FFGFYG. Fight, Fuck, or Go For Your Gun Society."

Nodding, a little disoriented, the politician turned toward the door. Looking at me, he couldn't decide whether to push his luck or just slide out the door. Then, deciding not to alienate a voter, he offered his hand.

Remembering his meaningless remark about the war, I showed him a clenched fist and shouted, "Power to the people!"

When he was gone, Stan exhibited the largest smile I'd seen, and he fell into the chair behind his desk, looking completely satisfied. Putting his hands behind his head, lifting his feet onto the desk, he said, "I've been waiting to get that son of a bitch for years. You know what he used to do? I'd walk down South First to Casey's every once in a while and he'd come by every time I did in his car and say, 'You tired of walking?'

And before I could tell him, hell, no, I liked walking, he'd say, 'Then run a while!' and peel out. Every time I went down there he did that. Endorse him. I'll endorse him, right across the head."

I laughed, because around his office were a number of plaques certifying him as a contributor to one cause or another, and our old friend from high school had probably thought this was a safe place in which to seek an endorsement. If he'd remembered harassing Stan on South First twelve or thirteen years ago, he had obviously believed Stan was too stupid to have done the same.

"Tell me you're back to stay," Stan said.

"Not yet."

"Hey, I'll make up your mind. You and Jill be at our house tomorrow at noon and I'll show you. I'll make up your mind."

"A surprise?"

"A surprise, damn right. What would life be without surprises?"

We sat and talked for a while. The oil business was stuck in the doldrums but he was fully expecting it to come back, thanks to OPEC. I started to interrupt and remind him he'd given me this spiel last night, but he was on a roll. In anticipation of the coming boom, he and Sally Ann were buying real estate south of town because south was the only logical way for the city to expand. When the city boomed, he would too.

He checked his watch and invited me to a tennis match, one with a man who owned a large chunk of land he wanted. "He'll sell it to me if I win."

"What happens if you lose?"

"We keep playing."

I watched the match with Sally Ann, whose friendly manner seemed to indicate she remembered little or nothing of the previous night's conversation. She wore a reddish orange pantsuit and had her hair pinned up rather loosely, and I knew she hadn't forgotten I liked seeing those loose strands of hair around her neck.

I decided I really was a Plains Indian at heart because I liked hair, and the Indians had associated hair with the soul, a belief that had been implicated in the practice of scalping. And now, even though I didn't want to get sexually embroiled with her again, I did want to reach over and touch those wisps of hair at her neck. I wanted to stroke her soul.

We sat where we really couldn't see the match very well, outside the courts on a bench, peering through the chain link fence, and I accused her of reversing the roles in her own production of *Pygmalion*. There was Stanley Gaines in an actual tennis outfit with an expensive racket, and his entire approach to the game had been polished. Occasionally he'd get carried away and revert to the old smash-and-bash technique, but overall he was smooth, impressively changed.

She shook her head. "I didn't do any of that. The tennis pro did."

"Yeah? Who suggested he take lessons?"

"I think he just decided on his own."

She sat forward, hands on her knees, showing me good posture on this unusually windless day. And I knew she had something on her mind because she'd been the one to suggest we sit here, outside the court, away from the players.

"What's Stan's mother like?" I asked.

She laughed and turned to look at me, seeming for a moment like my old friend. "She's a very unusual case. You need to meet her and decide for yourself."

"Do you get along with her?"

"Oh, much better than Stan does. Have you ever watched two goats butting heads? That's what they do; they butt heads. They argue about religion all the time, and Stan comes off sounding like an atheist and his mother sounds like a fanatic, and really she's not a fanatic at all. I've talked to her when she's never even mentioned religion." She patted my leg and added, "She likes you and she's never even met you. Now she nodded. "You've heard Stan talk about The Blest? Well, he got it from her. To Stan it's kind of a joke; to her it's very serious. The Blest."

Watching a long volley and listening to the *whop* of the ball, I remembered the question my mother would never answer—what had she known about Melissa Gaines and the two rich men, obviously The Blest, she'd worked for? I asked Sally Ann if she'd ever heard rumors to that effect, and for a minute she acted as though she hadn't heard at all. Then she sat back, our shoulders touching.

"Stan's never heard those stories."

She was obviously telling me I shouldn't bring them up around Stan, and I was touched by the protective nature of her comment. But she hadn't answered my question.

"Are they true?"

She shrugged. "I'd never ask about something like that."

I laughed. If she'd had personal conversations with Mrs. Gaines outside the presence of Stan, then she surely knew whether the stories were true. Sally Ann could glean a person's innermost secrets and leave the person sitting without a clue as to how much he or she had revealed.

99

"I know you wouldn't ask directly but you'd dang sure find out enough to make a sound assumption."

She gave me a look that said she accepted my appraisal of her talents while telling me I was also wrong, one of those contradictory looks at which she excelled. "You go see her and decide for yourself." Then, changing the subject, she said, "She thinks Stan ought to be a preacher."

"Are you kidding?" I all but yelled. "A preacher?" At first the idea seemed outlandish, but it wasn't outlandish at all. I could easily see Brother Gaines pacing the podium, pounding his Bible, exhorting the lost to be saved. All I had to do was change the words, "Let's make a deal," to, "Won't you accept Jesus as your savior?" And there was Brother Stanley in his ice cream—white suit. It was perfect. "You can't see him as a preacher?"

"Oh, yes, I can," she said. "That's what bothers me. I have this dream, well, really a nightmare—his mother finally brainwashes him and he comes home and tells me he wants to sell everything we own and give it to the poor."

"You'd make a great preacher's wife. Maybe you could sing."

"Preacher's wife, my be-hind. I'd give him a one-way ticket back to his mama."

I smiled, watching her watch the game. I didn't think she was really paying attention, but her head was turning, following the flight of the ball. It was a mindless sort of exercise.

Suddenly she looked at me and asked, "How's Jill in bed?"

The question made me very uneasy, and Sally Ann took my discomfort as that of a parent reluctant to discuss the failings of a child. She laughed right in my face, assuming Jill hadn't yet conquered the missionary position. It was a happy kind of laugh, full of enjoyment. I shook my head, embarrassed. She stopped laughing as suddenly as she'd started and looked aghast.

"You haven't even done it, have you? I'd forgotten what an old maid you are."

I'd discussed my feelings about sex with Sally Ann, like everything else, and now I regretted it. I fixed my eyes on the tennis court and tried to ignore her.

She tapped my leg and sang, "Bil-ly." When I didn't answer, didn't look at her, she said, "You're the one that ought to be a preacher."

I was no longer sure how I felt about sex; my beliefs had been formed in an earlier and simpler time. Under the best conditions, most often with Sally Ann, I'd found it to be the most intense personal, and impersonal, experience I'd engaged in, something like communion in church, a universal rite of celebration.

"Does Stan make love like he used to play tennis?" I asked.

"He did. Wham, bam, thank you, ma'am. He thanked me, like I'd washed his clothes or cleaned up his car for him." She gave me a smile of superiority, one that showed how advanced she was, how easily she could discuss this subject.

"How sweet."

"Do you still see pussies everywhere you look?"

I thought about getting up and leaving, but she was trying to make me mad, payment for my refusal to tell her I was glad to see her. She was talking about something I'd told her once, related to my attitude toward sex, over how amazing I'd found it that every woman, theoretically anyway, was capable of giving birth.

"Do you remember when we were friends?" I asked. "What happened?"

She leaned forward again to watch the game, shrugging as she put her hands on her knees. "Friends are friendly. You're just not friendly anymore."

I grabbed her shoulder and turned her around so I could see her face, doing so before I considered what this scene might look like to a passerby or, better yet, to her husband. But I was too irritated to think. "You know those places that cure you of smoking by making you smoke ten cigarettes at a time and sniff ashtrays full of butts? That's what the navy was like, but it didn't cure me of cigarettes, it cured me of bullshit. The day I got out I decided I wasn't going to take any more, I didn't have to. And I'm tired of your bullshit. If you've got something to say, say it, and quit playing these damn games."

Instead of protesting over my rough handling of her shoulder, she used the occasion to drop her hand into my lap as though I'd forced it into that spot and she had no choice. Smiling, she said, "All I want is for you to show me you're glad to see me."

We'd gone from "tell" to "show" and she'd keep raising the ante until I'd destroyed myself attempting to demonstrate my joy over seeing her again. In the end, she'd require a sacrifice. I disentangled myself and stood, looking down on her, wondering why on earth she was so persistent. She looked as lovely as I'd ever seen her, her hair parted in the middle and pulled to each side, arcing down over her forehead like curtains pulled back over a window.

"I'll tell you what," I said. "As soon as I see somebody I recognize, I'll tell her how glad I am to see her."

I walked off and this time she didn't call me back.

Jill and I arrived at the Gaines's house just before noon the next day so Stan could show us his big surprise, one certain to change my mind about returning to work. I assumed Sally Ann would be her usual smiling self, refusing to acknowledge any real difficulty between us, and she was, armed with a picnic basket and two bottles of wine. I thought at first we were going on a picnic but discovered we were taking a long drive, even though it wasn't a good day for a drive. A front was pushing across the state, black clouds leading it and unsettling the sky. But we set off in Stan's white Cadillac.

Jill was already exasperated. The fact that Stan wouldn't tell us where we were going put her in a bind because, ignorant of our destination, she didn't know what to wear. "He thrives on these *surprises*," she said. "Anybody who wants to *surprise* you all the time has some kind of personality defect. I *hate* surprises."

Jill and I each seemed aggravated by the presence of our opposites in the front seat, but I'd had a dream that had at least given me some insight into my predicament.

In the dream, I'd found upon waking up each morning I had a small circle on my face, something like one that would be made by a cigarette lighter in a car, only smaller. And each morning I was further puzzled by the appearance of a brand new circle. Howard Cosell—I never figured out what he was doing in my dream—told me that the country was experiencing a new fad. People were sneaking up on sleeping victims, spraying an anesthetic aerosol into their faces, and then marking brands on the victim's face. Most were much more elaborate than my simple circles.

I was astounded that such a thing could have been happening to me; in fact, I refused to believe it could. Until the next morning. I woke up to find a completed game of tic-tac-toe on my cheek, and the O's had won.

I woke up for real with a start. Sally Ann had taught me to play the game, and she'd always been the O, and she'd always gone first, and she'd always won. Finally I'd refused to play anymore, and then she'd refused to even talk to me until I had agreed to play one more game, which she'd won, of course. Then our friendship returned to normal.

And that's what she was doing now, except it wasn't tic-tac-toe, it was sex. And she wasn't going to resume any kind of normal relationship until we'd come back together on her terms, which meant I had to woo her sexually. Why, I didn't know. I did know she was making me mad as hell acting that way and preventing the resumption of the most meaningful friendship I'd ever had. Didn't she remember—or care about—what we'd had together?

Once we were on the interstate, headed east toward Fort Worth, Sally Ann distributed the contents of her basket—cheese and bread—and we began our mobile picnic just as the first drops of rain hit the windshield and the first gusts of cold air rocked the car. Everything meant for the back seat she handed to me. "Here's one for you," she said, giving me a plastic glass of wine. "And here's another one for you."

We drove through the cut in one of the last few hills of the Callahan Divide, falling into several miles of level prairie, and I asked Stan, "We must be headed for Dallas or Fort Worth. Is Brewster-Gaines expanding?"

He gave me a quick look, wondering if I'd broken the code, and decided I was only guessing. "How can I tell you anything without spoiling the surprises? See, I've got two surprises. Actually, that's three. The third was that you thought there was only one."

Jill gave a loud sigh. She'd worn a rather simple blue dress, which wouldn't be completely appropriate for many events but which also wouldn't be totally inappropriate either, not unless we were attending the Mayor's Ball in Dallas. But now Stan, with his unexpected revelation that we had a double destination, had increased the odds ten or twelve times that she'd be embarrassed before the day was over.

"So when are you two getting married?" Stan asked.

I sighed. "We'll let you know when we decide."

Sally Ann turned and rested her chin on her hand on the top of the seat. Looking Jill over as though she might be a peasant with grass in her hair, she said, "What's taking so long? Won't Billy ask you?"

"Shut up," I said, meaning it.

She turned around and said to Stan, "He hasn't asked her."

We munched bread and cheese with no enthusiasm at all in the back seat, both of us wishing that on this Saturday we were someplace else. Instead we were speeding through occasional rainstorms with people we didn't like. I tried putting Jill at ease when we finished eating by holding her hand, smiling at her, whispering conversation that Sally Ann couldn't hear. We formed the Anti-Gaines Alliance, and I found her company comforting, particularly when we were enclosed by a heavy curtain of rain.

I wasn't sure I wanted to marry Jill, but I seemed to have very little choice without hurting her. She'd waited, she'd been patient and longsuffering, and she wanted to be a Brewster. My mother had already bought her Christmas present, a diamond necklace that probably cost ten times more than anything she'd ever bought me. They had become fast friends.

We didn't stop in Fort Worth, although we did reduce our speed from ninety miles an hour, driving right through the heart of the city and getting on the toll road to Dallas. Fort Worth had always seemed like Abilene's big brother, a small town that had kept growing but hadn't changed a great deal. But Dallas was different. It was slick and energetic and efficient, the IBM of cities. It was generally misunderstood because of the events of the early sixties, when its loudest voices had been those of political kooks and when Kennedy had been assassinated. It was a city that always looked to me just as it did on a map because it arose from generally flat land, an impressive-looking downtown surrounded by older neighborhoods, encircled by the growing suburbs.

We drove silently through downtown Dallas, turning north, and I wondered how much farther we were going. To Oklahoma? Surely not. Before long, Stan left the freeway and headed toward Highland Park. But he made several turns and we ended up in the other park city, University Park. Both of them were incorporated cities within the corporate limits of Dallas, both desirable places to live, full of old homes and trees and neighborhood pride. We stopped in front of a three-story brick home that was obviously empty.

It was built with red brick and formed an elegant cubicle with three rows of windows equally spaced across the front. A semicircular drive passed under a huge portico where at least six cars could be parked. The house had a definite antebellum air and caused Jill to speak in spite of herself.

"I love it," she said, bending toward the window of the car.

Stan had stopped in front on the street so we could get the full effect and now pulled into the drive, stopping under the portico and opening his door. "It goes on the market next week. The lady who lived here moved into a retirement home, and I paid her son a few bucks to keep it off the market until we make up our minds."

"You are moving to Dallas then?" I asked.

Stan nodded. "Probably."

"What're you waiting on?" Jill asked. "I'd buy it in a second."

"I wanted you two to see it," he said, leaving the car.

The women apparently declared a truce on ill will, tacitly promising not to spit in each other's eyes until they'd seen the house. Suddenly they were acting like lifelong friends who could have been considering a joint purchase. I followed them in, thinking Stan was probably right when he talked about money bringing people together. Economics had even affected the Indians. They'd lost much of their interest in taking scalps when they'd discovered how much more fun, how much more enriching, stealing horses could be.

The house was impressive even though the decor was dated. The wood of the staircase gleamed, the stairs twisting upward from the entryway to the left, stopping at the second-floor balcony. The pattern was repeated to the third floor. Throughout the house there were ornate built-in bookcases, shelves, cupboards, and various compartments. It was the kind of house that made all four of us say, "You don't find them built like this anymore."

I ended up alone in a room designed purely for a pool table. The cue racks were built in to one wall, and four shaded lights hung low over an eight-foot table with felt that was faded but in good shape. I sent a yellowed cue ball rolling silently toward the far bumper.

"It's beautiful, don't you think?" Sally Ann asked, entering the room behind me. She wore a black pantsuit. The top was long and had a white yoke across which hung gold chains connecting two rows of gold buttons.

Being around the two women had made me nervous, and I looked toward the open doors on either end of the room, wishing I'd see Stan walk in. But the house was quiet, as though Stan and Jill had disappeared altogether.

Sally Ann didn't stop. I was standing, facing her, against the end of the pool table, and she bumped into me. Like a blind person with an unerring guidance system, she locked her mouth onto mine and then shoved me backward onto the table before I could move away. It was the strangest position I'd ever been in; we were half on, half off, the table, and she was giving my mouth and lips the most thorough workout they'd yet received.

I wasn't about to remain in that spot, so I slipped to my left and flipped her off to my right, not particularly concerned about the rough way in which I was handling her. After all, she'd started it. I looked at her, lying in something of a pitiful strung-out heap, and for a moment felt sorry for her. She was as out of control as a former movie star who couldn't land a part and didn't know what to do about it. She'd been overwhelmed by ego.

"Billy Boy!" Stan shouted from another part of the house.

I squelched an urge to help Sally Ann stand and beg her to simply talk to me, knowing that was a request she wouldn't grant at the moment, and went off in search of Stan.

He was standing reverently in a darkly paneled drawing room that adjoined the dining room, and when I walked in, I realized this wasn't my kind of house. It was a Rockefeller or Vanderbilt house, a place that wouldn't tolerate an irreverence toward riches or a sense of humor either.

"How about this?" he asked. "After a meal you bring the boys in here and maybe do a deal or two." He looked at an imaginary friend across the room and said, "Now what're we going to do about that block of downtown property, Clint? You know I want it and you know you're asking way too much." He looked at me and said, "Huh? Huh? I love it."

Stan waited for me to respond but I'd been rendered speechless by his wife. I didn't know what to do about her. Never in her life had she acted this way.

Stan changed the subject. "Bill Two is going to offer you the presidency of Brewster-Gaines Production, and you're going to have to decide whether you want it or not. Personally, I hope you don't take it. I want you to come to Dallas, which is why I brought you up here, not to the house. Not here. I haven't shown you the other surprise yet. But I'm hoping that'll make up your mind."

He looked at my face as though something strange had nested there, and I wiped my mouth, the back of my hand coming away streaked with red lipstick. God, I thought. She'd really smeared it around, and I probably had been tinted red from the nose down. I got my handkerchief from my back pocket and mumbled something about Jill's romantic nature having been stirred by the house. Stan smiled as though he knew all about spontaneous displays of romance.

"So what do you think?" he asked. "You coming along?"

"Stan," I said, not wanting to talk at all, "I've never taken a job I didn't know anything about. Let's talk about it later. I want to see the rest of the house."

I had to find a bathroom and decided the best spot was upstairs. Still wiping my mouth with the handkerchief, so vigorously I'd probably removed several layers of skin, I headed for the staircase, feeling suddenly a sense of foreboding about everything.

None of us belonged in Dallas, especially not me. It was a city too far removed from the ground to which I was connected. How could I drive 180 miles when I needed to see that stretch of empty prairie between Albany and Abilene, that spot I'd visualized frequently in the war to find the peace my soul required? That country was more than home; it was the place that gave me a sense of comprehension of something I couldn't consciously comprehend. It was the world reduced to earth and sky.

I entered the master bedroom, thinking surely it contained a bath room, and found Jill standing just outside opened French doors on a balcony. I stopped immediately, painted handkerchief in hand, and started to tiptoe backward from the room.

Of course she turned. "Come look at this."

"Well, I was looking for a bathroom."

"It's right over there, but come here a second."

I crossed the wide expanse of wood floor in this empty bedroom and walked out onto a small balcony. It looked out over an immaculately groomed yard. In a clearing in the center of the yard grew an unconnec- ted square of boxwood shrubs, and in the middle of the square were concrete benches and a birdbath.

"Don't you just love that?" she asked, pointing.

What I would have loved was a mirror, but I stood beside her looking out on the yard, feeling as though my face were blazing like the red light on a police car. The afternoon was quiet; we'd outrun the front, and the humidity hung in the air as heavy and as damp as Houston's. Winter seemed a season away.

"Did Stan say how much this place costs?" she asked.

"No. And I don't even want to know."

She took my hand and moved close to me, standing shoulder to shoul- der, and I felt a sense of kinship with her. She had, after all, waited for me, put up with me, and she'd never acted like Sally Ann. Never. She was a Brewster at heart. She had to be; my mother had taken her in. And what was her loyalty worth? More than anything money could buy.

I put my arm around her and said, "What would you think about getting married?"

She gave me her shy smile, that gesture that made her as alluring and desirable as a wood nymph peeking around a tree. "Is that a proposal? It sounds like one."

"It's a proposal."

"Okay," she said, kissing me on the cheek. "I'll marry you."

"What would you think about moving to Dallas?"

She wasn't quite as agreeable to this idea, and I couldn't even believe I'd suggested it. In fact, not only didn't I want to move to Dallas, I didn't want to marry Jill. But what was I going to do? I lacked the will to replay the night before I'd joined the navy; I couldn't rip the heart from her chest. And I couldn't very well court her into old age, leading her to believe that one day soon—maybe on my ninetieth birthday—I'd ask her to marry me. And I didn't want to be president of Brewster-Gaines Production. The old man and I'd end up wrestling on the floor. Like Sally Ann, he thought he was dealing with the prewar Billy. He wasn't.

Finally Jill said, "You know, in the last ten minutes, I've been asked twice if I want to come to Dallas, first by Sally Ann, now by you. Of course, she's just terribly interested now in what I do, even though while you were gone she called me maybe twice. Two times in four years. Now, though, I should be thinking of all the new and wonderful things she and I can do here, you know, going to the theater and museums and parks and on and on."

We walked to the car without having made a joint decision, and I still couldn't believe what I was doing. I liked Dallas but not as a place to live. It was too big. Life couldn't be the same here because the size prohibited it. Trips to the bank would be a race over busy streets, competition for a place in line, impatience over the need to be back on the road, off to another destination. People here probably never had time to talk.

Sally Ann was already in the car, sitting with her head against the window on the door as though she was suffering the world's most painful headache. She had nothing to say as we pulled out of the driveway, headed toward surprise number two, the one that was going to convince me I needed to move to Dallas. I hoped it would.

"Well," Jill said, taking my hand as we got comfortable in the back seat. "It's official. We're getting married."

Stan, half a block from the house, jammed on the brakes, the tires squealing and Sally Ann flying forward against the dash. She bounced off the dash, her head whipping forward, and ended up sitting on the floor. All I could see was the top of her head.

"Whoops," Stan said, offering his hand to help her back onto the seat. "I'm sorry about that."

She slapped at his offered hand and huffily pulled herself back onto the front seat, almost immediately closing her eyes and resuming her position, head against the window. Stan gave her a moment's more attention, then turned back toward us.

"You're telling me you decided right there in our new house?"

Jill, growing ever more happy and enthusiastic, nodded. "We certainly did, right on the balcony of your bedroom."

"Is that great or what!" Stan said. "Now we'll always have something to remember about this trip. The first time you ever saw our house, you decided to get married. I love it. That's great."

Sally Ann opened her eyes and fixed them on her husband, licking her bottom lip until she said, "Is there some reason we're sitting right in the middle of the goddamn street talking?"

"No, not really," Stan said. "I just got all excited when I heard the news. How about moving to Dallas? Are you going to do that?"

"We may," Jill said.

I was trying to keep quiet. It was words spoken at a time such as this that Sally Ann would always remember. In fact, she'd remember them for a much longer period of time than *always* implied. At the age of ten, she'd fallen and hit her head on a gourd, and I'd called her a gourdhead, and she'd brought up that breach of friendship over the years. I knew eventually she'd come around; she'd be my friend again. And I didn't want her delaying because I'd said something rude.

"Congratulations," Stan said. "I'm really happy. I hope you come to Dallas too. Come on, I'll show you where Billy Boy's going to work."

"Stan," Sally Ann said, her eyes closed again, her head in repose. "They have to *come on.* They're in the back seat."

We continued the momentarily aborted trip, farther to the north, and Jill squeezed my hand, leaning to whisper in my ear, "I love it." I didn't ask what she loved because at such times Sally Ann had ESP. If I ever even thought *gourdhead* or any similar derogatory comment, she knew it.

Surprise number two was on the northern outskirts of Dallas and it was worthy of its name. In the middle of a vacant field, not far from the road, stood the skeletal structure of a six-story office building. A big six-story office building. The project sign out front announced, "Future Home of Plaza North One, a project of Brewster-Gaines Properties, Inc." This grid of iron beams and metal conduit was to become the rather modern-looking office building depicted on the sign.

So we could get a good look, Stan pulled off the road, jumping the curb with the Cadillac and driving on the border of the field until he found a good spot to stop.

"My God, Stan," I said. "When'd this happen?"

"Over the last couple of years. Listen to this: I was out on a lease near Novice with the Barron Oil company man, and we were talking about Dallas. He said their computer people were all wanting to live out north and they didn't want to drive downtown every day. Just like that, that's how it started, computer people wanting to live out north and not want-

ing to drive downtown. These people are hard to come by, these computer guys. So I came up and talked to Ed Welch, and within a month,
we had a deal. I got this hotshot leasing agent to work out the details on
what they needed and how much rent we oughta charge. You know, I
needed somebody who could talk about horizontal and vertical considerations and all that.

"Barron's gonna have the first three floors, and we've got the rest leased
already. Just over a hundred thousand rentable square feet. So what do
you think?"

"I think I'm amazed," I said.

"The oil business is slow, Billy Boy, and it's given me the opportunity
to see a dream come true. All my life I've wanted to build something.
Shoot, I used to walk around to whatever part of Abilene they were
building houses in and I'd keep track of them. I had this little notebook
I carried. Roof on 1706, I'd write. Or framing finished. Whatever. I have
always wanted to build something, and here it is in the beginning."

I sat in the back seat with my mouth open again; that was invariably
the effect Stan had on me. He made my jaw drop. While his friends in
Abilene were sitting around debating the pros and cons of buying a
duplex, he was building a six-story office building in Dallas. Well, I
thought, maybe that's why I was moving to Dallas, to watch this guy.
That was probably reason enough.

"Putting this thing together was the most fun I've ever had," he said.
"A limited partnership in Abilene's going to own 60 percent, and a real
estate investment trust in Boston has the other 40. The REIT is going
on the permanent financing, and I knocked their socks off. Listen, I
walked in with signed leases. A hundred percent occupancy before a
spade of dirt was turned. They're not used to that.

"We're going first class. The building's not showy, and it's not a monu-
ment to the architect, but it's still beautiful. It's the kind of building
Dallas needs.

"You could do the calculations yourself, but I'll do them for you. Each
partner's got twenty thousand up front, and he's going to get about a
twenty percent return on his money. I mean, he'll be able to service his
debt on his return, take a profit, and watch this building appreciate
because you're sitting in what's going to be the hottest spot in all Dallas.
Man, the city's coming this way, and we're going to be here waiting on it."

"And you've already got a hundred percent occupancy?" I asked.

"You got it. Oh, we might squeeze in one or two more if they just had
to have the space."

I laughed. Trying to pin the guy down was impossible. After all, this was the same guy who'd been walking all over Abilene, making entries in his "Houses under Construction" notebook, dreaming of building something, all while telling his mother he wanted to go to work for Brewster Drilling and learn all about the oil field from the best there was.

He pointed toward a corner of the grid. "That's your office in the southeast corner. What kind of furniture you want?"

I didn't answer. Why speculate on office decor when you didn't know what kind of job you had?

He turned so he could see us in the back seat, reminding me of a child getting on his knees so he could see over the top of the seat. "So. You two lovebirds want to go look at houses or apartments or what?"

"Or what," I said. "We don't even have a date set. Hell, we just decided."

Sally Ann spoke for the first time since we'd arrived at the construction site, but she didn't open her eyes. "Take me home. I'm feeling like a gourdhead."

8

My mother reinstated the Thursday night dinners on Sunday at one o'clock, probably to encourage us all to attend church. The meals now included Jill, Stan, and Sally Ann. Since Jill and I had announced a February wedding (on Valentine's Day, of course), my mother had taken Jill in as a full-fledged daughter. She spent more time at my parents' house than I did. Every time I dropped by, I looked to see if she had her own bedroom.

And my mother and future wife seemed to be plotting against me. Every other sentence seemed to start, "If we stayed in Abilene . . ." or "If you stayed . . ." I was up against the sorority of women, but I wasn't staying, even though I would have preferred it to moving. I seemed to be at a point where something was required of me, and I couldn't do it in Abilene.

Boomer still made the meals with us but he didn't eat. He took his meal earlier in the kitchen before we gathered because his hands were so shaky he was embarrassed to eat in front of anyone outside the family.

Still, in typical Boomerish style, I thought he made the best of his degenerating physical condition. I'd eaten with him from time to time, and I thought he might be making his condition worse than it was because he liked seeing food fly. "Whoa, Billy, look at those peas go! All the way over the stove."

He sat with us through the group meal and wanted to hear stories about Vietnam, certain the experience had been similar to his in boomtowns, full of meaningless fights, rampant crime, long drunks, fortunes being made and lost on the streets. I was having too much trouble even thinking about the war to discuss it. Then too, Boomer was confused as to what war I'd been in.

"Did your beard ever freeze?" he asked.

"You're thinking about Korea."

"The hell I am. I know my wars."

"You're thinking of Korea, which is way the hell north of Vietnam. There wasn't a frozen beard in all of Vietnam."

Stan, much less emotional about the war, usually fabricated a few stories for him, stuff that would have made good scripts for "McHale's Navy," and usually threw in a frozen beard or two.

I was improving in one way; I wasn't getting that feeling on the back of my neck as often, and slamming doors didn't get my undivided attention as quickly.

On this January Sunday, with everyone seated and waiting on salads, my father, still dressed in his brown church suit, stood and said, "After a long and fruitful search, Brewster-Gaines Production has decided on a new president. As you know, Stan here is going to Dallas to open up an office for Brewster-Gaines Properties since the real estate bug's bitten him. And I'm happy to say we've decided the man to head up our lease operations is William C. Brewster the third."

Sitting between my mother and Jill, I froze. Rage seized me, just as quickly as a match flared. The old man hadn't even hinted he was going to invite me back, but he'd apparently discussed the matter with his favorite son, Stan. And now he thought he'd back me into a corner, offering the job in this manner, because he didn't think I'd turn it down. Well, he was wrong.

I stood up, looking at myself in the mirror across the room, and found the image distracting so I turned to stare the old man down. "I'm sorry to say your selection committee should've contacted the candidate before you made the announcement. You could've saved a lot of embarrassment because William C. Brewster the third isn't interested in getting back into the lease operations business. *Xin loi*, Pop."

Even though the old man was fresh from the Episcopalian church, I thought he was going to throw his butter knife at me. Instead he banged the table, causing the empty plates to rattle. "Well, *when* in the *hell* are you going back to work? And when you do, *what* in the *hell* do you plan on doing?"

Boomer was never able to avoid the excitement. He too smashed the table and said, "Why, hellfire, the boy is working. Anybody about to get married is working like hell to get out of it."

Stan, untouched by the raised voices and bouncing plates, stood up and said very calmly, "Let me take him to Dallas, Mister Brewster. He needs the change and I need his help. There's more going on up there than I'll ever be able to handle by myself. Besides, he's been around here all his life and he needs a challenge. I'll get him to Dallas and we'll both love it."

The old man, still standing and shaking his head, disgusted by what he saw as genuine laziness gripping his son, said, "What he needs is a kick in the ass."

I spoke before I thought about it, the wave of hostility peaking. Pointing my finger at him, I said, "I know one or two people who might kick my ass, but I damn sure don't see any of them sitting around this table. And anybody who wants to try is sure as hell welcome. We'll step outside and see how it goes."

Boomer jumped up and waved his arm. "I'm taking bets, right here. I'll give three to one on Billy Boy. Any takers? Anybody?"

Now my mother stood, throwing her napkin onto her plate as she did. "I *cannot* believe this. What are you? A bunch of drunken roughnecks? This is a family. A *family*. I don't want to hear one more threat or any more cussing at this table. Do you hear me? All of you?" She looked around, checking for defiant eyes, examining the guilty and innocent alike. It was suddenly quiet, but those standing were reluctant to sit. "And anyway, I don't know how Billy can go to Dallas when his mother's in Abilene."

Boomer was the first to sit. "Just like a woman. Get a little excitement stirred up and they'll go for a bucket of water every time."

Now my mother sat. "Jill may not want to go to Dallas."

Jill smiled and shook her head, too worried about getting dragged into the feud to comment on the possible move to Dallas.

The only person at the table who'd managed to remain uninvolved was Sally Ann, and she gave me the slightest of sympathetic smiles. In fact, I probably would have been the only person who would have noticed she did in fact smile. We'd been very polite and correct toward each other since the pool table incident. We hadn't mentioned it; we hadn't mentioned anything personal. But I thought she was on the road to recovery.

Now she mouthed, "Gourdhead."

Until the wedding, the only item on my "must do" agenda was a visit to Melissa Gaines, but I waited to go until Stan and Sally Ann had moved. I didn't want to get right in the middle of a young Stanley story and have the son show up to stop his mother in midsentence.

I'd gotten her address from Sally Ann. She didn't have a phone so I couldn't call her in advance. Her son, the guy who'd been contemplating buying her a house and car, hadn't yet even got her a phone. Apparently he'd decided that if he just kept his money at work, invested in white Cadillacs, tailored suits, and mansions in University Park, he'd soon have enough money accumulated to buy his mother a phone.

She lived in a deteriorating neighborhood. One house might be a neat frame bungalow, the next unpainted with greasy car parts and half-naked children in the yard. Mrs. Gaines's house was a light brown cubicle with darker brown trim, neatly kept. But the condition of the yard —barren—told me she not only didn't waste money on frills, such as telephones, but either couldn't afford to water her grass or chose not to.

She promptly answered my knock, and I wouldn't have recognized her from the time I'd seen her at school. She did have somewhat sharp features and gray hair that was as fine as I remembered, but I'd transformed her in my mind into a caricature of an overly religious shrew, her shoulders stooped from the weight of the burdens she willingly assumed. Actually, she looked very pleasant and self-assured.

I introduced myself and she invited me in, taking my hand as I entered and giving me a long appreciative look as though I might have been one of the wisemen reincarnated.

"Well, I've heard a lot about you, Billy. Stanley thinks a great deal of you, a great deal."

As I walked in I eliminated another expense—heat. The house was cold even though a space heater sat against the wall, unused. Still, this wasn't the house of an impoverished person. It had pale green carpet in every room I could see and furniture that looked fairly new. It was somewhat mixed, as though it had been bought a piece at a time—a blue couch with white flowers, a beige wingback chair—but it was all in good shape.

She motioned with her hand that I sit on the couch but I'd already found my objective—pictures on the mantle of a fake fireplace, all sitting in front of a mirror on the wall. The mirror, like the pictures, was old, but I felt as though I were on the verge of a big discovery.

"Mind if I look at your pictures?"

"Oh, if you want to look at pictures, I can keep you busy for days and days. I don't take many anymore, but when Stanley was little, I took them all the time."

The first photo I fixed on was a man standing beside a milk truck, probably twenty years ago, and I assumed he was Stan's father by the hint of Abe Lincoln in his face, a feature Stan had taken to the extreme. A certificate next to the picture told me Charles N. Gaines had been salesman of the month in March 1944. He hadn't been in the war, for some reason.

Mrs. Gaines, standing at my left, said, "That was taken not two days before he got killed in that truck. He got hit by a drunk that ran a red light."

She had a strong voice, too strong for this room, and she was standing close enough to me to make me conscious of where she was. And I wondered, was I imagining things, overly influenced by the rumors, or did she seem to be a woman with a real sense of herself as a woman? She moved and acted like a woman who knew a man had just walked into the room, and, I thought, she could very well have been the multidimensional maid she'd been reported to be.

The next picture down the line was one of Stanley Gaines himself, probably ten years old, dressed in a white suit with short pants, holding a big black Bible under his arm. Skinny legs.

"That was the day he preached his first sermon. Well, his only sermon. He was lovely that day, just lovely. I helped him prepare and we gave it the title, 'Keep Your Eyes Upon the Savior.' I still have our notes. And do you know, there are still people at church who remember that sermon?"

"What church was that?"

"Church of the Redeemer, just around the corner."

She reached for the picture, her arm coming into contact with mine and bringing with it the faint scent of something I couldn't identify —soap, maybe, or something homey. "He still has that Bible, I know he does, but I'll bet you he never reads it."

"He does," I said. "I saw it in a box at his house."

She gave me a knowing nod as though we'd confirmed some important fact about Stan, and she replaced the picture. "I don't think Stanley ever did accept the death of his father. He just kind of ignored it. One of his teachers told me once she thought it was nice that his father was helping Stanley with his homework, and I had to tell her the man had been dead for three or four years. And he kept telling kids that his daddy was taking him places. The Cowboy Reunion in Stamford, I remember that one." She shook her head. "He was the kind of boy who didn't let go very easy. He had a little friend in grade school that moved over to Winters, and Stanley wrote him for the *longest* time. The boy hardly ever answered, but Stanley just kept right on writing him letters."

She put her hand on my arm, her fingers draped over my forearm, and said, "I was about to have some tea, Billy. Will you drink a cup with me?"

"Sure."

She walked off to our left and I watched her go, suddenly more interested in her than I was in her son. I judged her to be in her midfifties, and although there was really nothing remarkable about her, she'd left me slightly buzzing from touching my arm. My God, I thought. I'm getting turned on by a friend's gray-haired mother. Or was it only the stories again?

I watched her take a brightly painted teapot from the stove and pour hot water into two cups. She wore a plain kind of dress that looked almost flannel, a blue plaid with a belt of the same fabric around her waist. So she wouldn't have to carry both cups, I followed her into the kitchen. The floor creaked beneath old linoleum.

"How do you talk to a boy like Stanley?" she asked, dropping tea bags into both cups. "I've tried and tried but never got anywhere. It's always been plain to me that he should have been a preacher, but—" She shrugged and shook her head. "He wants to be something he's not."

"Oh, I think he's doing real well. In fact, I've never known anybody quite like him, Mrs. Gaines. He's already accomplished more in a few years than I ever have. Or will. He's a real ball of fire."

We finished making the tea on an old white table in the kitchen and then took our cups to the living room, sitting, for some reason, fairly close to each other in the center of the long blue couch. It was one of those with cushions that made it difficult to get up once I'd sat, so I stationed myself near the front edge of it and put my cup on the coffee table. The tea had some kind of spice in it that both tasted and smelled slightly strange.

"Stanley needs to read that Bible of his," she said. "'Both riches and honour come of thee,' it says, and 'Every man also to whom God hath given riches and wealth.' It doesn't say anywhere that Stanley can arrange for his own blessings or change the way God works. He wants to be something he's not."

She gave me a small sad smile that said Stanley Gaines was barking up the wrong tree and nobody could do a thing about it. I started to argue with her but decided against it for the moment.

"I'll show you what I call Stan's book," she said, sliding down to the end of the couch and leaning to get a picture album from the lower part of an end table. When she returned to the center portion of the couch, she ended up much closer to me. Our hips touched.

People had thought over the years that I was crazy because I found beauty in the most unlikely females. The stronger a woman's sense of her own femininity, the more beautiful I thought she was. That trait had caused Sally Ann a great deal of trouble in understanding me, and I had just as difficult a time trying to explain it—just as I'd had trouble trying to explain my fascination with the Indians and the land on which we lived.

The first item in the book wasn't a picture but a piece of manila construction paper upon which Stan had written in red crayon, "I love the Lord and the Lord loves me. My mama loves the Lord and the Lord loves her."

On the next page were two report cards, both for the eighth grade, and I had to look closely to determine the difference. The grades were identical, but the number of absences were different. One showed perfect attendance, the other several absences every six weeks.

"This is Stan's book," Mrs. Gaines said, tapping it. "It's got the good with the bad. And this was when I found out he was skipping school. Some way or another, he'd finagled an extra report card. He brought me this one showing he was going to school every day; only problem was, he was filling it out himself. But you can see by the signatures, I signed this one, the phony, and he was signing the real one himself. But now, don't you think it's interesting that he didn't change any of the grades?"

I smiled and she turned the page. The book seemed to have photos in a random kind of order because the next had been taken in Laos. In one he was standing with a group of Americans, none of whom looked like they'd ever belonged to any branch of the military, and in the next he was beside a group of mountain tribesmen.

"Do you have any pictures of him in uniform?" I asked.

"Goodness, no. Brother Reed and I worked hard at keeping him out of the army. Not too long after he graduated from high school that business with the missiles in Cuba started, you know, with that Russian that used to take his shoe off. I just knew he was going to get drafted because he was working at a gas station, and we never believed in taking a life."

I started smiling. Stan had given me the report card he'd been filling out himself, and on this one the grade may have been the same but the subject was entirely different. "What was he doing in Laos?"

"He was a conscientious objector. He was there with International Voluntary Services, working at a school."

Here was the ultimate in fractured perspectives, mistaking his status as a conscientious objector with clandestine service as a CIA operative. I couldn't wait to see how he explained this difference. I'd been wanting to catch him in a contradiction he couldn't talk away ever since he'd told that bullshit story to the old man about having wanted to work for Brewster Drilling since the age of ten.

"Did he ever talk about any of the kids over there? Like a boy named Pham. Or Jimmy."

She thought for a moment, her eyes wrinkling in the corners while she stared at the pictures, and said, "Well, he talked about them but I don't remember any one child. I know he really liked the people over there. He thought they were gentle and kind. But I don't remember ever hearing about a child named Jimmy."

I wondered, had he ever talked about killing any of them?

The next picture was one of Stan with, of all people, a policeman in the sort of old-fashioned uniform the local cops used to wear. The cop had his hand on the top of Stan's head as though in the midst of tousling his hair, and his young friend had a grin of genuine enjoyment on his face. Mrs. Gaines, presumably, had taken the picture from the front porch.

"This man had a real strange first name, I never did figure out how to say it, but we called him Jay. He'd found Stan in front of a gas station one morning about three o'clock. The boy was just sitting by a gas pump drinking a Coke he'd gotten out of a machine. Jay brought him home, and after that, he took a real interest in him. Of course, he had to because Stan wouldn't stay in the house at night. I even nailed his windows shut, but he still got out. I never knew what he was doing, but he was wandering all over town at all hours of the day and night. And every once in a while I'd hear the front door open at four in the morning. Jay was bringing Stan home."

She shook her head, and I couldn't tell from this story if she'd had a high regard for the policeman or not. Since she'd omitted any verbal commendations, I assumed she'd resented him for some reason.

"I sent Stan the news clippings when Jay died—of a heart attack —and do you know, Stan never mentioned him again? To this day, I've never heard him mention the name of that man." She shook her head. "Stan can be the strangest person."

I came very close to laughing, but didn't. We looked through the rest of the album. Apparently the mother and son had taken their vacation every year to a church camp in west Texas, an austere and unattractive-looking place with metal buildings that would have been ideal in which to sweat sin from one's system. She had programs from the one-week affairs, and the activities were confined to church services of one kind or another, all featuring sermons with titles such as, "The Gifts of the Spirit" and "Armageddon on our Doorstep" and "The Baptism of the Holy Spirit."

Melissa Gaines wasn't the typical holy roller, not from what I knew of them, but her church seemed definitely bent that way. The women I'd known who had marched around the church and waved their arms at the sky while speaking unintelligible words had all gone without makeup and never did any more to their hair than brush it. Most didn't even cut it. But Mrs. Gaines had carefully applied makeup, and her hair was rather short.

She put the album down beside her and gave me a smile, one full of warmth and sudden good humor and . . . what? Attraction? Over the years Sally Ann had taught me to ignore speech in preference to more subtle means of communication, and I couldn't decide now if Mrs. Gaines was a woman who liked to touch or who liked to attract. I placed my hand on top of hers.

"Mrs. Gaines, I don't guess it would do any good for me to tell you that Stan's doing great. The guy's amazing, he really is. He works harder and thinks more about big deals than anybody I've ever seen. The guy's going to be a tycoon one of these days."

Melissa Gaines ended my speculation on her interest in men by turning my hand over and holding it with both of hers, flat between them, and rubbing between my fingers with her hand that was on top. She'd forever live in my memory as the first elderly (I thought she was at the time) woman who'd given me an erection. There was something so titillating, so blatantly sexual, about her fingertips sliding into the openings between mine that I simply responded.

"Stanley Gaines can't be a tycoon," she said. "That's what he doesn't understand."

119

I wanted to ask why he was ineligible, but I knew that I had to vacate the premises. Although there was a certain irony in the thought of making love to the mother of Stan Gaines—he had, after all, stolen my father—I couldn't even imagine the size of mistake I'd be making.

"I've got to go," I said, giving her hand a squeeze and then standing up. I helped her up, and she followed me to the door.

"Billy, will you come see me again?"

"Sure. And thanks for the tea."

Before I could open the front door, she'd moved to kiss me on the cheek, but she didn't kiss me. She brushed her lips and nose over my cheek, back and forth, back and forth, as lightly as a feather, and she continued to do it, standing close enough for her breast to push against my arm. It was the most obvious offering of sensuality I'd ever encountered, and I hoped I met no one on the way out of the house. I'd have to walk bent over or use my hands as fig leaves. I finally kissed her on the cheek, patted her arm, and said, "Thanks for *everything*, but I've got to go."

"I'll see you again," she said.

Not anytime soon, I thought, as I walked out the door.

I spent the afternoon wanting to talk to Sally Ann, and since she wasn't in town, I drove out to her grandmother's ranch west of town. I'd always had carte blanche to visit the place whenever I wanted, and over the past twenty years, I'd undoubtedly spent more time out there than anyone else with the exception of the pumper, who watched after the only things raised there anymore: pumping units.

On the metal gate in the barbed-wire fence was a combination lock —four dials on the bottom, all set to zero, opened it—that had never been changed that I could remember. I drove in and took the rocky road to the top of the mesa, bouncing and scraping my way up through the walls of cedar trees. The day was bright but cold, and I stopped the car after arriving at the top, right at the edge of a big clearing. The yellow grass, a real contrast to the bright green of the cedar trees, swayed in the wind.

I did what I always did—walk to the rim of the mesa and stand in a grove of barren red oak trees, looking down at the spot where two raiding Indians had been killed, that spot where I'd dug deep into the ground twenty years ago trying to find their blood. They'd been caught in a ravine, just where it turned north, and the spot was now marked by two cedars on either side of this deep gash in the earth, which was no doubt even deeper today.

From where I stood, I could see miles of the Comancheria, that vast stretch of land that had been claimed by the Comanches as theirs and fiercely defended against all interlopers. I'd always been fascinated by the Indians, even while knowing I'd never have made a good one. The thought of drinking the warm blood of a freshly killed deer or buffalo, or partaking of the raw tallow around the animal's kidneys, was thoroughly repulsive. And I *knew* I wasn't a warrior.

Still, they were my *wakan*, my guiding spirit, and I wished I'd paid more attention to their wisdom when I'd been a child standing in this same spot. I'd wanted to study anthropology in college and now wished I had. I was, after all, one of The Blest, and had a secure future; I could have done anything but instead I'd done nothing. And now I was having to leave the Comancheria.

Still, I thought, I had a relative in Dallas, a blood brother, the only female blood brother I'd ever known. Sally Ann and I had sat in this spot and she'd pricked our fingers with a pin so we could mix our blood, and I wanted to see her again.

For a long time, I stood, listening to the wind.

As the saying goes, all things come to he who waits, and I got my invitation to Dallas that night. Stan called as though he could feel me getting close, digging into his past. He wanted me to meet him for lunch the following day at the Pecan Grove Country Club. And as usual, he wasn't specific and wouldn't tell me why. He wanted to *show* me what he was doing.

I told him I'd be there.

"So what's new?" he asked.

"Oh, not much. By the way, did you ever hear of some organization called International Voluntary Services?"

There was a long pause and then he said, "Jesus. You've been talking to my mother."

"As a matter of fact, I have. But there was one thing she couldn't tell me, and that was how a person can get a counterinsurgent and a conscientious objector confused. Or was International Voluntary Services a front for the CIA? I can't figure all this out, Stan."

"Hey, do me a favor and don't say anything about that IVS stuff to *anybody*. I never was a conscientious objector. Never. I'll explain it all tomorrow."

I hung up thinking, if anybody can, you can.

•   •   •

The Pecan Grove Country Club was in a new subdivision outside Dallas, and the clubhouse looked as though it had been built overnight, just like all the houses surrounding it. It wasn't really a cheap looking place; it just looked similar to the homes surrounding it, all rock or brick fronts and frame sides. A developer with a very narrow idea of diversity had thrown the place up and set a huge sign out front that shouted, "Come Home to Pecan Grove!"

Inside the clubhouse, a gum-smacking hostess showed me to the table where Stan and an older man sat. The table was next to a big window that looked out onto the number-one tee box on the golf course. I assumed the membership belonged to the man with Stan, a rather used-up-looking guy who needed both his hair and the cuffs on his shirt trimmed. Both were frayed, and the huge gold cufflinks only drew my eyes to the condition of his shirt.

Stan introduced me to Art Cashion; Art seemed nervous but shook my hand anyway. He'd already filled the glass ashtray with cigarette butts.

"We're making deals, Billy Boy, making deals. Art here has an old building near downtown we're going to renovate."

"We are?" I asked.

"You betcha. I was waiting on you to go over this with Art, and since you're here, we might as well start."

I was more interested in Stan's past than in his future, but I sat and listened. He had a folder thick with legal-sized documents, and he placed them in a stack on the table. I was hungry but this "lunch" date with Stan was like everything else. Words to Stan didn't necessarily carry the connotations that the general public believed they carried. Lunch didn't have to involve food.

Stan explained the deal. Art's company and Brewster-Gaines Properties were forming a joint venture that would buy Art's old building. They were going to borrow $1,400,000. Of that amount, $1,200,000 would be used in the renovation, although $20,000 of that was going to Brewster-Gaines right off as a management fee. The remaining $200,000 was going to Art for his equity in the building.

Art liked that last part. It made him smile and rub the back of his neck, checking the length of his hair and wondering how much longer before he could afford a haircut.

Stan and I were going to the bank (obviously without Art) with a takeout letter on the permanent financing through a local savings and loan. The takeout letter was a commitment for the permanent financing based on several conditions being met, chief among them an adequate appraisal. It encouraged the bank to provide the interim financing. The other documents related to occupancy, leasing revenues, hard and soft costs, and cash flow.

"Hey," Stan said. "Did Art work a hell of a deal or what? He's going to have 50 percent of a modern office building that'll appraise for three mil, and we've already got our tenants. Listen to this: Dallas loves good Methodist boys from S.M.U., and I got us a former football player as a leasing agent. He's already got us a division from an insurance company and one of the city departments. We're leased up, Billy Boy."

He sat tapping his chin and smiling as if suggesting someone just try and hit him; it wasn't possible. I had to admit this was all much more exciting than the oil business in Abilene, but I didn't understand the concept as Stan did. He was borrowing money to pay himself a management fee? And debt obviously didn't frighten him. This was a brand-new way of doing business for me; the old man had never liked debt, and I couldn't believe he'd sent Stan up here to hock the company.

After the briefing, Stan cleared the table like a waitress and then packed me into his car without showing me even a cup of coffee. We rode toward downtown, and before he could get started on a real estate spiel, I said, "So tell me about the CIA, Stan."

He wrinkled his nose and shook his head, making me feel like a reporter who wanted to go over the same old stories. "Hey, I did everything I told you, and it was just like I said with one exception—I was with this IVS group. But I wasn't *ever* a conscientious objector. My mother was. And her damned old preacher. They got together after the Cuban missile crisis and ganged up on me. It was like one of these deals where everybody in church gathers around some poor sinner they want to see saved. You know what I'm talking about? Some poor guy is just sitting in church during the invitation, and then ten or fifteen people fall all over him praying out loud and begging him to be saved. Kinda like a spiritual gangbang. Well, my mother and this preacher convinced me I didn't want to get drafted and kill people.

"It was funny, the way it turned out. When I got to Laos, the school where I was going to work had been taken over by the PL. They'd kicked everybody out and they were using it for an artillery base. I mean, they had artillery pieces all over the grounds. And they'd really pissed off the people at the school. Most of them were helping USAID resupply the Meos. I couldn't believe it. Here I was supposed to be a CO, and they throw me right into a civil war. All these

123

COs fighting the PL. Damnedest thing I ever saw.

"Anyway, that was the only difference. I can't very well tell people I was a CO when I wasn't. And when I was fighting the PL. What kind of sense would that make?"

I smiled and shook my head as we took a crowded freeway into Dallas. Was Stan unusual, or did everyone have a history as difficult to interpret? Nothing that had ever happened to him was clear, nothing subject to the statement, "Now, this is the truth." There simply wasn't anything about Stanley Gaines that was simple.

We detoured by Art's building, an old two-story warehouse, built with dark red brick, that almost bordered the street in an area that almost fell into the shadow of downtown. The second-story windows had been broken, and the walls autographed by Mario, who loved Teresa. Someone with a can of spray paint apparently knew Teresa as well and had advertised her thusly: "She got a tongue like a lizard."

Stopped at a traffic light downtown, Stan said, "Billy Boy, you need to get up here fast. Somebody's got to help me out. There're more deals to do than one guy can keep up with. You found a house yet?"

"No. Maybe I'll look while I'm here."

"Get Sally Ann to help you. She knows where all the good neighborhoods are."

At times it seemed he was trying to pair me off with his wife, and I was glad for the suggestion. I felt a need to see her, to talk to her. Her mother had told me she'd undertaken to remodel the mansion on her own, and everything from her color schemes to her selection of wallpaper was making her sit in the middle of the floor and cry. Poor Sally Ann. She wasn't often bested.

"Promise me you'll find a house today," he said.

"I'll work on it."

At least one reason I was in Dallas became clear when Stan and I arrived in the bank, right in the middle of downtown. The loan officer was a young guy, probably underpaid, and his appearance almost matched Art's. He needed a haircut, and his shirt had a small cigarette burn in it. But unlike Art, this guy probably had better days in front of him. And when Stan started his spiel as we stood in the glass cubicle on the first floor of the bank, I began to see my function.

"This is William C. Brewster the third," Stan said proudly. "He's part of Brewster-Gaines, part of the Brewster family. They go *way* back into the west Texas oil field. Way back. In fact, his family's the cornerstone of the oil business in Abilene."

The loan officer looked appropriately impressed and shook my hand. Like Boomer, I mumbled something. I hadn't been prepared to be an exhibit in Stan's presentation. Now, sir, here we have the projections on cost flow, here we have the appraisals, and here we have Billy, who could be standing up a little straighter. Right, Billy Boy?

"I call him Billy, just like everybody else, but I introduced him one day as William the third. And I thought, hey, that sounds like the name of a king. And why not? We're talking about the House of Brewster. William the First, William the Second, William the Third; it's quite a line, let me tell you, and I've been proud to be associated with them. I came out of the service five years ago, and Billy's father, William the Second, gave me my chance, my shot at success. That was all I asked for, and that's what he gave me. And it's working out for both of us. But tell me how many well-established, well-respected businessmen would do that? I only know of one."

While Stan explained to the loan officer the package he had worked up and was putting on his desk, I tried to remember when he'd introduced me as William the Third. And I couldn't. Another Stanism. It could be true; therefore, it was.

"I'm going to leave all this with you if that's all right, and you can look it over without us standing over you. I want you to check out all our references. Brewster-Gaines Properties is a relatively small company, but we won't be for long. And you won't find anybody who's ever regretted doing business with us. Nobody."

I listened, thinking Stan's plan appealed to me. I wanted to see Mario's blackboard renovated into something functional and pretty; I wanted to witness the process, watch the old disappear and the new take shape. But I wasn't going to be Stan's exhibit, even though the listeners always seemed to respond to his line. This was the ten-year-old evangelist in his white shorts and coat, too childish and naive to sound broken and jaded. And maybe that's what kept him from being a hustler. He believed what he was saying. Or appeared to. And he wanted to put the kind of building on the street that would make people say, "Now, there's the kind of building Dallas needs." His designs wouldn't win architectural awards, but neither would they waste space and money.

I looked to see if the loan officer was listening to Stan, but the guy was staring at me. He was in the presence of William the Third and he knew it.

When I arrived at the Gaines's residence later in the afternoon, the day was cold but Sally Ann was sweating. She answered the door in

Levis and a T-shirt that said, "Mickey Mouse for Governor." The rodent's outstretched hands were damp, stuck to her breasts, and the hair around her neck was wet.

"Oh, no," she said, collapsing against the door jamb and almost wilting. "I just asked myself what else could happen, and now I know. Why didn't you call? Did you want to see me looking like this?" she asked, peeling the mouse hands away from her skin and holding the shirt out.

Before I could answer, she turned and looked back into the house and wailed, "Billy, will you please please help me decide what I'm supposed to be doing?"

I followed her inside, seeing a great deal more color than the house had possessed when I'd seen it before. The entryway that led to the curving staircase had light blue wallpaper, part of which had been ripped from the wall and lay in wounded strips on the floor, and a darker blue trim. It was a pretty combination but gave the house a cold look.

She pointed at the wall. "This is the third try and I *hate* it. I started out with the colors on a peach, kind of yellow and red, and it was *hideous*. Stan almost had to take me to the hospital when I saw it. And now the wallpaper guys just left and you can see what I'm doing." She pointed at the crumpled paper on the floor.

"I'm doing fine, and thanks for asking."

She looked properly chastised and gave me a brief kiss on the cheek. "I knew you were doing all right or you wouldn't be here." She pulled me by the hand across the paper and said, "Come on, pal, we need a drink."

I went, my hand in hers, wishing I could preserve the feeling of joy and giddy elation I felt to be touching her again. She stopped in the kitchen to make drinks, and I walked into a small breakfast nook that was just large enough for a table and something that looked like a church pew against the windows. I sat at the table, watching the day outside, and Sally Ann, bringing the drinks, took the bench. She sat on it longways, bringing her feet up.

"Still getting married?" she asked, gathering her hair at her neck and lifting it up as though hot.

"As far as I know," I said and explained why I was here—to eat a foodless lunch with Stan and now to enlist her help in the search for a house. "Stan volunteered you."

"I'd love to help you. I want *out* of this house. I don't even want to think about this house. You know, it's a good thing old Granny took care of me. If I had to work for a living, I'd starve within a week."

I'd seen her in this unusual self-criticizing mood rarely, the last time before we took college entrance exams. She'd been certain she was going to score so low she'd end up attending some unaccredited church school majoring in church nursery management.

"I have a new girlfriend," I said, watching her give me a questioning look, her fingers stuck into her hair like a comb. She was really working over that dark blond hair. "Melissa Gaines."

Her mouth dropped open and she immediately left the bench to come sit beside me, turning a chair so that it faced me and then sitting. She tapped my knee and said, "Tell me *everything*."

At first I was hesitant to tell her everything, but then I decided, if I couldn't trust her, who could I trust? So I recapped the visit from beginning to end, including the pictures—but omitting the story of International Voluntary Services, thinking that was something Stan ought to tell her—and explaining where we sat on the couch, what she'd done to my hand, and how she'd nuzzled me before I'd left. And I found that the subtly vibrating sexual energy returned in the telling. Sally Ann, who knew me too well, caught it in my voice.

"Billy Brewster," she said loudly, slapping me on the knee. "You wanted to do my mother-in-law."

"Yeah, but I didn't."

"You should have. It would've given her a thrill. And you know why? Because she has a scrapbook on you." She nodded emphatically over my skeptical reaction. "She does. She went to the newspaper and got everything she could find on you and Brewster Drilling. She has a picture of you that was in the paper when you were a *senior in high school*. It was a football picture; you were flying over the goal line like you'd been shot from a cannon. I'm serious."

I remembered the picture and had no reason to disbelieve her, but I couldn't quite comprehend her interest in me. In Brewster Drilling, maybe, but not in me. And now I remembered something Sally Ann had said the day we'd watched Stan play tennis—that Mrs. Gaines liked me and had never even seen me.

"You're one of The Blest," she said.

I nodded. "Big deal. I thought I turned her on naturally."

"Well, you do, just like gold would. Or silver."

"Hmmph."

While we finished the drinks, Sally Ann brought me up to date on her new life. Her neighbors, those younger, closer to her age, were somewhat reserved after displaying an initial burst of curiosity over the new occupants of the house. She'd been on her best behavior, so she wasn't sure why they were keeping their distance. I laughed, knowing why. She looked like the kind of woman their husbands would take to Acapulco for the weekend while the wives stayed behind to wipe noses and buy groceries.

She lapsed into a silence, finishing her drink and going for another before I was ready for a second. Then, moving back to the bench, she said, "I don't like it here. Maybe that's why I can't decide on anything for the house. Maybe, I don't know. Other than college, I've never lived anywhere else, and I want to go home. I don't want to feel like an ant in a hill of a million others. Ants, ants, everywhere. I want to come live with you."

An unhappy Sally Ann was a sight almost as rare as the self-flagellating one. And even though she didn't make an appearance very often, and didn't merit a lot of sympathy to start with, I still wanted to comfort her. I wanted to peel Mickey's drying hands away and replace them with mine.

"You and Stan not getting along?"

"Lordy, lordy, how could you not get along with Stan? Do you know how much he worries about people leaving him? Do you know how much he wants you up here just because you're his friend? No, if I told him I was miserable, he'd sell the house and move me back to Abilene. I think he'd commute if I told him I wanted to go home."

"You mean you're going to—" I paused dramatically, then finished. "Adjust?"

"Don't make fun of me, gourdhead. I'll come back over there and you'll have to smell me."

"I already smelled you. You smell like a salted-down grape soda."

She wasn't sure whether such a scent would attract or repel, so she silently finished her second drink and then crunched ice. I wanted another but decided against two on an empty stomach. Sally Ann, good hostess that she was, had heard I'd gone without lunch but still hadn't offered me anything to eat. I decided her home was mine and walked into the kitchen to look through her refrigerator.

I was bent over, thinking I'd spied a block of cheddar cheese behind a lettuce crisper, when I felt fingers poke me in the sides.

"I'm sorry. You told me you hadn't eaten."

I got the package of cheese and stood, finding myself standing with Mickey Mouse's right hand on my arm. I thought she'd move, but instead she began to nuzzle me, just as Melissa Gaines had, very softly, her nose and lips brushing my cheek. And she did smell like a salty grape soda.

"Is this what my mother-in-law did?"

"Yeah, but it was her other breast and my other arm."

She twisted a short strand of hair, just above my neck. "You turn *me* on naturally. I don't care if you're one of The Blest or not."

This, I thought, was a very tricky situation. I was standing with the refrigerator door still open, feeling cold air on one side, the warmth of Sally Ann on the other, and the effect of a drink on an empty stomach throughout my body and brain. What was I to do?

"You know what I was thinking about this morning?" she asked, still fiddling with my hair. "I looked out back and saw that swing in the tree, and I started thinking about the time I fell. Remember? In my grandmother's backyard? I fell and landed flat on my stomach and couldn't breathe, and you got so upset you didn't want me to swing anymore. Ever. The next time I got in the swing, you stood right by it so you could catch me if I fell." She laughed and shook her head. "I would've smushed you. Back then, I was bigger than you were."

She released my hair, patted me on the back, and took the cheese from my hand. "You're the best friend I've ever had and I tried telling you that marrying Stan wouldn't change that. I didn't want you to be hurt because I wouldn't marry you. Do you know, my grandmother told me once that some men were too important to marry. If I was on a desert island and could have only one other person to be with me, who would that person be? That was the acid test, according to her. If I could immediately think of a person I'd want to be with me, then that was the person I shouldn't marry."

I watched her cut the package open and pull out the half-moon of cheese. She started to slice several strips. I'd been comfortable she was telling me the truth, right up to the desert island stuff. Now I didn't want to comment at all. Maybe she was telling the truth, but I doubted it. Still, on the outside chance she was, I didn't want to accuse her of manufacturing bullshit right here in her kitchen.

Absently, I opened a drawer in the cabinets and found, of all things, a copy of *The Sensuous Woman*. In the kitchen? I slammed the drawer shut.

"Look in the one next to it," she said.

I pulled the next drawer open and found a vibrator with various attachments, at least one of which looked suspiciously phallic. Suddenly I felt as though I'd been transported into a shop that specialized in sexual paraphernalia. What were these things doing in a kitchen?

I hadn't come by to see Sally Ann with sex on my mind. Food, maybe, but not sex. But now, I doubted that I'd ever get to eat any of the cheese slices or crackers she'd carefully arranged on a plate.

"What do you want to drink?" she asked.

I shrugged. "Whatever you've got."

She brushed by me, headed toward the refrigerator, out of which she got a bottle of Coors. And then, after popping the cap off, she picked up the plate.

"I'm going to take a shower and I can't talk to you if you're down here, so you can eat up there."

The Voice of Morality told me to leave the Gaines's residence immediately, but then, the VOM wasn't as hungry as I was, and besides that, it wasn't thinking. I'd be getting married soon and I intended to practice full-time fidelity. This was my last chance at single adultery, and I wasn't going to engage in double adultery.

I took the plate of cheese and crackers and the bottle of beer from Sally Ann and walked behind her through the living room toward the stairs. Halfway across the living room, she peeled off her T-shirt, showing me a softly flaring back, the slight protrusions of her spine, and so much skin that I set the plate of cheese and crackers down on an end table, leaving it behind.

"Go up the stairs backwards," I said.

She complied without asking questions, carefully ascending one step at a time. She didn't have especially large breasts, but they were large enough to sway rather magnificently with her movements. And I thought, this isn't going to be good; it's going to be great. I could feel the mystery coming on. When I looked at Sally Ann, I saw not only her, but my ten-year-old friend as well. I could see beyond her. I could see the mother and wives and daughters of my favorite Comanche, Ten Bears. I could see all the way back to Mother Earth, hear her straining and groaning and giving birth.

"How long has it been since you screamed?" she asked, nearing the top of the stairs.

"A long time."

"Will you scream for me? Like you're happy, like you're just exactly where you've always wanted to be?"

I nodded, not wanting to talk anymore.

At the top of the steps, she stopped and removed her Levis and panties, sitting down not to make it easy but sitting because she knew what I wanted to see.

Mother Earth.

9

The year 1970 came close to proving Stanley Gaines was a prophet. His expectation that the oil industry would find itself revitalized because of events in the Middle East came close to fulfillment. In the first half of the year, the price of fuel oil rose 48 percent, primarily because of a shortage of tankers. A bulldozer, by design or not, ruptured the Trans-Arabian pipeline and the Syrians refused to allow repairs. Suddenly the oil that had been flowing effortlessly over land now had to be shipped by sea. And by summer, we were seeing shortages; utilities began cutting back power to industrial users.

The shortages had little effect on west Texas; our crude wasn't useful for the refining of fuel oil, and the drilling business continued in a decline. But Stan, convinced more than ever that a boom was just around the corner, kept buying property south of Abilene and listening to the news. Israel was engaging in border skirmishes with Lebanon and fighting outright with Egypt in the Suez Canal area.

Sally Ann was surprising me with her determination to work her way out of the ant hill. She was so determined that she was spending a considerable amount of money, donating it first to a symphony and then to a museum, attending clubs and luncheons and teas. I'd never really thought about society; every circle in Abilene had been open to us both. And my role as one of the ants bothered me in a much different way than it bothered her. It was the concrete beneath my feet, the buildings that blocked my view of the sky that made me feel like an ant. Sally Ann, though, didn't want to feel insignificant, and for the first time in my life, I began seeing that she and I weren't completely alike. She'd always known it; I hadn't.

She and Stan had already been accepted into the Preston Hollow Country Club, one of the relatively new clubs in town, and they swept Jill and me in when we arrived. But Sally Ann wanted into the Dallas Country Club, and she also wanted to work on the Mayor's Ball, a fund raiser for medical research and the main society event of the year. And here she was finding the going much tougher. Their application for membership in the Dallas Country Club was on a waiting list, where it could very well languish into Sally Ann's old age, and she didn't like that kind of delay any more than Stan did.

But what was really bugging her were the ladies who worked on the Mayor's Ball. And one night when we went to eat at the Gaines's house, she was ready to arm herself for an assault.

Jill liked visiting the Gaines Mansion only because she loved the house itself. She rarely talked while we were there, and I always assumed she was engaging in fantasies—she owned the house and Sally Ann was her maid and cook. Sally Ann facilitated the fantasy by cooking, lasagna on this night.

We were waiting for Stan in the den; he'd called Sally Ann earlier in the evening to tell her he'd be late because he was working on a "humongous son of a bitch of a deal," which he expected to have completed by eight. And now we sat, Sally Ann in an orange miniskirt with a sleeveless white blouse which showed her the-best-in-high-school arms.

"God, I hate these Junior Leaguey types with their singsong voices," she said. "'Hello, how are you? Well, aren't you just the sweetest thing for volunteering.' They sound so sweet and sincere and they're just about as sweet as pit bulls and about as sincere as insurance salesmen." She was upset, no question, her arms and legs crossed, a look of vengeance on her face.

"Who're you talking about in particular?"

"Mrs. Big Butt Baxter, the one you've got to start with on the Mayor's Ball. Oh, she's a bitch." Still irritated with the memory of Big Butt's voice, she sang, "'Well, aren't you just the sweetest thing . . .' If she really wants to help medical research, she could donate her body. Now. In fact, she could probably solve the fuel oil crisis single-handed by melting down all the fat in her butt."

I felt sorry for this lady with the large posterior. Sally Ann never forgot. If it were possible, she'd commit suicide so she could apply for the job of assistant keeper of the pearly gates. Then she could personally slam the gates in the faces of some chosen enemies. Big Butt would end up with pearl embedded in her incisors.

Jill had made no comment on Sally Ann's trials. Being a member of the Preston Hollow Country Club was the extent of her ambition for the time being. Besides, she was obviously deep in a fantasy. Sally Ann, wearing overalls, her head shaved, was asking if Mrs. Jill wanted her toenails done.

"'Hello, how are you?'" Sally Ann sang again. "You know, if somebody cut her tongue out, she could only go, 'Unh unh, unh unh unh?'"

Stan ended the conversation by bursting into the room in a supercharged manner, obviously having concluded his humongous son of a bitch of a deal favorably. He stood in the middle of the den, running in place on a Persian rug, his arms working like pistons.

"Talk about your deals, talk about your deals! I can't believe this one myself. Listen to this: I bought two hundred acres not far from Plaza North One four months ago. Four months ago. I paid three thousand an acre. And then I just started visiting around. I made every coffee shop and restaurant in the area, stopped at every store, I mean, every one of them. Hey, I'm not the one who decided North Dallas was going to be hot; I'm just talking about it. I've been going around out there at least once a week just talking. I might ask a couple of people if they're interested in selling. Selling? Well, let's see. For Sale signs start popping up. People can smell money, they can see dollar signs.

"A broker calls me about my two hundred acres. No, I'm not selling, I tell him. I've got plans. I talk about computer people who want to live north and don't want to drive downtown to work. I see housing developments, apartments, strip shopping centers, more office parks. Hell, I can even see a mall, a big one. I love talking about the future, love it. I can see all this.

"A couple of days ago two brokers called me within an hour of each other. An hour. They want my field. They've got clients who'll pay good money. One brings me a contract for five thousand an acre. I laugh; it's the funniest thing I've ever seen, this five thousand an acre. I already know how much I'm going to sell it for—eight thousand. I want a million-dollar profit. If I don't get eight thou, I keep it. One of these days eight'll seem dirt cheap. One of these days it's going to bring ten times that much, maybe twenty.

"Boom, boom, boom, I've got two brokers wearing out their cars driving between me and their clients. One of them calls me and asks how late I stay up. I tell him sometimes I never go to bed; what's he got in mind? He's got another buyer but the guy won't be in until nine that night. Well, he didn't make it at nine. He got fogged in in St. Louis. The broker's going crazy, calling me all night long. His client's lost in St. Louis. Nobody can find him. Finally, this afternoon, he gets his guy on the phone at the airport in St. Louis, and then he calls me and says he'll have a contract by six this afternoon for eight thou.

"Hey!" Stan said, snapping his fingers. "At six, he was at the club with a contract for eight thou, and I've made a million fucking dollars. One million buckaroonies, count 'em!" he said as though he were throwing dice. "Whoa!"

He bent down and gave us a fast version of the Twist. Then, looking at Sally Ann, he said, "Hey! We made a million bucks today. You hear me?" Then he asked me, "Hey, Billy Boy! What do you think? Are we doing all right? Are we? Mrs. Brewster, you have anything to say?"

I was finding Stan even more amazing, not because of his wheeling and dealing but because of his knowledge of real estate. He had tapes that he listened to in the car while he drove. He could discuss everything from riparian rights to demand-pull inflation. In Abilene he'd been watched over by the old man, but here he had no one and he was on his own. And he was learning it on his own.

We congratulated him, patting him on the back, shaking his hand, and we all moved toward the smell of lasagna. I'd never seen anybody as excited, and he seemed to even make Sally Ann forget her social problems. He'd at least changed the mood from one in which we were contemplating the singsong sound of a voice that was missing the owner's tongue to one in which victory swelled through the air.

"I was coming home thinking there were four people who've helped me get this far. Sally Ann, your father, you, and an old Frenchman in Laos named Charlie. Charles N. Sannier. We called him Charlie Insanity because the communists thought he was a religious mystic. They thought he was wandering around looking for God when he was really inciting riots. He was a holdover from French colonial days, he liked it there, and he'd never left. Charlie Insanity. He made me think I could do anything, but hell, even then, I never believed I could make a million bucks flipping one piece of property. I wish he knew what a hell of a good time I'm having."

He rested his arms on the table, forgetting we had gathered there to eat, and shoved his plate toward the center of the table. "He used to ask me questions. Can you make a million bucks in four months? I'd tell him, sure, it was possible. And he'd say, but can *you* make a million bucks in four months? And I'd tell him, hell, no, Charlie, I can't do that. And he'd tell me I was right, as long as I believed I couldn't, then I couldn't." He sat back, allowing Sally Ann to get his plate so she could serve him lasagna. "I'll have to tell you about Charlie some time."

I'd only heard Stan offer revealing information about himself three times, and two of those times he'd been inspired to do so by deals. The first had been when the two operators had started bidding for the Lowell B. Brooks Estate lease, and now a million dollars had him talking. What would he confess to if he'd made five times that much? Ten? That he was possessed by Kyklos, the god of deals?

"What would you have done after Laos if you hadn't met Charlie?"

"I don't know, but I did know I was never getting railroaded again. I was there because of my mother and her preacher, not because I thought I should be. I figured out we lived in a world where anything could happen, and that meant if other people could get rich, so could I."

I wasn't sure what I was doing for Brewster-Gaines Properties other than watching Stan. He spent his time chasing tips, and now money was chasing him. In some states, real estate investment trusts had to be 60 percent invested before they could go public, and there was something of a rush on to find mortgages. In some cases, REITs were approaching banks and buying part of their portfolios, leaving the banks and savings and loans with money for people like Stan. Interest rates were falling, and Stan was on the move. I never saw him eat, but he always had an abundance of energy.

When Sally Ann had filled all the plates with steaming lasagna, Stan looked at her and said, "You tell them the good news?"

She looked at him for a moment and then said, "I thought we weren't going to yet."

"Oh, go ahead."

She looked at me and said, "I'm pregnant."

No way, I thought. No way had she ever engaged in sex with Stanley Gaines. Hell, she wouldn't even have undressed in front of him.

"Stan had this big plan. We were going to talk you into having a baby and make it into a race. See who could do it first. Then, a week after we'd challenged you, we'd tell you I was pregnant and you'd be amazed." She looked at my mouth, which couldn't have been knocked closed with a sixteen-pound sledgehammer. "I guess it would have been funny if we'd really done it."

"Congratulations," Jill said. "Are you hoping for a boy or girl?"

"A boy," Stan said. "And you need a boy. We need to get started on the next generation of management for Brewster-Gaines."

"Until they're old enough to manage," Sally Ann said, "I presume they'd play together."

No, no, no! I wanted to shout. That was you and I who played to-gether. Billy and Sally Ann. We mixed our blood on the mesa in view of the sun and wind. You told me you'd never leave me and I believed you. We were together every day and taught each other everything we know. And now, shit! *You've been fucking Stanley Gaines!*

I'd stopped breathing and now I emitted a little yelp when I finally exhaled. Everyone looked at me.

I stood up and dropped my napkin, thinking I was going to faint because all the blood had drained from my body. I was lifeless, inanimate, useless.

"Are you all right?" Jill asked.

I wanted to speak but couldn't breathe, couldn't inhale. "Not—" was all I could manage.

"Not what?" Stan asked. "What's he talking about?"

I had to go somewhere. But where? Where could I go? I had no place.

"He's all white," Sally Ann said, rising. "I'll take him to the bedroom."

"No, no," Jill said. "I'll take him home and put him in bed."

I left, dumbfounded, unable and unwilling to speak, Jill's hand on my arm, guiding me to the car. She spoke for me, telling Sally Ann we appreciated the invitation and would have enjoyed the lasagna because it looked *so good,* leaving behind two confused friends who kept wondering what had happened to Billy. Maybe it was that virus going around. Let them know.

I was almost home before I figured out what had happened. My youth had been rudely stomped on and wouldn't survive the night. It suffered from terminal exposure to reality. Short of thirty years, it was a goner. It had survived the war somehow, maybe because I'd seen it as a re-enactment of the Indian wars. The Viet Cong had been the ill-equipped but exceedingly tough band holding out against the machine of military superiority, engaging in small unit hit-and-run raids to steal our horses.

But my youth couldn't possibly survive Sally Ann's bearing a child whose father was Stanley Gaines.

Jill wasn't stupid, but she now claimed to be the world's biggest idiot. "Why didn't I ever think about what you did when you found out she was getting married? You went off and tried to kill yourself in a war. Now you find out she's pregnant and you almost pass out. I never knew it, but you're obsessed with her. You're not in love, you're obsessed. And this is just a great time to be finding out, after we've been married six months. This is just the perfect end to my life."

I wanted to tell her she was crazy for saying such things but I couldn't. I knew I'd been unfair, but what could I do? Only part of me had married her. My emotions, which had always belonged to Sally Ann, had skipped my wedding because they refused to say, "We do."

"Now I'm the one who feels like passing out," she said.

Considering the fact that we were on a freeway, headed north to the promised land of massive development, I found my voice. "Wait'll we get home if you don't mind."

"Oh, shut up."

            •   •   •

I was apparently segmented. Part of me continued right on with life, the most useless part, the vice president of Brewster-Gaines Properties. I ran the department that manufactured tits for bulls. Even Stan wouldn't tell me what my job was.

"Hey, you're the vice president. Do something vice presidential."

So I tried. I tried to keep up with him and his projects but couldn't ever find him. At one in the afternoon he might be at the bank drawing down on an interim construction loan. At two, he was at the Plaza North One site, gazing in admiration at his creation, and by three he was having a drink with one of Art Cashion's friends at the Pecan Grove Country Club, some guy who wanted to make money like Art had. On his way out, he'd call his stockbroker, ask how a stock had done that day, then tell him to sell it before getting an answer. I visualized a hundred tiny whirlwinds blowing around inside his head, all individual projects and ideas.

Until Plaza North One was completed, our office was a corner of an empty bedroom at my house. That was all the room we needed because I had two boxes of incomplete documents, contracts, and plans. I didn't have *all* of anything, and Stan couldn't understand why this haphazard manner of operating bothered me.

"Okay," I asked him one day. "Where's the proposal on Wychwood?"

"It's in the biggest box, right under the bank papers on Live Oak Place."

"How about the contract on your million-dollar deal?"

"In the glove compartment of my car. See? I know where everything is. It's all under control."

He had six projects under way, over $13,000,000 worth of construction and renovation, he was running twenty hours a day, and I was idle. Each morning I got up, showered and shaved, and ate breakfast. I walked into the empty bedroom, paid homage to the incomplete records, and then I was through for the day.

I was very curious to know whether the old man was keeping up with him. On the one hand, I couldn't believe the old man had simply turned him loose to wheel and deal through every financial institution in Dallas, but on the other hand, I was in Dallas, supposedly working with him, and I couldn't keep track. As vice president of personnel, I didn't know if we had employees; as finance, I couldn't have begun to draft a profit-and-loss statement; as archives, I was doing moderately well.

And so partly out of curiosity and partly out of a desire to see the

Comancheria, I drove to Abilene, telling Jill I was going only on my way out the door and not giving her enough time to make the decision to accompany me. I didn't want to ride 180 miles with a statue, a replica of Sullen Ignorance. I knew she wasn't happy with the state of our marriage, but what could I say? I thought she'd only wanted to become a Brewster.

In Abilene, I surprised the old man and caught him in his favorite spot, standing at the window looking down on Cypress Street. He wore a suit, nowadays spending much more time in the office than out. But he didn't look seventy years old.

We got along better than I'd thought we would, even after my refusal to return to lease operations. He confused me. I never knew whether he was authentically mad or whether he was just falling into one of those poses he used when negotiating. He'd always been the kind to press a man simply to find his backbone.

"The prodigal son," he said.

I smiled and shook his hand. Here he was seventy years old and he was still engaging in contests of strength with his son. Who could squeeze the other's hand the harder? Little did he know that I carried a hard rubber ball in my car and exercised just for these occasions.

"I win," I said, having stairstepped his knuckles, figuring I'd have to break one or two if he didn't give up.

"The hell you do," he said, grunting, grimacing. "You grabbed my hand before I was ready. That's cheating."

I released his hand, a gesture of mercy, and I could tell he wanted to rub it but he didn't. Instead he sat behind his desk, and for a few minutes we talked about family. Boomer wasn't doing well; he didn't have any particular symptoms other than what old age brought, but he seemed to be losing interest in the world around him. All he did anymore was watch soap operas.

After the preliminaries, I said, "Listen, I'm watching Stan blow around Dallas like a tornado, and I don't even know the total amount of his debt. I don't have all the loan papers, I don't have all the proposals, I don't have all the contracts. He has some in his car, some at his house, some at my house. Some have probably blown out the window and some have probably fallen under the cushions on his couch."

I sounded more irritated than I was. Or thought I was. As vice president in charge of people who were acting in a manner contrary to my wishes, I wanted the old man to recall Stan and send him out to a rig.

Far far away. For a couple of years. And then roll back the clock and make Sally Ann barren.

The old man smiled and pushed away from his desk far enough so he could prop his full-quill ostrich boots on the surface of the desk. "I thought you'd help him get organized, and you will eventually," he said. "Stan can't stand still long enough to do it himself, but pretty soon it'll get too big for him to keep up with in his head. That's when he'll decide to listen to you. I talk to him at least once a week and he knows what his limits are."

"You have put some kind of limit on him?"

"Sure, I have. He's limited to ten million total debt, and, believe it or not, he's a long way from it. When we set the limit, I thought he'd go running off and blow it all on one deal, but he surprised me. The boy may make a businessman after all. On these six projects he's got going, Brewster-Gaines is in for a little less than three million." He gave me a big smile, going almost horizontal as he stretched, arms reaching out for the wall. "He's working on something big. He says it's a surprise."

Stan and his surprises. I was beginning to take Jill's attitude toward his surprises. Mr. Flabbergast Gaines and his confounding personality, appearing in person but not for very long.

"Keep in mind," the old man said, "he's not nearly as reckless as he seems. He's not throwing up houses on swamp land. He's particular about what he's doing and he's proud of it. He's concerned with his reputation. Hell, I wouldn't any more try to rein him in than I'd try to get you to act like him. Just keep working on getting him organized, and I'll keep an eye on the debt, and other than that, we'll just turn him loose. Personally, I want to see what the boy can do." Then, sounding and looking just like Stan, he suddenly flopped down loudly and threw his hands out. "Hey! If he goes bust, he goes bust. He won't be the first, and he won't be the last."

Right, I thought. The old man had always demanded the highest standards of businesslike demeanor from me. I had to arrive at the office on time, take no more than an hour for lunch, keep all my paperwork in order, and speak politely to the ladies in the office. With Stan, the old man had assumed the spirit of Boomer. Sloppiness was no big deal, nothing to worry about.

I told the old man I was coming by the office after work to make copies of all his Brewster-Gaines Properties files. Stan wasn't going to bite the hand that cinched the deals, and he'd made sure the old man had all the paperwork, a fact which made me wonder what my function was in Dallas, besides being over the accessories for bulls. Was I a paid friend? Two hands clapping? That was it. I'd finally become an Indian —Two Hands Clapping.

After leaving the office, I went by the house and spent the rest of the day with my mother and Boomer. My grandfather, according to my mother, had almost been done in by the sixties. He didn't understand black power, women's lib, or antiwar demonstrations. He remembered blacks as respectful, women as submissive, and citizens as volunteers for any war effort. And for some reason, he'd given up drinking, thirty years after the doctor had told him he was wrecking his liver, an observation to which Boomer had responded with, "It's my goddamn liver and I'll wreck it if I want to."

The old man had called to tell them I was coming by, and Boomer, trying to keep up appearances for his admiring grandson, had asked my mother to make tea so he could fill an empty pint bottle and pretend he was still drinking. It had taken several tries to approximate the color of whiskey. He might have quit drinking, but he remembered what color the stuff was.

Boomer's eyes and ears were getting weak, and I could hear his big-screen TV in his bedroom. He had peopled his world with soap opera characters, and he talked to them as though intimately acquainted with them all. "General Hospital" was his favorite.

He was sitting in a rocker-recliner, his favorite chair, the upholstery of which was long gone. He'd covered it with a sheet, unwilling to let it go for remodeling. The room was spacious and almost always hot, both winter and summer. As I walked in, he was shaking his finger at the TV. "Don't you go with her. She's lying to you, yes, she is. You go with her, you're less a man than I thought you were."

He'd always been thin but now he was bordering on a flesh-covered skeleton, his skin blotched, his white hair more yellow than ever.

"What's up, Boomer?"

"Nothing. I ain't had nothing up since 1951 when the boys down at the Abilene Club got me a dancing girl for my birthday. Where you been anyway?"

"At the office."

I sat on his bed, sinking into the mushy mattress he liked. He'd always traveled light and there was enough extra space in the room for a miniature-golf course. I told him I was on a "business" trip as though I was capable of such a thing, and then, knowing he'd love the story of Stan's million-dollar deal, gave him the details, much less dramatically than Stan could have. Boomer thought money made in any way that failed to demonstrate cunning and a very high tolerance for risk was tainted, unworthy of the recipent's time in handling it.

"So. The doughboy's doing all right, huh?" he asked with a smile. Then, without making a transition, he said to a man in the midst of a seduction on TV, "Hell, boy, get away from her. You couldn't satisfy that woman if you had Pinocchio between your legs and he was lying his ass off. What's wrong with you?"

He watched the man disregard the instructions and kiss the woman, and he changed the subject just as quickly again. "You want anything I got, Billy? You need a big TV?"

"Don't talk like that, Boomer."

"Hell, I'm just facing up to the fact that the golden years are getting pretty tarnished. I want to get things straight while I'm of sound mind. Even though your daddy'd argue about whether my mind's ever been sound. But what does he know? We're talking about a man that wants the government to tell him how many times he can shake it after he pees."

I hated to see the man as frail and as used up as he appeared to be. He wasn't just my grandfather, he was the last contact I had with the frontier. He'd seen the trail drives, had talked to the Indian fighters, had roamed the crowded streets of the boomtowns, and had remained an individual in a world growing less and less tolerant of them. He'd seen Abilene grow from a town started by the railroad to a modern city of 100,000. When he was gone, who would tell me stories?

We talked a while and then he turned serious, a condition he normally avoided at all costs. But he had nursing homes on his mind. "Listen, Billy, if I ever get of unsound mind and they try to put me in one of those damned death camps, you put me out of my misery. Just point a gun right up here and pull the trigger." He pointed his finger at the side of his head. "You do and I'll be grateful. And if I ain't of unsound mind, I'll take care of it myself."

"Don't worry," I said, knowing I shouldn't be giving him assurance I'd keep him out of a nursing home, but I did anyway. "Nobody'll ever put you in one of those places."

The prospect of such a fate made him gloomy, and he stopped talking even to his friends on the screen, letting them deal with their fates alone. We sat quietly for a few minutes and then I realized he'd fallen asleep, his chin on his chest. He had the opened pint bottle of tea between his legs, his hand on the neck, but he hadn't even feigned drinking. His breathing was so shallow I thought for a moment he'd died, but then I noticed his yellowed hair moving slightly.

After a few minutes, I tiptoed from the room.

. . .

The third floor was quiet, deserted when I returned, but the door to the offices of the Brewster-Gaines Companies was open, the light shining into the hall. Every time I saw that roll call on the door, all those businesses Stan had started, I was impressed all over again.

The receptionist was gone, but Sally Ann, of all people, was sitting on the gold couch to the left of the door, reading *Time*. She was dressed in a short black skirt that covered less than a third of her lovely thighs and a light green blouse.

"What're you doing here?" I asked.

She looked up and said, "Well, I kept thinking you'd call me and you never did. So this morning I called you and your wife told me you'd come out here. I thought, what a perfect chance to talk to him. And here I am."

I sat on the edge of the receptionist's desk, looking more closely at the decor than I had before. The coffee table was glass with a gold frame, and on top of it sat a piece of driftwood with a brass fish swimming through the air. Dime-store art in the office of Brewster-Gaines? The place was suffering with the absence of its guiding hand.

"And you knew I was coming back here after five?"

"Rita'll tell me anything. She knew you were coming by."

Rita was the receptionist. Again, I was fighting the sorority.

Sally Ann dropped the magazine on the coffee table, blowing the brass fish with an air current, and then sat back, hands in her lap, waiting for me to begin the conversation she'd driven 180 miles to initiate. But for the first time since I'd known her, I couldn't think of anything to say. She had irrevocably linked herself to another person.

"I haven't seen you, I haven't heard from you, I haven't even heard your voice in I don't know how long. Not since the night you were at our house."

I shrugged. "You decided on a name for the baby?"

She sat forward, suddenly earnest, clasping her hands and resting her chin on them, assuming her talk-to-me look. "That's it, isn't it? It wasn't a virus, was it? Well, not unless it's a virus of the spirit."

I got off the desk and moved toward the copy machine at the rear of the reception area. "I've got to make copies. Your husband hasn't seen fit to give me all the paperwork even though he's seen fit to make sure the old man has complete files. So Two Hands Clapping has to drive to Abilene to make copies."

I wanted to leave her sitting on the couch but I didn't know where I wanted to go. When she fell into that mode of concerned friend, I *wanted* to tell her my secrets. She made me think of the day we'd mixed our blood, and I could see that ten-year-old girl in shorts, without a shirt, sticking my forefinger with a hat pin. We'd smeared each other's blood, and I'd been overcome with the first of an untold number of inexplicable feelings for her. "I'm your brother now," she'd said. "I won't ever leave you." I'd been unable to speak, my throat constricted with emotion.

"Billy, if I'd known how you were going to act about all this, I would've married you instead of Stan."

The Gaineses would be the death of me, at least my mouth. They were going to turn it into a piece of wood, desiccated from exposure to the air because they were constantly making it hang open. "That's the most fucked up thing I've *ever* heard."

I was standing by the copy machine and she got up and walked toward me. The green blouse she wore was extremely thin as though worn from many washings, but it wasn't old. I could almost make out the details on the fringe of her bra. The buttons were low on the neck and the sleeves were large, and overall it qualified as a blouse but reminded me of a pajama top.

"It's the baby, isn't it? You're upset because I'm pregnant."

She was an expert at making suggestive and almost meaningful statements, such as she had about marrying me instead of Stan, and then dropping them in the dirt to be forgotten. It seemed important to me at the time to ferret out the means by which she held me, but as usual, I was more interested in giving in to her, donating my soul.

"Do you know," she said, "that I'm almost you at times? Remember when you came to my house just before you got married and we took a shower and then made love? Even though it'd been years since we'd done that, I knew exactly what position I needed to be in, I knew just how to squeeze to make you scream because I knew how it felt for you. I was almost you. I *knew* how it felt for *you*. Do you know how close we are? Do you know things can be perfect between us if only you'll let them? I've been trying to tell you for years and you won't listen."

She stood two feet away from me, brushing long strands of dark blond hair back from her eye with the ends of her fingers. I didn't say anything.

"What do you want?" she asked. "Tell me what you want and I'll do it. I don't care what it is, I'll do it for you."

She waited for a response, her hand pressed to her chest just below her neck, her fingertips inside her blouse. She knew I wouldn't make any irresponsible or unreasonable demands on her—to leave Stan, to abort her child, to run away to Mexico—and so she could offer to do *anything* I wanted. I should have surprised her, should have said, "Okay, Sally Ann, I want you to purify yourself like a plains Indian and cut your legs with a bone knife." And she'd merely laugh and say, "Sorry, I'll do anything but that," which would be her answer for any real demand I made.

"I have to make copies. Go sit down."

As if demonstrating her willingness to comply with whatever request I made, she promptly turned and walked back to the couch. Of course, she added her own twist. Picking up the magazine, she sat on one end of the couch and then turned, lifting her feet up on the cushions and sitting longways. Her knees raised, she showed a long slice of lime green panties.

"Pull your dress down. I can see your panties."

She raised her bottom off the couch and tugged on her skirt, tucking it below her cheeks. Then, properly situated, she wordlessly returned to the *Time* magazine.

I moved to the bookkeeper's desk outside the reception area where I couldn't see this woman so eager to please. I wanted to think about something else, and Boomer had provided me with the subject by asking whether I wanted anything he owned. Sally Ann seemed to be acquiring a portion of my inheritance, and I was curious about the size of it. And the first matter to determine was the size of Stanley Gaines's take from each of these businesses he'd started. I knew he was still getting a draw against the profits in the form of a check each month.

Sitting at a desk with a partition separating me from Sally Ann, I said, "My God, you people are getting almost eleven thousand dollars a month out of these companies."

"We were getting fourteen but we had to pay some back last year. Stan had it reduced."

I was surprised, but not by Sally Ann's lack of concern. "Eleven thousand bucks a month and he hasn't even visited this place since you moved to Dallas."

"So? Your father owns fifty-one percent of Brewster-Gaines Properties and he's never come to Dallas."

"I'm just making an observation."

"Me too."

I moved back into the office toward the CPA's assistant. She sat right outside his door. Stan had been more generous with private offices than the old man had ever been, and some of the old-time employees had moved from the second floor up here on the third just for an office.

It was the summary on Brewster-Gaines Production I was most interested in. When Stan had signed on six years ago, the production department of Brewster Drilling had working interests in about 600 wells. Some of those the old man had developed himself, some he had acquired by drilling for interests, and some he had bought outright. During Stan's tenure with what became Brewster-Gaines Production, another 250 wells had been added. Stan had started out with no ownership, acquired 3 percent, then 5. On an average, the wells brought in revenue of $186,000 a month, and each month Stan was drawing $7,500 just from the production company.

The remaining $3,400 came from the well-servicing company, the oil-field supply house, and the pump and testing companies, in which he had a varying interest.

It was easy to see why Stan was waiting for the Middle East to erupt in a war that would disrupt their exports. An increase of a dollar a barrel —which would be almost unheard of, but a major breach in supplies was going to send the cost of oil through the ceiling—would increase Stan's take from $7,500 to $9,500. And the increased activity in the U.S. oil field that would follow any prolonged disruption would have a beneficial effect on all the other companies.

Amazing. Charlie Insanity strikes again.

I put the records up and walked back into the reception area to make copies of all the Brewster-Gaines Properties files. The old man had directed someone to leave the files by the copy machine, and a stack of folders sat on a table nearby. And every time I looked at those brown folders, I got irritated all over again. Two Hands Clapping.

Unable to decide whether I even wanted copies of the files, I asked, "Why'd Stan want me in Dallas? I don't *do* anything."

Slowly, as if stiff from sitting in the same position too long, she turned on the couch and put her feet on the floor. "He knew how much I wanted you there."

"I'll tell you what—let's cut the crap. All right? You don't tell me how you think you should've married me. Or how you'll lay down your life if I want you to. Or anything else. Let's just cut out all the bullshit."

She smiled, a smile that reminded me how dangerous life could be without any bullshit, and she stood, stretching, reaching above her and pulling the tail of the green blouse from the skirt, revealing a bare midsection, a navel staring directly at me. She sighed and twisted, engaging in a slow and sensuous dance without music.

I knew exactly what I wanted to do; I'd been wanting to do it for a year and a half, ever since I'd been released from the navy. I wanted two bottles of wine, the Young Rascals tape I had in my car, and Sally Ann on the mesa. I didn't feel any particular loyalty at the moment to either Stan or Jill, and pretty soon Sally Ann would be a mother and I'd never make love to a mother. This would be my last chance.

"You think you could swipe two bottles of wine from your mother?"

"Sure," she said, approaching me. "Where we going?"

"To the mountaintop."

"Let's go."

I left the complete files for Brewster-Gaines Properties on the table where they sat. Two Hands Clapping would go with the flow.

Two hours and considerable white wine later, I knew what it meant to shout it from the mountaintop. We'd made love in this clearing before, near the red oak grove that grew to the edge of the mesa, but not since Sally Ann had learned I had good lungs. This was the exact scene I'd visualized in the navy when I'd thought about coming home, and it was eighteen months late in coming, but it was here, as wonderful as I'd imagined.

I lay flat on my back in the middle of a quilt that had come, like the wine, from Sally Ann's mother. The September moon smiled on me as it had on billions of other fools, as kind and untelling as a good friend. Sally Ann, dressed—or undressed—as I'd asked, was walking around the quilt, a near-empty bottle of wine in her hand, wearing only the green blouse, and it was unbuttoned. She looked like pearl, transparent and opaque at the same time, absorbing and reflecting the moonlight.

"Stand still," I said. "You're making me dizzy."

She stopped at my feet and looked down on me, smiling. She was twenty feet tall and had breasts as big as pumpkins. "You don't think a husband and wife would do this, do you?"

"My wife and her husband wouldn't."

"That's what I'm telling you. That's what I've been telling you for six years and you wouldn't believe me. When we were kids and came out here, you believed me. Now you don't. I told you I'd never leave you, and I won't."

I closed my eyes, listening to the bark of a coyote. The crickets had heard the Young Rascals so much they were now singing "A Girl Like You" back to me, and I didn't want to leave this place. Ever. It was the earth and sky I'd visualized when I'd been most worried, most frightened, because right here, infused with the *wakan*, the mysterious, I couldn't be touched. I could be killed or tortured but that part of me connected to this ground would go forever free.

Sally Ann was moving again, circling the quilt and making my eyes feel as though they were floating in pools of water. She passed down my left side, slowly as if trying to walk a straight line for a highway patrolman. The tail of the blouse swayed slightly over her bare ass like a small curtain in a gentle breeze.

"Melissa wants you to come by and see her," she said. "I called her while I was waiting on you."

"There's no way I'm going by to see her."

"She's going to get you, Billy. She's just like Stan, believe it or not. When she wants something, she's going to get it."

"She won't if I never see her again."

"The difference between her and Stan is that she can wait. Stan can't. That's what faith does for you."

She stopped circling and sat beside me, cross-legged, right at my waist, and leaned forward to rub my stomach. I reached beneath her, grabbing for a bone where her thigh connected to her hip. I didn't know why I liked feeling that bone, but I did.

"Who's this Charlie Insanity guy Stan talks about?"

She shook her head, leaning forward and running her hand over me as though smoothing a long piece of cloth. "Some French guy in Laos. He told you about him, didn't he?"

"Yeah, but, you know, nothing with Stan is ever as advertised. And his father's name was Charles. In fact, it was Charles N. and this guy in Laos was named Charles N. Charles N. Sannier."

"Maybe it's a coincidence."

Maybe. I moved my hand to her stomach, marveling at the fact that somewhere within her, a baby was being formed. Out here, it didn't bother me that Stan was the father; out here, Stan really had nothing to do with it except in an incidental way. We were talking about life.

"I can't wait to see you pregnant. I want you to get huge. I want you to look like you've got a globe inside you, the whole earth. A globe about two feet in diameter."

She bent forward now to kiss my stomach, having properly smoothed it with the palm of her hand. "I'm not going to show. I've already decided."

I laughed. "You mean it's optional?"

"With me it is."

With her lips she lifted me from the ground. I was levitating, free of

147

gravity, free of cares and woes. Nothing existed at the moment but the two of us, alone on the earth, alone beneath the sky. And with my hand on her stomach, I could almost feel the miracle occurring, the baby growing.

"Jill can get fat but I'm not," she said.

Just the mention of Jill's name caused me to skid slightly. My ability to levitate was hampered and my ass scraped the ground. And then I thought, why would she think Jill's pregnant? Or was she merely wishing some extra pounds onto her?

"I was surprised to hear it from her," she said. "Why didn't you tell me?"

I was experiencing a severe drop in altitude. In fact, I could see, as in an old movie, the needle on the altimeter spinning as I dove to the ground. And if I hadn't been drunk, I would have believed Sally Ann thought my wife was pregnant.

She rubbed her nose in a big circle on my stomach. "If you don't want to talk about it, maybe we should make love again."

I crashed into the ground, pieces flying everywhere. *My wife was pregnant!* I sat up and pushed Sally Ann into an upright position. I needed to see her face when I asked, "What'd she tell you?"

"That she's pregnant. She told me this morning when I called." Then, with realization flooding her features, she said, slightly awed, "You didn't even know, did you?"

"God, you're serious, aren't you?" I couldn't believe it. My child's father was sitting naked as the day he was born with a woman not his wife on a mountaintop 180 miles from home, in total ignorance. How in the hell could that happen?

I closed one eye, trying to ward off the headache that was already settling in behind my eyes twelve hours early. "Am I dreaming?"

"Billy, you're lucky, but you're not that lucky."

10

Jill was indeed pregnant, and I knew I couldn't possibly be the father. Only one of two could be responsible—either Sally Ann, because she hadn't wanted to be fat alone, or Stan, because he wanted a foil for the coming Stanley Junior. One of them had bought little voodoo dolls or something and had impregnated my wife.

I told her outright I'd learned she was pregnant from Sally Ann. Why hadn't I been the second to know, right after my wife?

She shrugged. "I figured you were so interested in what was going on in Sally Ann's body, you could've cared less what was going on in mine."

No question, I needed to try harder to be a good husband and father-to-be. My youth was dead as wet ashes and I had only one way to go. I didn't want to follow Boomer because I knew where the route led, but what could I do? Life was terminal. We were born to die.

One day at the store, picking up milk, I was hit with the kind of inspiration only a reformed husband could have received. I'd call my wife and ask for a date. So I did, from the pay phone near the "Community Bulletin Board" in the store. Some civic-minded person had pulled down every notice and swept the board clean except for about twenty million staples in the cork.

When Jill answered, in that reserved and formal manner she had of answering the phone, I said, "Two Hands Clapping, Comanche *pukutsi*, wanta bang maiden's box."

She hung up on me.

I was considerably less enthusiastic after waiting in the checkout line to get more change, right behind a kid who was buying a package of ice cream sandwiches with pennies, all of which had to be counted. When I got back to the phone, I said, "Don't tell me you didn't know who it was. What obscene caller would know about a Comanche *pukutsi?*" A *pukutsi* was one of those who did everything backward.

"If I'd thought there was even the *slightest* chance my husband would call and ask me for a date in a normal manner, I wouldn't have hung up."

"Give me some credit for trying."

"Okay. That's all you get. Credit."

I couldn't figure her out. Since we'd married, she'd acted exactly as a woman who had merely wanted into the Brewster family. We engaged in sex quarterly, and we were so far from the passionate hair-pulling madness that had enveloped us the night before I joined the navy that I didn't ever expect a replay of that. And yet she could turn around and exhibit acutely injured feelings when I got upset over Sally Ann's pregnancy.

Now she wanted to know, she said, she wanted to know *for certain*, that my first choice for wife was her and not Sally Ann. Finding that out would have to precede any improvement in the relationship. I gave lengthy consideration to what Sally Ann had told me—being friends and not spouses was the perfect situation—and decided I was in total agreement. "You're my first choice," I said.

She believed me for some reason. "Two Hands Clapping wanta bang maiden's box?"

She didn't pull my hair, but she did show a little enthusiasm in her kissing.

Still she wasn't happy about being pregnant, and I watched her mope and talk about dreaded visits to the doctor and how much she hated the thought of wearing maternity clothes, until I finally decided I had no choice but to invoke the hated name. "Listen, I hope your attitude improves. Even Sally Ann smiles and I know she doesn't like being pregnant. You're the type that oughta bloom and you're miserable."

She gave me an irate look and said, "I've been in competition with her for years and now I'm having a baby along with her. I don't know what I'm going to do if they're both girls. Theirs will be tall and beautiful, and ours will be short and ugly like me."

"If we have a girl, I hope she looks like you. I wouldn't want her to look like Stan. You want a girl who pops out of the womb looking like Abe Lincoln? Who says, 'Somebody here say they have some acreage for sale?'"

She had an amazing capacity to change her mood when she wanted to, and she did. She even smiled again, that half-shy wood nymph look that made me think maybe I really did want her for my wife. She was cheery again, happy to be a Brewster, and she frequently placed my hand on her stomach even though there was nothing to see or feel, just imagine. She was constantly in a book of names, checking roots. And the more time I saw her researching names, the more I worried our kid would end up with a strange name. I wanted to name a boy William Ten Bears, after my grandfather and favorite Comanche, but I figured he'd end up Reginald Frederick. Or worse.

Our lives were fairly smooth until I made the mistake of telling Sally Ann one day on the phone that I was making a fine husband. "You wouldn't believe what a good guy I'm being. I help her with the dishes, I take out the trash and pick up after myself. It's unbelievable. And she even puts my hand on her stomach and lets me make love to her. I mean, she even uses her tongue when she kisses."

I realized too late what a mistake I'd made. I never learned. She'd given me a black eye for a lesser offense twenty years ago, and when I heard the line go silent, I closed my eyes and hoped for the best.

She tried, she really did. Very slowly she said, "Billy, I'm glad you're happy, I'm glad your marriage is working, I'm glad—you know, you're a real *shit* for telling me that. Why'd you tell me? Why're you saying things like that?" She sighed as though willing to let the matter drop, but then there was another long silence. "Do you want to hear about the conception of our baby? Do you want to know where we were and how it felt?"

"I'm sorry, I'm sorry, I'm sorry. I get the point and I won't say anything else about it."

I made these calls from the bedroom with the door closed as though I was engaged in tedious work for Brewster-Gaines Properties that required total concentration. But Jill still walked in on them from time to time. She never made any comment on them but she was invariably cool for several hours, or days, afterward. But I was worried now. I was going to have to say things Jill couldn't hear me say to make amends for this error. So I knelt beside the bed, near the headboard, and put pillows over my head.

"Sally Ann, you know—"

"I was on his lap. I sat on his lap and made him scream. He made *me* scream. He's got a fourteen-inch *rod* and if he was an Indian, his name would be Satisfies Women. You wouldn't believe how loud I screamed. The neighbors thought we were being murdered and called the police."

"Okay, okay, okay," I said from the darkness beneath the stack of pillows. On the one hand, I was glad she could still feel jealousy, but on the other hand, I could hardly overlook the fact that I'd accidentally tweaked her nose and she was trying to castrate me with a corkscrew. "Let's talk about something else. Have you got on with the Mayor's Ball yet?"

"What do you mean when you say you're being a good husband? If we wanted to go out for a drink and listen to music, would you go?"

"Well, sure."

"I want to go tonight."

I felt a tap on my back and said, "Oh, shit." I tried not to visualize this scene Jill had walked in on, but couldn't help it. Her husband was on his knees half buried beneath a mound of pillows. "Just a minute," I whispered to Sally Ann.

I arose, dumping the pillows, just as Sally Ann screamed, "What do you mean, just a minute?" She could have been on a public address system. Jill stood beside me, two feet taller, biting on her bottom lip. "Are you going to talk to *her* or are you going to talk to *me*?" Sally Ann said, just as I turned the receiver over to press it against the mattress.

I couldn't think of a good explanation so I said, "The light was hurting my eyes."

Jill stormed from the room, slamming the door behind her so hard it compressed the air in the room and made my ears ring. And by the time I got back on the phone, Sally Ann had hung up.

I gave a long sigh and fell face forward onto the bed, suddenly tired. "Thanks a lot."

I didn't hear from Sally Ann for a week, and Jill was just about to recover when the Gaineses arrived on our doorstep one night. They were dressed for the first cold weather of the year, bundled up in coats and colorful scarves, wearing mittens. *Mittens.* I hadn't seen any since I was a child, but here were Mr. and Mrs. Upwardly Mobile in their high fashion winter clothes wearing mittens.

I invited them in but Stan waved his come-on-why're-you-standing-there wave.

"Let's go," he said, pulling Sally Ann toward the white Cadillac that was idling in the driveway, its exhaust vapor swirling off into a strong north wind. "I've got a surprise for you."

I looked at Jill, who was standing out of sight near the TV, and her face showed how much she disliked that eight-letter word. It was twice as bad as a four-letter word. I watched Stan and Sally Ann hurry back to the car, expecting us to follow now that we'd heard the enticing and magical word, and I wasn't sure what to do.

"Why don't you just tell them you don't want to go," Jill said.

"Well, I guess because I want to see the *surprise.*"

That was one area in which Stan couldn't be faulted. If a person said he had a surprise, it was normally a real disappointment, something mundane and uninteresting, like Silly Putty that had been lost for ten years. But Stan's surprises qualified for the term.

We went. Stan sped out of the neighborhood as though his surprise might leave for its next stop on the tour before we could get there. He tapped on the steering wheel as he drove.

"This isn't only a surprise; it's a secret. We've got to keep this quiet and I'll tell you why in a minute. But I hope this deal's done by June first so I can make an announcement on Stan Junior's birthday. That'd be perfect."

Amazing. We were already marking the birthday of a baby, gender unknown, who hadn't yet been born.

I settled back in the seat, leaning against the door and looking into the blustery night outside. The telephone and electrical wires looked like long jump ropes going mad between the poles.

Sally Ann turned to talk to us. "Stan had me on my back the other night, with a Coke bottle hanging from the ceiling. It was supposed to tell us the sex of the baby." She gave me a big gleeful smile, hoping I'd visualize this intimate and exclusive scene.

"So you have given some thought to the possibility that this baby could be female as well as male. Or do you plan on naming it Stan Junior regardless?" I asked.

"He made the bottle swing until it went in the right direction. God, I was on my back all night."

"Yeah? That's how you got in this fix to begin with."

Jill hit me on the leg with her knuckles, right behind the knee, almost frogging me.

"It all sounds pretty unexciting to me," I said, disregarding the warning from my wife. "Personally, I'd rather scream." I cleared my throat as though having trouble swallowing. "And I guess I've given myself a sore throat for the first time."

"You two have the weirdest conversations," Stan said.

Sally Ann gave me a dirty look and then turned around with a bounce that shook the car. "You *always* have weird conversations with gourdheads."

We ended up downtown, stopping along a block of small buildings, most of which looked like warehouses. The biggest appeared to be three stories. Stan left the engine and heater running, and we looked at these low dark buildings.

"Now, all this started with a toothache, believe it or not. I used to hate toothaches and now I love 'em. I want another one tomorrow. But I had this molar that was just about to bug me to death, and I finally decided I had to go to the dentist. So I looked one up in the yellow pages, and danged if there wasn't a Franklin Gaines. Hey, I thought, maybe we're cousins. So I made an appointment and went in, and we got to talking about one thing and another, and come to find out his mother owns this block. The whole damn thing. She not only owns it, she was thinking of clearing it and making a parking lot for the church over there."

I could see, beyond the flat roof before me, the lighted spire of a church.

"Can you believe that? A lady with so much money she's going to clear this block for a parking lot? For a church? I told Franklin to forget about the tooth even though he'd already given me a shot. I didn't care about the tooth, I wanted to talk to his mother. I went to see her and danged if she wasn't actually planning to do just that. I told her, hey, Mrs. Gaines, why bother? Let me do it. In fact, I'll do even better. I'll give the church covered parking with full-time security. I'll run a shuttle bus if the weather's bad. And I'll pay top dollar for this block.

"She said, 'Why, Stanley, would you do that?'

"I told her I certainly would. I'd put a fifty-five-story office building here, the biggest in downtown Dallas, and the church could have the parking any time they wanted it with the exception of seven in the morning to seven at night. Otherwise, it was all theirs.

"She kinda liked the idea but she'd already promised the church and didn't want everybody mad at her. So Sally Ann and I went to their business meeting the other night. Sally Ann smiled and I told them what I wanted to do. And I was ready for them because, God, I've been to church business meetings before, but I still couldn't believe some of the things they were asking.

"One lady stood up and said, 'Well, I thought we were going to use part of the block for a gym for the kids.' Wonderful. Great. No problem. I'll put in a health club and give everybody free memberships. No problem.

"Another guy gets up—and I couldn't believe this—he says if the property's going to be developed, then he thinks one of the members ought to get first shot. Why, I don't know, since the church doesn't own the block. And he even says, 'I think we ought to ask Jim Blob Blowbutt if he wants to develop it.' Well, I know every major developer in town, and Jim Blob Blowbutt's not one of them. Turns out the guy's eighty-four years old and converts garages.

"This other old bag gets up and wants to know if the swimming pool will be open to mixed swimming. Can you believe this crap? I told her no, it wouldn't be because I didn't believe in swimming at all. Swimming and dancing were nothing but a prelude to sex. There'd be no swimming pool in the health club."

He shook his head and sighed as though too much was required of him, but he was smiling; he'd loved every second of it. "Anyway, we got the church satisfied—mostly—and dear old Mrs. Gaines and I have done our deal, and Brewster-Gaines is fixing to put up the biggest building in downtown Dallas as soon as the new airport opens or the FAA gives us a variance, whichever comes first.

"Now look and tell me if you can see this—fifty-five stories of Italian marble and dark glass. Beautiful lines of windows all the way around the building, clean and sharp, like the edge of a piece of paper. Over a million rentable square feet of office space: seventy-five hundred windows, all automatically washed. High-speed elevators and energy efficient. The home of First Southwéstern Bank and managed by who else but Brewster-Gaines.

"I've got an architect in Los Angeles working on the plans, and I don't want the word to leak out yet. The damned Canadians are planning a fifty-story building and I don't want them changing their minds. I want the biggest building in Dallas."

Talk about surprises, I thought. How would he ever top this one? I was almost afraid to ask but did: "How much?"

"Ninety million."

I was overwhelmed by zeroes: $90,000,000. I decided then that it took a person with no regard for money to plan such a project. In fact, I was having trouble comprehending the project altogether. "How're you putting this together?"

"A syndicate. Twenty partners with five hundred thou apiece."

"And how much will Brewster-Gaines have?"

"Eight percent. The partners will have four each, and the bank twelve because they'll call it home."

I wasn't so awed that I'd lost my mathematical ability. Eight percent of ninety million was just over seven million, and the figure almost made me laugh out loud. People wondered how these deals were put together, and even I had wondered how Stan arrived at the company's extent of participation. But this one was obvious. If somebody asked how Stan had arrived at 8 percent, I'd tell them, "My daddy said that was all he could have." He'd just used the last of his allowable debt.

"How many partners you got lined up?"

"All of them."

At one time I would have questioned him closely on whether he actually knew twenty people with five hundred thousand up front, people who could acquire debt of over three million. But no more. If he told me he'd acquired rights to build on the moon, I'd believe him. There were too many people flocking around him, wanting a piece of his next deal, too many people who believed he could accomplish amazing feats.

I remembered another recent development that had puzzled me. Stan had been spending a great deal of time with a city planner, trying to woo him away from the city, luring him from public to private employment, and now I knew why. This project would take an enormous amount of coordination with the city and Stan wanted someone who had a map of city hall.

"Charlie Insanity strikes again," I said.

The less I had to do, the more determined I was that I needed an office. The *pukutsi* in me demanded one. Forget that I'd been omitted in the very small information loop in the company, that Stan had been attending church business meetings and talking to an architect in L.A. and negotiating to buy part of downtown, and Two Hands Clapping had known *nothing* about any of it. I wanted an office. I wanted someplace to go every day so I wouldn't feel like Stan's paid friend. His mother had said he didn't let go easily, and he was apparently willing to name a vice president in charge of amity to keep people around. Jill pointed out that I, as corporate officer, should simply go lease an office somewhere, but that wasn't the point. I wanted Stan to recognize the need for one.

He finally located one and called to inform me on the first day of 1971 at 8:00 A.M. I was asleep. When the phone rang, I knocked it off the nightstand reaching for it and then spent a minute trying to find the receiver, guided by Stan's voice saying, "Hello? Hello? Hello?" I reached through the fog of a hangover acquired in responsible fashion on New Year's Eve, right in my own living room.

"Hello? Hello? Hello?"

Finally, irritated beyond reason by this staccato introduction to the new year, I yelled at the floor, "Shut up, Stan! I'm trying to find the phone."

"You're what?"

"Okay," I said, locating the receiver. "What do you want?"

"I'm going to pick you up in thirty minutes."

"The hell you are."

"Come on, Billy Boy, wake up. I want to show you your new office."

"It'll still be there this afternoon, Stan. I'm going back to sleep."

"Hey, you're gonna love it. I thought one would be available before now, but the old tenant changed his mind. So I had to wait. And get this—it's on the thirty-eighth floor of the Southland Life Building. Billy Boy, we're gonna sit up there and watch the First Southwestern Bank building climb right up in the sky. What do you think of that?"

I sighed and watched Jill wake up. On her stomach, she propped herself up on her elbows and rubbed her eyes with her fists. This is what happens, I thought, when you don't follow your *wakan*. Some morning you wake up in a city of ants to spend your day walking on concrete or asphalt and working downtown where the movement of the wind was artificial. It was funneled between big buildings like that in a wind tunnel.

"Stan, if you'd ever listened to anything you said or I said, then you'd remember why I moved to Richardson. North Dallas is hot, remember? Nobody wants to drive downtown. Remember that? How about, hey, Billy Boy, if you move out to Richardson, you'll be right near the Plaza North One office. It's a great place to live. Do you ever remember anything you say, Stan? Anything at all? Well, remember this—I'm not driving downtown every day. There ain't no fucking way."

"You're right, Billy Boy, you're right. North Dallas is going to be one of the hot spots in the whole country. But you don't want to watch the tower go up? Man, we're going to have elevators on that thing that'll move entire trucks. It's going to be something else."

I admitted what I'd always known—this job wasn't going to work. I'd signed on only out of curiosity, and Stan had hired me only to be the audience for which he performed. It wasn't employment; I didn't know what it was.

"Stan, don't take this personally, but I quit. I just can't handle the job. It's either too big or too small, I'm not sure which, but I wasn't made for it. So I don't want to argue about it, and I don't want to be persuaded, and I don't want you to think I'm mad at you. But I quit."

There was a silence on the other end, and then he yelled, off the line, "Sally Ann! Come here!"

I shook my head and hung up, hoping he'd simply take my oral resignation and leave me alone. To make sure he couldn't call me back, I removed the receiver from the phone and covered it with pillows so I wouldn't have to hear the dial tone.

Jill, now sitting up, looked at me silently. I threw the sheets down and got out of bed.

"Hell," I said, "that felt good. That's the first thing I've done in months."

Jill's favorite topic of conversation was moving back to Abilene, but now she looked nervous. "Should you have done that?"

"Of course, I should have. Otherwise, I wouldn't have done it. Get dressed. We'll go get some chips and dip and stuff and snack all day and watch football. We can watch Texas beat the dog out of Notre Dame."

I went to the kitchen and made coffee, wondering why I was in Dallas to begin with. I liked our house. It was nothing close to the Gaines's but it was spacious and in a subdivision built on a slight incline. We were near the crest so our view of the sky wouldn't be blocked any more than necessary. I loved trees but I'd chosen this brand-new subdivision because it lacked them altogether. There were enough impediments to the view without living under the trees.

Jill walked in scrubbing her face with a wet washcloth. From behind the rag she said, "What're you going to do?"

"I already told you, I'm going to watch football."

But the day brought discouragement. Notre Dame put eight men on the line of scrimmage and stopped Texas's triple option dead. To take my mind off the Cotton Bowl, I read the paper and ended up looking over the want ads, which gave me additional reason to feel depressed. Entry-level accountants were drawing salaries of $8,000, and the only oil and gas accountant listed, a job that required knowledge I'd have to fake, wasn't doing much better at $9,000. And there wasn't an ad for a land-man in the entire paper.

So I kept hearing Jill ask, "What're you going to do?" I wanted to return to Abilene, but the oil field was probably at its lowest point ever. And I wasn't going to return to Brewster Drilling to work for the old man. It seemed the most fundamentally wrong thing I could do.

"Shit," Jill said.

We were sitting on the floor in the den with the newspaper spread over the entire room almost, and she was looking out the front window. She used profanity under extreme circumstances only so I assumed she'd just read in the entertainment section of the paper that Robert Redford had yet to engage in a fantasy that concerned a woman named Jill.

"I think it's Stan or Sally Ann," she said.

It was both. They walked up the sidewalk to the porch laden with bags and obvious good cheer on their faces. Well, Stan's. Sally Ann seemed rather disgusted, as though she'd been enlisted against her will to go party.

Dressed informally, they walked in and Stan shouted, "Happy New Year!" They emptied their grocery bags on the kitchen table, adding to the clutter of opened bags of chips and containers of dip and empty beer bottles. Sally Ann removed her coat to reveal an actual maternity dress.

"Happy New Year!" Stan yelled in my face, shaking my hand with gusto and pressing something metallic into my palm.

I looked at my hand, which now held a gold key.

"Your new office," Stan said, "just around the corner. We can go see it in about thirty minutes, just as soon as it's furnished."

Nothing normal had happened to me since October 1964, when Charlie Insanity had sent Stanley Gaines to see me in the offices of Brewster Drilling. I'd stopped a couple of times to offer him a ride and now I'd be paying for it the rest of my life. And so I had to believe the maxim I'd always heard—no good deed goes unpunished.

158

"There aren't any offices just around the corner," I said. We lived at least two miles, and maybe more, from any of the little office parks that were being built.

"Okay, okay, so maybe it's around two corners. Don't be so literal. But it's right out here and you won't have to drive downtown."

We settled into something of a party routine and watched Texas make numerous failed attempts to pass their way to victory in the Cotton Bowl. I knew how they felt because I was making numerous failed attempts at generating enthusiasm over my retention as vice president of Brewster-Gaines Properties. One of these days, when Stan became famous throughout the world, I'd write an article about my tour of duty and call it, "Being In Nothingness."

Sally Ann waited until Jill went into the kitchen to make cheese dip and Stan went to use the phone in the bedroom before she said, "Do you know what this is costing me?"

"What what is costing you?"

She was on the couch wearing blue pants with a matching top, and now she slid down toward the opposite end, where I sat. "This business with the office. We were supposed to go to Rene Landers this afternoon. Rene Landers can get us into the Dallas Country Club. So why'd you pick today to pitch a fit? If you'd just told me what you'd wanted, I would've gotten it for you."

Was all this being misinterpreted, or was I really as childish as they thought I was? Probably if a person felt childish and in need of appeasement often enough, then he was probably childish. I started to explain but I doubted that even Sally Ann would understand. Instead, I changed the subject.

"You finally started showing, huh?"

"You wanta see?"

I looked toward both doorways, one to the kitchen, one to the hallway, and saw neither Stan nor Jill. "Sure, I want to see," I said. Of course, I did. Jill was barely showing but she didn't want me looking at her, afraid I'd think she was merely disfigured rather than pregnant.

Sally Ann stood, lifting her top and lowering the pants by catching the elastic panel with her thumb. She looked as though she'd swallowed a small pumpkin, her belly bulging, making her navel protrude. With both hands, I tested the ripeness of this pumpkin, patting here and there, then holding it on either side.

"I love it," I said. "It's beautiful."

"Mother Earth?" she asked.

"Not quite, but you're getting there."

This too was the *wakan*, the mysterious, and I was always surprised when I thought that both women had gotten pregnant in Dallas. It didn't seem likely that it could have happened here, so far from the Comancheria, so far from the earth and sky. But it was a sign of how powerful the *wakan* was, that it could have happened so far away.

I kissed her stomach just before Stan returned to the room.

"So," he said. "Who wants to go look at an office?"

11

As it turned out, Robert William Brewster was born before Stanley Gaines, Jr. He won the race by six weeks but paid the price by spending the first weeks of his life in an incubator. Tiny and red and absolutely helpless, he brought me to my knees in awe. I couldn't believe he was capable of sustaining life. Any accomplishment that preceded him paled in the face of his. I'd look at him and rub his bulbous stomach and think, kid, if you can make it through this, you can do anything.

He weighed just under four pounds at birth and was to remain in the hospital until he managed five. Jill considered each gram a victory. Ounces for him were just too much to think about. She came home each night with a progress report—2,401 grams, up 16 from yesterday. I'd visit and wonder why we'd given him such a bulky name. Robert was just too big. Jill had agreed on William, after Boomer, but she wouldn't go along with an Indian name. Just the suggestion of William Ten Bears Brewster made her speechless. She wanted William Edmond because the latter supposedly meant protector of wealth, but I refused to agree to any name with overtly materialistic implications. Robert had been the only name we could agree on. It meant bright in fame, and I felt certain he'd be a great anthropologist.

Just as Robert neared the weight goal, Stanley Gaines, Junior, was born to a mother who thought the dirtiest words in the language were "natural childbirth." She looked on women who wanted to engage in such a sweaty, grunting, panting activity as true barbarians. Long before she entered the hospital, she made sure her doctor understood she was to be unconscious throughout. She hadn't invited me to look at her stomach, had forgotten the words "Mother Earth," and had been busy wondering how in the hell she could live with a basketball descending toward her feet.

When the ball hit the floor, I wasn't at all surprised to find a miniature Abe Lincoln in the nursery with a thatch of thick black hair. He bawled and squalled from the time he was laid in his plastic crib near the viewing window. Jill and I watched him one night as a nurse tried to calm him with the nipple from a bottle.

"She hasn't got the slightest idea how to shut him up," I said.

"You do?"

"Sure. Forget the nipple. Make him an offer."

Sally Ann wasn't nearly as comfortable in the role of mother as Jill was. For feeding, she laid Junior on the bed beside her and stuck the bottle in his mouth while she propped herself up on one arm as if waiting for a quart of oil to drain into the engine of a car. I watched her—I visited her more than Stan did—and wished I could help her toward motherhood. As it was, she'd probably only decided to have a baby because she thought the presence of a baby in their house would make her more acceptable in the social circles she wanted to enter.

Not that Jill was a perfectly relaxed mother. She was already worried about Robert's study habits, about whether he'd understand geometry, about the entrance requirements of the best colleges.

Stan's attitude was similar to his wife's. He appeared at eleven the night Junior was born, several hours after the fact, and didn't reappear until it was time to take him home. I found him at the window of the nursery on the morning of Junior's scheduled departure.

The two, father and son, were uncharacteristically quiet and Stan didn't immediately notice me. Stan had a strange look on his face as though he was simultaneously exhorting the child to top the father's accomplishments and threatening him with harm if he even made the attempt.

I brought him out of his trance by saying, "Congratulations. I haven't seen you to tell you."

He whipped a cigar out of his coat pocket and handed it to me. "I've been so busy with the tower I've hardly had time to sleep. But this is a heck of a kid, isn't he? A heck of a kid."

I nodded. Stan had delayed making the announcement on Toothache Tower, just as the Canadians had delayed theirs after supposedly revising their plans to a fifty-five-story building that would be higher than Toothache. The tower was Stan's obsession. We hadn't had a conversation on any other subject in months, not on potential children, not on other projects, nothing.

"So how're things with Robert?" he asked.

"Good. It looks like we may be going home tomorrow."

We walked together to Sally Ann's room, and I wasn't at all surprised to find a full-time babysitter already on the job. She'd been assigned her first task, that of clothing Junior for his first outing, and she had his clothes spread on the bed.

Sally Ann was prepared to exit the hospital with makeup and hair fixed to perfection, as though done by a professional. She was ready to campaign for a spot on the Mayor's Ball and appear sufficiently mature to wrangle an invitation to join the Dallas Country Club. The scent of her perfume caught the attention of a nurse behind Stan and me who peeked into the room as we entered.

Smiling, the nurse said, "Motherhood just brings out the best in a woman." Then she was gone.

Sally Ann waited until she was out of sight and then flipped her the bird. And then, looking at me, she said, "I don't want to hear a word, or any animal sounds, out of you, buster."

Since Stan hadn't been around, I'd spent much more time with her than anyone else had, and she'd taken the opportunity to tell me how miserable she was. She felt like a cow, she said, lifting her breasts to demonstrate their tonnage. I'd been mooing occasionally so she wouldn't feel alone in the pasture. She just couldn't believe what had happened to her body; she felt as though she'd been stretched sideways on a rack, pulled apart. I kept telling her I liked her new motherly shape, particularly the top-heaviness, which wouldn't last long since she wasn't breastfeeding, and her response usually was, "Mother Earth sucks."

Now this carefully coiffed and glamorous-looking woman sat on the bed, sighed loudly, and said, "I feel like shit."

"Hey!" Stan said. "You're doing great, just great. It'll get better in no time."

She looked at me and knew what I was thinking and hated me for it. She looked like a thirty-year-old mother, and the fact that I didn't miss the sleek racing form she'd once possessed made her question my taste and value as a friend.

"Billy likes cows," she said. "He wants something to *milk*."

"Moooo," I said.

With a vicious look and intent, she picked up one of Junior's tiny white shoes and threw it at me. I ducked and the shoe sailed into the hall. The babysitter scampered after it.

"I love it," Stan said. "One big happy family."

1974

12

S tanley Gaines was now a prophet, elevated by almost everyone in the Middle East. In the fall of 1973 the Syrians and Egyptians had surprised the world, and particularly Israel, by attacking on two fronts, along the Golan Heights and in the Sinai. Stan, having waited years for the fighting to erupt, watched the news with the kind of rapt attention usually reserved for football games. And the Israelis, used to fighting wars not much longer than football games against inept Arab armies, were amazed to find that not only did the Arabs attack but that they could hold their positions. Other countries, as though encouraged by the head cheerleader in Texas, were so exuberant over this display of military prowess that they joined the fight themselves.

Everyone Stan talked to regularly remembered his "deadly combination," that of religion and greed. Religion started the war, and greed took over. Saudi Arabia retaliated against the U.S. for its support of Israel with an oil embargo. They reduced production 10 percent. OPEC's Gulf states announced a 70 percent increase in price. Stan's favorite, Qaddafi, liked a 93 percent increase better. In December the Gulf states announced another increase, this one an additional 130 percent. Just like that, they proved the center of production had not only shifted, but the control of the price had as well, not to mention control of the oil company operations throughout the Middle East. Stan wasn't required to recall his predictions. Everyone remembered.

I was ready to collect his sayings and call a conference of churches to see if we should add First and Second Stanley to the Bible. The Book of Gaines. Stan, however, was too busy counting money to care. The price of crude oil, which had been hanging in the $3-to-$4-per-barrel range for years, almost tripled. Federal price controls, enacted to control inflation, kept the price of "old" oil in the range of $6, but "new" oil, any that was produced in excess of 1972 allowables, was averaging $10.50 by the end of the year.

Stan's take from the Brewster-Gaines companies in Abilene went from just under $11,000 a month to almost $18,000. And in the lackluster economic environment in which we found ourselves, with the stock market in the dumper, there was a magic word in investments—oil.

I finally acquired work, but my function was more of an administrative assistant's than a vice president's. I'd gone from Two Hands Clapping to Takes Notes, fielding calls from an enormous number of people who wanted in on one of Stan's deals. He was the darling of doctors and lawyers, all of whom greeted him in the same manner: "Hey, Stan, what've you got going? Let your friends make some money."

Stan felt a deep spiritual call, this one from St. Dino, harking him back to prehistoric formations deep below the surface of the earth. And Stan, being the spiritual person he was, not only heeded the call but became very selective about those to whom he issued invitations to join him in these pilgrimages. He politely but firmly pushed away anyone whose money wasn't quite big enough, and he didn't tolerate those who questioned his methods, called too often, or wanted updates. His favorite line was, "I don't have time to hold the guy's hand."

He called me one night and asked me to meet him the next morning at the airport; we needed to make a trip to Abilene. And although he didn't give me a reason for the trip, I knew why we were going. Brewster and Gaines were about to break their hyphenation and float off in different directions. The old man had seen it coming, of necessity, when Stan had expanded into the Los Angeles real estate market. My father believed that if plastic hadn't been developed, California wouldn't exist. His favorite statement concerning that state was, "Now that's the biggest waste of space I've seen since I was in California."

We met at the airport. Brewster-Gaines Properties had acquired a company plane, a candy apple–red Lear jet customized for the Shah of Iran, who for some reason had not taken delivery, and Stan had wanted this plane capable of carrying oil royalty more than the old man had considered it a total waste of money. Stan, however, believed that the father of the biggest building in Dallas (which wasn't yet completed) *needed* it, as he needed a leather briefcase and customized gold Cross pens and a Rolex.

I hadn't expected Sally Ann to accompany us, but she did. Both were dressed in business uniforms, mostly blue with some red and white. Rebuffed by the social circles into which she wanted to move, overloaded by motherhood, she was reacting against both by trying to become twenty years old again. She worked harder physically than anyone I knew, harder than most athletes. And the benefit was her former sleekness.

Our relationship had changed, as everything else had, not so much by design as neglect. We just seemed to have fewer and fewer occasions to meet.

"Hi," I said, kissing her when we met at the foot of the ladder into the aircraft that was as sleek as she was. I couldn't help but feel the electrical surges when I got close. I whispered into her ear, "You look good enough to eat."

She whispered back, "Are you hungry?"

"Ready?" Stan asked. "Your father said he'd have somebody pick us up."

I climbed into the plane, bothered by Stan's new attitude, one of outward calm dictated by his newfound status as brother of Jeremiah and Hosea. I felt as though I liked him only on those occasions when he was being honest and straightforward, as the night he'd told me about his Laotian nightmare. Unfortunately, as I always found out, the conversations had lacked the honesty I'd supposed they'd had, and even then, they were rare. I wanted to mess up his carefully styled hair and say, "Hey, I know who you are, under the pinstripes and hair spray. Knock off the crap."

We were in the old man's office before lunch. Almost seventy-five, he seemed to find pleasure in the company of younger women, especially when he got to hug them; but he shook hands with Sally Ann, not because she was there on business but because he saw her as part of Stan's problem, his propensity to squander money on Lear jets, to introduce himself in parts of the country where he had no business.

We sat around the old man's office for a few minutes shooting the bull. The office hadn't changed a bit except for one item—the old man had a new chair. My mother had come up one day and found it covered with gray duct tape patching splits in the upholstery, and she'd ordered him a new chair on the spot.

Stan sat with his legs crossed and his fingertips pressed together, looking like a psychiatrist who'd listen to your every problem. I watched him and decided he really was nothing more than a whore. At some point, the pursuit of the deal, the love of money, had to become secondary to larger considerations, such as peace in the Middle East. And although he'd never outwardly gloated, had never expressed sublime *delight* in the fact that a large number of people had been killed in the Yom Kippur War and that his fellow countrymen were having to sit in gas lines, he didn't have to gloat. His attitude said it all.

"Mr. Brewster," he said, bringing the small talk to an end. "I stood in this room ten years ago and asked you for a chance. And you gave it to me. I didn't have anything to offer but determination and a willingness to work, and I couldn't even prove that. Everything I've accomplished this far is because of you. Billy knows I've never forgotten that, and I never will."

He stood, some of the old Stan breaking out, demanding motion. He walked to the window overlooking Cypress Street, and I thought, he's the only person I know who could make a message of gratitude sound like an acceptance speech at the Academy Awards. He was about as grateful as a lizard.

"I know you're thinking about retiring, and I've got guys chasing me all over the country wanting into the oil business. So I've got two proposals. As you know, Sally Ann and I own a great deal of property south of town, and we're already seeing expansion in that direction. That's where Abilene's growing, south, just as I thought it would when I started buying property out there."

He walked back to his chair and picked up a briefcase from the floor, opening it and lifting out a document, a listing of property holdings. He laid it on the old man's desk should he want to look at it.

"That's a listing of the property we've talked about. It's here, where you're located, and we're fixed in Dallas, probably always will be. So here's the proposal. I'll transfer this property, along with all my ownership in the BG companies, with a million five cash, for all your interest in Brewster-Gaines Properties."

I hadn't seen the list of Abilene real estate and didn't know what it was worth, but I did know this—the prophet was approaching the old man as though he were just another investor or banker, using this formal tone he'd been using ever since he'd become Third Isaiah. I found it irritating and I knew the old man did, too. Abilene wasn't a town where pretense would get you very far.

"That's proposal number one," Stan said. "This isn't a package deal, but it probably should be. Anyway, number two is this: I've got investors who are more interested in the oil business right now than they are in their own families. They've just *got* to get in. And I've got a group that wants to buy Brewster-Gaines Production. That's why I asked you for the production runs, so we could put a value on it. Twenty-four months' production is slightly over eight million nine. They're willing to pay, in cash, nine million dollars."

Poor Stanley Gaines. He was about to get cleaned and pressed. The old man, who'd always found Stan about as interesting as I had, was now ignoring him, a sign of a coming squeeze. The last man who acted condescending toward him had been a company man who'd believed Brewster Drilling would grovel for business. The old man would shut down before groveling, and he'd never drilled another well for that company. Stan should have walked in and, in a normal voice, given the old man his best shot. He'd have come out of this deal saving millions.

Stan sat down, pressing his fingertips together and becoming an oracle. "If I was a betting man, I'd bet the price of land south of town's going to increase faster than the price of oil. Abilene's about to take off, just like it did when the population doubled during the boom of the fifties. That $640,000 worth of property will double, triple, quadruple. This is a big chance for you, Mister Brewster."

He turned to me and said, "We're talking about your inheritance, Billy, and that's why I asked you along. You're going to have to decide which way you go from here, Brewster or Gaines."

He wasn't talking to me; he was telling the old man they were going separate ways regardless. I didn't say anything.

Without further discussion, the old man stood and took his brown suit coat from a brass rack in a corner. "You're right, this is a family matter. Billy and I are going to get a cup of coffee and we'll be back in an hour."

I followed my father to the door, watching Stan give a look of consternation; he'd barely warmed up, hadn't even gotten to his sales pitch yet. And now the old man was going to pitch. A fastball. Outside the office, he guided me to the stairs so Stan couldn't catch us waiting on the elevator to continue his spiel.

Once outside, in a day that was typical early summer, windy and warm, the old man consulted his watch. "It's ten-fifty. Stan expects us back by eleven-fifty or before. He doesn't know I know it, but he's got an appointment at the Bank of Midland at two-thirty. And we're going to make sure he's late for that, which means we can't be back here before one. So let's go eat."

Even with the resurgence in the oil field, we weren't likely to get run over crossing the street downtown. Abilene wasn't a hotbed of activity yet. After years of a slow decline, the industry wasn't going to get off its deathbed overnight. Supplies were short. All the manufacturers associated with the oil field had been tapering production for years.

The old man and I were getting along better since Robert had come along and Boomer had died. My grandfather had passed on during "General Hospital," and the last words he'd spoken had been, "I *told* you to stay away from that woman." My mother had found him sitting in his ragged rocker-recliner, head forward, chin on his chest. As everyone had said more times than I cared to think about, it was an easy way to go.

We buried him next to my grandmother in the cemetery at Buffalo Gap, right between the hills through which the buffalo had passed on their migrations, where the cattle had come through on their way to Dodge City, along with Civil War veterans and the old pioneers. Stan had been in Denver at the time, but Sally Ann had come with Jill and me to the funeral. I'd stood between the two women on a rainy day in November, thinking that not only had someone close to me passed from my life, but an era had passed from the earth. Boomer had watched the cattle come up the Western Trail, had been part of those free-wheeling, nitro-shooting, leg-to-leg derrick days. Control over the price of oil had passed out of the hands of the Texas Railroad Commission—and out of the country altogether.

With the death of Boomer and the Arab oil embargo, I somehow felt cut off, drifting, even when I stood between the hills in Buffalo Gap, well within the Comancheria. It was a different world, one in which fortunes would be made in boardrooms using CPAs and lawyers, and Dallas no longer seemed like the foreign place it once had. I didn't think I'd be working for the pretentious prophet much longer, but I doubted that I'd return to Abilene either.

As the old man and I drove into the parking lot of a restaurant, I asked, "Well, you going to sell?"

"Probably. I'm not ready to retire yet, but I've been promising your mother for years we'd travel one of these days and she keeps pointing out I may not have many more days left. She doesn't bug me about it, but she damn sure lets me remember I promised. You know where she wants to go? China. Tricky Dick opened the door and she wants to walk through it. China. I've never been to a communist country in my life and don't really see why I ought to start now, but that's where she wants to go."

We left the car and walked toward the front door of the restaurant. "We'll have a nice slow lunch," he said. "Stan expects us back by eleven-fifty or before. By twelve, he'll be pissed that I'm standing him up. You know, now that he's acting and talking like some Wall Street lawyer, he'll take that pretty hard. He'll start thinking maybe he'll gouge me, cut his offer. By twelve-thirty, he'll decide I'm not fit to deal with, as little respect as I have for his talents, and unless I come back *right now* and bow down, he'll just leave. By a quarter to one, he'll realize he's going to be late for his appointment in Midland and he'll be walking in circles, madder'n a hornet because he's realized he can't make the deal in Midland without first cutting a deal here, and he's going to get me eventually. By one o'clock, he'll be back to the old Stan, worrying like hell the whole deal's going to fall through and everybody in Dallas'll realize there's nothing inside that stuffed shirt. We'll walk in and make us a good deal just a little after one."

I laughed as we entered the restaurant. The wages of pretense, in the offices of Brewster Drilling, were going to be high.

We were at the restaurant early and there were still some lagging coffee drinkers around, most of them retired, most of them well known to both my father and me. We made the rounds, shaking hands and making light conversation. After growing accustomed to Dallas, I always had trouble slowing down when I returned to Abilene. I hardly felt as if I could take the time to talk anymore. My mind kept telling me to talk to these people, be nice, but my feet were saying go.

We took a table and sat, and I asked, "Why's Stan going to Midland?"

"He's buying Walker Drilling. And he wants the production here to cinch the loan."

"How do you know?"

"Same way I know anything—somebody tells me. Walker told me part of it, and the bank called."

"What do you want for the production?"

"Oh, I might've parted with it for what he offered because the decline is pretty bad on some of the new wells. But he'll have to pay more than that now. And if he doesn't like the price, he'll have to go find some somewhere else. If the old Stan had showed up, I'd have been fair, but he's been preaching twenty-dollar oil's just around the corner, and he may be right, but I don't think it's the *next* corner. What I do know, he thinks it is, and that's all I need to know. He's going to leave my office a little shorter than when he walked in."

We ate a leisurely meal and talked about Robert. With his mother's refined looks and blondish-brown hair, he provided the perfect counterpoint to Stanley Gaines, Jr., the little Abe Lincoln with the coal black hair. Robert would have definitely been misnamed as Ten Bears because there was no Comanche blood in him. He refused to defend his property. Every time the two boys got together, Junior would collect every toy Robert chose to play with, exacting a hundred percent tax on toys. They played the same roles wherever they were, regardless of the actual ownership of the toys. Robert couldn't play with them. I'd watch, hoping eventually Robert would get tired of Junior's ways, would grow embarrassed over having adults step in to enforce sharing, and he'd simply coldcock the coarse-haired prick, but so far he hadn't. I tried not to push him, too close to my own youth and my father's frustration over my lack of fire in the gut.

Junior really wasn't a bad kid; he was just overly aggressive at times, and one of those times was when he spotted Robert with a toy. When I was around him, he was in my lap every time I sat down. He usually asked me to read to him, but he was in that regard just like his father had once been—he didn't care about the stories as much as he did the noise.

On the way back to the office to relieve Stan of money and his own sense of prestige, the old man asked who I was throwing in with. I told him we were established in Dallas, had made good friends, and Jill was involved with an amateur theater company, for which she made sets. We'd stay in Dallas but not necessarily with Gaines.

Stan was staring at his fingernails, next to the Cypress Street window, when we walked in, a frown on his face. I'd agreed with my father's estimate of how he had tolerated our absence. At this point, I thought nerves were winning out over disdain.

He stood. "Well, you're finally back. I hate to tell you this, but I've got an appointment in Midland and it looks like I'm going to be late. I hate that."

The old man walked to his desk reading phone messages, a toothpick in his mouth. "Well, it seems pretty obvious to me that you won't get to Midland if you're sitting on your ass in Abilene." Without looking at Stan, he pitched his toothpick at a trash can behind the desk and sat down.

"Did Sally Ann leave?" I asked.

"She's making some phone calls," Stan said, then looked at his watch. His prophetic demeanor was beginning to slip. He wanted to walk out, wanted to continue his role as one pursued, but he didn't want to leave a deal undone. He watched the old man wad up one phone message and toss it toward the wastebasket, then stood.

"On the extremely slim chance we might be able to make a deal in such a short period of time, what's the best you'll do."

The old man shoved away from the desk and propped his feet up. "Let me tell you something, Stan. You won't ever know what the best I'd do was going to be. You walked in here like a New York lawyer, like you forgot every damn thing I ever told you. You've been reading your own press, and you've made that fatal mistake—you believed it. Now it's going to cost you. I'm going to say this one time, and you can take it or leave it because I'm not going to fart with you. If you want my interest in Brewster-Gaines Properties, it's going to take your real estate and three million cash. If you want the production company, your high-powered investors are going to have to come up with, *in cash*," he said, mimicking Stan, "an easy twelve million bucks." He pointed his finger at Stan and added, "And if you give me any more garbage about what the value of real estate in Abilene's going to do, you're going to leave here with just exactly what you carried in that door. Or," he said, suddenly dropping his feet to the floor and leaning on his arms on the desk, "it's possible you'll leave here with even less than you brought."

The old man stared at his employee, daring him to present part two of his bullshit spiel. He seemed more irritated with the boy wonder than he had at lunch, and I didn't know whether he was just now giving voice to greater ire than he'd expressed to me, or whether he was simply acting. That was the problem in dealing with him, even for me, and Stan said nothing for a moment. The threat that hung in the air—that Stan could leave with less than he'd arrived with—was a rather rude reminder that the old man was and always had been the majority owner of Brewster-Gaines Properties and hadn't forgotten that the minority owner had expanded into southern California against the old man's wishes. It was entirely possible that Stanley Gaines could not only leave Abilene with a deal undone, but he could also leave as ex-president of Brewster-Gaines Properties.

Stan had almost gone white and he walked to the window to look outside. He rubbed his neck with his hand in the same position he'd have used to choke himself. I would have felt sorry for him but didn't

171

know how he was going to react. It had to be hell, walking in as wise as Solomon and leaving on his knees, as short as Zacchaeus.

There was a rather quiet and humorless laugh that came from the window. Stan turned, having lost his psychiatric omniscience. He looked at me and said, "You know, we spent an hour flying out here and you could've told me I was about to screw up."

"I can't tell you what I don't know."

He walked back to his chair in front of the desk and sat. With a wry smile, he said to my father, "Well, why don't you draw up the papers. You know how I am with paperwork. Hell, you know everything." He looked at me, untouched by the fact that he'd just cost his investors a million or two, the old Stan, naive and enthusiastic. "What about you, Billy Boy? You staying or going?"

"Let's go."

Walker Drilling in Midland had been in business about as long as Brewster, but Walker had never possessed the old man's touch. One thing he had possessed was a drinking problem; occasionally he went off on binges and occasionally he went off to dry out. And now, at the beginning of what certainly seemed a revival of the industry, he wasn't in shape to take advantage of it. He'd expanded in the early sixties, acquiring additional rigs with the capacity of drilling 20,000 feet, but he'd never been able to climb out from under his debt. He still owed the Bank of Midland almost $8,000,000, and the bank was glad to see a serious suitor who wanted Walker's twelve rigs.

As we flew to Midland, Stan was philosophical about his dealings with William C. Brewster, Jr. "He wasn't going to fart with me; you heard him say that, didn't you? Man, I caught it. I should've known better than to mess with him. He knows me from the feet up and he knows I'm no horse trader. You know what I should've done? I should've walked in there and made him my best offer right off."

"That's right, Stan."

"I probably could've saved a million, a million five. Maybe even more. Why'd you let me do that?"

"To teach you a lesson, boy. I don't ever want to hear any more garbage about what real estate in Abilene's going to do."

For people who'd just watched money being squandered, we seemed to be in a good mood as we whistled through the sky in the red Lear jet. Stan stood in the aisle, his hands on the seat backs on either side of the aisle, looking out the windows as though he wanted to see the city of

Midland just as soon as it appeared. Sally Ann sat across the aisle from me, looking like a world-class stewardess taking a break and relaxing. So far she'd ignored the decree from fashion designers that the mini was dead and continued to wear them. Unfortunately for me, Stan was blocking my view of her legs, standing between us.

"This is going to be a pretty big loan even for the Bank of Midland," he said. "They're going to have to have some participation, so I've already given them everything they need—financial statements on the investors, personal and corporate tax returns, and all that. There'll probably be two bankers out here from Chicago and Dallas."

He had to move to allow Sally Ann to get up. She walked toward the rest room, her long legs finally visible.

"Your job's going to be to put this drilling company together, Billy Boy. Walker's been making noises like he wants to stay under contract, but I want him out. He's a liability we're not assuming. We want to start brand-new, without any bad raps on our name. Which is going to be Gaines Petroleum, by the way."

He glanced at the closing door of the rest room and said, "I'm trying to get her to stay out here with you and get involved in this thing. She's been kinda . . ." He shrugged, searching for the right word. "Flighty. She's been kinda flighty. I think she needs something to occupy her mind."

"I'm staying?" I asked. I'd boarded this plane thinking we were going to and returning from Abilene the same day. I wasn't carrying clothes, much less a razor or toothbrush.

But the prospect of staying in Midland, even unprepared, wasn't quite as unsettling as the thought that I'd have company. I hadn't experienced the feeling Stan's words had given me in the past twenty years, not since I'd entered a haunted house at the fair. The door opened and the darkness creaked and the hair on my arms stood up. Was this something Robert Brewster's father should be doing, staying in Midland with Sally Ann?

She reappeared, looking at me as though we were conspiring against the world, and Stan, still in the aisle, moved so she could sit.

"I was just telling Billy you were thinking about staying and helping put this deal together."

She nodded. "You're damn right. By the time you see us again, we'll be cash-flowing this baby. *The Oil and Gas Journal* will have written us up, and Billy and I'll be in demand all over the world as consultants."

Stan punched me on the shoulder. "Hey, is that confidence or what? I like it."

It wasn't confidence I was worried about.

The Bank of Midland was one of the pioneers in oil and gas lending, renowned for large loans, but the meeting included, as Stan had expected, loan officers from Dallas and Chicago. We met in the boardroom, and the president's secretary, whose short skirt matched Sally Ann's, served coffee from a silver urn that had been installed. Stan made the rounds, meeting everyone in attendance regardless of position.

Sally Ann and I, representing the peasantry, sat along the wall in leather-bound armchairs, out of the action. I looked at her hand, resting palm down on her knee. Her fingernails were screamingly red.

"Are you really going to stay here?" I whispered.

"Sure. Don't you want me to?"

"Of course, I want you to, but . . ."

Our conversation was ended by Stan, who, standing before the assembly of bankers, said, "I brought William C. Brewster the third with me. I'm sure most of you gentlemen at least know who he and his father are. They got their start not too far from here in that, oh, that little bitty field, what's the name of it, oh, yeah, Yates." The joke got light but appreciative laughter. "Billy's signed on to help set up Gaines Petroleum. If there's anything he doesn't know about the oil field, it probably doesn't need to be known."

Stan was still making use of his assets. As all the bankers looked at me and smiled their acknowledgments, I smiled back and said quietly to Sally Ann, "Right, but what the hell does he know about running a company?"

She nodded as though I'd said something appropriately profound.

"Gentlemen," Stan said, "here's what I need from you. We're buying Walker Drilling for twelve million, everything from the iron to the pencils. Billy's going to find the best men there are to run this operation, and if anybody knows them, if anybody can find them, Billy can. My investors—and you have their financial statements and tax returns—want to put in two million and carry the remaining ten on a five-year payout. We want a million-dollar line of credit for the purchase of existing production, and we're coming in with production that's paying almost four million five at the present. We'll pledge all that revenue toward the note."

I knew more about Stanley Gaines than these bankers did, and I knew that here, unlike he'd done in Abilene, he was being himself. He wasn't telling all. I didn't know his plan, but I did know his philosophy, and it wasn't built on practices such as plugging all that revenue back into the bank. He wanted the maximum return on his money and he'd let inflation whittle away his debt. Whatever his plan, it hadn't unfolded yet.

"Last week," Stan said, "Mr. Medders said he'd see what he could do on those terms, and I hope you've got an affirmative answer today. As you know, the oil field is rebounding, and we're in it for the duration. I'd like to know the Bank of Midland is our bank."

The president, sitting at the opposite end of the table, nodded, the decision already made. "We can and will be happy to work with you, Stan. We want you to know you'll be a valued customer here."

The meeting became much less formal, and I kept thinking, somebody in Dallas had the bucks. A loan for $10,000,000 had just sailed right through this joint credit committee, and Stan had already committed $15,000,000 to the old man before announcing he had another $2,000,000 to sink into the new Gaines Petroleum. With that kind of money available, no wonder he didn't have time for hand-holding.

I kept looking at Sally Ann's legs, all that glistening expanse of pantyhose, hoping she'd stay, hoping she wouldn't. As we drove to the airport in the car I'd rented for my stay here, I tried my best to ignore her face in the rearview mirror. With her hair up, she looked prim, proper, as she watched the passing industrial scenery along the road, her face turned toward the window, but she always had that look that said, "You wish." By the time we got to the airport and I found a phone on which to call Jill, I'd end up telling her I was staying in Midland to put together a Sally Ann.

But then, I doubted that she cared. After we parked at the airport, Mrs. Gaines escorted her husband to the plane and I went off in search of a phone. And, typically, I couldn't tell whether Jill was at all disturbed over my staying in Midland.

"Midland?" she said. "I thought you were going to Abilene."

"Listen, we've been wheeling and dealing all over west Texas. Gaines bought out Brewster, Brewster bought out Gaines, Gaines bought out Walker. You name it, it's been bought." I explained the transactions, growing so conscious of my desire to avoid saying the name Jill hated that I was dead certain I would. Sally Ann. Sally Ann Sally Ann Sallyannsallyannsallyann. I stared at the phone as I talked as though I could see my carefully scripted and completely asexual role.

"Are you drunk?" she asked.

"What?"

"You sound drunk. This is the way you talk when you're drunk, like a robot or something."

"No, no, no," I said, trying to conjure up a chuckle that came out sounding like a one-syllable cry. This is what happened when your son was being held hostage. You had to appease the kidnapper whether you wanted to or not.

"Well, as long as Sally Ann's not there."

I started sweating; my skin turned hot. Damn, what hell, another person exercising such power. I didn't worry about Jill disappearing with Robert when I was in Dallas, but what if she managed to verify Sally Ann's presence in Midland before I could return home? I never had liked lying, but I said, "Sally Ann went to Abilene with us, but she stayed there."

Jill tch-tched the fact that I hadn't brought any clothes, and we hung up. I turned away from the phone, having stared at the silver plate on the coin box so long I couldn't see very well, but I could see that Sally Ann, as usual, had been listening in. She was standing right behind me.

"You poor baby," she said.

She offered her arm, I took it, and we set off for the parking lot. As we walked I said a brief prayer of thanksgiving that she was being tolerant and begged that she would continue in that mode. At one time, lying about her location, and thus revealing embarrassment to be caught in her company, would have brought swift and severe retaliation, anything from a black eye to a choke hold.

Although she hugged my arm tightly to her breast as we crossed the parking lot, she said, "You don't have to worry about me, Billy. I've become celibate."

"No more babies?"

"Oh, it's just all these unknown and incurable diseases floating around. I don't want one. Besides, it simplifies life. You ought to try it."

"I do, three months at a time. On the first of every quarter, if Jill can work it in between washing her hair and polishing the silver, she lets me have some. While we do it, she tapes a letter to her mother. 'Dear Mom, ho hum, let's see, nothing's happening . . .'"

Sally Ann laughed, but I was hardly exaggerating. Jill Brewster was the mother of Robert, the daughter-in-law of my parents, an acquaintance, or dear friend, of Stan Gaines, depending on who she was talking to, but she didn't seem to have much interest in being the wife of Billy Brewster. And although I may have been overly cynical, she seemed to have gradually lost that interest, if she'd ever had it, as Robert grew to be more and more the center of my life. Had we grown apart, or did she realize she possessed the key to the kingdom? I not only didn't know, but I didn't care very much.

We got back in the car, which had already turned hot on this summer day full of sunshine, and left the airport. The day reminded me of those in Mayport. Getting up and heading for the beach, anticipating the smell of salt air and hours of utter laziness. Drink beer or splash in the surf or soak up the sun. Whatever, it didn't matter. I didn't have anything else to do.

Headed back into Midland to find a hotel, I knew we weren't headed for the beach. We weren't in Florida but west Texas, on a prairie that was close to plains, flat and treeless. In fact, we weren't far from Notrees, appropriately named. We were in true oil-field country, the land of deep wells and big producers. The Yates Field had come in with wells capable of producing 100,000 barrels a day and more. This was the city of money; the work force lived in Odessa, twenty miles away.

Sally Ann looked at me and said, "I'm not interested in this drilling company business. I'm only staying to visit with you. How long has it been since we've had a good talk? There's always something going on or someone around who doesn't want us to say much to each other."

"Was this your idea or Stan's? You staying."

"Stan's, believe it or not. That's how much he knows about me, thinking I'd have any interest in a drilling company. But I've been talking about going to France and he decided my idle hands needed something to do." She gave me a wicked smile, held her hands as though she were gripping pipes and engaged in masturbatory movements. "Actually, it's easy to be celibate when you live with Stan. You make love to a woman taping letters to her mother, and I make love to a man staring at the telephone."

She turned on the seat, coming closer to me, and brought one leg up onto the seat, showing me the darker shades of the top of her pantyhose. Her short blue skirt draped between her legs, covering a strategic spot. I was glad we'd embarked on this voyage of celibacy because otherwise I would have felt bad looking at her exposed eighteen inches of thigh.

"Stan's either scared of sex or doesn't trust it, maybe because of his mother. I always thought he didn't know about his mother's messing around, but he does. He just never did say anything about it. But he got real upset with her one night because she always thinks he's successful because of you. She gives him no credit whatsoever, and he gets *pissed*.

Anyway, we went by and visited her one night and he got so mad he called her a whore, not to her face, but after we left, and said something like she was so screwed up she wanted to fuck her way into the kingdom of God."

"The mysterious Mrs. Gaines," I said, shaking my head. She thought Stan was successful because of me and was going to be carried into heaven on her back spread-eagle. She was a strange lady.

"So tell me what you've been doing," Sally Ann said, pushing her knee against my leg.

What had I been doing? Nothing. Take Robert out of my life and it would have been empty. I hadn't been doing anything, a fact which wouldn't surprise Sally Ann. She'd told me years ago to stop piddling, but I hadn't followed orders.

"I'm thinking about writing a treatise on procrastination."

"But you just haven't got around to it. Right?"

"I'm kinda like Stan. He was going to buy his mother a car once, but decided if he waited he could get her a house. Here it is ten years later and he hasn't even got her a phone."

"There's more to that story than you know," she said as she spied a tiny thread on her pantyhose, just below the hem on her dress. She wet her fingertips and rolled the errant string. "He's offered to buy her a house and car and she wants him to give the money to her church. And he'd *burn* the money before he gave it to that church of hers. And he obviously doesn't have anything against churches in general. He's a big giver at ours. He even bought a new organ not long ago. But he wouldn't give a penny to her church."

She pointed through the windshield. "There's a shopping center. Why don't you stop and we'll get some clothes. I'll let you pick out my panties."

"I'm glad we're both celibates."

"It does simplify things, doesn't it?"

I stood in the hotel lobby, just outside the door to the restaurant, waiting on Sally Ann. By now I was certain Jill had called to verify Stan had returned home alone and she'd either caught a plane to Midland or she'd hired a private investigator, maybe the guy reading the paper in an easy chair right near the fountain.

The suspicion had probably been precipitated by the clothes-shopping expedition earlier. I'd never in my life helped Sally Ann pick out clothes, never had such a difficult time keeping my hands off another person. "Here, let me see if that fits you in the hips. Oh, yeah, oh, my, that's a perfect feel, I mean, fit." Anything I liked, she bought, and the panties I'd selected were, of course, something I'd never see on her.

Now she came walking across the lobby in a simple black dress, drawing more eyes than mine, including those of the private eye, who folded his newspaper and sat back to enjoy the sight. Black and blond, contrasting colors I loved. The dress showed her arms, and the shape of her braless breasts, to advantage; it seemed to be merely draped over her, clinging in all the right spots. I was as emotional as if we were going on our first date, and it wasn't only because I was expecting the man with the newspaper to come arrest me in the name of all loving wives who were at home waiting on their husbands.

I took her hand when she reached me. "You look so *goooood.*"

"Thank you."

I had to do something about my life, had to put some excitement into it so I'd be immune to moments such as this one. I'd been living in the past for at least a year, listening to music of the sixties, staring back at that psychedelic haze of a decade that had been disconnected by all the turmoil. But the fact was, at times, I wanted to be back in the navy, at home on leave, my world in transition, everyone I knew taking off to, if not the war, at least the military. I wanted to stand around and drink and listen to the Stones and Rascals with those guys, eating, drinking, and making merry because tomorrow we might truly die. I wanted to relive my last night with Jill prior to the navy, wanted life to be sweet and bittersweet, tears and laughter, all at the same time. I didn't want to be past thirty, looking backward.

And now I was paying the price for my boredom, looking across a candle in a glass holder at a woman who was sending me into a dizzy kind of forgetfulness.

"Billy," she said. "When I look at your face, I don't see any real dedication to celibacy."

"To the day I die, I'll never understand how I can be so attracted to some girl whose hair is some off-color blond."

"You don't like my hair?"

"I love each and every strand."

She took a small sip of wine and said, "I thought we were going to flirt and have fun but remain pure. You sound like you're trying to seduce me."

I took a deep breath and said, "Okay, ask me about Jill and Robert. That'll remind me of who I am."

"How's Robert? I don't care about what's-her-name."

"Robert's my pride and joy. I go home in the afternoon looking forward to seeing him. He can talk but he'd rather use sign language. He's got all these signs he uses, one for car, one for airplane, one for hot or cold, just about anything he wants to tell you. He cracks me up. I don't think there's a thing on this earth cuter than a three-year-old boy."

She shook her head. "That's not a good antiseduction story. It makes me want to seduce you. I love you as a father. I watch you and Robert every time we get together, and you know what I think? Those two guys should be mine. I want them both. I want a father with your kind of patience and dedication. You're so sweet with Robert, I think, that's the kind of man I want making love to me."

"Well, hmmm," I said, thinking all roads led not to Rome but to Sally Ann's room on the sixth floor, the one with the outer wall of windows that looked out over the lights of Midland. "Why don't we just go on up to your room and get it over with? Then we can enjoy the rest of the visit."

She shook her head, making her hair swing. "No, we can't weaken. Besides, you're trying so hard—oh, I guess I shouldn't use that word. You're really trying so I've got to come, I mean, I've got to help you remain upright. You know, erect." She sucked her lips inward, trying to keep from laughing.

I sat back, shaking my head. There wasn't any way to win because all I could think about was that she was here, I was here, and we were free to do whatever we chose, regardless of the suspicious men in the lobby reading newspapers. Besides, where could we go when we left this dimly lit restaurant in which a pianist was softly playing the music from "Love Story" and the sight of Sally Ann had consumed me?

I attempted to make small talk but we'd been squashed by sex. It smothered us like a bully who refused to be ignored and wouldn't let us breathe until we'd paid our respects. The attempt to steer the conversation in another direction was so futile that I started laughing. My, my, we said. You don't say. Really? Huh, that's something. How about that.

"The hell with this," I said. We were sitting at a table for four, across from each other, and I moved around one setting so I could sit next to her. I wanted her within reach. Using the tablecloth to cover my movements, I put my hand beneath the table and grabbed her leg. The slick fabric of the black dress slid over her leg as though it were coated with oil. "I just can't stand it. I've got to touch you."

She sipped wine and looked at the pianist. "Does this mean we're not remaining pure?"

"No, this is the purest desire I've ever had. It's absolutely untainted."
My hand moved to her lower stomach. I had to lean forward and down, stretching, to touch her there, and as I moved my fingers smoothly from the slight rise of her navel, falling into the valley below, I discovered something missing. "You're not wearing those panties I picked out."

She looked directly at me and said, "I didn't want to get them wet."

My entire body was warm and flushed and glowing. I was probably radiating light. I felt healthy and lively, a newborn. Immortal. Beneath the table, I pushed her dress up to the top of her thighs, and, as she opened her legs, let my second finger probe the moist depths of Mother Earth.

"You're right. You would've got your pants wet."

She set her glass of wine down because her hand had begun to quiver.

How long had it been since I'd felt this way, since I'd felt connected to the ground from which I'd emerged? And why did I only experience that sensation in the open, beneath the Comanche's sky, or with this woman who had received my finger?

"You know," I said, "I'd rather eat in the room. We can call room service and tell them to send up something, anything, just as long as it has a ton of whipped cream."

"Oh, come, thou fount."

"Oh, God, let's go. Now."

13

After Sally Ann returned to Dallas the next day, I threw myself into the search for good people to man Gaines Petroleum. I had to work out of my hotel room because when I told Walker his services wouldn't be required, he downshifted and started moving very slowly in vacating the office at his yard and in getting the rigs back in. So, not unusually, I was without an office. I also submerged myself in work because when I called Jill I wanted the new venture consuming my mind.

I first consulted with Stan to find out exactly what he had in mind for this company, and he answered almost every question with a joyous shout: "Growth!" For the next three days, I was on and off the phone with the old man, coming up with the names of those we thought qualified and diligent. Then I began tracking them down. Some of them had gone independent or started their own companies with the new life that had been infused into a dying industry.

I began to understand what Stan had meant with his exultation over size. A lawyer called me from the airport, wanting to meet me at Walker's yard. I met not only him but a steady stream of people who were getting out of two vans that had ferried them from the airport. Some I recognized. The lawyer had done some work for us, as had an accountant, and for some reason Stan's stockbroker was also visiting the scene, but the others were all new faces.

One smiling and overly aggressive man pulled me by the sleeve away from the others as though we had highly important and confidential matters to discuss. We stopped and he turned me, situating me as a photographer might work with an uncooperative child. "Now look at that," he said. "We've got to do something about this. Jesus, man, we're right on the interstate. *Everybody* can see it." He waved his hand as though "it" might be the entire city of Midland and he wanted it remodeled. Or the backdrop of sky needed repainting.

"Who the hell are you?" I asked.

He introduced himself as a public relations specialist on a permanent retainer from Stan. That made sense. His hair looked just like Stan's, long sideburns, bushy sides, styled well down onto his forehead. They had to use the same barber.

And he was probably right. "It," the Walker Drilling yard, was something of a sight. It was partly graveled, partly paved, and it was filled with holes that ranged from small pocks to gorges into which a rig could disappear. The office was a wooden mobile home without windows, and it gave the appearance that the entire business had shut down. The shop, a huge sheet-metal building at the back of the property, was beat up and rusted.

My well-groomed adviser said, "By the way, I need two pictures of you yesterday. One black and white for the papers, a color for the brochure, both five by sevens. And really, you oughta do something about your hair."

"Hey, friend. Two things. First, get fucked; second, why do you need any pictures?"

"We don't have any time to waste. We've got to establish a strong public relations effort before we hit the quiet period because then you can't initiate any new PR efforts. So get me those pictures, and, no, offense, but with a little help, hey, you're Bob Goulet. Leave your hair as it is and you're Old McDonald. Know what I mean?"

I looked at this little guy with the big mouth, and a piece of the puzzle fell into place. Gaines Petroleum was going public and all its debt was going to be retired. Now I knew why Stan had pledged all the revenue from production toward payment of the note.

"Your part's important," he said, tapping me on the arm and making me slap his hand away as a child would have. "William C. Brewster the third, descendant of all those famous and incredibly successful wildcatters. I mean, you've got an ancestor who used to catch those tubs of saltpeter." He threw his hands out, unable to top that feat even in his imagination. "Man, this job's a dream for me. I love this kinda deal."

"It wasn't saltpeter; it was nitro."

"Yeah, whatever, I'm just thinking out loud. This is going to be the most exciting brochure I've ever done. Maybe we oughta get a shot of you standing with one of those torpedo jobbies. Or holding one. No, hell no. Catching it. Yeah, *catching* it."

I walked away from him, visualizing his brochure. The parking lot would be newly paved and striped, filled with Cadillacs and Lincolns and Mercedes. Probably a few tour buses stopping by to see our museum and the one o'clock demonstration of William Brewster III catching nitro as it blows out of the hole. Some midgets selling programs and beautiful blond girl tour guides. Admission reasonable.

I stopped. He'd never answered my question. "Why do you need my picture?"

He shook his head, exasperated by the simpleton before him. "I've got to have a picture of the president."

I wasn't surprised, not to find that I was president and didn't know it, not that I hadn't been told. There were two ways to persuade others —convince them of the wisdom of a course of action in advance; or take the action without any discussion, let events envelop the man who needs to be persuaded, and deal with questions later. Stan was now operating solely on the second method. Maybe it was the least time-consuming, the least likely to require hand-holding. But he was going to have a real problem if he expected me to move to Midland and handle the day-to-day affairs of Gaines Petroleum. I simply wasn't going to do it.

The next person to approach me was Stan's broker. He wanted information on the 30,000-acre lease Gaines was going to develop. This was past bizarre; we'd moved into some other realm. First, Gaines had a president who didn't know he held the position; now the president found out from a stockbroker that he had a 30,000-acre lease to develop. Next, I'd meet a shoe salesman who'd introduce me to the brother I never knew I had.

"I'll get you everything you need on the lease," I said. "By the way, what're you doing out here?"

"We're setting up a drilling fund. You need big bucks to develop a lease that size. I'm trying to come up with a name. You got suggestions? We need a really catchy name, something that people in L.A. can relate to. Every movie star with a dime's going to want in."

A drilling fund? They had more or less fallen by the wayside. Sold in units like mutual funds, they had the potential of bringing in untold amounts of money with skilled marketing, often much more than drilling prospects warranted. They forced the contractor to drill whether he should or not.

"Call it after one of Stan's friends," I said, walking away. "The Insanity Fund."

People were now stopping on the interstate to see what had drawn the crowd in the Walker yard. An accident, maybe. A station wagon stopped on the shoulder emptied its occupants, a load of children who ran across the grass toward the yard.

The only reasonable person in the crowd was a consultant who was to handle the process of picking an investment banking firm and act as a buffer. He and I stood off to one side and watched a highway patrolman stopping to investigate, and we talked about esoteric matters such as assets and liabilities, things that seemed to matter only to him.

I knew what I was going to do. I was going to get in my rental car, collect my brand-new clothes and toiletry items, and Stan and I were going to have a talk. A little mystery was all right, but to find out I was president of Gaines Petroleum from a PR flake who didn't like my hayseed hair was just too much. He couldn't treat William the Third, House of Brewster, in that manner.

It was early evening before I met Stan in a bar near S.M.U., one I'd chosen because it was unlikely to be populated by those seeking an audience with the prophet. It was an old saloon with scarred wooden floors and a long massive bar. I'd been in it once or twice and liked the atmosphere. You could flop down in a chair, stick your feet out, and yawn without anybody calling you Old MacDonald.

Stan arrived wearing a beige suit with a light blue shirt, looking as though he'd been designed by his PR man. And in his case, I couldn't disagree with the need for a new image; nobody needed to look like Abraham Lincoln.

"Hey," he said, spotting me. "How's Gaines Petroleum coming along?"

I gave him a very brief update, willing to spend about as much time keeping him informed as he spent with me. While we talked, we ordered beer, which we drank from the bottles. The bar was in a lull, and the bartender sat on a stool watching TV. I brought the small talk to a close because the morning's travesty was still fresh on my mind.

"Stan, I know there's some good reason you didn't bother telling me I was going to be president of Gaines Petroleum, but I haven't been able to think of what it is. So why don't you tell me?"

He looked surprised. "Who else would be president? Not me. I hardly know the business. And not somebody we don't even know." He shrugged, all but stunned by the need to even discuss the matter. "It's got to be you."

"No, no. You didn't listen to the question. Now think about this, Stan. Listen carefully. I've spent the last few days putting this thing together in my mind, and I knew exactly who I wanted to install as president. I even called him. You remember Roy Massey, worked for the old man? About the time you came to work, the old man helped him get started on his own. And he was doing fairly well until things got so slow he sold his rig to Brewster and went to work for the Western Company. He's been doing real well, moving right up the ladder with them. And what do I do but ask him to think about it, and then this morning I'm being descended on by brokers, lawyers, consultants, people driving down the freeway, the highway patrol, not to mention some little shit who doesn't like my hair." I stood up and leaned over the table, getting as close to his face as I could, because I didn't want him to miss what I was saying. "All these guys knew things I didn't. Now listen to this part, Stan. *Somebody* told the broker about a thirty-thousand-acre lease we've got, *somebody* told the consultant he needed to help with a public offering, *somebody* told this obnoxious PR man I was the president. Somebody had to tell them because they knew all these things. They knew and I didn't. Because nobody ever told me a goddamn thing, Stan. Not a goddamn thing."

I was breathing hard, getting excited, letting loose ten years' worth of frustration with the way Stanley Gaines operated. A few days ago, I'd been certain I was leaving his employment for all the reasons that now had me panting and squinting, and instead I was trying to do the impossible, planning for a man who didn't understand the concept implied by the word *plan*.

He laughed as though I was putting on a show for him, as though I'd gone all out to provide the evening's entertainment. "I never thought about it that way, but you're great, Billy Boy, you really are. You could pull off anything. Absolutely, you can handle anything that comes along. You just don't know how nervous I was when we were in Abilene and I asked if you were staying with your father or coming with me. I've hardly got time to breathe anymore, and I can't take the time to explain every little—"

Sitting back down, wondering why I'd bothered to call this meeting, I cut him off with a horizontal wave of my hand, slicing the air. "Stan, am I wrong when I remember being in the same plane with you flying to Abilene, then to Midland? That was you, wasn't it? You're telling me you didn't have time to tell me when we were on the plane?"

He threw his hands outward. "I did tell you. We talked about it before we got to Midland. Hey, you're putting the thing together. If you want to be president, be president. If you want Massey, hire him. This is your baby. And I can't tell you what I don't know. That lease is a farm-out from Exxon. I didn't even know about it until I got back here. And, hey, I'm serious. This is your deal. You won't get any interference from me. If you think Donald Duck would make a good drilling superintendent, hire him. Go to it."

I shook my head and sat back, taking a long drink of beer. Stan seemed to imitate, in some part, those around him, and he'd learned to communicate from Boomer. Never listen to the question, and if you do by mistake hear what was asked, answer some other question. And, most important, treat logic with the disrespect it deserves.

Stan, thinking I was relaxing, sat back as well and crossed his legs, turning toward the door so he could watch the pedestrian traffic. "This is great, isn't it? Just kicking back for a few minutes. By the way, Sally Ann changed her mind about getting involved with the new company. She came back the day after we went out there. I guess it didn't suit her." He gave me a focused look. "How'd she seem to you? Happy?"

I shrugged. "If she has what she wants, she's happy, and I think she's got everything she wants. I didn't hear any complaints."

He gave me a slight nod as though my opinion was just one among several hundred thousand he'd be taking under advisement. It was the same attitude I'd seen him take with Junior, the hope and fear of being exceeded.

"Take a few days off and go on a vacation, Stan. Take Sally Ann somewhere for a few days."

"I may do that. I'll tell you one thing. Old Charlie never told me there'd be so much pressure involved in success. Jesus, Billy, I never have time to even slow down anymore. Back in the beginning, I'd sit down every once in a while and think about what I'd done, and, hey, it felt good. I felt good. Plaza North One. Sometimes I'd go out and just sit in the car, open both doors and let the breeze blow through. I'd sit out there and look at the building and maybe even take a nap. Hell, if I sit down anymore, man, I'm wasting time. I *can't* sit down. The more I do, the more I feel like I've got to do. I've got to keep making bigger and bigger deals, and it's hard keeping up.

"You know, this all started out pretty simple. Charlie showed me, in this world, anything can happen. The people you're closest to can just up and die. And you can sit back and wait for the worst, or you can do anything you want. It just depends on how you see it. If anything can happen, that can be good as well as bad. Your best friend can die, you can build the biggest building in Dallas. I mean, I know that doesn't make any sense, but that's the way it works."

It made much more sense than he knew, I thought. I'd bet almost anything that if I called Abilene and asked if they'd ever had a policeman named Jay Sannier, who had died while Stanley Gaines was in Laos, say from 1962 to 1964, I'd bet anything the answer would be yes. Charlie Insanity had never existed. He'd been a mysterious combination of Charles N. Gaines, father of the tycoon, and Jay Sannier, a stranger who had taken time to teach Stan something when he'd found him out roaming the streets at three in the morning.

"What're you after, Stan? What're you chasing?"

"I don't know anymore, I really don't. When I started, I wanted people in Abilene to know I'd made it, I wasn't poor anymore, I'd done something. But now, it beats the hell out of me. I keep thinking, when the tower's finished, I'll quit chasing after these bigger and bigger deals, and then before you know it, I'm thinking, no, the tower's really not that big a deal. There're God knows how many buildings in the country bigger. I'll build one even bigger than that. I'll move into New York, where the big hitters are. But you know what? Once I got there, I'd think, no,

187

I've got to go international. I want London and Tokyo. So you tell me—what the hell am I chasing? Because I don't know."

He shook his head, surprising even himself by how much he'd said and how frantic it all sounded. And I thought, for the first time ever, I'm close to the real Stanley Gaines. He's under that hair spray and cologne somewhere. Still, there was something basically incredible about the conversation. Here was a guy who had done unbelievably well, whose company was managing five office buildings, had seventeen projects under way, including the Toothache Tower, which was going to be taller than the Canadians' by at least sixteen inches. He was involved in a large oil-field venture, was the subject of periodic news stories in a major Texas city, and he didn't know why he was chasing the carrot. I wasn't sure what I'd expected him to say when I'd asked that question, but it hadn't been "You tell me" because he didn't know. But then, what had I expected? Philosophy from Stanley Gaines? He'd never been high on introspection, or thought of any kind. He was a doer.

"So you recommend a vacation, huh? You know, you may be right. I bought into a condo on South Padre Island a few years ago and I've never even seen it. Why don't we go down there, see what it looks like."

I sat up, as alert as a wounded rabbit. A vacation with Sally Ann while Jill and Stan were around? "We?"

"Sure, let's all go. Hell, we deserve a vacation."

"Well, let me check with Jill," I said, thinking it was time I got out of the presence of Stanley Gaines. This was all getting too complicated. I had to worry about both Stan and Jill, although Stan was only a worry for what he'd do, what position he'd place me in. I could have said, "Yeah, the other night while I was wrapped around your wife like a spool of wire," and he'd have said, "I made some money on wire the other day. Did I tell you?"

We walked out together into a very pleasant summer evening and stood for a moment in front of the saloon, facing downtown, which was beyond some large oak trees across the street.

"You know," he said, "if it wasn't for those trees, I bet we could see the tower."

"Hell, Stan. Call the city and have them cut those things down."

He started to agree—yeah, that's a good idea—but realized I was joking. He gave me a sly, understanding grin and said, "Yeah, we need to go to South Padre."

•   •   •

I drove home, feeling the need for a buzz I hadn't acquired in the bar, something that would get me into the presence of my wife. I turned on a local news station to get my mind off Sally Ann, off joint vacations, off the prospect of getting her back to Midland alone, but all I got was bad news from the radio. The big oil companies had announced their first-quarter profits for 1974, and they'd probably incite riots. Texaco was up 123 percent over first quarter 1973, and Exxon, apparently sandbagging, had announced a mere 39 percent increase. They'd been accused of creative bookkeeping to hide the truth, which was supposed to be 118 percent. The Federal Energy Office was accusing them of having gouged the public during the embargo, and the House Ways and Means Committee was already drafting punitive legislation. There was some demand to repeal the depletion allowance, which had already been reduced to 22 percent, and the committee was working on a tax to take care of excessive profits. No way, I thought, was I going to tell my neighbors I was now president of Gaines Petroleum. They'd firebomb my house.

I walked into my suburban home and saw my three-year-old son, his tanned little body clad only in shorts, give me the sign for grasshopper, an expanding, hopping hand that bounced all over the room. He'd become a constant stalker of the little bugs and spent most of the day proving to his friends they did indeed spit tobacco.

Jill walked into the living room as I dropped my new luggage to give Robert a hug. She was dressed in a lime green pantsuit and she stood several feet away from us, making sure that if I wanted to hug or kiss her, I'd have to come to her. I didn't. I picked up my brand-new suitcase and took it to the bedroom.

"Did you get everything done?" she asked.

Right, I wanted to say. I put together a multimillion-dollar company in three days. I inventoried rigs that were still all over west Texas. Sure, I got everything done. Instead I said, "No, there's a lot involved."

Returning to the living room, I was accosted by a nearly naked boy and pushed toward the couch.

"He wants to show you his new grasshoppers," Jill said.

"I know what he wants."

"Well, I'm sorry I opened my mouth."

Robert went running after his jars of grasshoppers and I looked at my wife, who stood sullenly across the room, and I thought, dang, she's been screwing that old man. I couldn't remember his name, but he was a patron of the amateur theater company Jill was working with, and I'd learned she'd been to his house at least once. He was probably retire-ment age, very wealthy, and just oh, so sweet.

How was it I could be married to this woman and know so little about her? I wanted to say, "Sit down and tell me how your life's going," had in fact spoken those words to her before, and her answer was always the same. Oh, just fine. She may have talked to someone, but she'd never told me anything.

"I'm now president of Gaines Petroleum."

That got her attention. She crossed the room and sat on the other end of the couch. She was pretty, and the contrast of lime green clothes and light brown hair was an attractive one. It wasn't black and blond, but she'd undoubtedly catch the eye of an old man who supposedly threw parties for the theater company, which were somehow attended only by one woman.

"Are you getting a raise?" she asked.

"No, I told Stan since we were just starting out, I didn't want a salary at all. We're going to have to sell the house and move to a one-room apartment. We'll be so poor we'll have to give Robert to a rich family."

She stuck her tongue in her cheek, making a protrusion, and then bit it, obviously mad. "Why can't you just answer the question?"

"Why don't you ask a question worth answering?"

Robert returned with two jars that had formerly been used for the storage of peanut butter and were now the homes of several grasshop-pers. He offered me the captured insects. They were grasshoppers all right, dull-eyed with long hinged legs.

Robert pursed his lips and started to spit.

Jill covered his mouth, preventing the execution of the sign, and said, "He wants you to know they can spit."

"Do you remember, this is my son and I talk to him all the time. I know what the sign for spit is. He spit all over my hand the other night showing me."

"Well, I'm *so* sorry."

I looked at Robert, who was leaning against my leg. "What's the sign for 'I'm *so* sorry'?"

He slumped on my leg as though exhausted and unable to hold him-self up, giving me the penitent face of a puppy dog, its bottom lip stuck out, making a sorrowful whining noise as he did.

"Hey, that's good. How about the sign for Mama. You got one for that?"

He went spinning off across the room, his arms flopping, his head bobbing as though he'd been possessed by a voodoo god. For a moment he stood in one spot and shook all over before collapsing in a heap on the carpet. For several seconds he didn't move.

"Damn," I said. "He's got it exactly."

14

It was, I supposed, a tribute to Stan's energy and perpetual motion that we still had the two-person office in north Dallas. He'd never taken the space in the Southland Life Building downtown, and the corner office of Plaza North One, which he'd shown me in the steel skeleton stage before we'd moved to Dallas, had been leased to a land developer. And so the receptionist of Brewster-Gaines Properties had never seen Stan. After showing me the office on New Year's Day in 1971, he'd never returned. The receptionist had seen Stan's picture in the paper but never the living item.

Before I returned to Midland, I went by the office to check the mail. No one other than the receptionist or I ever looked at it. Stan was all over the city, often all over the country, almost always available on a mobile phone when he was in the area, but he wasn't any more centralized than our business was. We had two employees but a horde of partners, leasing agents, and contractors, and our records were scattered all over town. I'd given up trying to organize it all. I couldn't even get Stan to look at the mail when I was gone. He trusted the receptionist to determine what was important and to call him if necessary.

After looking over several days' worth of mail, I closed my office door and called Sally Ann. She didn't answer, of course. She never answered. A maid or babysitter was charged with that responsibility.

When I got her on the phone, I said, "Mrs. Gaines, this is Maxmillian Smell, gossip columnist for the Dallas *Morning News*. Tell me, dear, is it true you've acquired the nickname One Garment Gaines, for your, shall we say, propensity to wear nothing but a dress? Is that true?"

"Yes, I admit it. I have a very dear friend who likes wearing nothing but a smile and I *hate* to overdress. You know what I mean, Max?"

"Oh, yes, I do, I do. Sweetheart, tell me, if I was going to be in Midland tonight, would I catch your act out there?"

"Well, ordinarily, I'd say yes, but something's happening here I can't miss. My husband and I are shopping tonight. You see, there's a sale on congressmen, and we're going to buy one." She switched gears, going sexy, sultry, quiet. "But, Max. If you were in Midland tomorrow morning, oh, Max, what you could see right there in the hotel. Because I could be there before lunch. And I could order the whipped cream when I checked in."

"The large size?"

"Super Jumbo."

I went to Midland while Sally Ann went shopping for congressmen. The red Lear jet was making numerous trips between Dallas and Washington in an attempt to limit the damage done to the industry because of unbelievably higher gasoline prices. The Gaineses gave great parties, peopled with minor celebrities and stars. Of course, the parties served a dual purpose. When the stars showed up, Stan's broker could now sell them on the drilling fund.

I drove to the airport in high spirits, singing with the radio, in possession of that constitutional right guaranteed all Americans—something to look forward to. What would life be without something to look forward to? Intolerably boring? Would we all be suicidal? Life at times seemed one long intermission between birth and death, time to fill up the best way you knew how. Shopping for congressmen was one way to pass the time, but a futile one. The oil-producing states were outnumbered forty to ten and we'd always lose.

Walker had finally vacated his office, and I was working with my new drilling superintendent in an attempt to find tool pushers. Once we'd hired those who supervised the rigs, I was getting out of the personnel business. We'd discouraged the Walker employees from believing they'd have continued employment with Gaines; they'd worked too long for a shoddy operation. And since the word was out, we were experiencing the consequences. They were granting themselves severance pay in the form of hard-to-find equipment, which was growing more and more valuable as the demand far exceeded the supply. The only employee I would have retained was the one who'd climbed the fence one night to leave us this message on the outer office wall in black paint—"Gaines is to the oil patch what VD is to sex."

The president's office was too small for all those who tried to occupy it. The consultant who was coordinating the process of going public was there, as were the omnipresent PR flake and several accountants. The consultant was somewhat frustrated because he wanted specific capital requirements from Stan, and Stan had told him that was his job. Figure it out. So we pored over contracts and books and talked as we did.

"You know," he said, tapping his pen on the desk. "These new issues don't go over like they did in the sixties."

I nodded.

"But we can wipe out the debt on a company that's capable of drilling a hundred seventy-five wells a year and generating twenty-five million a year just on drilling operations."

I nodded.

Part of his problem was finding small drilling contractors among public corporations for comparisons on receipts, returns on equity, earnings per share, and a number of other points on which he needed figures.

"You know," the consultant said, "I don't think Stan knows how tough investment analysts are."

"You're right," I said, pointing at Stan's twin, the PR man. "That's why *he's* here."

He was carrying a phone around the room, having supplied a lengthy cord for it, and was talking to every newspaper in the country, telling the same story over and over, repeating it until I was having trouble remembering the actual facts. "A lot of people don't know Stan Gaines got his start in the oil business. They just know him as undisputed king of the real estate deal. But when he got out of the army—Green Berets in Vietnam, wasn't it—he went to work for Brewster Drilling. That's B-r-e-w-s-t-e-r. And by the end of his first day, he'd put together a deal that people in Abilene are still talking about. For the first twenty-four hours after he went to work, he searched over three counties for exactly the right spot to drill and finally found it down in Coleman County. That was ten years ago and the well's still producing. First shot, a million dollars in oil.

"What a lot of people also don't know is that William C. Brewster the third pointed him toward that first deal, and it's been pure magic ever since. In the past ten years, they haven't had a losing proposition, not a one. And why not? We're talking about the grandson of Willie Brewster, the old Indian fighter and wildcatter. There's stories about him you wouldn't begin to believe. He's the Paul Bunyan of the oil field. I've heard stories of him fighting the Indians with one hand and drilling with the other.

"So what we're talking about here is a winning combination, two young men who don't know how to lose. I heard one of the old-timers out here the other day say, 'Them's the luckiest two sumbitches I *ever* saw.'"

I would have stuck around to listen to my many accomplishments but Sally Ann should have arrived at the hotel by now, and there was one person I was interested in more than the legendary grandson of the Paul Bunyan of the oil field.

I must have been legendary myself because I was doing something even I couldn't believe—running off as though I were eighteen and unattached, as happy and excited over the prospect of seeing her as I had been fifteen years ago. And the closer I got to the hotel, the more certain I was that I didn't even need a car; I was capable of flying. I could take wing and land on the windowsill outside her room.

When I arrived at the room, she was wearing a sheet. She'd opened all the drapes along the outer wall of windows, giving the room a day-time look I didn't usually associate with hotel rooms, an atmosphere that seemed that much more wicked and delightful.

She threw her sheet off and said, "One Garment Gaines returns in the altogether."

I picked her up and threw her naked body onto the bed, then fell down beside her. She'd cut her hair short and I messed it up. I loved rubbing her scalp. She rolled me over onto my back and then mounted me, sitting on my stomach. She leaned down and kissed me while un-buttoning my shirt.

"Do you know how much I like playing with you?" she asked.

I looked up at her, at the swelling bottom sides of her breasts, sweep-ing up to the nipples. And she was right; she did like playing with me. Her nipples said so. I had to touch them; I covered them with my hands.

"Guess what?" she said. "We're taking a vacation together. And Stan said it was all your idea." She moved to sit beside me so she could work on my pants. "It's going to be wonderful. Dangerous. Exciting. We can make love in the bathroom standing up while Jill and Stan wash dishes. Just think about it. We'll all go to the beach and then you and I can sneak back into the dunes and watch them build a sand castle or some-thing while we just screw our brains out. Are we going to have fun or what?"

I wasn't even going to think about it at the present. She pulled my shoes off and absently threw them over her shoulder.

"Stan had me get him a prescription for Valium. You know why? We're going to be there two whole days. Two whole days! He doesn't think he can make it."

I sat up and she removed my shirt, throwing it as carelessly as she had everything else. I'd heard of bright-eyed people, and she now qualified

194

for the category, as excited as a thrill-seeker going after great white sharks. She could smell the potential of this vacation. The Voice of Morality was issuing a stern warning: tell her now you'll never go on any such vacation. But the VOM was dealing with a part of me that would have sat on an ice cube while I was nude. It was that part of me that thought I could fly to the hotel, that part that had enjoyed listening to the PR man spin yarns for the newspapers. Besides, it all made a crazy kind of sense. We lived in an insane world and had to adapt. We each had to listen to our own Charlie Insanity, go after bigger and bigger deals. The ultimate orgasm was out there somewhere; all we had to do was find it, claim it as our own.

"You and I are taking an early vacation," she said, running her hand up and down my stomach and chest. "We're not leaving this room until my plane leaves tomorrow night. We're going to stay right here on this bed until we're so exhausted we'll have to stand up and rest. When you leave here, you'll weigh less than a hundred and have an extremely sore throat."

We embraced, both on our knees in the middle of the bed, and kissed. She kissed me so hard I thought she'd drawn blood.

"Let's move the bed over to the window," I said. "I want to make love in front of the whole world."

"Oh, yeah, that's good," she said.

But the bed wouldn't move. It was either built in to the floor or bolted down. So I leaped back onto the bed and lay on my back, ready for a thorough ravishing. She again sat on my stomach, this time wiggling, pressing dampness against me.

"How loud can you scream?" she asked.

I remained as president of Gaines Petroleum because I was having so much fun performing as the legendary grandson of Wild Willie Brewster, but managed to lure my father's old drilling superintendent away from the Western Company as chief executive officer. He ran the show in Midland and I was a celebrity in Dallas. I couldn't believe the number of people who swallowed all the crap the PR man was cranking out. And some of it I only heard about third-hand. "I didn't know your grandfather taught Teddy Roosevelt how to shoot a rifle." Some were purely rumor, and I wasn't sure about the source for those. I was for a brief period of time linked romantically with Tuesday Weld, a rumor I laughed off with the comment, "Nah, she's too old for me." I did shortly thereafter get my hair styled, though, thinking I could do better than Tuesday

Weld. I also read in the paper once that I'd been in Vietnam on direct orders from the president, engaged in matters that couldn't be fully discussed yet, a rather elaborate statement that could have been made about anyone. But the PR man limited it: "The president, a fellow Texan, knew him more formally as William."

Now my name was magical. Oil, discovery, success, riches, they all added up to Brewster. The name had always been respected in west Texas as the symbol of hard honest work in the oil field, but now it became associated with the mysterious, the esoteric. I communed with St. Dino. People began calling our office and asking not for Stan but for Billy Brewster. They wanted a lead on a "good deal in the oil business."

I began casting a critical eye on the prospects we were drilling. The first was near Ozona and was a dry hole. It didn't matter that we were simply the contractor and got paid regardless, that we had no interest whatsoever in the well, that we had indeed drilled in a professional and competent manner. I didn't like being involved in these ventures that would end up in a newspaper column headed, "Area Dusters." This was conduct unbecoming the luckiest sumbitches in the world. We should be telling people when they were throwing money away.

Like Stan, I was now carrying a money clip fat with hundreds because, as Stan said, "People want to see your cash." I sent my press clippings to my mother with a cautionary note: "Don't believe *all* of this." I was a very gracious star, of course, one with time to speak to those who called seeking my counsel. But I was also an impatient one; I'd never liked rude store clerks or waitresses, and they now drew the frequent demand, "Let me speak to the manager."

I also began to appreciate some of the pressure on Stan to surprise, amaze, succeed. One of his investors, a plastic surgeon with an unlimited amount of money—his own as well as his family's—behind him, liked Stan's style. The doctor understood a brassy manner; he had pictures of his own delicate and skilled hands decorating the walls of his office. And the doctor, who had literally millions involved in Gaines Petroleum, was quoted in the newspaper as saying, "Some people just don't fail. It's not within them. And Stan's one of those people."

Our joint vacation was delayed several times, but in August we boarded the red Lear jet and ferried two three-year-old boys to their grandparents in Abilene and then headed for South Padre Island, a destination which I now questioned. Why did we want to take a vacation some place where no one would recognize us? We'd be ants again.

I did hope our PR man wrote a good news release. "The Billy Brewsters and Stan Gaineses jetted off to South Padre Island for a well-deserved few days of rest. The husbands have been toiling like slaves to make a success of their latest multimillion-dollar venture, Gaines Petroleum. The word is that only Billy (as he is called by seven of the nine Supreme Court justices) can make it work."

We sat facing each other in the plane, turned toward the aisle, and sipped martinis made by that old tycoon himself, Stan Gaines. My wife had just committed her most daring deed—she'd worn an orange sunsuit without a bra. I'd been suggesting that with our notoriety, she needed to loosen up, and her bra should be the first item of old conventionality to go.

This trip had more than the simple air of a vacation about it. It promised more wickedness than the Old Testament. I felt like a kid on his way to view, for the first time, a skin flick, a kid who'd been so lucky as to persuade the best-looking girls in school to accompany him. No telling what they'd do when the lights went out.

Stan lifted his glass in this compressed tube shooting through the sky and said, "One big happy family. This is great. Absolutely."

He was the ignorant father of this happy incestuous family, and everything was happening off away from him. He watched through a haze.

I asked Sally Ann, "How many Valium did he take?"

"Quaaludes. He decided Valium was for old women."

"Vitamin Q," he said with the same goofy smile. "Anybody need another drink?"

Stan, pouring in slow motion, refilled my glass, and as he did, I tried figuring out why Jill looked different. In her orange outfit, she sat directly across the aisle from me, legs crossed, bent forward with her elbow on her knees, and the loose neck of the sunsuit gave partial exposure to lovely brown breasts.

"Here you go, old buddy," Stan hollered as if I were a hundred yards away.

I made a megaphone with my hand and yelled, "Thanks," accepting the glass.

"We could be one big happy family," Sally Ann said, looking at me. "And sleep together. Jill and Stan and Sally and Billy." She wore bright green shorts and a matching top, one that was almost silky, and she was almost as tanned as Jill. But when she bent over and the top fell away, it revealed breasts that had been protected from the sun. They were creamy white.

And *that* told me what was different about Jill. Her breasts were brown.

197

She'd been sunbathing *in the nude.* Or at least topless. The realization made my hand go numb and I dropped my drink. Fortunately for me, the glass landed upright, didn't fall over, and only a little was jostled out. As I bent forward to pick up the glass, I whispered a question to my wife. "Have you been sunbathing in the nude?"

She gave me a mysterious shrug and sipped her drink.

Sally Ann said, "No secrets in this family. What're you talking about?"

"We're talking about brown boobs. My wife has brown boobs. She's been sunbathing in the nude."

This revelation would have embarrassed her to tears at one time; today it made her proud. She sat up straight and looked out the window opposite her as though she were beneath this kind of speculation and innuendo. And I thought, damn, she threw her bra away a long time ago. The only time she wore one was around me.

Stan gave a one-syllable laugh and then smiled as benignly as a monk would.

"Have you got a tan line anywhere?" I asked.

She gave me the smile again, and I knew what she'd been doing. She and Robert had allegedly been going to the home of her old friend, the rich patron of the theater company, to swim, an innocent-sounding outing for mother and son. The son hadn't been going. He'd mentioned the other day that he'd accompanied a friend to the zoo, and I'd said, "I thought you went swimming." "No," he'd said. He'd been to the zoo. I'd forgotten that exchange until now, and obviously I shouldn't have.

So, I thought. We had a modern marriage, an open marriage, and there was only one thing to do. "Sally Ann's right. We ought to all sleep together."

Just saying it shot a bolt of adrenaline into my loins, and I downed my martini. Sally Ann and I'd sleep in the middle, and Jill could hang onto my backside if she was able to hold on.

"In what order?" the brown-breasted stranger asked.

"What is this, the peace talks?" I asked. "If we have to negotiate, forget it. We'll just choose up sides."

"I think we ought to get the Cowboy cheerleaders for the road show," Stan said.

We all turned to look at him. We were talking about sex and he was thinking about business. The road show was the only acceptable new public relations effort the SEC would allow a business going public to mount during the quiet period. Theoretically, sales of the new issue were promoted only by the prospectus.

"Or maybe we could get Jill to appear in the nude. We could find out if she has tan lines *anywhere*," I said.

"I do, I do," she said, making a small offering to prepare me for her refusal to sleep as one big happy family.

"Yeah? We'll see."

The condo in which Stan owned an interest was plush, right on the beach, and was built around a four-tiered swimming pool, each emptying like a waterfall into the pool below it, and at the bottom was an Olympic-sized pool. Our unit opened onto a deck by the third-floor pool, and I could see the waterfall just beyond the sliding glass doors of the den. We had four bedrooms, four baths, and thick carpet the color of chocolate to hide the oil tracked in from the beach, oil that floated in on the tides from offshore drilling platforms.

I sat beside the pool, feet dangling in water, between Sally Ann and Jill. My wife, obviously concerned about the lack of tan lines on her body, had put on her pink two-piece suit in a bathroom away from my examining eyes. Sally Ann, sitting on my right, wore an authentic bikini, black and green, the colors flipping, twisting, pulling my eyes in. And Stan, needing movement even when he was zonked, was off trying to get recommendations on local restaurants.

The water overflowed the pool above us, crashing into ours, and it gave the impression that we were sitting beside a waterfall. It also kept the water in a constant turmoil, and Sally Ann had used the cover of this boiling surface to hook my right leg with her left foot. She was using her right foot to massage mine.

This reminded me of a sensation I'd had several times before, most often when I'd looked at the steel structure of Toothache Tower and closed my eyes and imagined that I was walking one of the uppermost beams. I'd stand on one foot and teeter, fifty-five stories above the tiny cars below. I'd pirouette, landing on my toes. And the feeling of lightness in my stomach would infuse my loins with that same titillation, giving me an erection. Which is what I was now experiencing, feeling the sole of Sally Ann's foot rubbing mine.

"Where's Stan?" Jill asked.

"Looking for a place to eat," I said.

"Why don't we just eat here?" Sally Ann asked, scraping the outer side of my foot with her toenails. "We can just choose up sides."

She had that look again, probably the same look the boys in Pamplona had before the bulls were turned loose. Her eyes were black liquid but still focused. She wanted to dance with me on the beams that would form the roof of a fifty-five-story building. I leaned backward as though propping myself on both hands, but with my right I touched the pants of her bikini. Then, with my forefinger, I pulled them down onto her right cheek.

"I think Jill might find Stan rather tasty," Sally Ann said.

"No," I said. "Stan's just aged. She likes meat that's about to rot. Something seventy or eighty years old."

I'd managed to pull the bottom of Sally Ann's bikini down all the way across her ass, and she'd decided to attack on two fronts, just like the Germans. So as she tried to pull my foot upward so she could slice the sole with her toenails, she also returned my pants-pulling favor. Her left hand slid between my back and the waistband, and she was attempting to force it outward and down at the same time.

"I only know one older man," Jill said, "and he's very, very sweet."

"The sweeter the meat," I said, "the closer the rot."

Jill was sitting as I was, hands back to prop herself up, and she decided to swat me. She did, right on the butt, but she hit Sally Ann's hand.

"Ow," Sally Ann said.

Jill was momentarily confused. She'd hit me but Sally Ann had protested. Leaning back to investigate, she saw a foreign hand that had succeeded in partly stripping me, had revealed white cheeks which rested on the deck around the pool, and the hand had partly worked its way under one of those cheeks. Worse, looking beyond her husband, she saw other cheeks shining at her.

"Good God!" she said.

"It's not what it seems," my bright-eyed friend said. "It's better than that."

Jill hopped up and left wet footprints to the sliding glass doors, which we'd left open. She didn't stop to dry her feet once she was inside, and she took a hard left toward the bedroom, disappearing into the luxury condo.

My brain befogged by several martinis, I was content to let her go and to sit half bare-assed by the pool, my leg entangled with Sally Ann's. But then it hit me—she was leaving. She was leaving and what would she do when she returned to Dallas? Take Robert and . . .

I disentangled myself and got up, pulling my swimming trunks up, following her inside. She'd suddenly lost her modesty; in the bedroom she stood naked —without the hint of a tan line—staring into her suitcase and obviously trying to decide what to wear. She was exceedingly angry but not so angry her mind had quit working. She was reviewing her options, trying to decide how she'd look in this particular outfit if the plane was hijacked to Cuba and she appeared on the evening news.

"Don't tell me what she was doing," she said, "because I know. She was looking for the perfect asshole and she found it. She found it. I found it, but I wish I'd given it back. I've been putting up with you two for—oh, God, it's been years and years. *Years.* And I'm *through*," she said, giving *through* an extra syllable, accenting the second as she grabbed panties and bra from the suitcase. She jammed one leg into the panties.

Stan chose that moment to return from his search for a restaurant recommendation. He entered the apartment in slow motion, hands in the pockets of dark blue shorts, his legs as white as the refrigerator in the kitchen. Spotting me standing in the bedroom, he gave me a nod of recognition and headed my way. "I thought of something better than the Cowboy cheerleaders," he said. "Let's take a drilling rig with . . ." He stopped when he saw Jill hooking her bra.

"Tell him why I'm leaving," Jill said. "Go ahead and tell him."

"You don't have to leave just because you don't have clothes," he said. "We can go get you some."

"Give us a minute here, Stan," I said, escorting him a few feet into the den and leaving him there unattended.

"I think that'd be a great idea because—" he was saying.

"Outstanding, Stan. That's great." I returned to the bedroom and closed the door behind me.

Jill couldn't decide what to wear. I turned her, my hands gripping her shoulders hard enough so that she'd understand I wasn't playing games with her, and shoved her into a sitting position on the bed. "I want you to understand something. You will never, and I mean *never* take Robert away from me. You won't because I won't let you under *any* circumstances. Don't even think about it."

This was how it felt to fall when you were dancing on the beam. One moment you were impervious, immortal, balanced on your toes, unable to do any wrong, and then you fell. And the sensation was a completely different one. It was nauseatingly abrupt.

"This is what we're doing whether you like it or not. We're going back to Abilene and I'm going back to work for my old man. What you do after we get there is up to you; I don't care. But you're not taking Robert *anywhere*. If you want to fuck every senior citizen in the city, you can. You can live wherever you want, with Robert and me, or someplace else, I literally do not care. Now put some clothes on because we're leaving."

This is what happened when you got away from what made you the individual you were, I thought. Life was screwed up enough without getting further assistance from me. Stan was on Vitamin Q because he couldn't slow down even though he didn't know why he was going so fast or even where he was going. I'd been in dreamland, playing the leading role in the fantasy of my life story, and Sally Ann had convinced me I wanted to screw standing up in the bathroom while my wife and friend washed the dishes twenty feet away. The ship of Gaines Petroleum had set sail on a sea of hype, and as far as I could determine, nothing I'd done in the past years made any sense at all. Nothing made sense because the president had resigned in disgrace, the Vietnamese were killing each other in record numbers, and the Cambodians were slaughtering their own. Nothing made sense in this absurd flow of events except one very small thing, one process I witnessed every day—the continuing evolvement of Robert William Brewster as a person. That was the only thing, that one innocent soul in this absurd world.

If Jill had other plans, she didn't specify them as I walked from the room. I was glad she didn't; I didn't want my resolve tested at the moment.

Stan had dutifully remained in the spot on which I'd left him a moment ago, and when he saw me, he said, "A lot of people haven't ever seen a drilling rig."

"Hold that thought, Stan," I said, crossing the rather large room to a telephone on the bar. There was a directory beneath the phone, and I started looking in the yellow pages for a cab, but then I realized I didn't know where we were. "What's the address here?"

"You gonna order supper?"

"No, Stan, we're leaving. I'm calling a cab. What's the address?"

"Hey," he said, approaching the bar. "Do what I did. Take one of these." He pulled his hand from his pocket and dropped a number of white pills on the beige formica. They rolled in every direction. "The guy told me to take five hundred, but I think he was probably joking."

"Stanley Gaines!" Sally Ann shouted, entering the doorway that led to the pool. "He told you to take *a* five-hundred. That's the size of the pill. How many have you taken?"

She grabbed his hand as she would have a child's, demanding to see if he was holding any back. And I could tell by looking at her that she'd fallen from the beam as well. Her eyes had gone flat.

Stan shrugged. "I don't know. Three, I think."

"My God in heaven," she said, scooping the tablets from the bar into her opened hand.

Stan, determined to finish his spiel, said, "Instead of a—" He flipped his fingers outward as though trying to dislodge a word that was stuck. "Instead of a, a kelly—that's it, a kelly—we can have a giant roman candle that'll shoot right up through the crown. We'll use that for the big finelly. The big *finale*. You know what I mean, the last thing."

Sally Ann leaned on the counter, looking at her handful of Quaaludes. "I've got a better idea. Let's just all go home."

Jill, who had entered the room and was standing somewhere behind me, said, "That's the first decent idea *you've* ever had."

"Shut up, bimbo, or you'll be walking." She looked at me and asked, "Is that what you want to do?"

I nodded. There was one other person here I knew, and it wasn't the man I worked for or the woman I had married. It was my oldest friend, who may or may not have realized we'd screwed up. Whether she did or not, she was going to cooperate with me and that was all that mattered. She'd known since we were children that our appetites had never matched; she wanted more than I did. She always had.

She pulled Stan by the arm toward the bedroom they'd chosen earlier. "Come on, Stan. Get your suitcase."

He looked at her, squinting one eye. "Has it been two days already?"

1 9 8 1

15

I could see Stan's car in the parking lot of the small motel, but I couldn't turn across the highway and get into the lot. His white Cadillac was surrounded by white Fords with the Gaines logo on the doors, and I counted them while waiting for an armada of oil-field trucks to pass, a fleet moving a rig, carrying mud pumps and substructure and sections of the derrick, followed by more rumbling trucks hauling tanks and dog houses.

The small town of Giddings had been turned upside down. What had been little more than a crossroads community of less than 3,000 people had suddenly expanded to the capital city of a geological formation called the Austin Chalk. And although the little town wouldn't have impressed Boomer, it was the closest thing I'd seen to an authentic boomtown. Stan was staying in one of the few actual motels in town, able to get a room only because he'd been willing to pay $1,000 a month for what usually cost $12 a night. People were sleeping in cars and campers, and one enterprising citizen had turned oil-field tanks into makeshift motel rooms. The town was overflowing with people searching for the honey-colored crude oil that lay within the chalk.

I had business with Stan that could have been transacted in Abilene or Dallas, but I'd come to Giddings just to see what was happening to the town. It was becoming known for rampant inflation, numerous wrecks, and extensive oil-field theft. Apparently a few hookers had tried to set up shop to service the transients, only to be run out of town by the sheriff, an act that would have certainly disappointed Boomer.

Stan had shown the world he'd been serious about growth. Since the company had gone public, the stock had gone from its original issue price of $13.50 a share to $76, and although Stan had eighty-two rigs, he wanted an even hundred. And Brewster Drilling had eighteen rigs, all of which Stan coveted.

The industry was supercharged, once again courtesy of the crazy politics of the Middle East. For sixty-eight days in early 1979, the second-largest OPEC producer had been shut down. The Iranian revolution had deprived the world of 5.5 million barrels of oil a day and given motorists long gas lines again, not to mention an incredible price for oil. Buyers were paying $40 a barrel. And when the revolution succeeded and Iran again started producing and exporting oil, the cartel again proved Stanley Gaines was right—people who didn't mind killing one another could be united by one thing: greed. In the spring of 1980, when a modest surplus of crude oil developed, OPEC reduced production to keep the price high.

Forty-dollar oil had brought more people into the business than it had ever seen. In Abilene, everybody was getting into the oil business. One day a man was coaching high school kids and the next he was performing some function in the oil business. I could hardly drive around town without being run over by a truck, very often one of ours, or by a brand-new tycoon driving a Mercedes and wearing a Rolex.

We couldn't keep experienced employees because they kept running off to better-paying jobs or starting their own businesses. Our drillers could hardly start a tour with a crew intact, and they were calling cafes and bars and asking the person who answered the phone to poll the crowd—did anybody need a job? We were getting accident reports on employees who were getting mangled because they didn't know what they were doing. Or because they were drunk. Or stoned. Or the driller called the office to report that an employee, whose name nobody knew but he might have gone by Spider, had been hurt the previous night and may have gone to the doctor. Or returned to Michigan. Or something.

Brewster Drilling, of which I was now 60 percent owner, had peaked at drilling four hundred wells a year with our eighteen rigs, and although we had operators and producers calling us daily, begging us to drill, we couldn't get to them all. Rigs were being built as fast as welders could get them assembled. The incredible optimism was tempered, in my case, by my old man, who'd seen too many cycles to believe we'd have ever-increasing oil prices, but my father's voice was a minority opinion.

The loudest of the majority was Stan Gaines, whose heart and soul were back in the oil business. He'd turned over his real estate operations to an associate and had assumed the helm of Gaines Petroleum. They marched behind the banner of "Growth!" Oil was going to $80 a barrel by 1985, and it would break $100 by 1990. Anyone with engineering reports showing proven reserves was welcome at a bank. They'd thrown underwriting rules out the window and had gone as crazy as many of us in the oil field. Once they spotted a competitor's deposits doubling, or tripling, they believed they had no choice but to join in the parade. Banks that had for years assumed conservative positions on energy loans were on the street wooing and seducing the same people they'd once shunned.

I finally found an opening in the traffic and darted into the motel parking lot. I left my car, stepping into the central Texas heat and humidity, just as the door to Stan's room opened and his landmen started leaving. They had their hands full. The county maps were incomplete and titles were unclear and almost any property they leased proved to be a problem of some kind.

Still, Gaines had been among the first to arrive several years ago and not only had more land leased but had been successful in cracking the code of the chalk. It was difficult to produce, and $40 oil had taken care of that, and it was even harder to find, and a geologist who understood the chalk's secrets had been unbelievably successful in knowing where to drive his stakes. He understood seismic and could find the faults and fractures.

"Hey!" Stan said, as though that were still my name. He walked out of his expensive but crumbling motel room to shake my hand. "Is it good to see you or what?"

"I guess that depends on what I tell you. Right?"

"No way, Billy Boy. I'm always glad to see you and you know that."

His room smelled musty; the furniture was old and unraveling, and I could see the bathtub from the front door. A steady drip from the faucet had turned part of the tub orange. But the room was at least cool, kept that way by a rattling air conditioner in the window.

He waved me into a chair and said, "People around here are *greedy*. We're having to pay a fifty percent royalty in some cases. Can you believe that?"

"Well, I guess you could wait until oil goes back down to ten bucks, and then you wouldn't have much competition."

He made a face and a rude sound. "Ten bucks. We won't ever see ten-dollar oil again. No way."

"Never say never, Stan. Didn't your mother ever teach you that?"

"The only thing my mother ever taught me is that she's impossible to please."

He was dressed like a man working in the field, wearing khakis, or what looked like khakis, except they were tailored. Overall, he looked good. Finally his age matched his face. If he could always appear to be forty, just as he had up to this point, he could die happy.

"I heard you were getting rich in real estate," he said.

His voice had a slightly accusatory tone. In the transaction to acquire the old man's interest in Brewster-Gaines Properties, he'd transferred all the real estate he and Sally Ann had bought south of Abilene in anticipation of the city's expansion in that direction. And his vision had proven accurate. All those hungry developers, envisioning housing additions and small office parks and a big mall, had paid the old man handsomely. With profits in the neighborhood of $4,000,000, the old man had bought existing oil properties.

"We've done all right with it," I said. "Of course, it's not like having the production you got on that deal where you just keep making money off the property. Once you sell raw land, it's gone." But if you buy up production with the revenue, I said to myself, you get to keep making money.

Stan smiled, thinking he'd come out a winner, and maybe he had. I'd never tried deciding who'd won.

"How's Sally Ann?"

"Great," he said, automatically withdrawing his wallet to show me recent pictures, as though I didn't see his family frequently in Abilene. "She looks great, feels great, is great. She and Junior go round and round sometimes, but you know how that is."

I looked at the pictures. Junior was indeed a junior, Abe Lincoln with another thirty years to go before he looked as good as his father did. There were now two more children, here, I'd thought, because Sally Ann had decided that the route into the social circles she wanted to enter was to be more matronly. The little girl, three, was most fortunate to have acquired her mother's looks, and the youngest, a two-year-old boy, looked different from them all. When I'd first seen him, I'd suggested that Sally Ann must have taken a vacation to the south of France about nine months prior to his birth. Otherwise, how did she explain his

Mediterranean looks? "Revolt of the genes," she'd said.

"So what do you think?" Stan asked.

"Good-looking kids," I said. Especially the younger two.

"No, I mean about the sale."

"Stan, I haven't decided."

He'd assume I was holding out for more money, but I was stalling for other reasons. His offer was $31,000,000 for Brewster's trucks, yards, buildings, rigs, and production. Another $31,000,000 in debt for Gaines Petroleum, which was expanding faster than good sense would ever have allowed. Forty-dollar oil had turned the world upside down; it had also given us double-digit inflation and wildly fluctuating interest rates. In April 1980 the prime had been at 20 percent. As the country fell into a recession, the prime had dropped to less than 11 percent in four months. And four months after that, it had been up to 21.5 percent. The world seemed convinced we were headed toward ever-higher oil prices, but I was listening to the voice in the wilderness, that of my old man, who simply didn't believe it. And a sudden reverse in the trend toward higher prices would flip Brewster Drilling onto its back overnight; we'd be flopping belly up with the rest of Gaines Petroleum, which had acquired incredible debt right along with its eighty-two rigs.

Sitting in a wooden chair with worn cushions, Stan said, "You don't like the money, do you?"

"Stan, this really hasn't got anything to do with money," I said, avoiding the argument over $80 and $100 oil we'd already had several times. He was a true believer, caught up in the frenzy. Nothing touched him, not high interest rates, not the windfall profits tax, nothing. We couldn't see because the piranha were causing the water to boil.

"Then what do you want? Let's make a deal," he said in a sweetly cooing tone. "Door number one, two, or three. It doesn't matter to me, just tell me which one. But we can't deal if I don't know what you want."

He started all over again on his spiel, which I'd already heard, once in Abilene, once in Dallas. He'd leave Brewster Drilling as it was presently operating, with William C. Brewster III at the helm. I could name my own salary; his suggestion was $200,000 annually with a bonus that would meet my approval.

I tuned him out. I still held the photos of his family, and his wallet. A symbol, maybe. In the picture, Sally Ann smiled at me. She now drove a station wagon, and the first time I'd seen inside that car, I'd been appalled. Comic books on the floor, loose diapers flapping, open containers of Handy Wipes that were probably desiccated, gum and candy wrappers ground into the dirt on the floorboard. The car had been so trashed it had even embarrassed its owner. "Talk about getting your image blown," she'd said.

But I'd never been influenced by the evidence. The added weight on her racing-style frame was only the disguise of a siren masquerading as a mother, a woman with short hair who couldn't hide the fact that she was possessed by the spirit of sensuality.

"You're acting like your father," Stan said, leaning forward, trying to bridge a gap. "You don't like the numbers but won't say so and you want me to guess. Right?"

"I already told you, the numbers are fine. And I'm not holding out; I'm undecided. A drop in the price of oil and I get to preside over the funeral of Brewster Drilling, dead after forty years. And those three hundred people who work for us—what'll they do?"

The pessimism brought Stan out of his chair shaking his head. "Billy Boy, you're the only person in the world who thinks about cheap oil. Forget it, we won't ever see it again. Listen, you're not even as conservative as banks, and you know what they're doing? They're factoring in increases of ten to fifteen percent a year. They love oil; they'll loan you money. Everybody in this state loves oil. And the price has been going up for years. OPEC's talking about a ten percent reduction in production, and the Saudis are saying if we don't let our stocks drop down, they'll give us *sixty-dollar* oil. Hell, Billy, if Iran and Iraq close the gulf, what happens? What do we get? Five hundred a barrel? A thousand? Billy, Billy, Billy, forget the words cheap oil. They're out of the vocabulary."

I had to laugh. Here was Brother Stanley Gaines, preeminent evangelist begging me to trust Jesus. All he had to do was slip into a white suit, alter a few words, and he was fighting for my soul, not my company. He obviously didn't understand any hesitation, so I took another route.

"What's so important about a hundred rigs?" I asked.

"A hundred is a good round number. One hundred. Listen to the way it sounds. One hunnndddrrreeeddd. There's a hundred pennies in a dollar, a hundred years in a century, and there's always a hundred days involved in getting you to do anything." He paced, getting worked up, the preacher with a reluctant sinner on his hands. Why not trust Jesus? What did I have to lose? "Billy, you don't ever want to make a business deal. Everything's personal with you. Everything. Just make a deal with me, that's all I want. Let's do a *business* deal just once."

"What's wrong with eighty-two rigs?"

"Eighty-two's an odd number."

I laughed. "Eighty-two is an *even* number."

He fell into his chair and knocked it against the wall, slumping as if I'd exhausted him. I had to admit, I enjoyed trying to slow him down. The world had been unable to succeed, but occasionally I could.

"Look in the briefcase by the chair," he said.

I looked. The papers were already drawn up. The family had an equity of $22,000,000. Sixty percent of that, my part, was $13,200,000. Half of that, invested in nothing more than CDs paying 14 percent, would bring me almost a million a year. Jill wanted to sell, wanted to be a cash-in-hand millionaire. Rigs were selling at a premium, and twelve of our eighteen were free and clear of debt. Since January 1, 1976, my old man had been passing 10 percent of the company to me each year, and although I was now majority owner, I hadn't yet gone against his advice. I kept asking what he thought; if we were going to sell, now was the time, while we were moving up. And he wouldn't say anything but this: "If you sell, don't tote the note."

Occasionally at night, I'd lie in bed and think about having the ability to do whatever I wanted. I could go back to school and get a different education. I could buy the ranch that had belonged to Sally Ann's grandmother and become my own kind of archaeologist. The most exciting discovery of my life had come at that ranch, on the east side of the mesa, in a crevice at the highest point. I'd found the remains of an Indian, buried with his lance, bound with rawhide thongs, his legs drawn up before him. Even a piece of his burial blanket had been preserved. The rain had eroded the soil and rocks over his grave, the white surface of his skull peeking through the ground and giving away his final resting spot.

With a small pick and knife, I'd dug around him, finding the lance, the blade of which had apparently at one time been a sword, but I hadn't disturbed this Indian who'd been left to face the rising sun. Maybe this mesa had at one time been his; this had been where he'd found his guiding spirit. I'd left him otherwise undisturbed, still bound in a sitting position with his legs up, and covered him back up.

There were times when life made sense to me in an intuitive way, a way that I could never explain, and it never happened anywhere except beneath the open sky, and it had never happened to the extreme that it had the day I'd discovered the grave. At that moment, I could feel my place in life.

But I'd also realized something rather unsettling now when I thought about that buried Indian. One who had fought with a lance had been accorded the kind of awe he'd deserved because he'd chosen to fight close in, on the brink of death. And I'd always known I'd never have been a warrior, but I realized I was even farther removed from this particular warrior because had I been offered a lance, I wouldn't have accepted it, and had I been forced to, I would have purposely lost it.

My father had tried to kick me into action, and of course he'd failed, but I was beginning to get as frustrated as he was with my lack of action. Basically, I had never made a decision; I'd reacted—joined the navy after Sally Ann had announced her engagement, returned to Abilene when I thought Jill was leaving with Robert—but I'd never freely made a decision and acted on it with gusto.

And now I really didn't want to decide on the sale of Brewster Drilling. I not only wasn't related to the Indian with the lance, but I really hadn't been Boomer's grandson. His thirty-third cousin, maybe.

"Billy Boy," Stan said, "tell me what it'll take to convince you to sell. Tell me and I'll do it. I don't care what it is. Just tell me. I can't do it if you won't tell me."

"Sell two of your rigs and you'll have a nice even number. Eighty's a good number."

Stan pushed himself out of his chair as though catapulted, charged with new energy. "Okay, you're going to tell me, right now. What do you want? More money? A guaranteed management contract? A bonus up front? What?"

I shook my head and stood. "Stan, I'm feeling paternal today; I'm going to do you a favor. You'll be a better man for it. I'm going to wait a day or two before giving you an answer."

"A day or two? A *day or two*? Hey, we're sitting here eyeball-to-eyeball right now. We're ready to deal, so let's deal. Take out the contract and make whatever change you want. Mark it out and write in your own figure. I'll give you a blank check, just fill it out, that's all, just fill it out. But whatever you do, don't walk out that door before you give me a decision. Don't do that to me."

I thought he was going to try to block the doorway or grab my leg and anchor me to the floor, but he didn't. "Seriously, Stan, I'll let you know in a day or two."

He saw that I was serious and took a deep breath, then offered to shake. He tried squeezing my hand, but he had gone too long without physical exertion to win.

"I'm sure you have a real good reason for doing this to me," he said. "Your horoscope said, 'Stick it to a friend today.'"

I shook my head and stepped outside into the heat. "No, that's close, though. It said, 'If you see a friend rowing by in a boat that could sink at any time, don't throw rocks at him.'"

He gave me a good-natured shove out the door and said, "I can't believe you. But then, I never could. You beat anything I've ever seen. A boat that could sink at any time. You've always been going against the flow, Billy Boy, and you still are."

I told him good-bye and left, glad to be out of his overpriced motel room with the rusted bathtub and ratty furniture, glad to be headed northwest.

To the Comancheria. I thought I'd lost contact with it when I'd moved to Dallas and Boomer had died. But it was still there, always waiting, never calling, just waiting.

16

It seemed to me, after watching Robert William Brewster for ten years, that kids should go into a holding pattern at the age of five. Up until that point, they were charming, innocent, and loving. Thereafter they developed pronounced tendencies toward obnoxious and disrespectful behavior. Robert, at the age of ten, had somehow attained the knowledge required to merit a Ph.D. from a major university. I'd never seen a child who, based on his own estimation, was smarter. And anyone who doubted his shining brilliance had only to listen to him.

"Why would *anybody* vote for Reagan? You want a president who's always on vacation? The guy's a moron. He never knows what's going on.

"You know why we have school all day? Because parents don't want their kids at home. So they made these prisons and called them schools."

I wasn't sure how he'd attained this wisdom, because for the past year he'd done nothing but watch TV and read science-fiction comic books. And my desire to name him after Ten Bears certainly hadn't endowed him with any native wisdom. If there was ever a child who didn't deserve a Comanche name, it was Robert. He was horrified that I required him to mow the yard when we could pay "some poor kid" to take care of the yard. He hated sweating. He equated sweat with the symptoms of disease. After he mowed, he got a wet rag from the refrigerator, laid it over his face, and spent an hour recuperating beneath a ceiling fan running on high.

He'd been begging me to agree to Stan's offer ever since he'd heard about it, not only because he wanted the money but because his antipathy toward physical labor extended to every aspect of the drilling business. "It's just like digging ditches. It's not *any* different. The only difference is that you're digging a skinny little ditch straight down instead of a big fat ditch along a road or somewhere. It's just like digging ditches."

His avowed enemy was Stanley Gaines, Jr. They were the polar opposites of Sally Ann and me, repelling to the same extent that the parents attracted. Robert was obsessed with the greater privileges of Junior. Stan, deciding Junior would never be deprived of those material comforts and gadgets that had been so foreign to his own childhood, had showered Junior with a great number of items that Robert didn't have and wouldn't have any time soon. Junior not only had his own horse and dirt bike on a ranch outside Dallas, but he went to a private school and had the promise of a red Corvette when he turned sixteen.

Their visits resulted in Robert cast as the loser in the one-upmanship contests.

"I wouldn't live out here in the sticks," Junior would say. "You don't even have a Six Flags or White Water. What do you hicks do for a good time?"

"Who needs Six Flags or White Water? At least we don't have gangs running around killing everybody."

"Gangs? A gang came in our neighborhood, we'd call the cops and, whammo, they'd be in jail like that. Besides, I'm getting a red Corvette when I'm sixteen. I'm getting a hardship license. My father said so."

Robert had been living with a barely tolerable vision, that of a sixteen-year-old Junior in a red Corvette, and the thought of this child of ultimate privilege getting, of all things, a *hardship* license almost caused a complete loss of faith. He moped and lost his appetite and lay around uninterested even in his comics. Finally he very carefully printed a letter to his state representative and senator demanding that hardship licenses be limited to card-carrying welfare cases.

Both of them were basically good kids when separated from each other. In some ways, Junior was more affectionate toward me, his "uncle," than my own son was. Robert's affection, except where his mother was concerned, was of a general kind. He had given more signals that he was a Democrat at heart than just deriding Reagan. He always rooted for the underdog, and he only maligned minorities when Junior was around.

When I returned from Giddings, he and a friend were sitting in the shade of a large pecan tree on this warm April day. They were exceptionally still, possibly fearing an outbreak of dreaded perspiration. Robert seemed to look more and more like his mother as he grew older, even down to the half-shy smile.

When I got out of the car, Robert, ten feet away from the driveway in the San Augustine grass he hated, said without rising, "Tell him, Dad. Tell him we're millionaires. He doesn't believe me."

I walked over to him and offered to shake. "How are you, Robert? Good to see you. Thanks very much for the greeting."

He shook my hand, partly sheepish for having neglected to say hello, partly impatient with my refusal to confirm we were rich. "Hi, Dad. Now tell him."

The child beside him looked up without expression from beneath the bill of a Texas Rangers baseball cap.

"The best I recall," I said, "you're not a millionaire. You're a pauper and a debtor. You still owe me five bucks for all those funny books you got at the mall."

"Dad," he said in a whining, pleading voice. "*Tell him.*"

"Mow the yard," I said, heading for the front door.

"No way!"

I entered the house shaking my head, wondering what my father would have done if I'd ever told him, "No way!" when he'd given me an order, even if he hadn't really meant it.

Our house would never rival Stan's for the front of a postcard, but it was still big enough for a family four times the size of ours. It was two-story, in the same established neighborhood where my parents lived, and it had all the touches Jill wanted in a house: beveled glass in the windows, a winding drive, columns to the second story so she could pretend she was Scarlet O'Hara, and a gazebo in the back yard.

She descended the stairs as I walked in, dressed for dinner out should I give her the news she wanted to hear, that we were loaded with cash. Her friends were now calling her R.B., for Rich Bitch, and she seemed to like those initials just fine.

"Why's Robert telling the world we're millionaires?" I asked.

She stopped at the bottom of the stairs and shrugged. "Family pride, I guess."

She crossed the room and gave me a formal little peck of a kiss on the cheek. Formal described our relationship. Nonexistent would have described it the first two years we'd been back in Abilene, when she'd let

215

me know that she was incapable of forgiving me for having joined the navy and putting her through a four-year delay and two years of waiting to see a navy representative coming to advise my parents I'd been killed in Vietnam. I believed her, maybe because I wanted to think we'd been in love at least briefly. Now we got along in a meaningless kind of way, sleeping in separate bedrooms (an arrangement necessitated, she'd told Robert, by my snoring) and engaging in sex that was infrequent, silent, and by the book.

"You bring home cash?" she asked, rubbing her fingers together.

"No."

I walked into my study, that space I claimed completely as my own, which was really a shrine to the Plains Indians, complete with art and artifacts, the room of an amateur anthropologist. I wanted respite from all those people who wanted immediate decisions and the resulting benefits. I was so tired of thinking about Stan's offer that my back suddenly ached and I never had back trouble.

Jill followed me in. "You're slowing me down. I've got shopping to do."

"Then go shopping."

"Oh!" she said, misinterpreting what I'd said and emitting a short shriek of happiness. "You mean we're selling?"

"No, I don't mean that."

"Well, when are you going to decide?"

"If one more person asks me that, I'll decide, and you won't be happy about it. Now I'm asking you very politely to shut up."

She turned on her heel, a move of military precision, and stomped from the room, a move I was more likely to see from Robert than a forty-year-old woman.

Abilene was bombarded with Gaineses the next day in separate cars from two different directions. I learned Sally Ann was in town when Robert called me at the office to report seeing Sally Ann and children at the store.

"Godzilla returns," he said. "I saw him at Super Duper. Can he own a monkey? Isn't that a wild animal? He said he has one that lives in his bedroom and it screams when his mother comes in. Can a monkey scream?"

Never had one child said so much that was subject to such extensive verification. Junior had scarcely opened his mouth to say hello when Robert went off in search of a dictionary. "See? He didn't say it right. He accented the first syllable. He said, '*Hel*-lo.'"

I told him I could answer neither question; I was given the opportunity to confirm that the father of the zookeeper was in town, ready to turn up the heat on William C. Brewster III, when I saw him on the evening news, on all three channels.

The local media loved him. He'd been written up in *Time* and *Newsweek* and was an authentic celebrity. He was often quoted in the *Wall Street Journal* and in oil-related publications. Mr. Stan Gaines, the oracle of old, dispensing wisdom and a positive mental attitude. In fact, he was well known to the extent that he appeared in public-service announcements on TV. The first time I'd seen him on the screen, in an interview in the pre-PR era, he'd squinted at the camera as though it were an instrument of evil trying to steal his soul. But his PR man had taken care of that by eliminating the real Stan, and now he was as comfortable in front of a camera as a TV news anchor.

That night he appeared in my living room, standing in front of an indoor swimming pool at a new motel in town, talking to the reporters as though they were meeting at a class reunion.

"As you folks know, I got my start with Brewster Drilling almost twenty years ago, and one of the associations I've valued most in my life has been knowing the Brewster family. They're the first family of Abilene, fine, fine folks. Bill Brewster gave me my start, and his son, Billy, is the best friend I've got. I mean, they've always treated me just like part of their family.

"And it's going to give me great pleasure to enter into another business arrangement with them. We should have an announcement tomorrow."

One of the reporters asked about the rumor he'd heard for the first time about five minutes before turning on his camera, when Stan had let him in on a secret. Was the business arrangement the purchase of Brewster Drilling by Gaines Petroleum?

"Boy," Stan said. "That's one attractive rumor."

Then Gaines was buying Brewster?

"Oh, we've crunched some numbers and I think we'll probably have an announcement within"—shrug—"say, twenty-four hours."

I was on my way to the phone before the segment was over, shaking my head, knowing my old man had just witnessed Stanley Gaines's ardent wooing of the first family, who owned the eighteen drilling rigs he wanted so badly. And the old man, who never missed the news, wasn't at all surprised to see Stan turning up the heat, but he was disappointed that his numerous attempts to develop negotiating skills in his old employee had failed to take.

"You can make your own deal," the old man said. "He's right there in your living room begging."

"Well, I don't want to gouge him. Or I should say, gouge the banks," I said, watching the tycoon hold forth on the effect of Iran and Iraq making war on each other in the Persian Gulf.

"He doesn't know that for sure, so he shouldn't be looking for a TV camera to take pictures of him on his knees."

I spent the next few hours on the phone, talking to employees who wanted to know if they should show up for work, and from people interested in buying anywhere from one to all of our rigs. Or part of our production. Robert and Jill sat on the floor in the den listening to these conversations with pencil and paper and calculator. Robert cut out pictures of BMWs and Jill filled out coupons requesting information on exotic vacation spots.

Once after hanging up the phone, I turned to see them both on their knees, hands held prayerfully beneath their chins, saying in unison, "Say yes, Daddy. Say yes to cash money."

The first Gaines I heard from directly was Melissa, not long after the six o'clock news had gone off. She wanted to confirm the story—was Stan really buying Brewster?

She was, to say the least, something else. She now accepted money from her son without making any demands that he support her church, and although she lived in the same house, on which siding had been installed, she did drive a new car, a Toyota, of all things. And she didn't drive it very well. Both front fenders were dented from her lack of depth perception or care. But the biggest change had come in her appearance. She'd had her hair dyed blond and she wore clothes that Sally Ann helped her select. I found her to be a strange sight, walking out of her neat little house in the slums, as stylish as her daughter-in-law.

I saw more of her than any of us thought necessary. She appeared at our house at odd hours as though she were Robert's grandmother, often bringing him trinkets and toys, often simply visiting. There was something eerily, almost deathly, beautiful about her. Her skin seemed so thin, especially around her eyes, that the lightest touch would bruise it. And in places it had a tint that reminded me of the surface of pearl; it was lustrous, almost blue at times.

She loved to touch, Robert as much as me, and she played with my sense of the macabre, this thin and thin-skinned woman. She always gave me a grandmotherly kiss upon arriving or departing, but her hands weren't grandmotherly at all. They pushed and probed, thoroughly checking out the contours of my arms, back, shoulders. And remembering my first visit with her, I never gave her any encouragement at all.

She'd come to visit on Saturday night after supper and gave me a long talk about a new mission effort her church had undertaken in the valley. She'd spoken with such fervor and conviction, painting an emotional picture of impoverished Mexican-Americans, that I'd been truly impressed with her desire to help. I'd been in the den watching TV, and she'd left the room, going, I'd thought, to the kitchen where Jill was ostensibly cleaning up supper dishes but where in reality she was attempting to avoid Mrs. Gaines.

I'd gone to the study to use the bathroom in there since it was the closest, and I'd entered the room to turn on the light when I saw Melissa Gaines in my bathroom, standing in front of the sink, as naked as the day she'd been born. For a minute I'd stood just inside the doorway of the study without turning on the light, watching.

I would have thought her breasts were flat, deflated from age, but they were small and almost perfectly round with prominent nipples. And although they were round, they seemed to have been inflated with the minimum amount of air and they looked as though they could have easily been mashed flat against her chest.

She picked up the soap from the sink and smelled it, held it to her cheek, then ran it over her body as though it was coated with some kind of valuable residue. She picked up a small glass and held it to her mouth, rolling the rim across her lips. She smelled the hand towel, pressing it against her face.

This lady is looney, I thought, absolutely looney. I didn't want to admit what she was doing, but she obviously knew that she was in a bathroom used primarily by me. And her actions didn't give me a lot of encouragement over the future course of our relationship. Eventually this elderly lady was going to do more than sniff my soap.

I quietly left the room and met Jill as she was leaving the kitchen. She asked in a whisper if the "old bat" was gone, and I shook my head. "I don't know."

Ten minutes later, Melissa appeared fully dressed, completely at ease, and sat to drink a cup of coffee. She'd asked earlier if I'd consider contributing to her church's mission effort, and I'd given her a hundred-dollar bill along with her coffee, thinking she could do with it as she chose. She could keep it and buy some clothes that would stay on her body or she could donate it to the mission fund.

A few days later I received an acknowledgment for my contribution from the church.

Now she wanted to know if Stan was actually buying Brewster Drilling.

"I don't know, but I do know this—we're not within twenty-four hours of an announcement."

"He'll never learn, will he?"

"Learn what?" I asked, sitting, thinking this could be a long conversation.

"'Except the Lord build the house, they labour in vain that build it,'" she said, quoting some verse in the Bible.

"Mrs. Gaines," I said, thinking this was the perfect time to defuse a situation that was sure to arise eventually. Although she certainly intrigued me, just as her son had at one time, I had no desire to get sexually involved with a woman past retirement age.

"Melissa," she said. "I don't know how many times I've told you, call me Melissa."

"My parents always insisted that I show respect for my elders. And I don't understand where you got this concept, this idea of The Blest. My father went out just like Stan has, and made all this money I've got, every penny of it, except he probably wasn't as creative as Stan is. I'm no more blessed than anybody else. Lucky, maybe, by birth, but that's it."

"Billy, there're many blessings from God, and prosperity is only one of them, and not everyone with money has been blessed. Do you ever read Revelations? 'Because thou sayest, I am rich, and increased with goods, and have need of nothing; and knowest not that thou art wretched, and miserable, and poor, and blind, and naked.' Billy, I believe with all my heart you've been visited by angels. I knew it the first time I saw you. And Stanley, poor Stanley can buy a drilling company, but he can't buy the blessings of God."

I didn't know what to say. She sounded so reasonable, so assured, that I couldn't believe this was the same lady who'd been naked in my bathroom. Sally Ann had been right—she was impossible to figure. So, rather than trying to dissuade her, I asked, "How can Stan receive the blessings of God?"

"By following his leading. He was called to preach at the age of ten, and he preached one sermon and then turned his back on God. He's never followed the leading of the Lord."

"Neither have I, Mrs. Gaines."

"Oh, you have, you have. Some people are so in tune with the Lord that they never even have to mention his name."

I laughed. "Mrs. Gaines, I believe in the Great Spirit of the Comanche Indians, and I'm no more in tune with him than I am with Jehovah in the Old Testament."

"Billy, I can *see* it in your eyes, I can *feel* it in your love. You've been blessed, and one day when the time is right, I'm going to ask you to share with me."

I stood up, prepared to slam the phone down. There wasn't any way to discourage her, and now she was going to seduce me. Was the fact that a seventy-year-old lady wanted to seduce me a sign that I'd been blessed? Would I know I was doubly blessed if a horde of nursing home residents descended upon me, kissing me with dried and ancient lips?

"You're wrong about *all* this," I said and hung up without telling her good-bye.

The second Gaines to call wasn't the celebrity but his wife. She waited until I arrived at the office the day after Stan had appeared on the news to call and invite me to coffee. By then I was slightly crazed, tired of questions, tired of finding magazine ads in the refrigerator, a bright red Ferrari taped to a carton of milk. I was tired of employees who had heard we were moving to Hobbs, New Mexico, who had heard they could travel to Singapore with Gaines Petroleum, who were already de-manding raises to stay on with the new company. I wanted to flee to the safety and friendly comfort and understanding of Sally Ann's arms, but she sounded as though she'd called to lobby for her husband. Surely not.

"This hasn't got anything to do with the possible sale of Brewster Drilling to Gaines Petroleum, does it?"

"Well, if the subject comes up, we can talk about it, can't we?"

"What if I said no, I'm tired of talking about it."

"Then my feelings would be hurt because I'd know there was some-thing you wouldn't talk to me about."

I agreed to meet her for coffee, hoping she could give me some hints on how to handle Melissa Gaines, the lady who wanted to share in my blessings when the time was right, but I found myself sorely disap-pointed after I hung up. Damn, had Stan enlisted the help of his wife to persuade me to sell? I didn't think Stan would hesitate to use any avail-able resource, including his wife, but I didn't want to think Sally Ann had willingly agreed to cooperate. So why had she sounded coy on the phone?

She'd suggested a small cafe ten miles from town, a place truly out of the way—a fact that further stimulated my suspicion although she could also have been demonstrating good judgment under the circumstances. When I arrived I saw the monstermobile, as Robert called it, a blue station wagon, parked in a line of pickups in front of the cafe. The building was long and not very deep and had always reminded me of a mobile home. And although we may not have been known inside the cafe, we certainly weren't going to blend in among these ranchers and retirees, not with me in a suit and Sally Ann in a sleeveless yellow sweater and bluejeans, looking like a glamorous woman who wanted to appear frumpy but was failing altogether.

She walked to meet me, passing in front of the windows of the long frame building and drawing stares from inside. Using my line, she asked, "So how the hell's your life going?"

"As usual, it's being complicated by your husband," I said, adding silently, and you, not to mention your mother-in-law.

She gave me a restrained kiss and then took my arm, at first hugging it against her breast, then deciding the gesture was too intimate for either the occasion or the watchful audience in the building.

We'd always been able to determine the mood of the other within a matter of seconds upon meeting, and as I opened the door for her, she gave me a quick glance as if to confirm what she thought—that I was distant. Not that I wanted to be. But I didn't seem able to whip myself into shape. I never wanted to waste a meeting with her because I didn't see her nearly as often as I wanted, but some part of me insisted I maintain a reserve until I determined the reason for this visit. Whoop-de-do. I was a man of principle.

We took the only empty table, which happened to be in a corner, right by the window in front of her blue station wagon. I could see markings in the dust on her hood, one of which looked like a stick figure with a smiling face.

She said, "Guess who's this far from chairing the decorations committee for the Mayor's Ball?" She held her thumb and forefinger an inch apart.

"Congratulations. Your new motherly appearance must've worked."

She shrugged; she'd never admitted having made the attempt to adopt a matronly appearance.

"I don't really see how it could, though," I said, wondering why I sounded somber enough to be delivering a eulogy. "You used to look like the kind of woman every man wanted to take off for a weekend in the sun. Now you look like the kind they want to dump their wives for and marry. That'd be more threatening, not less."

She recognized my interior struggle without knowing its cause, saw her old blood brother winking at her from behind the stern face of the puritan before her. She encouraged the blood brother to come out and play by touching my finger, tip to tip, two fingernails meeting near a sugar shaker.

A waitress appeared with coffee and empty mugs, appraising us and wondering probably if we wanted the breakfast special, bacon and eggs for enthusiastic adulterers.

"Just coffee," I said before she handed us menus.

After she'd poured coffee and left, Sally Ann asked, "Did Stan tell you about his latest problem?"

"What?"

She got comfortable as though she had a long story. "About two months ago, this reporter from a Dallas paper came to see me. Stan knew the guy was writing an article about him, a long one, because they'd already spent several hours talking. So the guy comes out and brings a photographer and takes pictures of me and the kids and all that. And we kept looking at the paper to see if the article was in it, but we never saw it. A month went by, two months, nothing. Then the other day the same reporter called Stan and told him he'd been out here, and he'd been talking to—guess who?"

She didn't have to pause for dramatic effect. I remembered too well not only my conversation with Melissa Gaines from the night before, but my first visit to her house. Not only was there a conflict in the information the mother and son disseminated, but if I were Stan, I'd never want a reporter talking to my mother. I wouldn't want to see in print, "Even at the age of seventy, Mrs. Gaines still enjoys sex with rich men."

"So he talked to dear old Melissa and discovered Stan had not only never won the Medal of Honor but he'd never even fed the five thousand, right?"

Sally Ann laughed. "When the guy called back, Stan told him he'd spent all the time he could answering questions and anything more would be self-serving." She mugged, raising her eyebrows. "So now Stan's dying to know whether they're going to run the article or not, but at the same time he's trying to act like he's not at all interested. But you know the funny part? He got mad when he found out the reporter was questioning whether he'd ever been one of those Green Beret guys."

"Never believe your own press."

"He thinks anybody who doesn't believe that has doubts about his manhood. Isn't that funny?"

"No," I said, shaking my head because I remembered how easy it was to fall into the pit of your own press.

For a few minutes, we sat and sipped coffee and talked about children. Junior did indeed have a monkey, and while they were in Abilene, the pet store from which the creature had come was under orders to proceed to the Gaines home and liberate the thing. It was the dirtiest, foulest, most obnoxious animal she could have imagined. Whenever she walked into Junior's room, the monkey screeched and showed his teeth and played with himself until she left.

"You sure it's a monkey?" I asked. "Maybe it's a baseball player."

"Either that or he's a New Orleans Saints' fan."

The waitress refilled our cups, and she seemed to be lingering near the table, maybe attempting to eavesdrop and hear the details of the night we'd spent together.

When she was out of earshot, Sally Ann asked, "Are you going to sell?"

"Who's asking?"

She smiled and tapped the back of my hand. "Stan said you were playing mind games with him."

"Bullshit. Stan thinks if he doesn't immediately get what he wants, somebody's playing games. He thinks deferred gratification is waiting until you get up in the morning to eat breakfast."

I sounded much harsher, more judgmental, than I felt. Or thought I felt. Who was I? Jerry Falwell? I didn't want to act as if I possessed the mean spirit of a puritan; I wanted to take her to her grandmother's ranch and hold her.

"Did Stan tell you he'd sold his interests in a bunch of the Brewster-Gaines buildings to his partners?" she asked.

"No, but with interest rates the way they are, it doesn't surprise me."

"Most of his loans are fixed where the interest rate floats with the prime. Some of them are one point above, some even one point below. And we all know what's been happening to that. And if you want to know what I really think, I think he's back in the oil business because he knows real estate is going—" She turned her thumb down. "He was in the middle of a mall deal when the rates shot up. And now there's just a great big scraped-off lot just sitting there."

"So answer the twenty-one and a half percent question: why does he want more debt when he's having to sell his interests in the Brewster-Gaines buildings to people with cash?" I asked.

"I think he wants your production. It gives him more leverage. The banks love oil. They can take engineering reports and project higher oil prices in the future and then just loan all the money Stan wants. The value of oil is infinite."

"Tell me something else. Why're we sitting here talking business?"

The question, and my tone, caught her by surprise, and she sat back in her chair as though she needed the additional space for perspective. And she wasn't quite the mellow mother I wanted to think she was. Deep down, she was still my brother, too quick to accept a challenge, too determined to say, in one way or another, "You can't make me." She struggled with her emotions for a moment, and she might have succeeded if I hadn't been feeling overly mean, pressured, kicked, and abused.

"Here's an even better question. Why're we here at all?" I asked.

"Because I wanted to see you."

"So you could do your part for God and company?"

She shook her head. Maybe she was the mellow mother; a few years ago, she'd have taken a spike heel and crucified me to my chair for saying such a thing. Now she just looked sad. "My mother-in-law was telling me last night what a wonderful loving boy you are, but what she doesn't know is, you're only wonderful and loving when you want to fuck." She stood up, leaning over the table and whispering in my face, "Which means I hope you two get together soon because you're just alike."

Before I could decide how to respond, she'd fished two dollars from her purse and said in a formal voice, "Stan wants you to go with him tomorrow on a frac job near Midland. If you'll go, meet him at the airport at nine in the morning."

She walked toward the front door, sliding between tables and chairs in a cafe that was filled with morning coffee drinkers. I didn't want her to go. Whenever we were together, an electrical field activated, causing our electrons to jump and twitch and quiver. I hurriedly got up to follow her, thinking as I went that a marriage to her never would have worked. It would have been a contest, a continuous experience too exciting and draining and fulfilling for either of us to have survived.

Once outside, I said, "Hey! Aren't you going to take me into the country and say, 'Sell or walk'?"

She stood by the opened door of the car, shaking her head. I rounded the car, seeing that the stick figure drawn on the hood had either three legs or a very long sexual appendage that drug the ground. Probably Junior was already trying to impress his friends.

She said, "You know, I did have a reason for asking you out here, and it didn't have anything to do with what you think. And you'll go to your grave without ever knowing why I called."

She got in the car and slammed the door, starting the engine and backing out of the gravel lot onto the highway without ever looking at me again. I was left standing by myself with a peculiar feeling, one I remembered having before.

Not long after getting my first BB gun, I'd walked into the backyard and taken aim at the first bird I'd seen. It happened to be very close, a mockingbird sitting on a lower branch. I pulled the trigger and the bird dropped like a rock. And a sudden burst of pride over my marksmanship was quickly snuffed out. I stood over the dead bird, which had a drop of blood on the tip of its beak, and realized I'd murdered the state bird. And besides expecting to be arrested by a game warden hiding in the shrubs, I experienced a more painful emotion. I'd hurt something that had meant no harm whatever.

And that was how I felt as Sally Ann drove off. I'd miscalculated her intentions and hurt her feelings. Life was too short for that kind of crap.

17

I arrived at the airport the next morning with heavy eyelids. The Gaineses (all of them) were making me an insomniac, an all-night philosopher, sending questions rolling over and over in my mind while I stared at the dark side of my eyelids. Besides the obvious considerations on the sale of Brewster Drilling, there was a question that had really bothered me: was I Melissa Gaines's spiritual twin, just somebody hanging around wanting to get vicarious thrills, afraid to arrange for my own? Is that all I amounted to, someone waiting, always waiting, to be filled by another? I really hadn't wanted to think about it but couldn't fall asleep to get away from the thorny little question.

Stan was already waiting in the private terminal at the airport, dressed in his tailored khakis. He was obviously hiding out from the media, a darling on the run from his suitors, those people with cameras who had believed they were going to hear an announcement on the sale of Brewster Drilling within twenty-four hours. When I opened the door of the terminal, he glanced around quickly, expecting to see a horde of frenzied reporters rushing in, microphones extended, shouting his name.

He got me a cup of coffee from a big urn on a table and handed it to me. "Well, Billy Boy, we're going to convince some people they need to invest in the drilling fund. And a frac job'll do the trick every time."

I nodded. Every time I starting questioning myself, I ended up engaging in unrelated diversions, most often talking myself out of faith of any kind, and last night it had been faith in Sally Ann. "You're good at convincing people, Stan. How'd you get Sally Ann to come find out what I was thinking?"

He looked actually surprised. "What you were thinking about my offer? If she was asking you questions, she must not've found out anything. Or if she did, she didn't tell me."

I thought he was telling the truth, but then, who knew? He never told outright lies; he compressed the truth from statements. Or performed his own frac jobs.

"She said you were having to sell off your interest in some of the Brewster-Gaines deals."

He gave a bitter little laugh, one of the first I'd ever heard pass his lips, and I was so surprised to hear Mr. Optimism turn sour I was shocked. In fact, I gave him such a long openmouthed look that he began to get uncomfortable. He set his Styrofoam cup next to the urn and cleared his throat and looked around.

"I'll tell you something else," he said as though I were forcing him into an admission he didn't want to make. "Toothache Tower, as you call it? It's next."

"You're kidding."

"I'm not kidding. I wish I was, but I'm not."

No way. Stanley Gaines was selling his beloved tower, the structure that rose sixteen inches higher than the Canadians'? How could that be? That building defined Stan; it reminded him of who he was every time he saw it. He'd never be able to drive downtown again.

He had no experience in handling the stunned reactions that failure brought. He wasn't accustomed to hearing, "Say it ain't so, Stan." And he was suddenly irritated.

"Hey! The prime hit twenty-one and a half in January. You try paying loans on that kind of interest. It won't eat your lunch; it'll gnaw your gonads off."

I threw up my hands to show I meant no harm. "I don't ever remember serving on the Federal Reserve, and I can well imagine what kind of problem you're having. It's just a shock to hear you say you're going to sell your interest in the tower."

"Give me an alternative and I won't."

The problem, as he explained it, was that the First Southwestern Bank, which had called the tower home and had been the other general partner, had joined the *Growth!* parade and merged with another bank. In 1979 they'd sold their interest to a property management firm, which believed as Stan did that booms never busted. If '78 and '79 were good years for the real estate business, then 1980 would be even better. But it hadn't been. The same incredible interest rates that were eating Stan's gonads were chewing on everyone's. And when the bank vacated their seven floors, the building manager had to drastically cut rents to find new tenants. Toothache Tower was no longer cash-flowing. The general partners were getting hit with capital calls to make up the difference between the tower's revenues and their expenses and debt service. Stan was getting hit twice some months. The interest rates had added as much as $350,000 annually to his note payment, and the capital calls almost that much. He was using $40,000 monthly from Sally Ann's trust, which was fat with $40 oil, but he wanted out. Unfortunately for him, none of his partners wanted his 8 percent at the moment.

He walked to the other end of the table and looked at a display for American Express credit cards, stuffed with applications.

"If your partners don't want your eight percent, who're you selling to?"

"Oh, it's kind of a hush-hush deal right now."

How could selling his 8 percent be a hush-hush deal? His agreement required approval of all the partners before he could transfer his interest. *Son of a bitch.* I suddenly knew what he was doing. He wasn't selling his interest in the tower; he was selling Brewster-Gaines Properties, and I knew who his buyer was. I'd seen Stan in his company when we'd first talked about the possible sale of Brewster Drilling. Donald Gleghorn, who may as well have been a slumlord. News crews in Dallas were always chasing him to ask questions on some of his many apartment buildings around town, trying to verify numerous complaints about faulty heating and cooling systems, plaster that fell from the ceiling on sleeping tenants, even rat infestations in what appeared to be nice apartment complexes. He was the personification of the Reagan era—big was best and nothing mattered but the bottom line.

I asked, rather calmly, "Do your partners know you're selling?"

He unfolded one of the applications. "Some of them."

"Donald Gleghorn."

He folded the application and returned it to the cardboard display. "You know, I didn't have a father when it counted, and I haven't asked you to take the job."

I couldn't believe it. I knew the investors he'd told, the ones who wouldn't care. The others would have a hell of a time getting rid of Gleghorn.

"You sorry son of a bitch. You're selling Brewster-Gaines Properties to a slumlord. My name's going to be on the news when the tower gets run down because he won't spend any money on it. I can't believe you'd do that."

He didn't respond since I wasn't his father, but I had something more important to him than fatherly counsel—a drilling company with eighteen rigs, not to mention extensive production. And I had a legitimate interest in his judgment, or lack thereof. I wasn't going to give him more than three hundred employees for whom Brewster Drilling was a big part of their lives, only to watch them deserted later when times got tough. He was either going to explain his situation or we'd forego any further dealings.

I refilled my coffee cup even though I'd drunk very little, and I explained my position. "I've been watching you for almost twenty years, Stan, and I've always thought you treated your investors right. Now you want to buy Brewster Drilling, and whether you know it or not, there's nobody who can force me to sell, not to you or anybody else. So I'm putting you on notice: until you've told me the whole story about the tower, don't even mention your offer on Brewster."

He wanted badly to tell me to go fuck myself. No question, the words were forcibly pressing against his lips. But he didn't say anything, still looking over the display, now testing it to see if it sat level on the table. And I thought, a guy who wanted to approach perfection with his appearance, with styled hair and tailored clothes and handmade ostrich boots, maybe even a manicure, would have a difficult time admitting weakness to Old MacDonald. After all, one of the richest, most egotistical, and outspoken doctors in Dallas had pronounced him transcendent, immune from human failings.

He finally turned back to me and said, "Do you know how long it's been since I've been able to tell whether the pain in my stomach's from hunger or just pain? I throw up almost every meal I eat, even when I've gone a day without eating anything. I still throw up. Now, I've done *everything* I can, so get off my back."

Impressive words, but I wasn't feeling sympathetic. We'd never see Stanley Gaines on a poster publicizing hunger relief, never see him with a belly bloated by starvation. I doubted that he'd lost a pound. "The demand stands."

Bent out of shape was what we'd called it in high school. Some part of his body was applying torque to another, and he was almost twisted with the desire to tell me what he thought.

Outside, a blue King Air landed in the middle of the plate which the city of Abilene occupied, and I walked to the plane following Stan, looking at the line of blue hills to the west. How the hell would the Comanches have handled 21.5 percent interest rates? Maybe that's why the civil chief was superior to the war chief, because war was simple and peace wasn't. I didn't blame Stan for hurrying to the plane, refusing to walk with me. And maybe I was wrong. Maybe once Reaganomics took effect, it was the only system that worked.

On board the plane I found eight men, all conservatively dressed, all representatives of trust or pension funds, potential investors in the drilling fund. They were in the care of a middle-aged blond woman, a hostess for a Dallas restaurant who freelanced these kinds of functions for Stan. She was apparently performing her job very well because by barely after nine in the morning, every necktie in the aircraft had been loosened. A cheery mood prevailed.

Stan was all smiles, now bent back into shape. He introduced me to the crowd and the blond pressed Irish coffee into my hand. The plane started taxiing almost immediately.

In Midland we'd catch a well-equipped motor home and take these gentlemen to a location so they could witness a frac job. It was a sight that influenced emotions, one that made people believe oil could be produced from any well. Blood could be squeezed from the smallest turnip.

Stan and I sat in a Winnebago on a lease road thirty miles from Midland, right in the middle of the plains. The country was brushy, almost as flat as the panhandle, and there wasn't a tree in sight. We were probably 150 feet from the location, looking at one of Gaines Petroleum's rigs towering over the landscape. In a line stretching away from the rig were fifteen red and gray Halliburton trucks, all arranged along a massive manifold system through which they would force water, sand, and gel down into the well and out through the perforations of the casing almost 10,000 feet in the earth. The idea was to fracture the formation and stimulate production. Stan's eight potential investors, all provided with plastic ear protectors, were lined up along the lease road watching.

Stan and I sat at a small table at the rear of the motor home drinking a cold beer. He looked rather depressed, one foot resting on the table.

"I don't have any choice," he said. "I've got to sell. I can't believe a year ago I had interests in over a billion dollars' worth of property. Now I've got almost nothing. Twelve years ago none of it even existed, unless it was some run-down warehouse or dilapidated office building nobody'd rent. I mean, I built that stuff where it'd never existed. And then along came these ridiculous interest rates."

"Stan, you know why we have these ridiculous interest rates? Forty-dollar oil. If it wasn't for forty-dollar oil, inflation wouldn't be anywhere close to what it is. So if you're losing your ass in Brewster-Gaines Properties, just remember, you're getting it all back in Gaines Petroleum."

He wasn't listening, as usual. He was talking. Before I'd got my moral on the table, he was saying, "I've got two people interested in the tower. One's Gleghorn and the other's some lawyer for a corporation out in California. Windstream. Gleghorn's offer is on the table, and this hippie lawyer wants to know everything. What subs we used, everything. I asked him if he wanted to know what kind of Kotex the maids used. Hell, he'd be impossible to deal with. But Gleghorn's from Dallas and he's got a lot of property around the area."

"Stan! You make him sound almost respectable and we both know he's no better than a slumlord. What's he offered you?"

"Forty percent of the note."

"Hell, that's no offer, that's giving it to him. For forty percent, you may as well keep it. Interest rates won't be high forever and the economy's got to improve. What's the balance of the note?"

"About three million five."

"And what's your equity?"

"Slightly over ten."

Damn, I thought. Inflation and some very good years for real estate had been kind to Stan. A $90,000,000 building was worth something like $170,000,000. There had to be a way to avoid giving away property, even in the present climate. "Did this lawyer look *you* up?"

Stan sighed and sat up, dropping his foot from the table. He peered out the window at his investors along the road. Occasionally one would look back at us, hoping we hadn't deserted them in the middle of nowhere.

He sighed again and said, "Yeah, he looked me up. I got the impression he's representing some foreigner, but I don't know who. Anyway, I don't have time to fart with him. I've got to do something *now.*"

This was, I thought, the kind of behavior I'd always expected from Stanley Gaines; it had just been longer in coming than I'd thought. He'd give his property away before looking at what could be a legitimate offer, only because, as he said, he wanted out. He couldn't wait, just as a child couldn't wait.

"You're telling me you'll saddle your partners with a slumlord and won't even wait to see what the other offer is?"

"Hey, nobody said there was another offer. Have you checked the prime lately? How about seventeen fucking percent? You take care of the interest and I'll see what else I can do."

"It doesn't show a hell of a lot of regard for your partners."

"Hey! Fuck 'em if they can't take a joke."

Further conversation was impossible because the frac job was beginning. Several of the large dump trucks had already been running, and on a signal from the treater, the ringmaster of this performance, the remaining trucks cranked up. Ten diesel engines revved, the noise blasting across the silence of the plains, pushing water and sand and gel through the manifold system and into the well. The eight observers now realized why they'd been provided with the plastic earmuffs. The sound was deafening. It was an experience that made one believe that with modern technology and sufficient power, every drop of oil beneath the earth would eventually be recovered. We'd get it all.

The sight reminded me of military demonstrations of firepower, and it was impressive, as impressive as flyovers of jets at 200 feet, as the *New Jersey's* sixteen-inch guns lobbing shells twenty miles, or as the shock waves echoing along the ground during a B-52 strike.

The investors, lined up along the lease road, pointed and punched each other and nodded, in a state between adult solemnity and childish excitement.

I got up early the next morning, leaving before either Jill or Robert was awake, thinking that if either left me one more picture in their continuing effort to attain riches, I'd run away from home. I'd lifted the lid on the toilet seat to find a picture of a yacht taped there, smiling people lining the rail and watching me take a leak. Beneath the pillow on my bed had been another magazine ad, this one of a castle in England. And one fell from the refrigerator when I opened the door, shouting in bold print, "Buy Your Own Island!" I was going to locate a picture of a man giving every dime he had to charity, make at least a thousand copies, and drop them from an airplane.

The office was mercifully quiet, primarily because it was empty, and I made coffee and enjoyed the solitude before employees started arriving. I had only one compulsory task for the morning, and that was to call Sally Ann. I had not only squandered a visit with her, but I'd accused her wrongly of spying for the former real estate tycoon.

About eight I called her, assuming she'd be up with her brood, and got Junior, who wanted to tell me about his monkey. I didn't inform him that he was no longer a monkeykeeper. He finally called his mother to the phone, and she answered with, "Hello, Gourdhead."

"Call me whatever you want. I deserve it. Forgive me, brother, for I have sinned against our bond."

"That's not a bad start. Can you crawl?"

"I can crawl all the way to the ranch this morning, and if I knew you were going to be out there, I'd run."

"The Trysting U Ranch?"

"We missed the sunrise, but we could catch the morning breeze."

"I'm glad you've repented. I'll see you in a little while."

I drove through the mesquites and scrubby oaks, watched occasionally by the pumpjacks, which reared their heads every few seconds. The gate at the highway had already been opened, and I assumed Sally Ann had beat me, probably so she could choose the spot. I banged and scraped up the incline to the top of the mesa and found my friend waiting, strolling around, enjoying the warm April morning. She'd come in a little blue Toyota, which was parked near the grove of red oaks near the edge of the hill. Our spot.

I stopped in the shade of the trees and watched Sally Ann approach the car. She'd come dressed as Two-Garment Gaines in blue and white gym shorts and a matching tank top that revealed more skin than I deserved to see. And she'd been overly kind in calling me Gourdhead. Such a breach of trust would have brought ocular bruises at one time. Maybe, I thought, she really was mellowing.

She walked to the door and rested both hands on the window opening, leaning forward just enough to make me want to sit up straight and crane my neck. I could see maybe an inch of unbound breasts and the darkness of her cleavage. How did she know exactly how far to bend?

"You used to accuse me of being more than one person," she said. "Who were you the other day?"

233

"I was Arthur Asshole and I really am sorry."

She gave me a long look, one that bordered on sadness, and it made me feel lousy. I started to tell her again I was sorry, but apologies were no better than excuses. And I'd behaved inexcusably.

"Get in," I said.

"I don't want to get in. I want you to get out."

"Ah. Intrigue at the Trysting U."

"What would life be without it?" she asked, opening my door.

I followed her to the pickup, walking behind so I could watch her walk. Her hair was barely blond, too dark to be called that anymore, and the long legs didn't belong to a forty-year-old woman. Her ass wasn't the tight little affair it had once been, but I didn't care. It was soft and inviting and made me want to put a bumper sticker on my car that said, "Mothers make better lovers."

She pointed to the passenger's side of the pickup and I got in.

She turned behind the wheel and faced me. "Okay, here's Arthur Asshole's punishment. You have to look at me and you can't look away. And you can't close your eyes."

I could tell by her tone that she was going to be gentle enough to make me cry, and I was exceedingly curious about this method of punishment. I turned toward her, bringing one leg up onto the seat. Without looking away from me, she reached and hit a button on the little pickup's radio/tape deck. And within an instant, upon hearing the first beat of the drum, I knew she'd found "Be My Baby" on tape somewhere. The music reached back across all those years, almost twenty of them, and stirred the same emotions it always had. The vision of two kids swinging through a crowd, watched as they went, almost did make me cry. For a few moments, I didn't know where I was, didn't even care. I forgot the relative wilderness that surrounded us and for a minute was a kid back in Sally Ann's bedroom.

> We'll make 'em turn their heads
> Every place we go

She smiled and took my hand, as kind and warm as a friend should be, and pulled me toward her, leaning at the same time. I expected one of those intense electrical kisses, but she surprised me again. This was one of the summer variety, slow and languid and designed for pure enjoyment.

"I hate it when you're stupid," she said, kissing me on the tip of the nose. "You can be a lot of things, but you can't be stupid."

234

I returned to my side of the cab, pulling her with me. She turned her back to me and then leaned against my chest. I *had* been stupid, I thought, because for the past year I'd wondered why I preferred the feel of this fleshier matronly breast over the apple she'd once had, and I hadn't been able to decide. And the answer was obvious—it was a nurturing Mother Earth breast.

"I used to think you knew me better than anybody," she said. "Better than anybody ever could."

"I didn't understand the timing."

"If you work for Gaines, you'll have to come to Dallas at least once in a while, won't you?" She added, as though uncertain she should voice such a thought, "Maybe once a week even?"

I started to ask what had made her less cocky, Dallas or age, but didn't. She sounded vulnerable, so I just pulled the tail of the tank top out of her shorts and put my hand beneath it, holding her breast. It filled my hand.

"Do me a favor, will you? Don't give me a reason to sell, not that kind of reason. God, this is getting murky enough as it is."

I blew on her hair, watching the short strands of near-blond hair jump, giving me tiny glimpses, ever so briefly, of white scalp. She shivered and drew closer to me, squeezed my hand against her breast with her arm, and said, "Don't. You give me chills."

"I know another favor I want," I said. "You can't ask why I want to do this because I made a vow fifteen or twenty years ago I'd never give it away. But I want to make love on the other side of the hill."

"I came prepared," she said, pointing to the bed of the pickup with her thumb.

I leaned back, away from her, and looked toward the rear. The bed was a bed; someone had put a thick sheet of foam rubber back there.

"That's good. I can carry it."

"I'm ready if you are."

We left the pickup and walked toward the east side of the hill, following a road that hadn't been used in so long it could only be felt, not seen, the old ruts now long overgrown. Carrying the foam rubber beneath my arm as though it were a huge book, I led her to the crevice where the Indian had been buried, winding through the cedar trees and across grass that was once again green. The sky looked as though it would never know another cloud; it was a shallow blue bowl over us, not very deep but as big as time.

When we reached the edge of the mesa, I was glad the Indian remained buried. In that great crevice against which his back had rested, he remained secure, swallowed up, his legs drawn up before him, facing the rising sun, which was now filling the sky, warming the city below it, in the lake bed beyond us.

I laid the sheet of foam rubber, our bed, on a gray shelf of rock, the side of which formed the beginning of the crevice. Sally Ann, as though in a hurry, pulled her shirt over her head and stepped out of her tennis shoes.

"This is where the Indian's buried, isn't it?" she asked.

I gave the normal reflex action; it happened almost every time a Gaines said something—my mouth dropped open. She may as well have read my mind as I was contemplating an unspeakable perversion. "How'd you know that?"

She laughed and continued undressing me since I'd stopped. "You told me and you don't even remember. Billy, you told me everything. You never kept a secret from me." While she unbuttoned my shirt, she kissed me. "Don't you know that women have always been wiser than men?"

I couldn't believe she knew the most important secret of my life, or what I'd thought was a secret. And she had to be right; I must have told her everything. Everything. How could I have done such a thing? "You're probably more cynical than men too, aren't you?"

"Wouldn't you be cynical if you knew what I knew?"

I didn't answer her. Instead I took over the disrobing duties and watched her step back in the spring sun. She'd gained ten pounds probably, and her stomach tended to look round rather than flat. Her frame was fleshier.

Once I'd shucked my clothes, which formed a considerably larger pile on the gray rock than hers did, we came together, two sparks generating a considerable fire. Twenty years ago I'd thought making love to her was wonderful, but we hadn't known anything. The tautness of youth may have looked better, but it sure as hell didn't feel better. Besides, there was something else involved, trust maybe, or faith in each other, faith in the wholeness of the act.

We lay on the cushion in the sun, joined in an eternal way, passing into and out of each other, the one flesh of the Bible, of the Indians, and of every other culture.

She whispered into my ear, "Let's finish sitting up."

"I thought you'd never ask."

We sat up without breaking our most intimate connection, Sally Ann on my lap, her hands on my waist. She leaned back and moved for both of us, remembering exactly how it was done. I was patient through this exquisite pleasure until I could wait no longer, and I grabbed her around the waist and pounded as though I could send us both flying from the hill.

And then, looking at the sky, I screamed as loud as I could.

The sound floated across what looked like an endless valley, finding no obstacle upon which to echo, and as I finished, shuddering, I visualized people in Abilene looking around, shocked and fearful of this wonderful, terrible cry passing over them.

"I didn't know you could scream that loud," she said.

"I didn't either. That's what inspiration does for you."

For some soundless minutes, we lay beside each other, petting, touching, loving. I didn't want to move. I wanted to lie forever beside her, feeling the sun and air on parts of my body rarely exposed to either. But before long, other matters returned to my mind.

I rose up, propped on my elbow, and said, "Why does Stan need a hundred rigs when he's losing his butt on Brewster-Gaines Properties?"

"I'll tell you what I think," she said, on her back, stretching with a limberness she was probably too old to possess. "But you can't let it affect your decision. I think he wants a hundred rigs because he's so depressed about losing the tower. It's like shopping when you get depressed. Some people go out and buy a dress or an end table. Stan buys a drilling company." She turned toward me, matching my pose. "He's sick over losing all the property. I mean, literally sick. And even though he's taking forty thousand a month out of my trust, he still can't make it. Every penny Brewster-Gaines has isn't enough pennies."

I recapped my conversation with him, telling her about Donald Gleghorn and Windstream, including Stan's fuck-'em-if-they-can't-take-a-joke line, which bothered me more than anything I'd ever heard the guy say. I waited to hear some shocked indignation from the woman beside me, but she said nothing. Apparently she'd heard it all before. Or just wasn't shocked.

"Stan tells me I can't make a business decision, and I guess he's right because I don't know what a business decision is. Unless it's made by a computer."

"You're about as businesslike as this Indian under us," she said, smiling.

There was something to what she said, and there was something to

237

the feeling I'd just experienced, of feeling joined to this vanished culture below me. I'd been intrigued with the Indians all my life, but I'd never really learned anything from them. Or if I had, I'd pretty well ignored it, as I had all other lessons.

18

If I was having trouble making a business decision, my wife was not. I came home in the afternoon with the expectation of returning to the office after supper since I'd twisted off the morning, and I found a quiet house. Not only was there an absence of suppertime smells in the house, there was an absence of people. Jill and Robert were gone.

I discovered that the war of the pictures was picking up, but instead of magazine ads, these were professional eight-by-ten glossy color photographs of my wife in a black negligee in a bedroom I'd never seen. At first I was confused—had a private detective taken these to prove Jill was involved in an affair? Had I hired one and forgotten, as I'd forgotten telling Sally Ann about the buried Indian?

The packet of photos was in a plain manila envelope on the kitchen table, six of them, followed by a sheet of white bond paper upon which was written in Jill's careful script, "This lady will be home—*alone*—at 7:30 to make you happy."

Jill looked better than good; she was stunning, carefully attired and made up and wholly seductive, which she'd never been. In fact, she looked like her ideal, the would-be Princess Diana. The black gown was sheer but not transparent; the shadows played tricks on my eyes. Was she naked beneath it? She seemed to be. In one she sat on a bed, looking shyly at the camera as if waiting on me (or anyone else who happened to look at the pictures) to ravish her. The most revealing was a close-up. The gown had slipped from her shoulder and caught on her breast, which was only partly exposed.

"Who the hell made sure that thing caught on her tit?" I asked the empty room.

Obviously a professional photographer with an elaborate bedroom set, but I didn't know anyone in town who took such pictures.

I shook my head and made myself a drink, checking the clock because I didn't want to be home when she arrived at 7:30. I'd heard her tell a friend the other day that she'd dreamed she'd married her boyfriend from college, the one she almost married. She'd said, "I felt so much better about him. He had a Jaguar instead of that ugly old green Ford."

I took several quick sips of the drink, wondering how in the hell I was going to make a rational decision on the sale of Brewster Drilling. I resented the hell out of Jill for the pressure she was attempting to exert, and I didn't want to make any deal that would materially benefit her. She'd probably file for divorce the day after the sale was closed so she could claim her half of the cash.

After finishing the drink, I searched the house until I found a black Magic Marker. Then, sitting at the table, I clothed Jill, turning her sheer black gown into a Victorian dress with a very high neck.

I carefully placed all six pictures back into the envelope, leaving the envelope in the same place I'd found it. And then I went back to the office.

Stan was back in Abilene on Sunday for a meeting with me and the old man in our office. For whatever reason, Stan had asked the president emeritus, through me, to handle the contacts with the "hippie lawyer" from Windstream Corp., a man named Ray Lynn Hobbs, who had again called Stan about Toothache Tower. Since Stan had never seen Ray Lynn Hobbs, I wasn't sure why he kept referring to him as the hippie lawyer. An even more interesting matter to consider was this —why had Stan decided to give Windstream an audience when the other day he'd already decided he was taking Gleghorn's offer? Because he wanted Brewster Drilling? I didn't know, but the prospect of a sale seemed less and less likely all the time.

Stan had talked to my father in the middle of the week, requesting that he handle the contacts with Hobbs, since Stan was well known throughout Brewsterdom for his lack of negotiating abilities. The old man had readily agreed, hoping for the opportunity to do battle with California, and said he'd find out before the meeting today who the actual owner of Windstream was. We couldn't decide the nationality. The Mexicans were broke, the British didn't seem to care about the Southwest, the Arabs dealt through banks, and the Japanese seemed to handle their own deals.

I thought I'd beat Stan and the old man to the office when I went to unlock the building just before noon, but Stan was already waiting, pacing the sidewalk in front of the main entrance. Wearing white duck pants and a bright blue shirt, he looked as though he were ready for a day of sailing.

I expected him to hit me full in the face with a brand-new assault on Brewster Drilling, now that he was exhibiting responsible behavior. Wouldn't I want to reward him with a drilling company? But all he said was, "Thanks," when I opened the front door of the building. And we rode the elevator to the second floor without his offering a word of rationalization about why he'd chosen to deal with Gleghorn to begin with. What was wrong with Stan? Was his game off? He wasn't going to tell me that Gleghorn was really a fine fellow, that the news media had conspired to make him look like a slumlord, and that Stan had been incensed over the injustice of it all?

But we were off the elevator and inside the office before Stan said anything, a span of silence that may have set a record for him.

We sat in front of the desk, my desk, which was reserved today for the old man. It had changed into wood since my father's retirement, but otherwise the room was pretty much the same.

"Think he's found out who Windstream really is?" Stan asked.

"Probably. All those years when he was attending conferences and conventions all over the world, from Singapore to Amsterdam, he was making contacts. Hell, he could probably find out if Charles and Di were engaging in premarital sex."

Stan crossed his legs and checked the crease on his pants. "I saw a cute cartoon the other day. A kid on his knees praying. He said, 'Dear Lord, please give me patience. And I want it right now.'" He waited for me to laugh and then gave me a sad smile. "I knew how he felt. I'll tell you, Billy Boy, even if this Windstream deal turns into something, I just don't know if I can afford to wait."

This was all getting sticky. Here I was, the Voice of Morality guiding Stanley Gaines through the intricacies of ethics, while I was screwing his wife. I wanted to say, "Stan, make this easy on all of us. Sell to Gleghorn." Then I could forget about selling the company, resign as VOM, and go see Sally Ann.

The old man walked in, still in his church clothes. Closing in on eighty-two years of age, he looked no older than sixty-five. He was tanned from his travels with my mother, just back from the Mediterranean. His bald head was as brown as if it had been soaked in coffee.

I hadn't mentioned to him my suspicion, which I felt certain had been correct, that Stan had planned on selling Brewster-Gaines Properties to a slumlord. The old man not only would have refused to help, but he'd have strung him up by the ankles and field-dressed him.

He shook hands with Stan, glad to see him, and then checked the view from his favorite window to make sure Cypress Street was still down there. Without formality, he gave us the results of his inquiry.

"You're dealing with an old Japanese gentleman named Uesugi. Very rich old boy who loves two things—farmland and big buildings right in the middle of cities. I guess he likes extremes. Anyway, he figured out a few years ago there was a hell of a lot more farmland here than there was in Japan, and buildings in the U.S. were dirt cheap compared to Tokyo.

"Windstream can't be traced back any further than the Netherland Antilles. Unless of course you know the right people." He smiled as though prepared to bow. "Uncle Sam wants to monitor the ownership of farmland, but these bashful foreigners are using corporations down south to hide behind.

"Windstream usually wants the whole thing, not just your eight percent. Good for you if you're selling. He'll take yours and then work on your partners. You can sell them on that. Personally, I wouldn't sell a turd in a doggie bag to a foreigner, but if you've got to get out, this may be your best bet."

Stan obviously didn't want to hear this information, any more than I wanted to hear the same ethics that applied to others also applied to me. He wanted to hear Windstream was in chapter eleven, so broke it couldn't pay attention. He'd have no choice but to deal with a slumlord. It wasn't his fault, was it? What could he do? What could I do? Stay away from his wife? No way. Impossible.

"The Japanese will own the second-biggest building in downtown Dallas. What kind of sense does that make?" Stan asked.

"It makes the same amount of sense as the price of oil being controlled in the Middle East," I said.

He surprised me by saying, "Well, Mr. Brewster, if you'll agree to see what these people have to say, I'll tell this hippie lawyer to come out and talk to us."

The old man nodded. "Tell him we want to talk to him here, in Abilene. Let's get him out of a big-city environment. Dallas is too big. If he complains about all the connections he'll have to make flying, offer to bring him on that little red plane of yours. But we want him out here in the boonies so he won't know exactly who he's dealing with. All he needs to know is that he's across the desk from some old fart in a podunk Texas town."

"Okay," Stan said. "He's supposed to call me tomorrow."

The Voice of Morality demanded that I now speak up. A sense of fairness, if I possessed one, required that I advise Stan his responsible

241

behavior would probably not get him a drilling company. But, what were voices if you couldn't argue with them? I told the VOM I couldn't tell Stan what I hadn't decided. Oh? the voice said. You can't tell him you have serious reservations? Hell, no. What was I supposed to do, give Stan a call every time I shifted one degree? Hey, Stan, I'm leaning toward selling, just slightly though, a little more than yesterday. No, no, wait a minute. Jill just pissed me off. Forget it. I'm back where I was.

Really the problem was the same old one, a lack of decisiveness, the irresolution of my life. I wanted to wait for someone else to decide and then I could successfully avoid having to do anything. This was getting ridiculous.

We adjourned the meeting and Stan, for some strange reason, wanted me to accompany him to his mother's. Was he afraid to visit her by himself? I was, but I didn't know why Stan would have the same worry. Anyway, we drove in his car, and along the way, I discovered, as usual, that this was more than a visit to his mother's. He wanted to explain his behavior.

In the white Seville, we parked in front of his mother's neat little house with the pale yellow siding. Someone, apparently a neighborhood kid, had abandoned his bicycle in her front yard. It was missing its front wheel, the unused forks pointing at the sky. Stan removed the key and looked at me.

"I want to tell you something, and I don't want to make you mad, but I think you ought to understand something." He paused for a moment, looking at the front door of his mother's house. "I see you as having a real easy life, always have, always will. You started somewhere forty years ago and you'll end up on a direct line from there when you die. There was never any question about what you were going to do because you had all these people around expecting you to do this, that, or the other.

"My life wasn't like that. I started here," he said, pointing at the red leather seat and establishing point one, "and there were all these places where I could go right or left, right or wrong. Hell, I didn't know, one way looked about as good as the other. If my friends were stealing hubcaps, I stole hubcaps. It they were on the overpass throwing water balloons at cars down below, I was too. I didn't have all those people around expecting me to stay out of trouble."

I nodded, impressed by the fact that Stan thought at all. I rarely saw any evidence that his mind functioned if it wasn't closing on a deal of some kind. In some ways, he was incredibly creative, but in others he was downright stupid. But I asked the question that came immediately to mind.

"Stan, there's a lady in the house right there that had very high expectations. Why'd you have to learn this on your own?"

"My mother's crazy as a loon, in case you haven't noticed. Hell, she used to make me listen to her read the Bible for hours. After a little of that, I'd just leave the house. Then she got to where she'd lock me in the bathroom. She'd put me in there and she'd sit on the floor with her back against the door and read to me. I tuned her out a *long* time ago."

Still he surprised me, because I was waiting for the sequel and it didn't come. Now that I understood the root of his irresponsible behavior, and the length to which he would go in correcting that behavior, I could now feel easy over selling him Brewster Drilling. Okay? Or was I only getting paranoid?

As if in answer to that question, Mrs. Gaines stepped out her front door and walked to the car. She looked dressed up, ready to go somewhere, in a white suit. And it seemed typically strange that her prosperous appearance had come courtesy of her son to whom she granted no credit.

How was anyone to make sense of human affairs, sexual or otherwise?

She came to my door, which was on the curb side of the street, and opened it, taking both my hands as I got out. Her face had truly started worrying me because the last few times we'd met, she'd gotten an otherworldly look in her eyes as though she was approaching a state of ecstasy. Maybe that was what a holy roller looked like right before her eyeballs rolled upward and she passed out.

"Hello, Billy," she said, kissing me right on the mouth while she continued to hold my hands. She smelled of Clorets.

She gave Stan the same sort of brief kiss, his on the cheek, and they seemed genuinely glad to see each other. His hand on her shoulder, he escorted her back to the house. I followed, remembering Sally Ann's characterization of them as two goats butting heads. Invariably they started out the loving mother and son, both surprising those who'd heard either's somewhat sulfurous opinions of the other. And as long as they avoided any meaningful conversation, they continued in a pleasing kind of tranquility. But neither of them could avoid the sulfur for long.

We sat in the living room and, as always, the former hubcap snatcher positioned himself so he could see his car outside. He had good reason to distrust this neighborhood.

Mrs. Gaines, in the middle of the couch should someone choose to sit beside her, said, "I'm so glad you came by. Both of you."

She was proud of her white suit, which Sally Ann had helped her pick out, and had kept it on after this morning's church service.

The absent daughter-in-law wasn't experiencing the same moral qualms as her blood brother in Abilene. I'd talked to her the previous day and she'd been too excited about discovering she wasn't under consideration for the chair of the decorations committee but the more prestigious entertainment committee. And in a hyper, ball-bouncing way, she'd described her opponent, her competitor for the job. "Oh, God, you wouldn't believe her, Billy. She's got this coal black hair, I mean, she must rub it with black shoe polish every morning. And she pulls it back so tight it looks like her face would split right down the middle, just zap, it splits between the eyes and rips open." She was very worried about this lady lying in wait at Neiman-Marcus, waiting to accidentally run into some other chairperson so she could politic, and I lost track of what she was telling me. I could feel her manic energy though, and I was glad for her if that's what she wanted.

Her presence was here too, in the clothes Melissa Gaines wore, in the perfume I could smell across the room.

"I didn't know you were coming to town, Stanley," Mrs. Gaines said, looking first at him, then at me, as though trying to decide if we were there for social or business reasons.

"Oh, every once in a while, you need a Brewster to get you out of a jam," he said. "Mr. Brewster's doing a small job for me."

She raised her eyebrows and placed a small brown pillow on her lap, on top of which she placed her hands. "You're not in trouble, are you?"

"No, but it wouldn't surprise you if I was, would it?"

There it was again, that strange combination of emotions, an acknowledgment in one breath that he'd asked the old man to get him out of a jam, followed by his irritation over the necessity of doing such a thing. He thought I'd experienced an easy life because of the constant expectations, but he didn't realize the flip side to that alleged ease, which was a pain in the ass. And he should have realized my situation because he was in a similar one, that of trying to please his admirers with ever bigger and bigger deals. The result in his case was exhaustion and not simple irritation, as it was in mine.

"Well, I wasn't going to say it, but I will," Mrs. Gaines said. "The good Lord above you gives you direction on how to get out of jams, and the easiest way is to avoid them to begin with." That said, she slapped the pillow in her lap as though it were trying to rise up and she was there to make sure it didn't.

Stan gave her a I've-heard-all-this-crap-before nod. "I guess you'd rather see me in jail somewhere."

"You know that's not so."

"Or maybe living down by the railroad tracks in a piece of cardboard. I could drag all my maggots along when I came for a visit."

"Stanley, what is wrong with you?" she asked, glaring, her face focusing inward on him. "All I asked was, were you in trouble, and I never said I expected you to get in trouble. And no, I don't want you living in a piece of cardboard *down by the railroad tracks!*"

Their battles tended to escalate more quickly than any I'd ever seen, with the possible exception of those that had been fought between Boomer and the old man. But those had been part of a forty-year war that never had a ceasefire.

Stan stood up, too energized to remain seated but not so distracted he'd forgotten to watch his car. "Maybe there's a commune around somewhere, like those back in the sixties, and I'll let my hair grow down to my asshole and smoke dope all the time."

"Actually, Stanley, if you're not doing what God wanted you to do, then you're right, I suppose it really doesn't make any difference where you are. Maybe you should go join a commune. Maybe you should live in a piece of cardboard. Maybe you'd have time to listen to what your heart says."

Stan's mouth dropped as though he'd been struck by a bolt of understanding. "That's it. That's what I'll do. I'll listen to my heart. Maybe that's what tells women on the north side to go find a rich man and fuck his socks off."

I was watching this fight and now looked at Mrs. Gaines to see how she responded to this mother-bashing. What did I expect? She was a Gaines. Instead of standing and chasing her son from the house, she picked up the small pillow and hugged it to her breasts, assuming that blissful look I'd seen before. What was she doing? Remembering A. J. Ford's socks?

Stan shook his head. "She's crazy. You talk to her."

And with that he walked out the front door, slamming it behind him, and causing the windows of the small house to rattle. There was no way I was going to remain in a house with Melissa Gaines when she looked as though she was off on a search for a religious orgasm.

"Billy," she said.

245

"I've got to go."

She patted the cushion beside her without looking at me. Her gaze was fixed on nothing, or something I couldn't see. Until she seemed to have received her vision and then she turned her eyes to me.

"Billy, there's only been one woman ever blessed. The Virgin Mary. She swelled with her blessing. She was a vessel, a woman, a cup to be filled. I told you there'd come a time when I'd ask you to share with me, and this is the time. The Lord works in mysterious ways, and he's revealed to Stanley what I never told him. And so I know, this is the time."

What was I supposed to do, run from the house screaming, "Help! I'm being chased by a vessel"? I had to make her understand she was seeking what she couldn't find. And now she was walking toward me, as strongly influential as her son, radiating a desire so consuming I understood what had happened to A. J. Ford and Buck Hendrix when they'd lost their socks. I could resist Melissa Gaines at seventy; thirty years ago I probably would have sacrificed my socks too.

I started to speak, but when she reached me, this woman of surprises placed her hand on that part of me with which I would assist in filling her cup.

"You're so generous, so kind," she said, her fingers acting like snakes. "So loving."

I took her wrist and lifted her hand, kissing it. "Mrs. Gaines, I can't do what you want. I'm not capable," I said, meaning one thing but instantly realizing the comment could, and should, be taken in a different way entirely. I'd been emasculated in the war. Or by my wife.

The problem was that I didn't want to leave. I wanted to stay, without actually fulfilling her desire. There was something unearthly about that blue tissue-thin skin around her eyes, about the intense way she stood beside me, now in contact from top to bottom with me.

"I want to carry part of you, Billy. I want to be filled; I want you to fill me."

She rested her head on my shoulder, waiting, I suspected, for me to relax and release her wrist so she could catch me by the blesser. Instead I kissed her on the forehead, still smelling Clorets and perfume, and snuck out the door backwards, my hand on her shoulder, until I got the door closed, to keep her in the house.

She didn't follow me out.

When I got into the white Seville at the curb, I was blowing out a great breath.

Stan started the car and said, "You tell me, what the hell does she expect out of me? What does she want?"

"She expects you to preach," I said. I knew what she wanted out of me, too, but I didn't say.

19

I decorated the office for Ray Lynn Hobbs. From the files, I'd dug out several color photographs of a blowout, a big one we'd had near Ranger several years ago, with flames shooting high over the twisted remains of the derrick. I'd framed them and hung them around the office with three of Toothache Tower. I figured if Ray Lynn was observant, he'd assume we were fearless people who took incredible risks, even when it came to protecting a building in downtown Dallas that had never belonged to us.

Stan, my old man, and I sat around the office waiting on the arrival of the hippie lawyer. We'd sent a derrick hand called Mickey Mouth to fetch him. Mouth worked in the derrick partly because he was an experienced hand, but also because he talked endlessly about anything and everything and no one wanted to listen. The driller could put him ninety feet in the air and the wind would blow his sounds away.

The old man was ready. Wearing one of his older black suits, he sat behind his updated desk, looking like a retired admiral returned to his command. He was tired of traveling and being nice; he wanted to bite somebody.

Stan, at the window, unable to sit, said, "I always knew there was a reason I didn't change the name of Brewster-Gaines Properties. I should've known I'd need a Brewster somewhere down the line."

We heard Mickey coming. "WhenIwasintheairforceouttthereworkingon thoseKC-135s . . ." But Hobbs walked in before Mouth did, oblivious to the oral stream of consciousness following him. He was dressed Stan Gaines—style in a beige suit with a blue shirt, carrying his coat over his arm. And as soon as I saw him, I decided none of our tricks was going to work; this was a guy who'd be as comfortable in Ecuador as in Los Angeles. He was, if nothing else, smooth, and when I introduced myself, he looked me in the eye and squeezed my hand, giving it a good shaking, and made me think he'd been waiting at least forty years to make my acquaintance.

He walked immediately to one of the blowout pictures and said, "Well, here I am deep in the heart of oil country looking at a blowout. Did you call Red Adair in?"

"No," I said. "Boots and Coots. And that's not a blowout. That's several hundred thousand dollars worth of natural gas. But it turned out all right. That one well paid the drilling costs on the other twelve on that lease, once we got it under control."

He nodded and took a seat in front of the retired admiral, who was sitting quietly behind his desk, measuring his opponent. He was content to wait.

Hobbs put his valise beside his chair, extended his feet, which were clad in tassel-bearing loafers, and looked at Stan. "I was going to buy some Gaines Petroleum stock but my broker said you're carrying too much debt."

Stan laughed. "Hey, the best buy on the market is Gaines Petroleum. I'll tell you what. I'll guarantee you can double your money. Buy all you want and I'll personally make up the difference if you don't."

Hobbs shook his head. "I'd rather take your money on real estate. That's what I get paid for."

We talked for a few minutes about deregulation and the price of oil, which was hanging in the $40-a-barrel area. Apparently the American motorist had decided anything, even $40 oil, was better than the gas lines of 1979, which, in some cases, had been over a mile long and brought outbreaks of violence, even murder. Hobbs claimed he'd known a woman who had decided ten minutes with the station owner in his back room was preferable to a two-hour wait in line.

"She said when she really put her mind to it, she could get in and out of the back room in less than ninety seconds."

Hobbs smiled and we laughed, and the conversation died. Time to get down to business.

Without sitting up straight, the lawyer, comfortable in his chair with his feet still extended, said, "Well, you know why I'm here. I've got a client that likes the looks of your tower."

The old man, as if on cue, stood and walked across the room to check his favorite view. "Mister Hobbs, you realize Dallas is a conservative place. Lots of insurance companies, some oil business although there's not any production there, lots of Baptists and Methodists that go to church regularly. If you look in a Dallas phone book, you'll see Smiths

248

and Jones and good old American names. Being from California, you may not properly understand the atmosphere of that city. And I've got a problem. I've got a problem with Brewster-Gaines going down as the folks who sold the second-biggest building downtown to the people we dropped the big one on almost forty years ago. What I'm saying is, you look in the Dallas phone book and you won't see one Uesugi there, not even under the Ys."

Hobbs said nothing but I could feel Stan squirming. This was the way to sell 8 percent of Toothache Tower, trying to discourage your buyer's agent? The problem Stan was experiencing was a familiar one to me. We both knew the old man didn't like the idea of selling out to a foreigner, so Stan couldn't tell whether he was negotiating or attempting to squelch the deal.

"I've got another problem, Mr. Hobbs. These interest rates have created a distress-sale smell in the air and the buzzards are out. We got an offer on our interest in the tower, and it smelled like week-old lizard. So if you've come on the assumption that we're interested in giving away property, you wasted a trip. I've seen more cycles than they've got riding around Tokyo; everything that goes up comes back down, and everything that goes down comes back up. The best way I know to lose money is to sell in the valley. I haven't made it sixty years in the oil business by getting panicky every time the wind shifts." He turned his gaze onto Hobbs, his bald head shining in the light from the window. "Now, I've said my piece, you say yours."

Hobbs looked at Stan and said, "You know, I see the name of Stan Gaines in *Time* and the *Wall Street Journal*, and for all I know, it may be in the Kremlin as the prime example of a capitalist pig. I come out here to see him and I end up across the desk from an old man who sets me up and then knocks me down. Who's the wizard here, Brewster or Gaines?"

The old man returned to his desk and sat, lifting his feet up and placing them by the telephone. "You're implying we're not all wizards here, Mr. Hobbs? Hell, I've got a son sitting beside you who started with nothing seven years ago and he's thinking of selling his company to Stan for thirty-one million. Keep that bit of wizardry under your hat, by the way, or you'll get indicted for insider trading." He shrugged. "As far as I know, we're all wizards around here."

Hobbs gave me a skeptical smile, which irritated me, probably as Stan was irritated by those who refused to believe his Green Beret story. He turned his attention back to the old man.

"You've done your homework, I'll give you that. You're the first person who's known the identity of my client without being told. And even though I'm curious about how you found out, I won't ask. But I've got to tell you, my client is very thorough. Pain-in-the-ass thorough. I plan to spend the next few days in Dallas getting the information I need. I hope I won't have any problems."

"If we don't have it," Stan said, "we'll make it up."

"Keep the figures conservative."

Only someone who knew Stan well would realize he was about to pop his cork. He wanted to stand up and make a demand for an immediate offer right now, right here. If Hobbs would only say 50 percent of the note, they'd have a deal. We could all go home and relax and Stan wouldn't have to walk around with a barf bag in his pocket.

"I guess we can get started if you've got the time," Hobbs said, looking at Stan. He picked up his valise and from it got a small tablet, which he flipped open. "What kind of sanitary napkins do your maids use, Stan?"

For possibly the first time in my life, I saw Stan Gaines at a loss for words. He thought Hobbs was serious and had forgotten he himself had suggested the ridiculous nature of some of Hobbs's inquiries.

We all laughed and the lawyer stood, replacing his pad.

"If you boys will show me to a bar, I'll buy you a drink."

The old man shook his head. No way was he turning Stan loose with this man. "Thanks for the invitation, Mr. Hobbs, but we're on our way west." West, to his house. "But our man Mouth will be glad to take you anywhere you want to go."

Even when I talked to someone I didn't know, the conversation was still related to Stanley Gaines, the shrinking tycoon. I got a call from the reporter who'd been disturbing parts of Stan's well-rehearsed biography entitled, "The Rise of a Former Green Beret." He asked, in a low-keyed way, which immediately made my ears prick, if he could come visit with me in the next day or two. But he didn't identify himself as a reporter associated with either Dallas newspaper.

"I thought you were writing this for a Dallas paper."

"I was, but I left and took the story with me."

Um hmm, I thought. We'd gone from "The Rise of a Former Green Beret" to "The Lies of a Fraudulent Gringo." I told him I didn't have time in the next day or two; what did he want to talk about?

"Oh, you're a friend of Stan Gaines and I'd just like to get another perspective. And verify some information."

I remembered almost twenty years ago being asked by a waitress if

I'd vouch for him, the former Frank Dick, hubcap hustler. I didn't want to be in that position again, and I certainly didn't want to be asked if I could confirm or deny any of his stories.

"You know this guy Stan talks about, the old Frenchman in Laos? I went to Vietnam to do one of those what-it's-like-after-the-fall stories, and I spent some time in Laos. It may not mean anything, but I couldn't find anybody who'd ever heard of this guy Charles N. Sannier, not the immigration office, not the embassy, not any of the old French colonials. Obviously, I didn't poll everybody in the country, but it looks like some-body would've at least heard of him. I thought I'd look him up and get a reaction to Stan's success, but there wasn't anybody to look up."

If the reporter was actually looking for Charlie Insanity, if he believed such a man existed, he wasn't as close to the truth as I'd feared. Since returning to Abilene, I'd managed to verify the existence of a policeman named Jay Sannier, who had been well known for his interest in kids, and who had indeed died while Stan was in Laos. He'd reportedly been bad at remembering names and had greeted everyone with a loud, "Hey!"

"You ever hear Stan talk about the guy?"

"Sure, I have, but I'm like you. I've never seen him. But then, I wasn't in Laos twenty years ago, either. Hell, there were people in Abilene twenty years ago nobody remembers."

"Let me run this by you. Mrs. Gaines—that is, Stan's mother—told me some strange things. She's of the opinion that Stan would step on his dick every time he turns around if it wasn't for you. In fact, she speaks more highly of you than she does him."

I laughed. Here was some real irony. The old man had wanted Stan for a son, and Mrs. Gaines preferred me. That was a good example of desires that could never be fulfilled, a concept Sally Ann had recognized long before I had. If everyone had possessed the insight of my wise blood brother, there'd be more happy people in the world. Richard Nixon, for example.

I wasn't going to comment on Melissa Gaines at all. "What else have you got?"

"The other Mrs. Gaines—Sally Ann—she's something else. Man, what a classy lady. She said she was engaged to you before she met Stan; y'all were planning a wedding that was to set Abilene on its ear, when Stan came in and just swept her off her feet. Is that the way it went down?"

I barely caught myself, barely prevented myself from admonishing this guy. Remember, I wanted to tell him, you're not writing a story;

you're building legends. Quit trying to verify such information. Instead I said, "If she remembers it that way, why then, it must've happened that way."

"One other thing. Sally Ann Gaines said she thought you were probably still in love with her. Do you have any comment on that?"

"Sure, I do. Everybody's in love with Sally Ann."

Jill hadn't taken kindly to being redressed with a Magic Marker, and she hadn't spoken to me since, other than to ask if I would pass the corn or get her car inspected. I had, however, put an end to the war of the pictures. The planning sessions—where to shop and what to buy—continued with the rich bitch's friends, presided over by R. B. herself. These ladies sat around and drank coffee and priced condos in Vail and islands in the Caribbean. They were even researching the cost of flying lessons since the purchase of a plane would involve a hefty amount of cash.

Robert had given up. He told me he couldn't handle the ups and downs and didn't even want to talk about it anymore. "If you sell it, I guess I'll know, huh?" I told him regardless of what happened, his life wasn't going to change. He wouldn't catch Stan Junior, he wouldn't get a monkey, and he'd keep right on mowing the grass. "Great," he said. "What's the use of money?"

Stan decided that the sale of the tower would be an ongoing process, lasting until the world ended. Hobbs hadn't misled him; he had a breezy-looking young lady in Dallas who wanted to see everything from utility bills to leases, and she measured the distance to the closest restaurants.

Stan considered me responsible for the misery he was experiencing and felt free to call and let me know how often he was throwing up. I got tired of hearing his complaints and asked, "How is it you haven't eaten a thing in months, have been throwing up on a regular basis, but you don't appear to have lost a pound?"

"I'm lucky, I guess. I'm just one of those people who don't need to eat."

I couldn't figure out why he had yet to bring up his offer on Brewster Drilling again. I'd already made a decision, but he hadn't asked. Time had a way of distilling reason, and there was really only one consideration—even a slight reversal in the price of oil was going to toss a large number of businesses into bankruptcy. And only those without debt would survive a crash. I wasn't astute enough to predict the price of oil from one day to the next, but my advisor, William C. Brewster, Jr., had convinced me it was indeed coming back down. And we were taking advantage of the prosperity by getting the bank paid off.

Besides, Stan had other matters on his mind. He hadn't seen Hobbs's girl in over a week.

"Hobbs must've lost interest," he said.

I knew where the conversation was headed, and with good reason. Although the inflation rate had fallen below 10 percent, the prime was bouncing off the ceiling again at 20.5 percent. And I knew what Stan wanted to do; he wanted to call Hobbs.

"Stan, look at it this way. Number one, you know Hobbs is interested and a week isn't enough time for the old man in Japan to look at all the figures. I mean, hell, you told me yourself the girl walked all over the building with a stopwatch, timing the elevator, timing everything that moved. Number two, good old Mister Slumlord offered you a whopping million four, which leaves you on the hook for two million. What're you going to do, file chapter eleven? What happens if Hobbs comes back with an offer of, say, eighty percent of value? What if he offers you eleven million? Stan, do some fucking arithmetic. Subtract one point four from eleven and then multiply by a million. What if he offers you only half that? Consider it a salary. You're going to pay yourself a couple million to wait another week."

"I'll tell you what. Let's just call him and tell him we're going to have to have a sign of real interest because we have another buyer interested. That's only reasonable. That's what your old man taught me, let two people bid the price up."

I shook my head and wanted to take a hammer to the phone. I would have if the impulses would have carried to Dallas. "Get your head out of your ass, Stan. You don't have two bidders and Hobbs'll know you're lying. One phone call to him will cost you a couple million. He's a big leaguer and you're talking about a T-ball stunt. And aren't you the one who used to understand inflation? You don't remember what's driven the value of your building from ninety million to a hundred seventy? You're going to forget everything you used to preach? I'm telling you, *do not call him.*"

"So I'm supposed to sit up here and wait forever, is that it? Gleghorn's probably lost interest too. What am I going to do in a week when I haven't heard from anybody?"

"You're going to call the old man and say, 'What do you think?' And you're not going to call Hobbs at all. If anybody calls him, the old man will. You're the one who asked him to help, remember."

He exhaled a great sigh, not of relaxation but of concession. I knew he was standing, knew he was pacing. His phone had a cord long enough to stretch between telephone poles, and he occasionally got it wrapped around furniture, even his own legs. And I had to smile even though I sympathized, because dealing with him at times was no different from dealing with my own son. They were both a bundle of wants barely tied together with string.

"Breathe in a paper bag, Stan. Just hold on."

"Easy for you to say."

He didn't have to wait long. Hobbs called him the next day and invited him to sunny southern California to talk about selling his interest in the tower. Stan somehow managed to muster up every drop of patience and discipline he possessed and told Hobbs he wasn't sure he'd have time for a meeting at all, much less one in California. And so Hobbs was flying back to Abilene to meet the old man, who was pissed at his opponent's attempt to sneak by him. And so we dispatched Mouth in the oldest pickup we had to get "that California chickenshit" from the airport. The pickup rode like a buckboard and had no air conditioning. And as though God were on our side, Hobbs arrived in the middle of a dust storm. The wind was out of the west and the horizon was red, filled with the powdery topsoil of Midland and Odessa. Even inside the office I could taste it.

The lawyer arrived dressed once again Stan Gaines–style, this time in blue pants, a white pullover shirt, and deck shoes. He walked into the office trying to determine what color his shirt was.

The old man, standing at his favorite window, said, "Look at this, Mr. Hobbs. Look how pretty the sun is shining through the dust."

Hobbs nodded without going to look. "It'd be a great time for an eclipse because you can look directly at the sun. How do you people live out here?"

"It's the Comancheria," I said. "What do you expect?"

"Well, personally, I prefer living some place where I can breathe."

Hobbs took his former chair, in front of the admiral's desk, and, dropping his valise on the floor, looked around. Stan, beside him, was wearing a three-piece suit as though he didn't want to be outdone in the matter of casual dress. Then after looking me over, Hobbs turned his attention to the old man. "You know, with you sitting behind that desk, I never would've suspected you were retired. You have to come back periodically to keep the boys here in line?"

The old man returned to his desk and sat, pushing the chair back and stretching out. He folded his hands on his stomach and said, "I'm almost twice your age, Mr. Hobbs. That doesn't mean I'm twice as smart, but in your case, it's a damned conservative assumption. By the time you leave here, I may be twice as tall."

Hobbs laughed, stretching out as well, showing the old man he could match his relaxed air. "I like you, Mr. Brewer," he said, purposely mispronouncing his name. "You're a hybrid, a cross between Will Rogers and Al Capone."

"Let's not engage in a battle of wits, Mr. Hobbs. I don't like fighting unarmed men."

Hobbs could take care of himself, but I still felt sorry for him. Negotiating with the old man was hell. He never gave his adversary an opening, and he'd stomp all over your dignity. And the assaults were personal, never directed toward an offer or the terms of an agreement. He'd never give a man a legitimate reason for walking out by insulting the offer. If you stomped out of a negotiating session, you ended up feeling personally inadequate, bested, beaten.

The old man looked as though he was about to fall asleep, his chin on his chest, but his voice was as loud as usual. "Brewster Drilling and Brewster-Gaines Properties both carry my name. That's where the Brewster comes from. In Texas, we don't need majority ownership in something to feel personally about it. Hell, that's what makes us different, that's what makes us Texans. When your name's on the door, that makes it personal. Stan here will be the first to tell you, till I check off on a deal, it ain't a deal."

Hobbs nodded in appreciation of this bit of insight provided by the protector of the state's heritage. "I always wondered what made a Texan. My wife showed me a bag of cow manure the other day, and the instructions said to apply sparingly unless you lived in Texas, and in that case, you were to eat the whole damn bag."

"As much as I enjoy your conversation and casual clothes, Mr. Hobbs, I guess we ought to get down to it."

Hobbs, enjoying the exchange, seemed reluctant to get down to business, but he picked up the leather valise. For a minute, he dug through his papers. The old man had sat up, crossed his arms, and now looked like a Buddha, his bald head shining. He dared Hobbs to hit him with a low offer.

"You know," Hobbs said. "I can't remember what building we were talking about. Oh, yes, Toothache Tower as you call it." He pulled a manila folder out and opened it. "Here's what we've got. We're willing to make a very generous offer considering the market and interest rates. For Brewster-Gaines Properties' eight percent, we'll offer you a nice round seven million." He handed the old man a contract with a cashier's check stapled to the top. I couldn't see the amount.

I wanted to look at Stan although I didn't. His 8 percent was worth somewhere in the neighborhood of $13,500,000. Gleghorn had offered him 40 percent of his note, or $1,400,000, and Stan still would have been indebted for $2,100,000. I had no urge to say, "I told you so," because such matters were impossible to predict. But by waiting, he'd made at least $5,600,000, and the two negotiators hadn't yet arrived at a suitable figure.

The old man looked at Hobbs as though he'd just discovered they were talking about two different buildings. "You must've found a cracked foundation or some major structural defect, Mr. Hobbs. And if you did, we'd appreciate knowing what it is so we can fix it. Hell, we don't want this building falling down and blocking traffic."

Stan gave a sharp grunt as though he'd been kicked in the stomach. He was white-faced, close to passing out, and he jumped up, hand over his mouth, and ran from the room. Hobbs watched his exit, then turned to the old man for an explanation.

"He's had the flu," I said, getting up to follow him.

By the time I arrived in the men's room, Stan had already thrown up and was sitting on the floor, his back against the wall, wiping his face with a brown paper towel. He was a strange sight, sitting there in a three-piece suit, sweating, his head rolling back and forth.

"Just tell me when it's over," he said. "I can't take it."

I wet a paper towel at the sink and handed it to him. "You want to make more than five mil every two weeks? That's not enough?"

He shook his head, his eyes closed, looking weak and tired. "That's not it, that's not it. I just figured out what was making me sick. It's *losing* these buildings, especially the tower. I can't believe I'm losing it. *Jesus*, Billy Boy."

He sounded as though he were pleading for help, as though he wanted me to do something, and I wished I could. But I didn't have an extra half million to pay his interest and capital calls. I felt for him. He could take his father and his policeman friend and combine them into Charlie Insanity, who somehow had lived without having been born, but I didn't know how he'd keep his building.

He crossed his arms, rested them on his knees, and then bowed his head. I suspected he was crying but couldn't verify it. And I thought, he's really not very far away from the kid he was, the one who'd kept writing his friend who had moved away and never answered the letters. He was an easy person to misinterpret because all he wanted to do, on the surface, was wheel and deal. But what he wanted most was to keep his friends. I knew because he'd paid me to stay.

He looked up and seemed to have grown as angry as he was sad. And he had been crying. But now he pointed his finger at me and said, "I'll tell you something. Gaines Petroleum is going to make it. There ain't no way I'm losing that too. It's going to make it because I'm going to be as tough as your old man. If I have to sit around and burn myself with cigarettes, I'm going to be as tough as your old man."

"If you're selling somebody else's property, you can be tough. It's nothing to him, just a game to see how much he can squeeze out of California. If I asked you to sell something of mine, hell, you could be tough too."

He leaned his head back against the wall and breathed deeply several times. "No, that's not what I'm talking about. I'm talking about how he handles everything. You know, he gets as excited as I do, but he's always just like that," he said, showing me a tightly clenched fist. "He's always like iron, always under control. That's how I want to be, tough as iron." He dropped his hand and almost smiled. "If this was a movie, they'd be playing the theme from *Rocky* and I'd go dancing out. Damn, I wish this was a movie."

"That's the problem. We always wish it was."

He pushed himself up and stepped into the stall where he'd thrown up, using his paper towel to wipe the top of the bowl. "You ever hear the saying, 'Difficulties are things that show what men are'? I figured out what I am. The last meal I ate. And I must love water because I spend most of my time floating in a toilet."

After straightening his clothes and checking himself over in the mirror, we returned to the office and sat in the reception area. But the anguish Stanley Gaines was experiencing seemed to dictate that we go get a series of drinks. I told the receptionist where we were going and requested that my father call upon completion of the negotiations.

We went to one of the new night spots in town. The boom had changed the face of Abilene, had even taken it wet, much to the dismay of its more conservative citizens. The flow of alcohol had been delayed by a long legal battle, which had ended in the state supreme court, but we

257

now had a host of new restaurants and motels and clubs. Building had been fast and furious over the past few years, with new office parks and shopping strips and housing additions. The streets were more crowded, the traffic faster, the out-of-state license plates more numerous.

We went by and got Sally Ann at her mother's. She had accompanied Stan to provide moral support even though she was heavily into her duties as the chairperson of the entertainment committee for the Mayor's Ball. And every time she did something unselfish and supportive of the guy, I was always slightly amazed, but no more amazed than I was when we were all three seated at a table in a bar and I found her hand on my leg. Dressed in designer jeans and a bright red T-shirt, she looked brazen enough to do such a thing.

Stan ordered a screwdriver, thinking he needed the nourishment it contained, and since we'd walked in during happy hour, he got two. The bar was crowded with people trying to avoid going home after work.

"You know something," Stan said. "There's nothing that ever happens that's completely good or completely bad. Why is that?"

I laughed and started on one of my two Seven-and-waters. "Your mother'll be glad to know you're here preaching tonight, Stan. Of course, when she finds out you're either a Comanche or a Taoist, she might not like it."

He reached around Sally Ann and patted me on the shoulder. "You know what I like about you, Billy Boy? I never have any idea what you're talking about."

"It doesn't matter. Nobody's paid attention to me since I started talking."

Sally Ann pinched my leg. "That's a lie and you know it."

Stan took a drink as though the glasses were full of nothing more than orange juice and he'd just arisen from bed in the morning. At this rate, he'd be drunk in twenty minutes.

"Gaines Petroleum is about to issue another million shares of stock," he said. "We're going to pay off debt. And I hope you don't mind, but we're not interested in Brewster Drilling. Jesus, can you believe the prime's headed back up? What if it hits twenty-five, like some people are saying? What's to keep it from hitting thirty?" He closed his eyes and shook his head. "I don't even want to talk about it."

Hmm, I thought. I just lost $13,200,000. Of course, if I took out Jill's half, which would have disappeared in the divorce settlement, and a chunk for taxes, I wouldn't have ended up with more than a couple million. Hardly enough to worry about in this kind of inflationary period.

258

No, really what I'd lost was the opportunity to do something, to have made a decision that mattered. Billy Brewster was still sitting on the sidelines, waiting, waiting, waiting. How long could I wait? Until I died? Until some kid found my white skull shining through the dirt, giving away the location of my grave?

The old man called before I finished my second drink, and the waitress called me to the phone behind the bar. Holding one finger in my ear and watching two bartenders madly mix drinks for the growing crowd, I listened to the result of the battle between the states. Stan's 8 percent now belonged to Windstream Corp., and 7.76 million of their dollars belonged to Brewster-Gaines Properties. "You tell Stan that seven point seven five's his, but that extra ten thousand is for the dignity of the state. Hobbs told me he'd decided before he got here that seven point seven five was as high as he was going. I had to squeeze out another ten thousand for Texas."

I laughed, congratulated him, and returned to the table with the news. Stan's profit before taxes was $4.25 million. Not bad for a Taoist from Abilene.

I patted him on the back and gave him the news, which he accepted silently. He was staring at a huge salt-water aquarium in which bright blue and yellow fish swam, slipping through the bubbles. I thought he was having trouble deciding what had happened. Had he lost his tower? Or had he made $4.25 million? Or both. How could one gain and lose simultaneously?

I thought again of the old Indian buried in the crevice on the east side of the mesa. And I knew he'd never been bothered as I was, knew he'd never worried about whether he could hold his head up because the lance had showed him to be a tycoon, a man with a storehouse filled with acts of courage. And, maybe, I thought, that was my problem—I'd been born into money and had always assumed my inheritance could give me what I needed. It couldn't. No one could be born into courage. In that regard, we were all equal.

After a surprisingly long silence, Stan stood and announced he was going to take a leak.

Sally Ann watched him go and said, "You're fixing to take me dancing. If Stan doesn't want to go, we can take him home. He needs to be by himself anyway. He's learning something he needs to know, and since I already know it, I can go dancing."

She sat holding her drink before her, elbows on the table, displaying all the rings on her fingers. I counted eight on her left hand. One reason she liked returning to Abilene was the opportunity to wear all her rings. Her friends in Dallas would have considered it bad form, a gaudy display, but Abilene was booming. We played I'll-show-you-my-Rolex-if-you'll-show-me-yours.

"I kept thinking you'd turn up in Dallas since I was too busy to come out here," she said. "But I haven't seen you."

"Really? I didn't think you'd notice."

She slowly pivoted her head and gave me a look I hadn't seen since high school, one of pure skepticism. All the expression shifted to the left side, the side toward me; she squinted and drew her mouth back toward her ear.

"It seemed like since I appointed myself Stan's voice of morality I didn't think I should be banging his wife, if you know what I mean."

When she made no comment, I decided to ask a question that I hoped would change the course of my life. I had to kick myself into action because I didn't think I'd ever assume an active role otherwise; I needed to push myself into a state of acute regret. I said, "Tell me something. If I hadn't been such a piddler, would you have married me?"

She gave the slightest of smiles and said, "If you hadn't been a piddler, you wouldn't have been Billy Brewster."

I returned her slightest of smiles, this one without any amusement. She was merely trying to save my ego, keep me from worrying the rest of my life over what my lack of action had got me when I wanted her to do exactly that. But I knew, had always known, why she'd married Stan and not me. And she'd just confirmed it whether she'd intended to or not.

She resumed her watching-the-crowd pose, looking over her glass. "I told Stan before we ever got married that you and I would still get together. We might even take a vacation now and then, and he'd just have to deal with it. He had to understand I wasn't cutting you loose and never would."

One thing about the Gaineses, they loved seeing my mouth open. Did they want to count my fillings? Estimate my age? When I finally managed to get it closed, I said, "Oh, bullshit."

She shrugged. "Ask Stan."

"Maybe I will."

"I'm sorry I forgot to tell you."

1 9 8 6

20

I couldn't tell if Stan was about to panic or not. We were sitting around a glass coffee table in his cavernous office, waiting on Sally Ann so we could go eat. He seemed calm, a state which should have been impossible considering the news his secretary kept giving us on this cold January day.

She was monitoring the New York Mercantile Exchange, specifically, the price of West Texas Intermediate crude oil, which had been trading there since 1983, and every time she was given a price change, she announced it over Stan's speaker phone, which sat across the room. It seemed appropriate, this disembodied voice calling out the price.

"Twenty-three fifteen," the voice said.

Stan sipped his drink. "It won't break twenty dollars. No way. As long as it stays in the twenties, we'll survive."

I didn't argue with him since he was voicing a popular belief. The Saudis would never let the price fall below twenty dollars. After all, they were even more dependent on revenues from crude oil than we were. The old man didn't buy that argument, and although he didn't like the idea of crude oil trading on the Merc, he was, even at eighty-seven years of age, a realist. We'd contracted to sell our 1986 production at $27 a barrel. The old man had suggested Stan do the same but he hadn't liked $27 a barrel. For years that had been the low end of the trading range and Stan decided to wait until the price went back up to $30 or above.

After all, Gaines Petroleum had at least five times the production of Brewster Drilling.

The old man had asked Stan, "You know the difference between a professional trader and an amateur? The professional's the first to panic. You better take what you can get now."

Stan had held out, and the Saudis, tired of trying to support the price, had opened the valve. They were flooding the world with crude.

"Twenty-three twenty-five," the voice said from across the room.

"Hey! All right!" Stan said, clapping. "Keep on going up."

Stan's profile had been so low the past years that the article from the Dallas reporter had never appeared in print. There wasn't much interest in a reformed wheeler dealer. Not that he'd completely reformed, but he was trying his best to learn how to be a CEO. He forced himself to sit at a desk and pore over financial reports, to weigh evidence before making decisions, to plan and budget. The proof that he hadn't totally repented was the office he now occupied. As a sop for his new program of austerity, he tore out a number of walls and expanded his office to at least 2,000 square feet. The space occupied by his former office was still his working area, but now he also had a sitting area and a bar and a more formal looking conference area with a long wooden table.

We were getting closer together. He thought before he decided, and I decided after I thought. I was much more determined to accomplish *something* before I ended up in my grave, and I was presently working my butt off trying to save jobs for the people who worked for Brewster Drilling. I'd never worked so hard, and the irony, of course, was that no matter how hard or wisely either Stan or I worked now, our fates, and those of the people we employed, were for the most part beyond our control.

He was still on the forty-second floor of Toothache Tower, and his outer two walls were mostly window, giving a rather breathtaking view of Dallas, its suburbs, and Stan's favorite sight, all those freeways. He liked to stand at the window and say, "All those cars burning gas. I love it. What I really love is rush hour when they're all down there idling, not going anywhere, but burning lots and lots of gas. Please, all you people fill up on your way home."

The voice said, "Twenty-two ninety-seven."

Stan was up immediately, running for the phone. "Jesus Christ, you've got to be wrong!" he yelled at the phone. "No way!" He picked up the phone and shouted, "Theresa! Double-check on that."

"Let's go get a drink," I said, thinking there was something masochistic about listening to the price fall.

Stan was already in trouble; the state was. The drilling boom had ended in mid-1982, almost overnight. All spring the demand for crude had been weak, and the optimists like Stan had believed that an improving economy would have vacationers out in record numbers and substantially increase the demand. But the soft market stayed with us, and changes in the tax laws had combined to relieve receptionists of their duties by the middle of the summer. The phones of drilling contractors simply quit ringing. No one wanted a well drilled. We'd been charging about $15 a foot, and that price fell quick as the glut of drillers started scrambling and bidding the price down to $12, then $9, as low as $7. They forgot profit and hoped merely for cash and time from the bank. Gaines had forty-three out of eighty-two rigs stacked, out of commission.

Stan slammed the phone down and yelled, "Goddamn. Twenty-two ninety-one. What the hell do the Saudis want? They want to be back living in tents and eating camel turds? Hellfire, they're already propping up their own banks with interest-free loans. What're they trying to do?"

"They're trying to figure out the laws of physics."

I wasn't at all sure Stanley Gaines was going to survive a collapse in prices. Shaking his head, he walked to the windows and looked down forty-two floors. "Man, there's got to be a floor at twenty bucks. There's got to be."

A large number of drilling contractors had already fallen by the way, and Gaines had managed to survive only because they'd issued a million shares of stock and reduced their debt by $60,000,000. The expansionist firms had been the first to fall, but now, after almost four years of greatly reduced demand for drilling, some of the older established businesses were slowly rolling onto their backs.

OPEC had learned, like we all had, that life cut both ways. Forty-dollar oil had enriched them, but it had also created a great deal of conservation and exploration in other countries. They'd lost a substantial share of the market. Their share of global production had been cut in half.

Stan, still at the window, said, "What the hell will happen to this state if the price collapses?"

"It won't be good."

"Twenty-two seventy-five," the voice said.

Stan went running toward his desk, and for a moment I thought he was going to destroy not only the phone but the desk as well. But he punched a button on the phone and said in a voice so calm it surprised me, "Theresa, that's all. I don't want to hear any more prices."

I sat back down and picked up my drink, relieved I wouldn't hear that disembodied voice anymore. In fact, I only realized how tense I'd become now that I decided I could relax. Knots between my shoulders dissolved, and I took a long drink of Seagram's.

Stan joined me, and although he didn't relax, he too seemed more at ease. "Hell, I've got to go back to the bank tomorrow." He laughed without amusement. "One time we were a valued customer; now we're a classified credit."

He'd had to ask for a moratorium on principal payments. And pleading for time was relatively easy; the bank certainly didn't need drilling rigs. If nobody wanted a well drilled, then it followed that no one wanted drilling rigs. So not only was Stan having trouble servicing his debt, but the assets pledged to the bank were rapidly losing their value. Not only were rigs cheap, but the value of oil and gas reserves was falling as quick as Theresa could punch the button on her phone. So Gaines Petroleum was paying only the interest on their debt.

The voice spoke again, but this time it brought good news. "Your wife's here, Stan."

Sally Ann walked into the room removing a coat. She looked great with a shaggy mass of hair newly tinted blond and a layered dress that was orange and brown. I didn't know if the sight of her cheered Stan, but it certainly improved my spirits. Now in her midforties, she looked better than she had at eighteen.

"Did you know," she said, "that a bank in Midland is giving new customers their choice of a drilling rig or a toaster when they open a new account? But you better hurry because the toasters are almost gone."

She gave us a smile and made herself a drink.

"That's an old one," I said. "You know how you get the attention of an oil man? Yell, 'Hey, waiter!'"

"I can beat that," Stan said, getting up and going to the bar for a refill. "You know the difference between an oil man and a pigeon? The pigeon can still make a deposit on a Mercedes."

I was glad she was smiling, joking. The tough economic times had been hard on her. She'd been busted back from the entertainment committee to the decorations committee by that "political bitch" she'd told me about, the one who put black shoe polish on her hair and then pulled it back tightly enough to endanger her face. The rival had ascended to the omnipotent Ball Committee (where they all grew balls, Sally Ann assured me) and decided Sally Ann was no longer in need of a chair. "You did such a *marvelous* job on that—oh, what was it—oh, yes, the Palace of Versailles theme, I just can't stand the thought of your talent being wasted." Sally Ann had left the country for a week, and when she'd returned, she hadn't so much as hinted that she'd ever been associated with the Mayor's Ball. She no longer knew what it was. I suspected that politics hadn't been involved; she'd been demoted to a position commensurate with her falling economic status. Dallas wasn't a city where failure was tolerated very well.

"Theresa said you didn't want any more reports from the Merc. What's wrong? Can't take the pain?" she asked. She sniffed her drink, then added ginger ale.

"It seems a little self-abusive," I said.

"I knew a boy named Billy Brewster who loved self-abuse. He used to tell me all about it."

"I was only testing to see if it made me go blind."

Husband and wife returned to the sitting area and sat on the couch across the glass table from me. The entire staff of the home office of Gaines Petroleum could take a break here. Four champagne-colored couches were arranged in a square around the table, and chairs were scattered around in this living room without walls.

"Is Brewster still busy?" she asked.

I nodded. "But I don't know how much longer."

We were still riding the old man's reputation, and we'd experienced little change in rig utilization. Eighteen rigs were still making hole in west Texas, but we'd had to cut our rates as everyone else had. We'd make it because we were debt-free, but with much smaller profit margins and fewer employees.

"Where're we eating?" she asked. "Someplace expensive, I hope."

Stan abruptly excused himself, saying he had to go see if a contract was ready to sign, but I knew where he was going. He wanted to check the price of West Texas Intermediate crude.

When he disappeared, I asked, "How's he doing?"

She shrugged. "Well, he's not throwing up, if that's what you mean."

"He said he was going to be tough."

She laughed and set her drink down, remembering something. "I forgot to tell you this. The other night one of his large and worried stockholders called, and Stan told him a story about how tough you have to be to make it in the oil business. Now, listen to this. He said you and your father were arguing once over who was the toughest, and you decided there was only one way to decide. You stood facing each other and

265

pressed your forearms together. Then you laid a lighted cigarette between your arms where it touched both of you. The first one to move lost."

I shook my head. Pure Stanley Gaines. He'd taken the hand-strength contests the old man and I had engaged in over the years and given it the Stanley Gaines twist. Make it worth telling, was his philosophy. The lesson was more important than the reality. And Stan probably wasn't the first to engage in such alterations of the truth.

"Who won?" I asked.

"He didn't say, but I'm sure your father did."

I laughed, watching her. She'd given me an oldies tape for my forty-fourth birthday, and I'd listened to it driving up here, listened particularly to "Be My Baby," and I'd discovered a change in myself while listening to those heart-stopping lines.

> We'll make 'em turn their heads
> Every place we go

That lightness of spirit, that sense of well-being, the smile those lines brought to my lips came not from a desire to display her on my arm; the sensation went deeper than that. It came from the strength and attitude of the alliance, the combination of our energy and emotion. I'd always be connected to some part down within her, down where that ten-year-old girl still lived, the one who'd been running around without her shirt thirty-five years ago, burnt by the sun, with just enough hint of the woman she'd become to keep me slightly in awe.

"I guess you finally made Stan into a Taoist," she said. "Somebody asked him the other day what was wrong with the oil business and he said, 'Too much *yang* in the Middle East.'"

I laughed. Stan had become a Taoist, but a Stanley Gaines Taoist, making all the definitions fit his purposes. *Yang*, for Stan, encompassed the traditional masculine qualities, but primarily aggressiveness, and *yin* was the traditionally feminine characteristic of passiveness.

"We need more *yin*," I said.

"Are you getting any *yin* these days?" she asked.

I shook my head. "We used to do it quarterly, but now we're always six weeks away from the first of the quarter. It's kind of like, tomorrow never comes."

Stan walked back into the office, more upright than when he'd left, and I figured we had to be over $23. He picked up our glasses and took them to the sink behind the bar.

266

"Okay, folks, where're we eating?" he asked.

"Over twenty-three?"

"Twenty-three oh one, Billy Boy. We're going to make it, I can feel it in my bones."

Although I wasn't overjoyed to be leaving Stan and Sally Ann, especially the latter, after lunch, I returned to Abilene and was glad to see the open skies and rugged land that lay to the west. A big perspective seemed to lessen the effects of the damage, and the old man took circumstances much more calmly than I did. Of course he'd been fixed financially since the Yates Field had blown in, and that kind of buffer between a person and the possibility of collapse always helped a tiny bit.

At eighty-seven, the old man was a little slower, but he still got around, and he'd been to visit Stan in his giant-sized office a few times. He was proud of Stan's attempt to get a better handle on his debt and to improve his abilities as a businessman, but he didn't approve of the office. "Worst case of wasted space I've seen since I was in California."

The person least able to tolerate the present state of affairs (with the exception of one she was having with a lawyer) was my own dear wife. I thought she watched the news reports of the revitalized north with an unusual amount of interest, and I kept expecting her to depart with a sticker on her suitcase that said, "Yankee Bucks or Bust." She'd used her forty-plus years of experience in selecting her lawyer friend, who, in my opinion, had lousier taste in women than I'd shown in selection of a wife. But his family fortune was immune from the nauseating cycles of the oil industry. His was secure in the food business.

She was sitting at the kitchen table when I got home, her chin in her hand, staring at the pecan surface of the table as though it were her future and all she saw was emptiness.

"You look cheery," I said, heading for the liquor stock, in need of a drink if I was going to have to actually engage her in conversation. My only interest in my wife anymore was that she function as Robert's mother. Otherwise, she could do as she chose.

"I don't guess the company's worth anywhere near what Stan offered for it, is it?"

I could tell by the way she asked the question that she hoped against hope I'd tell her Brewster Drilling was swimming against all prevailing currents and appreciating daily. She wanted to know that God was in his heaven and all was right with her world.

"It's not only not worth thirty-one million, but it could very well be worthless. If you can't find a buyer for something, then it has no financial value. If I had to put an appraised value on it right now, I think thirty-seven dollars would pretty well cover it."

She made a mark with her finger across the table as though scratching something out. Nothing was working for her. She'd lost millions but Diana was still a princess, and now some fat redhead was marrying into the royal family. What was going on?

"I just can't forget you waved all those millions in front of me and then took them away, just like that. I wouldn't be this miserable right now if you hadn't done that, if you hadn't talked about how much money Stan was offering."

Poor girl. She hadn't held up as well as Sally Ann; she was closer to the raw dough than the baked biscuit she'd once been. She had to get up every morning and cover the brown blotches on her forehead with a thick cake of makeup, and she'd given up aerobics for depression. I'd often wanted to install a clandestine video camera in the bedroom of her attorney friend to see what they did. I had to assume they were involved in one of the most boring affairs of all time. Metronomic sex.

"Since you're the one who made me so miserable, I think you ought to do something about it," she said.

Then she started crying. This state of serious emotion had to have a source other than the sorry state of the oil industry, and although I was only guessing, I said, "Your lawyer friend dumped you, didn't he?"

She was so unhappy she made no attempt to hide it. She slapped the table in frustration and anger and despair and gave into the sobs she'd been holding in reserve. Her body bucked with spasms, and I looked around, hoping Robert was outside.

Her hands pressed flat against her face, she said, "The bastard's getting married. To some teenybopper with a twitchy little body."

"Oh, don't worry about it. He'll make her sign a prenuptial agreement, and when they get divorced next year, all she'll get is a TV and microwave."

The thought failed to comfort her. She leaned forward and rested her face on her arms and cried out her money-grubbing heart.

"Now, now," I said, patting her shoulder before I left the room. "Maybe you'll win the Publishers' Clearinghouse Sweepstakes and get on TV."

"Ha!" she shouted.

I talked to Stan several times over the next weeks, but I didn't make the trek to Dallas to participate in the death watch. The price local buyers were paying for crude was changing often enough, and I didn't feel the need to listen to changes every five minutes.

By February we discovered the floor of $20 a barrel was more a horizontal spider web than anything else, and the price broke through it like a falling tree. Suddenly the price of oil was the only topic of conversation around town. How low could it go? Would the Saudis close the taps at $15? There was a macabre sense of fascination in what we were seeing. We were not only watching the slow death of an industry and of our state, but we were watching the noose slowly tighten around our own necks.

The truth of the situation began to sink home. The Saudis were not only resorting to harsh disciplinary measures aimed at OPEC members who'd disregarded quotas in order to recapture market shares, but they were intent on destroying competition worldwide. And we were going to be one of the first to go.

There was way too much *yang* in the Middle East.

I tried to adopt a philosophical attitude toward the economic death I saw occurring all around me, but we were faced with a domino effect daily. One company couldn't pay, and everyone down the line saw their ability to pay impaired. We sent out bills and in return got a "Notice to Creditors" filed with the bankruptcy court. We spent more and more time on the phone, trying to collect, and we kept hearing statements such as, "You can either take twenty-five percent of what we owe or we'll just file chapter eleven. We don't have it."

My greatest source of unsolicited support came from none other than Melissa Gaines, who had read only part of my mind and none of her son's. She was certain I'd seen the collapse coming and like a good father had stayed to watch over my children. That was in fact what I was doing now, but only after Stan had made the decision not to buy. "I'm so proud of you, Billy," she told me over the phone. She had to tell me over the phone because I steadfastly avoided any personal contact with her. "You could have sold out but you didn't."

"I didn't sell because Stan withdrew the offer."

She ended up crying, overwhelmed by her own sympathy. "You're a dear sweet boy, Billy, and I know God will always bless you."

It was the last time I talked to her. She died in March.

She went as she probably wanted to go, while dancing around the auditorium of her church in a religious conga. One minute she was praising the Lord, lifting her shaking hands toward heaven, and the next she was on the floor, causing those behind her to trip and fall. Rather than trying CPR, the minister rubbed olive oil on her forehead and called on God to raise her from the dead. A member observing this ministration decided EMS might offer more assistance and called an ambulance. Neither God nor the paramedics managed to revive her.

At the funeral in that same small church around the corner from her house, the Gaines and Brewster families almost outnumbered the rather emotional members of the church. Stan was obviously uncomfortable returning to the church after a twenty-five-year absence, and he sat beside me on the wooden pew, pulling at his collar as if he were being choked. His knees bounced up and down like pistons.

"Talk about unpleasant memories. I hate this place."

I could see the topmost configuration of Melissa Gaines's face as she lay in the gray casket. The lustrous mother of pearl skin around her eyes that had at times seemed almost blue was now pasty white with makeup. Stan had yet to mention her name.

As we sat between our wives, listening to the dirge of soft organ music, I said, "You did the right thing, having the funeral here. You know this is where she would've wanted it." He'd considered a funeral home chapel, a comfortable and colorless place that had no memories, but he'd settled on the church, showing that he could respect her wishes when she'd so openly disrespected his.

I experienced a strange thought while sitting between my wife and Stan. Melissa Gaines hadn't been the emotional mother of Stanley Gaines. They were in many ways similar, but Stan had found and listened to those moderating voices that led to balance. He had even provided those voices himself. Melissa Gaines had been the emotional mother of my wife.

There could also be too much *yin* in the world.

The minister, an uneducated man in his early twenties, displayed a rather unspiritual bent by eulogizing Mrs. Gaines primarily in relation to the accomplishments of her son. Her purpose on earth had been to conceive and give birth to a tycoon. The preacher had done a minimum of research with almost no understanding. He'd seen the figures on Brewster-Gaines Properties at one time, knew that they had possessed interests in properties with an appraised value of over a billion dollars, and he pronounced Stan a billionaire from the pulpit.

"Folks, we worship a God who not only knows the number of hairs on your head, but he can tell you the serial number on every dollar bill Mr. Stanley Gaines has in the bank. Praise the Lord?"

While the church members praised the Lord, some with their arms

270

raised, I intercepted a note passing behind me, from Robert to Junior. The boys sat on the outside of their mothers.

The two boys were getting along much better since Stan had instituted his new austerity program. In order for the son to learn survival, Stan required him to mow the yard, rake leaves, take out the trash, and, in short, to act like the "poor boy" Robert was.

I opened the note.

Robert: Are you staying in town? If you are, my mom will take us for pizza.

Junior: I have to hang around because of this funeral. You can come to my other grandmother's. I'll sneak off.

Robert: I know where we can go. Remember that girl named Ashley? I told you about her. She said if I came over she'd show me something.

Junior: What is she going to show you?

Robert: A dance she does to Def Leppard. She said it would curl my hair.

I handed the note to Jill. There was too much *yin* in the world.

After the graveside service, during which the young minister finally mentioned Mrs. Gaines, Stan and I drove to his mother's house, arriving simultaneously with the first spring rain of the year. It fell hard, straight down, and we were both soaked by the time we got to the front porch.

Sally Ann had performed a humanitarian act the previous night by finding and removing the scrapbooks Melissa Gaines had kept on A. J. Ford, Buck Hendrix, and Billy Brewster. They were rather simple and impersonal, mere collections of newspaper clippings related to any activity we'd been involved in, everything from community service to wells drilled.

The house already smelled musty, vacant, and everything seemed to be covered with a film of age—the furniture, the pictures, even the air seemed old.

Stan squatted to light a space heater set in the fake fireplace, adjusted the flames to their bluest point, and then stood before it, trying to dry his clothes. But the manic activity his body was engaged in seemed to derive from something more agitating than the wet clothes he wore. He couldn't stand still.

"You know what I want to say?" he asked. "I want to say I hated the fucking bitch. That's what I want to say. But I didn't just hate her, I couldn't have. If I'd just hated her, I wouldn't have kept waiting on her to say, 'Hey, Stan, you've done real well. I'm proud of you.'" He stopped, attempting to hold back tears, attempting also to restrain himself. He wanted to throw something, wanted to shout with frustration or pound the walls of his mother's house. "That was all I ever wanted, man, that was all."

But then he was off in another direction, his entire manner quickly changing, and he shouted at me, "But maybe she was right. Maybe it was all a fluke. You listen to this and tell me what the chances are of this happening. This is what it took for me to get where I am: Khrushchev had to put the missiles in Cuba, Kennedy had to bring it to a crisis, and my mother and that preacher of hers had to convince me I was a conscientious objector. And then IVS had to get me to Laos. Because if I hadn't ended up in the middle of somebody else's war, I'd never have decided I'd been railroaded one too many times. And I decided that was it, I was through with that shit.

"So you tell me," he said, now getting even louder and waving his hands, "why I've had to do this all myself? Why? Sure, I had help from you and your father and Sally Ann, but I'm not talking about that. I'm talking about when I was a kid. I needed somebody the first twenty-three years, and I didn't have anybody. Why in hell did I have to do all that by myself? Is that supposed to be fair to a kid? Oh, sure, I had my mother, and she'd lock us both in that fucking bathroom right there and read her Bible until I fell asleep over by the toilet. She was one hell of a lot of help, all right."

He walked to the window and looked outside through the rain dripping down the glass, now as determined to be quiet as he had been determined to rock the rafters of the house. He stood at the window, rubbing his forehead.

I could have told him a similar story but he didn't want to hear it; he didn't want to hear it partly because he was just wanting to talk, I thought, and partly because he'd never see any parallels between our lives. But the truth was that the events required to spur him to action had occurred much more quickly in his life than in mine, and although I'd never have told him he was lucky—because all any of us thought about was money—in a sense he was. He was the one who could hold his head high when the sun rose every morning, and he'd been able to long before I had. Still it would have been an insane thing to say. For me to say.

Stan, still looking outside, said, "You know, I used to sit on the porch and wonder how I'd get away from this neighborhood. I never knew exactly how I'd do it, but I always felt like there was a way. It was kinda like faith. I don't mean religious faith; I mean just a belief that I'd get away." He looked at me, squinting and blinking against tears. "You know how ridiculous that was, for me to be believing that kinda shit? Talk about naive. I had to be crazy thinking I'd get away. You know what I was doing when my mother decided I was about to get drafted? Working at a gas station. Changing tires, changing oil. And about to change my mind that I'd ever get away.

"You know, as much as you were gone from the office, you could've been gone the day I came by. And the secretary could've said, 'I'm sorry, but we're not hiring anybody.' And I could've gone around looking for a job until I'd gotten discouraged and ended up back at that gas station."

He walked to me and leaned forward, putting his hands on my shoulders and squeezing. And with just as much intensity, he said, "It would've been *so fucking easy* for me to have fallen through a crack just because I came from this house." And then, screaming right in my face from a foot away, he said, *"What kind of sense does that make?"*

He seemed to bring himself out of the fit of rage with the shouted question, and he released my shoulders, then smoothed the fabric of my coat. He offered me his hand and pulled me from the chair although I didn't know why since we weren't leaving yet. He walked back to the window, passing a big clay pot that held dried flowers, and he kicked it, sending it onto a leg of the coffee table. The pot broke, cracking into large chunks, and the dried flowers scattered across the floor.

I walked to the mantle and looked at the same pictures I'd seen on my first visit over fifteen years ago. Charles N. Gaines, salesman of the month in March 1944, was still there.

I told Stan about the Indian; he was out there still facing the rising sun, facing every morning that symbol of the Great Spirit. I told him because for me that Indian himself was a complex symbol—he was not only sitting there all alone, facing the rising sun, as we all had to do, but he fit the purest definition of a tycoon, one who had accumulated a vast number of acts of courage. His lance made me believe it.

I started to enumerate Stan's acts of courage, but didn't. He knew what they were. I just walked across the room and patted him on the back. "Come on, you old tycoon."

After the funeral, and Stan's emotional outburst, I was even more worried about his mental health, particularly when oil broke the second hoped-for floor, the $15 one. It didn't even stop to pay its respects, but continued right on down to thirteen. I began to imagine that one night Stan had walked outside, taken his shirt off and beat his chest and dared the fates to test his newfound toughness. And they'd taken him up on the challenge.

The strange thing was, he seemed almost calm. He'd stopped listening to reports on what was happening in the World Trade Center, home of the New York Mercantile Exchange, which was, to many in the oil business, the home of the devil himself. I was afraid he'd grown suicidal, and I called Sally Ann several times to get her evaluation.

"I don't know," she said. "He seems almost peaceful. I don't mean peaceful like you'd be, but peaceful for Stan. Now when he sits down, only one leg's hopping, not both."

I picked up the paper every morning expecting to see an article about a man who had plunged to his death from the forty-second floor of a downtown Dallas building. Instead I found evidence of other deaths. In the booming city of Houston, 29 percent of their office space was empty, and they were racking up record mortgage defaults. People couldn't make their house payments and were abandoning their homes. In Midland and Odessa, those wishing to move couldn't find U-Haul trucks to rent; they were already all on the road. Auctions of oil-field equipment were bringing anywhere from five to twenty cents on the dollar, and unemployment was reaching double digits all over the state.

We got $12 oil and still Gaines hung on. He wasn't among those crying out for help, demanding an oil import fee, because he was a realist. He was from the Comancheria, and he knew that when forty states liked cheap oil, when the month of February had recorded an actual decrease in the wholesale price index, a minus 1.6 percent, actual deflation, nothing was going to happen in the way of assistance for the oil industry.

Besides, we'd learned a hundred years before, when the people of Albany had issued a request for help from the Red Cross to make it through a terrible drought, and Clara Barton had personally visited the area and chided the citizens for requesting assistance. She'd generously contributed $500 of her own to a relief fund and then politely told the people of Albany that she couldn't possibly use Red Cross funds, money contributed by hardworking people, when there were so many in actual need.

Gaines hung on into the summer, through threats from creditors to throw them into bankruptcy. They hung on until August, when the last of the true believers realized there was no floor on the price of oil. In August it busted $10, and Gaines Petroleum filed for protection under chapter eleven.

21

Sally Ann opened the door of the Gaineses' manse wearing a pink dress at least six sizes too large for her. She'd been swallowed by the color for little girls. The shoulders of the dress hung almost to her elbows, but as usual, she was only masquerading. No matter how hard she tried to look poor, she'd never succeed.

"Halloween in August," I said.

She pointed at me and asked, "That's the kind of clothes you wear to a bankruptcy party? Get serious."

Stan had called earlier in the day and asked if I wanted to help mark the day on which the chapter eleven petition had actually been filed. Why didn't we have a bankruptcy party? As with everything else Stan had told me in the past twenty-two years, I didn't know whether to take it literally or not. Robert and I had come dressed casually in slacks and pullover shirts.

The former tycoon himself appeared behind his wife, and all I could see was the upper half of him. His old green work shirt seemed to have been worn last by a man checking a car battery that had exploded. Or maybe moths had nibbled tiny holes over the front of the shirt. He was, however, smiling.

We walked into the house behind our impoverished hosts, passing through the professionally decorated entryway, that area of the house that had caused Sally Ann such problems. The wallpaper was pale blue with a faded red hearts-and-pineapples design. *Warm* was how Sally Ann described it. Whatever, it was still on the wall.

I hadn't brought Jill even though she'd shown some interest in attending this party, the first enthusiasm she'd shown over seeing the Gaineses. She had a desire all right, a desire to gloat. I'd left her in Abilene with the suggestion that she ride around town and look at empty buildings and parking lots filled with weeds. Or maybe she could go visit her lawyer friend, who'd been indicted for the possession of cocaine with the intent to sell.

Stan put his arm around Robert as we walked through the living room and said, "I hope you brought your appetite, Robert, my boy. We're having biscuits and bacon grease, collard greens, and black-eyed peas. That sound good?"

Robert gave me a nervous glance. Here was a kid who thought the Colonel's chicken was a gourmet item, and he considered poor people's food anything cooked at home. He had no idea what Stan was even talking about. Was the man speaking English?

We entered the kitchen to see a huge aluminum pot on the stove, and Sally Ann said, "Actually, we're going to boil shrimp. Stan's secretary thought he needed something special, so she sent her husband flying to the coast after fresh shrimp. Besides, I don't know how to make biscuits, I hate black-eyed peas, and I'd just as soon eat Johnson grass as collard greens."

Stan motioned me into the den and handed me the copy of a letter given him by a loan officer of a local bank, a man we both knew and liked. It was one of those anonymous letters that turned up from time to time, this one authored by a humorous bank employee. It was a form letter denying a developer's request for a loan restructure. The end of it read:

> We're telling you now that your deal is dead,
> And a couple more things need to be said.
> We're taking your project and firing your crew,
> Plus we're taking your yacht and your Rolex too!!
> Don't deny that you own them; your accountant confessed.
> You purchased them out of the first draw request.
> We're going to court to get what we're due,
> And we'll nail your ass before we're through!!
> The light at the end of the tunnel you see
> Is a freight train called "Deficiency."
> And in conclusion we simply must say,
> Thanks for your business and have a nice day.

I handed the paper back to Stan, laughing, although there really wasn't much to laugh about. The banks were in as much trouble as the oil industry simply because oil and gas loans made up such a large part of their portfolio. Banks all over the state were increasing their loan loss reserves.

"So how the hell are you?" I asked.

He nodded. "Good. I'm even surprising myself. I haven't thrown up, and it's been a couple hours since I cussed the traders at the Merc."

I was talking to Stan but watching a conference between teenagers in the corner of the den. Robert and Junior were sitting on a couch, the volume on the TV turned down, and Junior was apparently attempting to sell Robert on an idea. Or that's the way it looked to me.

"How's Brewster?" Stan asked.

"Good, considering. We've got twelve rigs working." I didn't tell him that I expected those twelve to be operating through the end of the year. After that, who knew?

Robert had now been fully informed and he approached me, obviously wanting something. I always knew when he was needy because he prefaced his request with a smile and some physical sign of affection, trying to make me believe his love for his father was as vast as the universe. Standing beside me, he hugged my shoulders.

"Dad, Junior and I are going into business. We're going to sell T-shirts, you know, customize them and stuff. He knows a guy who can make a design for anything, and we can get the shirts for four bucks. Then we're going to sell them for ten." He wiggled his eyebrows and enlarged his smile, making sure I understood what a grand idea this was. "So, is it all right with you?"

"If you can afford it, you can do it."

"Well, see, I'm going to need some help. Just a little."

Witnessing his partner being diverted by the mundane and irrelevant, Junior took over. He'd just sold $600 worth of T-shirts to a fraternity at S.M.U. The younger Stan, the truest junior I'd ever seen, explained as earnestly as he could the tremendous potential of his idea. Every group he could think of, from Little League teams to the regular patrons of any bar, was a market. The profits could be infinite and the need was immediate. He finished his spiel by holding out his hands and saying, "Hey! No way can we lose."

"So can I borrow a measly five hundred bucks?" Robert asked.

"We'll talk about it later," I said. "Right now we're celebrating bankruptcy, and you need to work on your timing."

"Oh, Dad," he said.

I dismissed him with the universal parent look, the one acquired on the occasion of a child's first tantrum, and in return, I got the universal child look, which was polished by the second time a parent said no, just as though it were the thousandth. He and Junior adjourned to the bedroom to confer on the best method of dealing with the unwarranted bullheadedness of parents.

Stan got a call from a stockholder, and while he talked, I wandered the den, thinking the house was relatively new in my relationship with Sally Ann, but it still contained memories, some of which had been transported from Abilene.

Her grandmother's rolltop desk sat near the end of the couch, a large piece of furniture, one the granddaughter had used herself. At the age of nine or ten, she had adorned clothes that fit just as loosely as the pink dress she was now wearing, put on pink plastic sunglasses, and interviewed me for various jobs. I'd had to approach her humbly, "just like a real person," and ask if she needed any help. She had slid her sunglasses down to the end of her nose and looked me over and asked, "Do you have experience?" If she was interviewing me for the opening of boss of her dime store, she always played the part of the customer in a skit called, "The Customer Is Always Right." She'd then seen just how much abuse she could heap on this lowly job applicant before making him mad. And she'd even reduced the idea to the absurd. If the customer was always right, then she could steal whatever she wanted.

Stan was still on the phone, so I returned to the kitchen, looking into the big silver pot of water on the stove. It was heating; little bubbles had gathered on the bottom, waiting for more heat to send them to the surface. Sally Ann was deveining the shrimp.

"Stan seems to be holding up pretty well," I said.

"Does that surprise you?"

Did it? Yes, I was surprised, after babysitting him through the sale of the tower, after observing his hyperactivity for twenty-two years, after confirming that he was plagued by the same internal conflicts as we all were.

Sally Ann was taking shrimp off the ice in a big blue cooler and cleaning them on the counter by the stove. Now she stopped, placed her fist on her hip, and looked at me. Her forearm extending from the enormous sleeve of the dress looked tiny. "You don't have much faith in him, do you?"

"Well," I said, wanting to buy time, wondering why she was suddenly interrogating me on the subject of Stanley Gaines.

The two younger children, eight and seven, came bursting into the room through the door that opened onto the patio. The girl, the older, not only looked like a replica of Sally Ann, but she was dressed only in shorts, as her brother was, her chest as bare as her mother's had been when she'd been that age. Both kids were covered with a film of dust.

She jumped up and down on her tiptoes and shouted, "Is the shrenk ready?"

"No. I'll call you," the mother said.

The two little ones shrieked and simultaneously turned, making an exit that was as rapid as their entrance.

I wanted to talk about this bare-chested girl, but her mother had other ideas. As if closing every subject but the one she'd chosen, she dropped the lid down on the cooler and came to stand right in front of me.

"You know, of all the people he's ever known, he's less certain about you than anybody. He thinks you may be like his mother, somebody who'll never approve of him, but he isn't sure."

"Why does he care?"

She shook her head, moving her wild jungle–blond hair, the style that had come into fashion. "Because, Bozo. For the same reason I care, the same reason your son cares. We love you and want your approval."

I wanted to think she was joking, wanted to say, who cares what the third person in line thinks? And at times, I could have hidden behind that particular dodge. But not with Stan. I knew my approval was important to him.

"Do you know," she said, "that we were married probably two years before he ever said he loved me? And it was probably two years after that before he really did?" She looked at my face, monitoring it for comprehension, and when she didn't see any, she shook her head. "I always think you're smarter than you really are. What I'm telling you is, even if you don't approve of him, tell him you do. Then eventually, you really will."

If even she didn't know whether I approved of Stan, then I did have a problem, a need to say something. I'd originally found him an amusement, an object of curiosity, but he was a light year advanced from his first blundering days as a huckster of the oil and gas packages he didn't even understand. He'd taken himself from the June-bug stage, buzzing around and flying into walls, not quite to that of a butterfly but at least to that of a bee, his flight purposeful and straight. He'd always worked hard, but now he worked smart. But I simply didn't know how to walk up to him and say, "Hey, Stan, old buddy, I approve of you."

As if reading my mind, Sally Ann said, "God, Billy, just tell him you're proud of him. You don't have to make love."

As though paged, Stan walked in from the den, rubbing his hands together and talking about how much he liked boiled shrimp. Sally Ann had returned to her previous task, that of shelling and deveining the shrimp. And for a few uncomfortable moments, I simply watched both of them, feeling as I had the first time I'd asked Sally Ann for an actual date. What if she said no? What if she made me feel stupid? Did I want to risk embarrassing myself?

"So what's the plan, Stan?" I asked.

Peering into the vat of water that was beginning to boil, he assumed I was speaking of long-range plans and said, "Hey, I'm staying in the oil business. From the day—night, really—I met your grandfather, I was hooked. It got slow and I veered off into real estate, but I'm not leaving it now. And anyway, Gaines isn't done in yet. We've still got production all over the place and we may have to shut some in with the price like it is, but, hey, we haven't closed our doors yet."

He moved away from the stove as Sally Ann started dropping shrimp into the boiling water. I preferred it with the shell left on, vein and all, but I hadn't said anything since she thought they were unclean in their natural state. Stan hopped backwards onto the counter of the island in the middle of the kitchen.

"You know, I was thinking about your grandfather. He made me feel like I was in the middle of something important, some old tradition, not just the oil business, but exploration in a bigger sense. And he kept the big picture in his head. When God Help Us busted, he didn't sit down and cry. Or throw up. He'd gotten everything out of the experience he could, and he looked for his next opportunity. I know he liked the excitement, but he liked the achievement too, the creation.

"And something your father told me once has always stuck with me. He said, 'It's not how fast you go but how long you stay.' And, by God, I'm staying. I worked hard on Gaines, and I'm not giving up yet. Paying off that debt in '81 gave us an extra four years probably, because if we hadn't, we'd have been one of the first to go in '82. We got an extra four years, and I'll squeeze all the life I can out of this company. Man, we've got a bunch of stockholders out there hoping to get their money back."

I nodded, thinking Stan was the only person I knew who could have listened to both Boomer and the old man and come away with a balanced, hybrid philosophy. He made my father and grandfather sound as though they'd both been on the right track, two good men in harmony.

There was a silence and I could feel Sally Ann's eyes boring into the side of my head. Shit, I thought. She was going to require an act of courage from me; she was standing there asking silently if I wanted to be a real tycoon or not, and she wasn't going to take as a substitute just my trip to Dallas and my offer of moral support. That was too easy. She wanted an act of courage, which, in this case, was so simple it was incredibly difficult.

"Well, Stan, I'll tell you something. Boomer would've been proud of